The Third Coming

Vincent Redgrave

ISBN-979-888627647-3

Printed in the United States of America

Dedication

A heartfelt thanks to my close friends for listening to my insane ideas and then reading various iterations. Good readers and meaningful critics are hard to find, and even harder to keep. The lure of coffee and alcohol should not be underestimated.

A further thanks to those same beautiful souls for not calling the authorities and having me carted off to a padded room. In no particular order of preference, color, creed, ability, or persuasion: Randy, Heather, Jeanneane, Martin, Darlene. Thanks to my editor, Craig Bourne, for his patience and invaluable insight.

To anyone who has ever made a mistake or two - at least you can say that you lived.

For those of you reading the dedication I can assure you that the best is yet to come.

CONTENTS

Table of Contents

CHAPTER ONE

He stroked the reddish hair of his beloved creation and softly whispered, "I shall unite that living tissue as one so that it becomes an ocean of singular loving magnificence. I'll turn their dreams into hope so that they may dream again. There is opportunity in dreams." Levi D, Grey kissed the lips of his loved one and bid him, "Go now. Shine bright."

The crowds of pilgrims drifted slowly through Medina and paid their respects after saying their prayers at the holy site. The tomb of the Prophet Muhammad was the focal point for their thanks — an esteemed prophet who delivered the words of Allah.

The men sworn to protect the holy religious site watched carefully. Their backdrop was a testament to the creative labors where the masjid's towers spiraled toward the heavens, epitomizing man's aspirations to sample divinity at God's feet. Medina was the jewel surrounded by a maze of palatial modern hotels on a scale matched only by the Las Vegas strip. But the only bets placed in Medina were to score entry into abundant eternal life.

The last of the day's visitors ambled with a patient reverence across the highly polished tiled squares. Thousands of worshippers shuffled outside the high walls. Nearby streets bustled with cars, people, buses, and taxis that moved in all directions with a cacophony of busy horns. The departing pilgrims blended with the two million residents of the Saudi Arabian city.

Medina shone as a truly glittering metropolis of marble, tile, and stone rising from the sun-scorched sands. The delighted faces of the faithful evidenced its majesty.

Yasser Al-Temyat stood at the main gateway and listened to the instructions from his Captain coming through his small earpiece. He was a proud security officer at the beautiful Green Dome, the epicenter of the architectural Masterpiece and the resting place of the Prophet Muhammad. He looked across at Saeed, his colleague, and they briefly locked eyes. There were just a few more stragglers to go, and they could close the gates for the night. Yasser and Saeed nodded graciously at the happy departing pilgrims. Medina worked its magic.

The last few pairs of feet shuffled through. Yasser exchanged a thumbs up with Saeed. They pushed the metal gates towards the central meeting position, locking the deadbolts into the ground, securing the two gates together by wrapping through the large, gold-colored chains, and padlocking them tight around the metal bars. Yasser used his mic and confirmed to the Captain that the gates were sealed and all visitors had gone. A voice confirmed that the security cameras showed the Al-Masjid an-Nabawi was secure.

The daily debrief had been pushed back as the weather threatened a storm, and the captain wanted the pilgrims off the site. "Always messing with us," Yasser complained.

Yasser spun around and waved to the camera, knowing those inside the security office watched him as he saluted the 'all clear.' Yasser and Saeed went to the security office to attend their 5:30 debrief. Once the dayshift guys went home, the nightshift team consisted of eight armed staff to guard the entire facility, per their usual protocols.

The meeting concluded quickly. By 6:05 pm, the night crew performed their regular duties. The locked-down complex was bathed in the lights from the minarets that automatically switched themselves to full blast in the unusually dim light. The skies suggested a terrible storm prepared to unleash.

Yasser noted in the logbook that everything had transferred over without incident, and he noted the date: April 21st, 2019. Then, looking out of the security office windows at the strangely darkening gray skies, Yasser grumbled, "This wasn't part of the weather forecast. Twilight is another hour away, but it appears as if the sun has already set. Bloody weathermen can't get anything right!"

Saeed saw his colleague staring worriedly at the horizon. "My wife texted me and said my kids are scared because the birds have gone quiet and the air is still. My weather app does not say there will be a storm." He held out his phone to prove his point.

Yasser looked at his computer. "It should be a clear evening." His cell phone started to ring. "It's my sister." He checked that the Captain had left the office and then answered, listening to her frantic chattering. He tried to calm her, but she wouldn't listen. Finally, he shouted at her, but that made matters worse. Yasser hung up the call, shaking his head. "My sister is crazy. She said the sky is an omen, caused by the Christian celebration."

"What's that?" Saeed asked.

"She said it's Easter Sunday."

"So, what?"

"It's when Jesus Christ was supposed to have risen from the dead. She's losing her mind over there – all those kids running around. Her husband went off with that woman from the fruit market. I've asked her not to call me when I'm working unless it's an emergency."

Saeed remarked, "She may be right. I swear it's getting darker by the minute."

Yasser checked the camera feeds. Then, he contacted the six guards who patrolled around the courtyards, and each verbally confirmed their 'all-clear' status.

Saeed continued to play with his phone. "Our local news says there's not enough pressure for a storm to hit Medina tonight."

"Have they looked outside?" Yasser angrily replied. "Those guys don't know shit."

"Social media says it's Allah's way of acknowledging the importance Jesus played in the history of Islam. Brothers are showing their respect to God." Saeed's face held a childish delight. He stared at the mass of dark clouds. "Why do you think it is that God wishes mankind to remain on full alert at all times?"

Yasser shrugged his shoulders without replying. Something was brewing. They all felt it. It was time for him and Saeed to go out and patrol.

"Let's hope our Prophet and the Christian Prophet can sort it out, so we don't get struck by lightning. Inshallah."

"Grab the waterproof jackets." Yasser pointed to the changing room. Saeed dutifully took what they needed.

They proceeded outside to the jeers of their colleagues telling them they'd undoubtedly drown. The thickening cloud had become black and sat directly overhead. A shiver passed through Yasser. "Something's wrong here, my friend. Look at this!" He gestured with a clenched fist at the sky.

Saeed pulled on the rain-proof jacket. "You should put yours on, too."

Yasser looked at the clouds and reluctantly pulled on the jacket. "Let's go through the center and inspect the South Makkah gate. We can't risk another madman breaking in. Remember the eclipse?"

"Don't remind me. I nearly lost my job."

"You were lucky you didn't lose your head!"

They marched purposefully through the center of the site. The inner floors of the complex reflected the eerie colors from above. Outside the masjid walls, the busy hum of people had mostly vanished, with only a few passing cars heard on nearby roads. The security center reported all outer quadrants were free of pilgrims, and the inner mosques were clear. Alarms and sensors showed they were fully operational. Both men's furrowed brows felt the atmospheric pressure bearing down upon them. Yasser instructed the men who were inside the comfort of the security office to quit their gibbering and focus on doing their jobs. An angry thunder rumbled loudly across the skies, drowning out all audible noise from the ground. Yasser and Saeed ducked as the vibration shook through them. The dark clouds circled over the center of the complex, forming a deep central spiral that looked as if it would swallow them whole.

"Stay up against the mosque wall," Yasser instructed Saeed.

The Captain returned from his break. He grimly observed the skies and called on the team for calm, but his expression told a different story.

Yasser and Saeed progressed cautiously with their shoulders against the wall. "There should be another hour of regular daylight," Yasser observed. The complex lights blazed to their maximum, but the darkness ruled. They inspected the gate area and confirmed to the Captain that the south sections were clear. Yasser and Saeed moved up against the side of the Prophet's mosque. The Green Dome above was barely visible in the dark. The earlier light breeze that stirred throughout the southern courtyard quickly became a swirling wind that circled high plumes of sand.

"There's something wrong with the storm," Saeed shouted as his raincoat flapped wildly against his sides.

"What do you mean?"

"Three times we've heard thunder, but no lightning."

"Maybe we just missed it?" Yasser rationalized.

"It's the blackest sky I've ever seen! We need to get back inside. I'll radio the Captain."

"No!" Yasser firmly replied. "Our duty is to Allah and protect his servants' resting place. We stay here."

4

"Feel the air," Saeed cried out, waving his palm around. "There's no humidity – it's impossible." Saeed was right. Anytime a storm hit Medina, you could taste the moisture on your tongue long before a raindrop hit the ground. They held firm in the doorway as dust clouds twisted in all directions, forcing the fine sands to dance to impossible rhythms.

A flash of lightning zig-zagged across the black sky and exploded in a shower of sparks, striking the top of Muhammad's resting place. The Green Dome buzzed under strain. They crouched low in the doorway, covering their heads as pieces of tile scattered on the ground. Debris quickly filled a forty-foot area around their feet. When they dared to look up, wisps of light gray smoke drifted upwards from the top of the dome.

"It took a direct hit!" Yasser radioed the control office. "Call the fire brigade, now – the dome is struck."

"We are already on the phone. The security cameras show no sign of fire."

"We can see smoke from the outside," Yasser explained.

"Stand by," the Captain instructed.

The winds picked up, and delicate veils of sand swept against them from all directions. Saeed recited an ancient prayer of protection with his eyes shielded by his hands. A second later, the winds ceased. He firmly fixed his sights on the smoldering dome.

Yasser listened to the frantic voices in the control room.

Saeed speedily prayed aloud.

"Be quiet," Yasser told the babbling Saeed. "I cannot hear myself think. We wait for our instructions." The commotion and screaming from the men inside the control room increased. Their tone revealed a degree of terror, and Yasser's stomach knotted. Saeed's eyes were almost hanging from his head as he anxiously awaited an update. The cries of panic grew from inside the control office.

"Control? What should we do? Over." Yasser waited.

"Should we run back?" Saeed asked.

Yasser held out his hand to remain steady. "Captain, do we need to return to base? I repeat, do we need to return?"

There was a long gap before the Captain's slow, steady voice spoke. "There is a man inside the Prophet's tomb. Proceed immediately. Approach with caution; he could be armed. Sending backup right now. Go!"

Yasser and Saeed exchanged a petrified glance. The Prophet's tomb was directly under the Green Dome, where the lightning had struck. It should be impossible for someone to sneak past the cameras or the multiple motion sensors without triggering the alarms.

Yasser signaled Saeed to follow closely behind as they ran to the main doors. Yasser removed the Master key, his hand visibly shaking as he unlocked the door. He turned the handle and partially opened the door. He peeked inside, then pulled his head back, saying, "Remember your training," and silently prayed that he would remember, too.

"Allah help us," Saeed kissed the crescent moon necklace, a good luck symbol and precious gift from his late mother and stuffed it back inside his uniform.

"Hold your position," the Captain instructed. Yasser grabbed Saeed by the arm and kept him still. The silence lasted half a minute.

"Captain, are you there?" Yasser gently asked.

"Yes, I'm here. Stand by."

Saeed bounced on his toes, and Yasser shook him to get him to stay still. Thunder growled overhead, and the sonic rumbling rattled everything around them. More loose pieces of tile slipped from the dome, and shrapnel splintered nearby on the ground.

"There's a man beside the tomb, but there's something else," the Captain said. "Hold firm."

"Hold firm?" Saeed repeated as if the order was insane. Saeed's face had gathered in a tight ball, and his eyes were on the verge of tears.

"Captain? What is it?" Yasser whispered into his mic.

"We're looking at the worldwide news – lightning has struck the Vatican, Rome, and the Dome of the Rock in Jerusalem. India, too. We are all hit."

"Terrorists!" Saeed stated.

The Captain swallowed the last of his cold coffee. "Mustafa and Ibrahim are two minutes away. They will support you, but you must proceed. Go now."

Yasser drew his sidearm and stood back. "Whereabouts in the tomb is the intruder? We are entering through the main door."

Saeed tucked the butt of his rifle into his shoulder, aiming at the entranceway.

"He is beside the Prophet's tomb. Part of the golden grill is missing." The captain's voice faltered.

"Nobody can remove the golden grill!" Yasser snapped.

Their captain cleared his throat and reiterated, "It is gone! The tomb is exposed. He is right there on the south side. Assume he is armed. Shoot to kill. He could be carrying explosives. Keep a safe distance."

"Go here, go there, keep your distance – what do they want us to do?" Saeed mocked.

"Do your job," Yasser hissed.

"How did he get in there?" asked Saeed. "It's impossible. India, Rome, and Jerusalem, too? The dome is hit! Is it the Americans with a laser from outer space?"

"Shut up," Yasser hushed him. They made their way through the central part of the mosque to where the body of Muhammad lay at rest. They tiptoed over the highly decorated marble floor, which magnified the slightest sound. In the dim internal lighting, Yasser saw the man sitting cross-legged in front of Muhammad's tomb. Concealed in the shadows, it was impossible to tell if the man was armed. Yasser was struck by how calm the man appeared, as if he were sitting prayer like many thousands had done earlier in the day.

Yasser motioned Saeed to move around and approach from the other side. Extremists had never gotten this close before. The Captain was right that a section of the large protective golden grill was gone without a trace. The marble tomb was fully exposed. The sweat on Yasser's body soaked through his cotton shirt. At any moment now, he and Saeed could be scattered into a thousand pieces.

Saeed signaled his readiness. They positioned themselves at a slight angle to ensure they did not hit each other in an exchange of gunfire.

The Captain's voice ordered, "Have him stand up and raise his hands above his head."

Yasser swallowed hard to lubricate his dry throat. "You there! Stand up and put your hands above your head. Do it now!"

The man sitting on the floor slowly raised his head. His features were undetectable in the darkness of the tomb's shadow.

Yasser's backup team, Ibrahim and Mustafa, appeared with their rifles ready. Yasser signaled them to hold. "Stand up with your hands in the air." The man ignored him. Yasser bellowed, "This is your last chance; stand up slowly. I am Sergeant Yasser …"

"I know who you are, Sergeant Yasser Al-Temyat. I have known you your whole life," the intruder interrupted. "Cease with your demands. Your weapons are of no use to you now."

Yasser instinctively moved forward to see if he recognized the intruder. In his ear, the Captain's voice demanded an update. Yasser commanded, "Whoever you are, I need you to stand up and raise your hands. You are not authorized to be here."

"Authorized? Who are you to step into my house and tell me about authority?" came the firm reply.

Saeed softly whispered into his mic. "I have a clear shot. Advise?" The Captain gave the order to fire. Saeed squeezed the trigger.

The man rose to his feet as though pulled by invisible strings from above. He half-turned around towards Saeed. "I told you that your weapons are useless. Throw them down."

Saeed checked his weapon. Quickly he unclipped the magazine and re-engaged it. Again, he took aim, pulled the trigger – and again, nothing happened. Mustafa got the same result. Ibrahim was too afraid to pull the trigger on his weapon.

Yasser did not know why the words left his lips but said, "Stand down. Do not fire." In their ears, the Captain screamed for them to kill the intruder. Yasser stepped five paces forward. As he did, the man moved from the shadows into the light. He was six feet tall, medium build, and had dark brown shoulder-length straight hair with a reddish hue. His face was angular, with a full-sided, short, cropped beard; his eyebrows were thick and perfectly arched over his two deep-set reddish-brown eyes. He was wearing a long yellow thaub that covered the entire length of his body.

"You know who I am. Put down your weapons and prepare yourselves."

Yasser had never seen this man before, but he felt that he did indeed recognize him. The strength disappeared from his body, and he dropped his sidearm to the tiled floor. "It's you," he mumbled.

The Captain watched on the cameras. "Open fire!" His team paid no attention to him. Instead, he looked on helplessly as his four highly-trained guards put down their weapons and dropped to their knees. The light inside the tomb rapidly increased until it was too bright to see anything. The Captain and his team were forced to look away from the monitors.

One of his men said, "Captain, I think we should call the General and the Grand Mufti."

The Captain noticed that his officer was crying. "The Grand Mufti? He'll have my head!"

His officer then pointed to the external cameras. "Look, Captain, the sky."

The Captain thought it must be a trick from the overhead storm. He rushed to the window and looked out. The clouds were gone. Above was a brilliant blue sky, with the sun ready to set on the horizon. He turned and ran to the opposite side of the control room and looked to the East. All blue skies. "It cannot be. The storm was right over our heads sixty seconds ago."

"We should call the Grand Mufti."

"And have our clerical leader telling me that I'm wasting everyone's time?"

Yasser's voice came over the radio. "Captain, you need to come down here. Allah be praised."

The security screens went blank, and the control room was blind to events inside the Prophet's tomb or anywhere at the Al-Masjid complex. The Captain released a tiny groan.

"Captain?" his officer begged.

The captain snapped from his daze. "Call the General – call the Grand Mufti – call everyone! Do it now."

Carrie Carter was about to enter the advisory council meeting in Washington, DC, when her phone message alerted her. A text message from Senator Garofalo stopped Carrie in mid-stride; *Carrie, I need to speak with you urgently. Someone will come for you. Bob.* She hadn't heard from Senator Garofalo for months. The urgency of his text excited her. She barely had time to straighten her jacket as the two men in dark gray suits approached her. "Miss Carter, we have an urgent request from Senator Garofalo that you contact him immediately. If you step this way, we have a private space for you to call him."

Now, what do I do? she thought. The Senator had been instrumental in helping her rise to her position today, along with her brains and unmatchable work ethic. The two government suits gave her less than a warm and fuzzy feeling. However, direct contact with the Senator was always beneficial. "What's so urgent? I'm about to chair this meeting."

"We know," the lead man stated. He held up his cell phone and showed Carrie the same text message on his phone. "This is urgent. Please, follow me, Miss Carter."

"Why didn't he call me directly?"

"It's a delicate matter. Airwaves are compromised."

Carrie recognized the Senator's number and knew it was genuine. "Okay, but we need to be quick."

"Thank you. This way." He led her through three doors, two that the first agent unlocked, and the agent behind him locked as they passed through. The fourth doorway was surrounded by dirty old brick, showing Carrie they'd entered an adjoining building.

"How far is it?"

"Just another minute," the suit behind her answered. They went up three flights of stairs, turned left, and came into the vast, shared office at the end of the hallway. People dashed in all directions, with distressed chatter filling the space. At least three dozen people talked on their phones or checked computer screens as others anxiously watched news reports. The government agents showed Carrie into a side office. Sitting behind the desk was a large man with thin graying hair, wearing a dark blue suit.

"Good morning, Miss Carter. I just spoke with Senator Bob Garofalo, and he says you're the person I need to speak with." He shuffled some papers inside a folder.

Carrie looked at the two men who'd accompanied her into the room. "You said I was going to speak with the Senator. What's going on here?"

The large man in the blue suit stood and offered his right hand. "My name is James Gordon; I'm head of security here in Washington, DC. I'm like the internal affairs branch on behalf of our Homeland Security." They shook hands. "Security within security," he remarked with a forced small laugh.

Carrie guessed James was in his mid-fifties. His round face was etched in deep stress lines, and his pale cheeks gave him a sickly appearance.

"Please, take a seat and let me explain. We'll be on the phone with Senator Garofalo in just a second. We have something of a crisis unfolding. But, first, I wanted to get a quick notion of what you do here in Washington. Your resume is quite impressive," he said, holding up the folder.

"If you have my resume, you'd already know," Carrie suggested.

"All these titles and letters after somebody's name — it's hard to get to the core of what they do. I'd like to hear the abbreviated version from you." He gestured for her to sit.

"If you're a bit like security within security, then there's no need to ask me," Carrie's reply was caustic. "What do you really want?"

She lowered herself onto the edge of the seat opposite his desk. The two men in gray suits exited and closed the door. Everyone wore security badges pinned to their pockets or hanging from lanyards around their necks. "Mr. Gordon, I have a lot to get through today, so please tell me exactly what you want from me, or in sixty seconds, I'm going back to my meeting."

"Your file indicates a high level of expertise in theology." James Gordon looked her up and down.

Carrie stared him down. James held her penetrating gaze. She pulled her long brown hair and tightened the ponytail. Her dark green eyes were purposefully observant. Her face was long, and her jawline sharp. The solid and sleek lines of her frame indicated she was in excellent physical condition, echoed by the flawless tone of her dark skin. James Gordon had read every word in her file. She excelled in her college studies as well as athletics. She competed nationally in the four hundred meters – no doubt helped by her five-foot-ten inches in flat shoes. Carrie Carter had chosen to go into politics, quickly climbing her way onto the top of the education advisory committee. At thirty-two, Carrie looked, acted, and operated as though she belonged in the nation's capital. Her defiant attitude exuded a quiet confidence.

"Miss Carter, I just spoke with Senator Garofalo and the President of the United States. In case you hadn't noticed, a lot is happening." He pointed to the commotion in the main office. "We have something that requires someone with your background and expertise to help provide some insight. We've yet to establish the origins or motives for what's happening."

Carrie looked around his office, full of files and old government-related memorabilia. The walls were a horrible green. The certificates on the wall contained James Gordon's name, most with an eagle emblem behind the glass frames. "What exactly do you need my help with?"

James swiveled around in his chair and switched on the flat-screen TV. "I guess you haven't seen the latest news."

"I don't watch the news in the morning. Never have," she replied.

James frowned as if such a thing were impossible in Washington, DC. "An hour ago, severe weather patterns resulted in lightning strikes that hit several important religious sites simultaneously around the globe. Right now, we're trying to figure out what's going on. Nobody can make any sense of it — governments are getting twitchy. Including ours. The strikes are not a coincidence, but we don't know the source."

Carrie looked at the multiple feeds in the background. "I'm not an expert in weather patterns, so I'm not sure how I can help you."

"Your file says that you have a master's degree in theology and one in political science."

Carrie leaned over his desk; her glare full of agitation. "Why do I have a file? Who the hell are you people?"

"We're the people nobody wants to deal with. Miss Carter, you work here in DC. Of course, you have a file. Everybody does. Even I do." His smile lacked warmth.

James hit a button on his desk phone, and immediately the call picked up at the other end. "Senator Garofalo's office, how can I help you?"

"Hey, Margi, it's James. Can you get the Senator back on the line for me, please? He's waiting for me. I have Carrie Carter with me."

"Sure thing, just a second."

There was a small click. "Hey, James, do you have Carrie with you?"

"I'm here," Carrie replied, with some relief at hearing a friendly voice. "What's going on? I'm pulled from one thing to another with no explanation." Carrie scowled at James Gordon.

"Hi, Carrie. Sorry to drag you away from what you were doing, but we're in an almighty pickle, and we need your help. Apologies if it all seems a bit cloak and dagger."

"I'll say it does," she interrupted.

"This is something that requires urgent care. I think you can be of help to us and service to your country. James, what have you told her?" the Senator asked.

"Nothing yet. We just started. I wanted you on the line, so Miss Carter knows she's here because you recommended her. If you'd like to bring her up to speed?"

The Senator began, "Carrie, I'll give you the high-level view on what's happened and what we are doing about it, okay? The media is going berserk."

Carrie leaned closer to the phone. "Got it. I still don't listen to news feeds in the morning — but, you remember …" she held the rest of the thought. "I don't want to start my days off on the wrong foot. It puts me in a bad mood."

"Smart idea," the Senator conceded. "Here's what we know: six important religious sites have experienced a simultaneous lightning strike within the last hour. I know it sounds implausible but hear me out. There's heavy security surveillance on all these locations, most of which we're monitoring — that's a whole other conversation — but suffice to say, the lightning strikes happened in coordination. So it suggests some kind of manufactured assault."

"What do you mean by manufactured?" she asked.

"I'm no expert in this, but my advisors tell me that we, the Chinese and the Russians, all know how to meddle with the weather, and we have the resources to create certain weather situations. But we can't coordinate six exact lightning strikes, and we're sure neither can they. So we are all scrambling, and anything is possible at this point. Everybody suspects everyone else of doing something, but nobody is admitting to anything. We're looking closely at the North Koreans, but we don't believe they have the technology needed for something like this. We are talking with the other nations as we speak."

Carrie glanced at James Gordon; he rolled his eyes and shrugged. "Have you got a pen and some paper?" Carrie asked. James slid some across the desk. "I need to take a few notes. Give me the exact locations that took a hit." She adjusted her chair closer to the desk, "I'm ready."

The Senator continued, "In no particular order; Medina, Saudi Arabia; Vatican City in Rome; Golden Temple, Jerusalem; Angkor Wat, in Cambodia; Prayagraj, India, and last but not least, Amritsar, also in India. We have people close to those locations feeding back information as fast as possible. Nobody is claiming responsibility."

Carrie sat upright in her chair. "Do you have the exact locations that were hit within each of these sites? For example, some have multiple Holy places of reverence, and some don't. Get me that, and I can make a better estimation as to what or why."

"I don't have that in front of me. Hang on, and I'll have somebody get that right away." There was a brief silence at the end of the line.

The Senator looked at the team in his office. "Stop staring at one another and get me the hell what she asked for!" he barked. Half a dozen people scrambled from the room. "I've got all these damn people around me and not one of them with any common sense. Carrie, what's your gut reaction? I know it's not much to go on."

Carrie stared at the names and locations he provided. "Based on what you told me, it's not random."

"We figured that. But why these locations?"

"Well, these places are what you might call the accepted spiritual center for specific religions worldwide. These six sites are the predominant spiritual homes for Christians, Muslims, Jews, Buddhists, Hindus, and Sikhs."

"Jesus Christ, are you kidding me? No pun intended," he said.

"No, I'm not kidding," Carrie replied. "If you look at that on a global scale, you have something that's just affected the vast majority of the world's population. Roughly speaking, you've got about 5.7 billion people who worship some kind of religion. Specifically, 5.3 billion people connect to the six sites you mentioned through their faith. And you've got about 1.3 billion people with no religious affiliations."

"A war on all religions," the Senator stated. Then, he shouted through the open door of his office, "Get me those exact damned locations, down to the last inch. Now!"

James Gordon spoke: "Carrie, we brought you in here to help us decipher who might be behind this and predict their next moves. The Russians think it was us, the Chinese think it was the Russians, and they don't seem to care, and we don't know what to think. The Europeans think it could be any of us. Everyone is looking at each other and pointing fingers. In the meantime, we have millions of nervous people all over the planet. A war between religions is as unthinkable as divine intervention."

"For all of our sakes, you'd better hope the last one's not right," Carrie said, raising a pair of perfectly threaded eyebrows.

Senator Garofalo's tone sounded less friendly, "Carrie, can you work from there with James and his team? He'll make sure that you get all the resources you need. I'll have to call you guys back; I've got the President on the other line. Carrie, we need you on this."

The call ended. James Gordon leaned back in his seat, his face ashen and an unhealthy blotchy red to the middle of his cheeks. "Miss Carrie Carter, what do you say? If you're in, then tell me who and what you need."

Carrie understood the gravity, if not the entire scope, and how easily this could escalate out of control. Her body fizzed with a massive knot in her stomach, bursting with anticipation to get her teeth into something with global significance.

The view from the window behind James Gordon showed an overcast, drizzly day, making the buildings opposite appear dreary and lifeless. Everything else in her line of vision contained the same level of tedium. Nevertheless, the chance for such a call to adventure felt as though it would lift the gloom and take Carrie to a world of perpetual stimulation.

Her day job was stressful, and she was making great progress, but this puzzle that Senator Garofalo presented was on a worldwide scale, and Carrie had visions of writing her bestselling memoir on how she helped solve it to keep the world at peace. The President was calling the Senator about this. She was supposed to be chairing a meeting on religious education for an advisory committee of Washington district schools and colleges! The drizzle softly drummed against the windowpane. "I'm in."

"Thank you," James Gordon replied and puffed his cheeks in genuine relief. "Tell me what you need, and it's yours."

Carrie's internal surge pushed higher than the day she had her first government assignment – one that Senator Garofalo had helped by vouching for her. It had been Carrie's proudest day and one where she'd wept over the phone, telling her parents the news.

Carrie sensed something similar in this but on a much grander scale. There were more than thirty people busy in the main office in the name of national security. Those were just the ones she could see, and she was at least three floors above ground level. James Gordon and the operations were directly connected to the White House!

This was the kind of opportunity she'd dreamed about after spending the last seven years making a solid reputation for herself in Washington, DC's education sector. No more was Carrie the tall, gangly, dark-skinned girl with mixed-race adoptive parents whom the kids teased at her primary school. No more the nerdy kid who learned to sprint because other kids chased her. Carrie had figured out that her intelligence and strength set her apart from the crowd and made her who and what she is. Carrie had proved many people wrong. Now, Carrie could show that she was worthy of looking in the mirror and being satisfied with who she was. If executed correctly, it would align with her ambitions. The big time beckoned.

It was irresistible. She couldn't wait to call home.

Carrie scribbled a list of requirements and slid them across the desk to the sickly-looking James Gordon. "I'll need all these just to get started," she said.

CHAPTER TWO

Yasser Al-Temyat sat cross-legged in front of the man in the yellow robe. The man's hair was dark brown, but it had this glistening red hue. It was a shading Yasser had never seen before, and it was most pleasing to the eye. Yasser had never considered himself an ultra-devout Muslim, but suddenly the urge to pray seemed more powerful than ever before. His actions now, and that of his team, would surely land them a court-martial or worse. Yet, he felt a warm peace staring at the beautiful man. Punishments seemed unimportant. His internal satisfaction assured him that he'd made the right choice. Yasser's heart told him he would love this man for the rest of his life. His mind was joyful with a giddy sense of hope, and his body held a lightness, feeling like a child ready to take a mid-afternoon nap. An invisible but tangible pulse emanated from the yellow-robed man, filling Yasser with perfect contentment.

Yasser's devotion was confirmed the second the man called out his name.

His three colleagues had joined him, cross-legged in a line on the tiled floor. All were silent. Their weapons, wherever they'd left them, were forgotten. The guards prayed fervently until the man in yellow bid them to sit silently and meditate with him. The guards were serene with pleasant smiles, like a proud parent looking into the newborn's crib. Yasser and his colleagues had pulled their communication devices from their ears, not wishing to have the Captain's angry threats distract them.

General Salah leaped from his bed, waking his wife as the frantic call came through. The one day he finally spent some private time with his good wife, and now this. The general and his wife had enjoyed a stroll at the mall, followed by a light afternoon snack, before returning home and sharing their eager bodies. It had been too long since they'd been intimate. Finally, they had dozed off, wrapped together in beautiful post-coital happiness.

The unwelcome call from the Captain alarmed him. But today of all the days! He quickly dressed, with no time to shower. General Salah focused on getting the Captain to relay a clear message. A quick kiss on his confused wife's lips, and within five minutes, he was in a car, driven by one of his guards, taking him to the holy site. He learned that the Grand Mufti, Abdul Aziz, was alerted, and he, too, headed to the Prophet's tomb. He chastised the Captain for being so hasty. The general's job was to assess the crisis and secure the Holy site. Abdul Aziz was a most learned man, a good ally, but his presence would complicate an already complex situation. General Salah wanted order and having to play politics would not help his cause.

General Salah had great respect for the Grand Mufti and the messages he delivered to the faithful, but zealots surrounded the old man, who quickly descended into chaos. It would require all of the general's persuasion to keep the religious leaders from agitating the gathering crowds. The general must quickly secure the complex and all of its artifacts.

The Captain's garbled message told of a direct lightning strike and an unauthorized man inside the Green Dome. An outside threat had never made it this far. God help them all if anything happened to the resting place of the great Prophet. It was dangerous for everyone concerned. He hoped there was no damage to the ancient relics. General Salah was more a soldier than a scholar, but he understood the significance of anyone desecrating Muhammad's tomb. The threat must be nullified. The Captain spoke of a mutiny within the Green Dome, where a section of his guards had surrendered. General Salah was frustrated at the captain's lack of clarity and competence under pressure. Boots on the ground were needed and fortunately, the general lived only ten minutes away from the Al-Masjid.

From around the city, sirens converged towards the holy site. As the general's car arrived at the gates of the Al-Masjid, a couple of thousand people had gathered outside in the streets, with more approaching. "Get reinforcements, right away," he ordered his officers. "Make sure that no one gets into the complex without my approval. Keep the crowds back five hundred feet from the gates and walls. We cannot afford a stampede of ardor."

They entered through the gates. General Salah saw the trail of smoke spiraling from the Dome. Two media helicopters circled above. "Get those helicopters out of here and let no one come within five miles of this airspace.

17

If they do, shoot them down." He went upstairs into the control room. General Salah shook hands with the Captain. The men inside the security office were grim-faced and barely able to concentrate. The Captain's downturned face accompanied his thick eyebrows, which molded together at the crest of a deep permanent frown. He could not look his general in the eyes, embarrassed by the unfolding mess.

"Show me what you have," General Salah ordered. Then, using all of his six foot two inches, the general stood tall, looking around at the terrified faces, and giving each man a firm nod to let them know it would be okay. His medium brown eyes narrowed, already sharp like a giant predatory bird, set above a long straight nose and high cheekbones. The general's stature epitomized stoicism: his broad shoulders were straight, his mustache neatly trimmed, and his presence reassuring. Although some feared him, the men respected his reputation. The general's part in the Gulf war was a thing of legend. A warrior general, fearless of death in the pursuit of his enemy.

The Captain wiped a fine layer of sweat from his brow as he pointed to the camera feeds from inside the Dome. "Sir, we lost visibility for a moment, but as you can see, I have four security guards in there."

General Salah interrupted. "Be precise in your language. Four men, where?"

"Yes, Sir. My men are inside the tomb of the Prophet, the Green Dome. All other mosques within the site are clear, and we've performed physical checks. My men are not following orders and have laid down their weapons. I told them to shoot the intruder, but instead, as you can see, they are sitting on the floor as if having tea. I have two other men outside the main door so that nobody else can get inside. The tomb is secured."

"Then how did the other man get inside?"

"We don't know. The man just appeared after the lightning hit. The complex was locked. No alarms triggered. We checked the motion sensors, and they are fully operational. So he was not there before the lightning came."

"How can you be sure?" the general asked.

"We saw nothing on the cameras, and none of the motion detectors showed any sign of someone moving around. He just appeared." The Captain leaned over and pulled up the replay. "Watch. One minute there is no one, and the next, he's sitting in the middle of the tomb. The golden grills that covered the tomb disappeared, too. The men are saying the Prophet has returned."

General Salah scowled at him. "You should stop your men gossiping like old wives at the market. Show me."

18

They replayed the footage. "Probably some kind of magic trick," General Salah concluded. For now, the intruder's access route was unimportant. He looked at the bank of cameras facing nearby streets and the swelling crowds. "We cannot allow common hysteria from outside to permeate inside. Has he made any demands? Is he armed, or does he have any explosives on him?"

The Captain looked down at his boots. "We don't know, Sir. My men inside appear to have fallen under some kind of spell, and they will not speak to me. He does not appear to be armed and has made no demands. We do not know if he carries explosives."

"Perhaps his device has failed, and he is stalling for time," General Salah suggested. "Give me the mic," General Salah demanded.

"This is General Salah. I am ordering you, men, to take the intruder into custody immediately." He watched and waited. The four guards stayed rooted in place.

"They are no longer wearing their earpieces," the Captain sheepishly admitted.

General Salah's disgusted glance let him know that he should have already told him that. He threw the mic on the table and ordered, "I want six men at every entrance to the tomb of the Prophet." The size of the building was so great he was taking no chances on anyone getting in or out. "Send your best snipers up onto the roofs of the adjacent mosques and into each of the minarets. I want to know as soon as every angle of that building is covered." He selected his four best men and headed out the door. "Follow me," he commanded and strode quickly towards the Dome.

As General Salah walked around the corner, the Grand Mufti and his entourage arrived. He looked at his Major and Lieutenant. "Why wasn't I told they were already here? I said no one comes in without my authority!" They looked at their laces and made stifled apologies. "Don't let anyone inside unless I order it," he repeated through clenched teeth.

He waited patiently for the Grand Mufti to get out of the SUV.

The two men greeted each other, and the general informed the old man of what little they knew. "I am going in there myself to make an assessment. We will have everything back to normal shortly."

The Grand Mufti told him, "Other Holy sites around the world have similar incidents, but there is no word of a man inside another sacred space. We are blessed." The old man gave a rare hint of provocation.

General Salah liked the old man, even if he didn't fully trust those in religious positions of authority. But, as the senior authority on religious thoughts, laws, and edicts, the Grand Mufti must be obeyed. "I want to speak with this intruder personally."

The general explained, "I am concerned the intruder could be a threat. We have not yet confirmed if he is armed."

After a lengthy exchange, the Grand Mufti agreed that the general should determine if he considered the man a genuine threat. Then Abdul Aziz, choosing his words carefully, said, "The man in yellow must not be harmed. At the very least, we should understand how one man can bypass our security devices. This is important, beyond all our titles or rank."

There was an assurance to the old man's voice duly noted by the general. "I will do what I can. If the intruder poses a threat to the Prophet's tomb, I will personally finish him," said the general

The Grand Mufti gave a wizened smile that suggested he somehow knew the outcome would be satisfactory. "I shall await your return, general. In the meantime, I would appreciate your expediency, as it is difficult to keep some of my dogs on a short leash."

General Salah nodded his appreciation. The Grand Mufti's entourage was already restless.

The general saluted the guards at the outer door and ordered his men to approach from different sides. He showed no regard for his safety as he marched directly towards the robed figure. General Salah stopped six feet away, pistol ready in his right hand. "Who are you, and what do you want here?" he demanded.

The man in yellow cocked his head to one side and quizzically observed the soldiers. Finally, he slowly raised his arms, saying, "You can see that I'm not armed." He slid off the yellow thaub, dressed only in a small cloth covering his genitals. "I have nothing to hide and everything to give, General Salah."

The general flinched. "How do you know who I am?" He looked accusingly at the four guards sitting on the floor, convinced they must have said something.

"I've known you your entire life. You can tell the Grand Mufti he is safe to come in and speak with me. I know he is here. If it helps to put your mind at ease, I will not be here this time tomorrow, but I will return. You will help me. We'll meet again less than forty days from now," The man put his yellow thaub over his shoulders and straightened the material. "If the Grand Mufti wants to know who I am, let him know Jesus is here."

The man's confidence unnerved the general. How could he know the Grand Mufti had arrived?

General Salah's men had five weapons trained on the man in yellow, but Abdul Aziz wanted this man alive. The general could quickly rush him and drop him to the ground, but he could not bring himself to do it. The opportunity beckoned, but his heart said there was no need. The realization filled him with dread.

General Salah had seen the horrors of battle firsthand, but this was something new that rattled him to his core. He did not enjoy the unexpected. His years of training and military instincts were of no use. His inner voice demanded a kindly approach. The general signaled his men to stand down their weapons and hold their positions. "I will speak with the Grand Mufti. What should I tell him when he asks why you are here?"

"It is for his ears only. He's been expecting me." Jesus' gaze penetrated the general's flesh. "Have no fear, general." With that, Jesus lowered his head onto his chest and closed his eyes as if he were peacefully in prayer.

General Salah looked at the four guards sitting on the floor, it was as though they were hypnotized. Their gazes were firmly fixed in adulation on the man claiming to be Jesus. General Salah backed away. His mind incomprehensibly buzzed. His soul screamed the truth of what he'd witnessed, but his stubbornness held it in denial. Duty called as he marched through the mass of people surrounding the Grand Mufti. Their raised voices were like the buzzing of angry insects. Abdul Aziz waved away his entourage, patiently waiting until he and the general had privacy.

"They are anxious to get this over with," the old man said, as though he were tired. "I don't believe they know what we're dealing with." He studied the proud general. "You have seen something that has burned your heart, and you will not be the same again. Your eyes give you away, General Salah. Walk with me."

Abdul Aziz was a wise man. He'd been Grand Mufti for fifteen years, and, at the age of seventy-three, he'd seen and heard about everything the modern world could throw at him. Considered a moderate by the Arabic world, he took his time to make informed decisions. The old man knew the fierce reputation of the general and trusted his recommendations, if not always his motives. Abdul Aziz motioned for him to remain silent and follow across the yard. The two men stood alone inside the empty mosque opposite the Green Dome.

"It is beautiful here, is it not?" The Grand Mufti extolled.

General Salah could not bring himself to look around; instead, his head dropped to his chest, with his emotions throttling him, and he was suddenly overcome with something unexplainable. "I don't know how to …"

21

The Grand Mufti patiently waited.

The general twice cleared his throat. "He says he is Jesus. He knows you're here and wishes to speak with you. He knew my name before I said anything. I had the chance to arrest him, but I couldn't. He said he will be gone by tomorrow and return in less than forty days."

The general couldn't prevent the tears that escaped his eyelids. His head dropped closer to his chest as he fought the urge. His heart ached as if tortured with an enormous loss, worse than when his dear mother had died a few years earlier. "I do not have the words."

Abdul Aziz patted the general on the shoulder. "No time to waste then, my friend; you are soon to become a soldier of God. Saudi Arabia is no longer the kingdom for which you will be our blessed defender. I think you will be a warrior for the planet," the old man concluded with a slight chuckle. He patted the general's shoulder some more. "Say nothing of this to anyone. I will speak with this man. Inshallah. I know who he is." The old man steadied himself on his walking cane and slowly walked away.

General Salah wiped his eyes. "Who is he?"

The Grand Mufti smiled. "He is everything, and he is everyone." Then, he headed across the tiles as fast as his aching old legs would take him and entered the tomb of the Prophet.

Yasser Al-Temyat knew enough of the Koran and its teachings to ask the robed man, "Are you, Jesus? Who are you?"

Jesus lifted his head. "What words can I give you that will give you comfort? Listen with your heart. You will find the answers you desire."

Yasser closed his eyes, a broad smile spreading across his lips. Intuitively, he knew words were unnecessary. He swiveled his body around, got on his knees, and began to pray. Yasser knew precisely what it was that surrounded him. A beautiful and infinite source. A source revealed the moment he looked into the eyes of the olive-skinned man before him. Seeing Jesus provided a sensation that poured over him as if he were standing beneath a waterfall that flowed with pure penetrating love. Yasser's body shivered as he became drenched in the feeling that infused his veins. His three colleagues copied him and got to their knees. The feeling passed through them as they knowingly exchanged glances to affirm. Words were unnecessary, questions were irrelevant, thoughts meaningless, as they bowed their heads and floated in reverence.

General Salah spoke with the gathering of deeply animated clerics who demanded revenge for the attack on the sacred Green Dome and called on him to have his officers launch strikes against their enemies. Typically, the reserved general would have let them wave their arms and cry for the blood they thought was owed, but something snapped inside him as he pushed the gathering apart. The men splintered under his mighty shoves. "And who will you launch against? The Israelis, the Iraqis, the Americans? Who? You know nothing except the importance of hearing your own voices. Be silent, or I will launch the first strike here in Medina!" He slowly turned within the semi-circle of men and eyed each of them. "Enough with your sermonizing." The angry general pointed at his officers, "Have your soldiers be about their duty." His team scattered to carry out their orders. General Salah waited, before he addressed the clerics. Through a clenched jaw, he advised, "The rest of you should pray. You have no idea what awaits us."

The Grand Mufti walked through the Al-Masjid. He smiled at the decorative walls, floor, and ceiling. "Allah built you for this," he told the ancient structure as he ran his fingers against the inner walls. Abdul Aziz grunted as his age and rheumatism plagued him. The closer he got, the more his tingling abdomen convinced him that he approached the one he had never expected to meet. Once he came within fifty paces, the tingling increased, and the pains and tribulations of old age once slowing him down suddenly dissipated. His remaining steps were painless.

Four guards busily prayed on their knees. The Grand Mufti surveyed the bizarre scene. Then, Abdul Aziz spoke softly to the men on the ground, as well as the guards in the shadows, "You can all go now. I will talk with you all shortly. Report to General Salah. Be quiet now, my brothers. Go in peace."

The old man, who could barely get out of the SUV minutes earlier, dropped easily to his knees as if he were a young man. He looked upon the face of the man in yellow. The man he'd seen in his dreams was standing in front of him. "Allah be praised." He raised his arms above his head, tilted his head back with tear-filled eyes, and saw the hole in the Dome that led to the heavens beyond. He afforded a laugh at the sight of the star-lit sky through the six-foot hole in the tiles.

The Grand Mufti lowered his gaze from above and observed the reddish-brown eyes before him. There was another color in the man's eyes, but the old man couldn't tell what the light speckles were – something light, reflective, and filled with mystery. "God is Great," the Grand Mufti whispered the words – the words from his recurring dreams. The man in yellow smiled at him, and the old man's residual fear fizzled away like a morning mist. Abdul Aziz clasped his hands together and said, "I've seen you in my sleep."

The man in yellow opened his arms wide and replied, "For good reason. I am Jesus, the messenger of God. My brother Muhammad is buried here." He cast his gaze toward the tomb. "There is much to do and little time. Stand up and listen to what I have to say."

The Grand Mufti was able to stand upright without the help of his cane, and for the first time in years, his body was not screaming in agony. "I have called the Imams and scholars to come here," the old man said.

"God has called all men to bear witness," Jesus said, looking up at the hole in the Dome. "Night is here, but together we shall banish the darkness. The spiritual men that came with you bring them in here, so they can hear my words directly. Once concluded, I will speak to the world and declare my purpose. It is God's will."

CHAPTER THREE

James Gordon walked briskly through the busy office, placed his security badge in the card reader, and pressed the elevator for subterranean level eight. The aluminum cage rattled as it descended through exposed brick layers and shook as it settled at the bottom. James walked carefully through the dimly lit passageways towards the old infirmary. The walls were full of decay, and water dripped steadily from the ceiling. He turned from one passageway to the next. Dark empty spaces were on either side. The pitch-black watched his every step. The rooms contained bits of broken furniture, with debris scattered throughout the exit tunnels. Nobody used any of the underground floors of the building, not since Woodrow Wilson's administration in the early 1900s. Wilson made all his senior staff have their medical treatments and operations under the building, not wishing to expose their medical histories to anyone outside. The lower floors were abandoned when Truman took office in the 1940s. Since then, darkness held power.

James felt contaminated at being here, but ambition called equally loud as duty. At the very end of the hallway, he entered the old infirmary filled with pools of rancid water.

"You smell that, Jim?" the man with light gray speckled eyes asked him.

James was in no mood for Mr. Grey's games.

Mr. Grey stuck his long nose in the air and sniffed with satisfaction. He had perched himself on the edge of an old operating table, his legs dangling over the sides, and his expression was filled with gleeful expectancy.

James was tired. Coming here was a risk. He wondered why Mr. Grey rarely set foot on the ground, but he'd given up trying to figure out these oddities. "All I can smell is damp and decay," he flatly replied.

Mr. Grey's satisfaction disappeared. "Temporary species," he suggested. He flexed his eyebrows at James, and his thin lips curled upwards across his long face. The smile barely creased his flawless pale skin. "I smell anticipation, with a hint of fear and the faintest trace of pathetic hope. Quite a combo. It's the anticipation I like the most. Lots of it. The only thing sweeter than the collective sigh of disappointment is that of despair."

Mr. Grey crossed his long legs over one another, his rear carefully balanced on the table's edge. His bare feet stayed a foot above the murky water. He waited for James to react.

"That's not what I smell."

"That's because you have no imagination, Jim," Mr. Grey accused him with a pointed bony finger. He tutted loudly and sprang straight from the table into the tattered swivel chair. His agility was that of a missing link in the Homo Sapiens evolutionary trail. His light gray pinstripe suit looked too big for his wiry, long frame. He pulled some stuffing from the arm of the chair and scattered the fragments through his fingers. He spun the chair around in circles like a fascinated five-year-old.

"I want you to show some balls, Jim. You're an educated man, of high esteem, trusted, even respected in some places," he said with great enthusiasm. "Forgotten in others," he sighed with deep sadness. The smile left his face as he looked with dismay at the dirty water below the chair. He sighed as if he was disappointed not to see something besides his reflection.

"I know you hate the way they ignore you and use you like a shoe-shine boy. It's time to step up. Fire up those neurotransmitters and show 'em what you've got." Mr. Grey's gusto returned as he punched a hand triumphantly through the air. "You have the potential to be a Renaissance man – like me. Personally, I'm painting a Masterpiece. My creativity is way more than I'm given credit for."

James saw the delight in Mr. Grey's twinkling eyes, which permanently mocked him. His tone delivered fluctuations with a taunting regularity that had worn thin over time. He constrained his reply, "I could be better utilized." James conceded.

"And that's why we're here, Jim. You and me, a team that's going somewhere. What's the use of a security advisor if everything's too damn secure?" Mr. Grey pulled a small pipe from inside his suit pocket. "Mind if I smoke?"

"Knock yourself out." James observed the pools of stagnant water around his feet, where giant rats scampered against the rotten baseboards.

"We're underway. It's more exciting than a launch at Cape Canaveral." Mr. Grey confirmed, tossing his shoulder-length black hair behind his ears. "Going well, I'd say."

"It is. Liftoff in a few minutes," James implied.

Mr. Grey slyly smiled. "That's the spirit. Where your focus goes, so does your fortune. Do you understand what I want you to do?"

"I know what you want me to do, but I don't get why – it seems counter-intuitive," James said.

"Aha!" Mr. Grey wagged a finger at him like a kindergarten teacher to an unruly student. "There you go again – all orders, procedures, policies, and strategies – there's no creativity among any of you." He tapped the pipe on the side of his skull. "Think yourself lucky you have me. A creative genius. It's like a rollercoaster ride. Most people are afraid of the sharp drop, but the climb preceding is what gets you. The downhill whoosh is fleeting, merely a distraction before the next ascent where the true thrill begins. Humanity likes the struggle of climbing uphill. We're applying some additional G-force." He lit the pipe.

"Seems like an awfully big distraction you're providing."

"Who doesn't like a distraction?" Mr. Grey took a couple of puffs on the pipe, straining to curb his bursting excitement, as his lean body twitched, flexed, and pulled itself tight. He rotated his shoulders and momentarily appeared to fill his pinstripe suit. He puffed some more on the pipe, with his long bare feet dangling over the edge of the ruptured leather. "Bigger the better. I'll let you know why when we get nearer the time. By then, you'll be much closer to a seat in the Oval Office – maybe not the big chair, but at least you'll be at the adults' table."

He spun the chair in a full circle and faced James. "I like big chairs; they make you feel kind of important."

James disdainfully glared at Mr. Grey. He wondered if this partnership was worth the aggravation. "I prefer influence over big chairs."

Mr. Grey looked disgruntled. "Can you hear that, Jim?" Mr. Grey asked, cupping a hand to his ear.

"I don't hear anything except dripping water."

Mr. Grey leaned forward in the old chair, and his gaze penetrated deeply as if it was boring a hole through James' skull. "I hear the sound of your ambition calling you. It's irresistible, isn't it? It comes to all of us. Second thoughts are for the weak. Don't be so dull, Jim."

James wondered if Mr. Grey somehow had read his mind. "I never said anything about second thoughts."

"You didn't have to. You forget who I am," Mr. Grey coldly smiled. "I've had my share of disappointments, Jim; don't be one of them."

"And I don't like surprises. We have an agreement."

"That we do." Mr. Grey puffed out a cloud of smoke that expanded into the shape of a heart. "Cool, huh?" There was no reaction from James. "Surprises?" He repeated the word like it held significance. "I'm a planner, Jim. The fruits of my labors merely appear as surprises. Once a showman ..." he teased.

"Then what's the big deal about keeping the end game from me?"

"Unnecessary inquisitive minds are tiresome. While you and your two-legged ants clamor for answers to everything and humanity increases its universal understanding, you're simply widening the boundaries of your ignorance. You'll still be gazing at the stars as the earth explodes around your ears." Mr. Grey's long face sneered in disgust. "Stick to the plan."

"I need to get back upstairs."

"Say hi to Carrie for me."

James motioned with a flick of his head for Mr. Grey to elaborate.

"Oh, Jim, don't bother yourself. She'll be fine. A good girl. Thighs on her like a thoroughbred, and she probably rides like one, too." He sighed at James' concerned expression. "You really are a bore. I would have expected some banter and at least a mention of her nipples! Guys in the locker room together and all that." Mr. Grey despairingly threw his hands in the air. "Some other time. Carrie Carter is critical to pushing our agenda. I have no designs on her – can you say the same?" Mr. Grey licked his lips. "She's pretty hot, isn't she?"

"My focus is on the safety of the American people and the future of my country."

"I gave you two opportunities to express what you desire, and you passed them by. Pitiful!"

"I care about my country!"

"Spoken like a true patriot, Jim. You go ahead and save the day and get a little something for yourself. Everybody wins."

"I hope so."

"Run along, Jim, to boldly go where no man has gone ... ah, you get it," Mr. Grey laughed. "And use your damned imagination!" He stopped laughing, and his long face pulled tight as he whispered loudly, "I am the provider. They barely know who you are, but I'll make sure they never forget you."

James was already walking away through the awful stench of things that had spent years festering below the surface. The putrefied state felt like a contagion and one where he would need to scrub below the surface of his skin to disinfect himself. He worried that the stain might be permanent.

"It's not easy being an original!" sang Mr. Grey as his words followed James along the dreary corridor.

James stepped into the elevator, wondering if he could live with his conscience and hoping it would turn out for the best. They had made the deal, and assurances were given from both parties. James wanted what he deserved. There was no turning back.

CHAPTER FOUR

Carrie's world, Washington, DC, perpetually buzzed about something. It was a city that lurched from one crisis to another– where it became rare that anyone focused on a single storyline for more than a week. Instead, Washington and the entire world focused on the events in Rome, Medina, Jerusalem, India, and Cambodia. Carrie predicted that the lightning strikes would become a long-term focus for her and James Gordon's team. Her belief was held tight in a bundle of excitable stress, powerful enough to inform her that this was more than her keen sense of intuition. She called her bosses to let them know she was working on something urgent for the government. They already knew and wished her good luck. The hectic pace suited Carrie, who fancied herself at her brilliant best when things were hot. The items she asked for came quickly; James' team showed impressive resources. Carrie knew nothing about James Gordon, and she decided on a cautious attitude towards him.

Time was against her. She had to press on with minimal guidance to make this venture a success. She trusted Senator Garofalo, and for now, that was good enough. Carrie understood that whatever she asked for would be provided, from toothpaste and underwear to shoes, clothes, and her choice of approved electronic gadgets. She was also given a keycard to a hotel room a block away.

She found herself in a private corner office within the non-descript four-story brick building on Wisconsin Avenue. Carrie was informed it would take twenty minutes to get her a laptop and the other items she'd asked for, so she used the time to orient herself. Like many prominent buildings in that area, it contained oversized rectangular windows to allow natural streams of light to penetrate the gloom. Outside was an ornate stone entrance, giving it the appearance that it could have been a school, a factory, or an administration center. The reception area was less than ordinary at street level, as if nobody cared about the gaudy, late seventies décor.

The lady behind the reception desk paid Carrie no attention, and a guard checked her access badge before allowing her to ride the elevator up to the fourth floor. She continually adjusted the lanyard hanging around her neck. Carrie learned that everyone on every floor worked for James Gordon.

A shared workspace was outside her office, filled with desks and hallways connected to identical office spaces, worn-out carpets, and drab pastel-colored walls. When Carrie passed by what was to be her office, a group of technical assistants were organizing two temporary desks for the two people assigned to her. They busied themselves connecting their equipment and awaited her instructions. Within an hour after arriving, Carrie had her laptop, printer, and TV screen all patched into the major news feeds from around the globe. She assigned one of the new people to take notes on happenings in Rome, Jerusalem, and Medina, and the other to do the same for India and Cambodia. "Get me only the facts," she said. "No speculation or hearsay. If any country mobilizes military forces, let me know immediately." Both assistants got to it.

Carrie had to pinch herself at the company and elevation she was in. It was a stark contrast to the humble surroundings where she had grown up on the north side of Detroit. She knew little of her biological parents. Her adoptive parents had had a tough time being an interracial couple living on the border between an all-white neighborhood on one side and all black on the other. Carrie, along with her parents, never belonged, caught in the middle – never entirely accepted, but never shunned. Her mom was a lunch lady at a local school, and her father worked supplying parts to the auto industry. Every Sunday, they went to church, mainly on the back of her mom's love of all things Jesus, and her father tagged along to show support. Carrie loved attending services, feeling the story of the crucifixion and resurrection spoke to her personally. She wanted to live a life of good service and meaning.

She attended service most weekends, but the machine that was Washington sometimes kept her away. The adopted daughter of an African-American mother and a Caucasian father taught her a lot about people, perceptions, and reactions as she progressed through life, giving her an inner determination to strive and prove herself. She'd often exceeded her expectations and had surprised herself with her resilience.

This situation wasn't something for which she could prepare. Carrie was bright, her intuition highly attuned, and her Ph.D. helped her shine in her day job. However, theology and politics were not easy companions in the modern social realm. Her work contained plenty of stress and diversity, but Carrie felt a staleness. Despite many people applauding her contribution, her self-satisfaction reached a minimal level. This new environment had unknown elements and held a dangerous excitement. The risks were high, but the rewards were higher. The unfolding story, particularly in the Middle East, filled Carrie with trepidation.

Nevertheless, it was a challenge worth accepting. This was the first time Carrie had called into question the world as she understood it. Yesterday she was in control, rising steadily through the ranks of the Washington maze – now she was walking head-first into the unknown.

Make the most of it, she thought.

The outer office was pulsing to the chaotic beat of rushing bodies and rapid-fire conversations. That same energy was rooted in the exposed brickwork. Carrie imagined that decades of busyness acted like mortar, holding the whole thing together. She closed her office door and looked as if she was occupied at her desk. Carrie's adrenalin gave her the jitters. She wanted to take a run, or kick the bag, like she was in a kickboxing class, to clear her mind. She closed her eyes and said a prayer, asking God to look over her, help her shine, and mostly, make sure that the world's citizens held it together. People were scared. Nobody had answers. She crossed herself and whispered, "You can do this. Come on."

She marched through the main office, ignoring the noise and frantic activity, to speak with James. He'd given her an outline of what he wanted, but it wasn't entirely clear what she was doing and for whom. Anything she asked for arrived in double-quick time. "Come on, Carrie, keep it together," she said. On entering his office, she noted his complexion was ashen. "James, I need a couple of interpreters for each of the following languages: Urdu, Arabic, Hindi, Punjabi, Khmer. Modern Hebrew, Ancient Hebrew, and Italian. How soon can you get them here?"

James' bleary eyes peered over the top of his glasses. "An hour or two." He pointed to the chair next to him. "Sit down for a minute. You need to see this." He pointed at the two young men frantically working away on laptops in the corner of his office. "These fine young people are the best system hackers on the planet. Technically, we are not supposed to hack anyone, anywhere, at any time, but special occasions call for special measures," he explained.

He turned his screen so she could view it. "There's an almighty commotion at each site, but especially at Medina, in Saudi Arabia. Our sources have informed us that anyone who's anyone is converging at the holy site. Religious, military, and government leaders are all heading that way. Thousands of people are filling the streets outside the complex walls." He looked to the corner of the room. "Theo, have you got that feed up yet?"

The slender African-American man with short-cropped hair raised his right hand and held up his index finger. "One minute, Chief, and we'll be online." He went back to tapping furiously on the keyboard.

"Hurry up. Feed it out to the team. I want every face identified within the next five minutes."

"Yes, Sir."

James pointed a stubby finger with a horribly chewed nail at the screen. "Carrie, this is our live satellite feed, showing Medina."

"It's a mess," she observed. Vehicles jammed the streets, and thousands of people were approaching on foot.

"We guess there are twenty thousand people in the nearby streets. There are no reports of damage, riots, or anyone hurt, but something is happening."

Theo shouted, "Sir, online in ten seconds. It will be on the other screen to your left. We've gotten into the security cameras from inside the complex."

"Well done, Theo!"

James and Carrie moved closer. Seconds later, they looked at security feeds aimed towards the outer gates of the Medina complex, where armed guards urged the vast crowds to retreat.

Carrie suggested, "Theo, can you find the inside feeds for the Green Dome? That's where the lightning hit."

"Looking now. Give me two seconds."

James winced. "It's like a powder-keg. Look at them." The screen flicked through the different camera feeds at a rapid pace.

Theo declared, "This is in the Green Dome – hang on, they've got more than one view there … here we go."

Carrie moved within inches of James. "What are they doing?" The feed showed twenty men in traditional Arabic clothing sitting on the tomb's floor. In front of them, a man in a bright yellow robe spoke to the group.

"Theo, does this have audio? Can you zoom in a little?" James asked.

"I can zoom, but anyone watching this feed in Medina will know they've been compromised."

"Make sure we're recording and get the translation on the audio." James typed a message that went to the team outside in the shared office: "Get me the names of everyone in that room."

"Already recording. Audio coming up, now."

33

Carrie pointed at the man giving the lecture. "He doesn't look like a Saudi. His features are softer, and his hair is reddish-brown. I've asked my stylist to give me that color for two years, and we still haven't nailed it," she observed. As she retracted her finger, the figure in yellow gazed straight at the security camera through which they were observing. Carrie and James looked at one another.

"Looks like he heard you," James nervously laughed.

"If I didn't know better, I'd swear you were right," Carrie responded as her breathing tightened and goosebumps ran all over her flesh. "Do they know?"

"Definitely not," Theo replied. "If they did, we'd be offline, and James would be answering calls from the embassy in Saudi Arabia."

The audio came through. The man's voice was rhythmically smooth as it echoed through the burial chamber. The men gathered before him hung on every word.

"To say they have a hole in their roof without an explanation, they look pretty relaxed," Carrie suggested. "Probably a good thing."

"I need to know what he's saying. Who's translating this?" James asked his assistants.

"Two minutes," Theo responded.

"You've got thirty seconds!"

Carrie observed the men sitting on the mosque floor. The details of the headbands and ghutrahs indicated the importance of those gathered. "Can we see the faces from another angle?" she asked.

"We have one from the opposite side. Ready whenever you need it," Theo replied.

"Do it, please." The view switched. Carrie looked along the line of men. "There. The older guy. He's the Grand Mufti, Abdul Aziz, their most senior religious scholar, and the one people look to for guidance in observing the Koran and how the faithful relate to God. He's as powerful as it gets in Saudi Arabia, religiously and politically."

"An important man," James muttered.

"Very important, not just to his country but also to the Islamic world. He's not a radical fire-breathing nut but more of a thoughtful and dedicated idealist to the Koran's true teachings. Unfortunately, he's often been at loggerheads with the radicals."

"Who's the guy doing the talking?" James asked.

"I don't recognize him, although there does seem to be a strange familiarity. He looks out of place." Carrie shrugged.

James' grimace asked her to expand.

"His thaub is different, his complexion, his hair, and there's something about the eyes, but it's too hard to say with the resolution on these cameras." Carrie let out an exasperated groan as the explanations stayed out of her reach. "It's something important – I mean, they're inside the tomb of the Prophet – right next to it!"

"Meaning what?" James said.

Carrie wrung her hands together, unable to take her eyes off the screen. "Nobody has that level of access to the tomb! Muslims don't worship things like Christians do – like the cross or an object, but if you were going to consider a focal point of importance in the Muslim world outside of Mecca, it doesn't get any more significant than this. Muhammad's tomb would be like having a tombstone for Jesus. Millions visit Medina to pay homage."

"I get it. Like Catholics gathering in St. Peter's Square."

"Much bigger than that. Give us the other angle again," Carrie asked Theo, and immediately it changed over. In the same instance, the man speaking turned his head and stared straight at the camera again.

"How does he know?" James asked. "That's twice he's done that."

"He could be receiving comms from someone?" Theo suggested, "But we're invisible … we'll double-check."

Carrie said nothing. She placed a hand over her abdomen to curb the sweet sickly feeling. The yellow-robed man stared for ten seconds and then focused on the clerics. The man in yellow gave Carrie the impression he looked through her biological structure and into her soul. Her underarms broke into a light sweat, her skin was clammy, and her face was flushed. For a full minute, the noise in the office and bedlam outside disappeared as she focused solely on the man, like in a tunnel, looking straight ahead, and he was the light at the far end. His voice drew her in, and, despite having no idea what he was saying, she took comfort from his words. She only shook out of her haze when James tugged on the sleeve of her jacket.

"What now?" he asked, looking desperately at her.

"Get me everything you have from the other sites. Do they have someone lecturing religious leaders? I need to know if other countries have explained the lightning strike. Has anyone mobilized their armed forces? We need video and audio from all the affected locations, and I need translations. Now!" Carrie stammered.

James groaned as he observed the latest intel coming through his emails. "Islamic extremists are wanting to start a holy war. Christian radicals are protesting and saying this hoax is blasphemy. As if we haven't got enough to deal with."

The two agents in dark gray suits, who'd escorted Carrie into the building, knocked and entered James' office. "Sir, this is Mohammed Yousaf." They saluted and left the office.

Carrie looked as surprised to see Mo as he did her. His lean body stood over six feet tall, with jet black curly hair, which had grown longer, and looped wildly over his collared shirt. His perfectly round eyes had big brown, fully alert pupils. His handsome square jaw was peppered in a light stubble. He wore wrinkled khaki pants, a checked green shirt, worn sneakers, and a light blue woolen jacket, presenting himself as an archetypal professor. He looked panicked, as if the government had kidnapped him off the street and brought him here.

James was already on his feet and shaking Mo's hand, "Carrie, let me introduce you to Mohammed Yousaf. He's just arrived from Harvard. Could you explain what you lecture in up there, Mohammed?"

Mo gave a token shake of Carrie's hand. "Please, call me Mo; everyone does. Miss Carter and I have met before on several occasions. The theologian world is pretty small," he explained to James.

"Oh, you have. Well, that should save us some time," James unconvincingly noted.

Carrie figured that James knew that Carrie and Mo were well acquainted if they had files on everybody. She considered it might have been a test to see if they would admit to having worked together in the past, but there was no time to dwell on the question. Mo's incisiveness, and his detailed insights into the ways of religious studies and social psychology data, made him an obvious choice. "Welcome aboard, Mo," she said. Carrie knew her face had tightly fixed itself into a frown. Mo appeared tense. "You speak fluent Arabic, don't you?"

"I guess I do."

She motioned at the screen. "What's this guy saying to the clerics?"

Mo stood rigidly in the center of the office. He looked at the chaos of the shared office. "Guys, I just got off a government helicopter to translate something into Arabic? What's really going on here? They told me there was something of national importance, and you needed my expertise. You can find translators a dime a dozen in Washington!"

"You know theology, and in-depth understanding of Muslims, Hindus, Sikhs, and Christians," James explained. "And you came highly recommended as someone who can keep something in confidence."

"Who told you that?"

"That's confidential. Mo, we need you to help – now! We need you and Carrie to decipher potential repercussions based on what the religious leaders advise their political leaders. We have to get in front of anything that could pose a threat to national security," James insisted.

"You want me to guess what they're going to do?"

"An educated guess – but yes."

Mo looked at Carrie. "You're on board with this?"

"I want to help. Based on what I've seen so far, I guess I can. So can you." She waved a hand for him to join them.

Mo's eyebrows molded together in the middle of his head, and he rubbed the stubble on his chin. "I'll stay and help, but on one condition: Whatever we discover – only a peaceful solution is considered." Mo pointed at the number of gray suits outside the door. "I don't like people with guns; it makes me think they have bad intentions. I won't have any part in aggression or violence."

"You have my word that that is the least of our intentions," James confirmed. "We don't want anything to escalate into violence. This is why we need your help and the likes of Miss Carter."

"Call me Carrie," she said with some exasperation.

James nodded. "There are thousands of people on the streets in Saudi Arabia. In Vatican City, it's going the same way. Jerusalem is a minefield at the best of times. Our sources in India have informed us that they don't have the infrastructure to control a mass gathering, and Lord knows about Cambodia – that's anyone's guess."

Mo pointed to the computer screen. "If the guy talking is correct, you have a much bigger issue on your hands than you think."

"Why, what's he saying?" Carrie asked.

Mo moved around the desk to join them. "I didn't catch all of it, but he's telling those guys he's here to do God's work, and they need to do as God commands. He said he was the new Prophet for all religions. He also said something about returning to Medina, but I missed the end of it."

"This video feed is live, from the Prophet's tomb, in Medina," Carrie explained.

"You're kidding me?"

"Nope."

"Wow. Do you know how long I've waited to see what the inside of that place looks like?" He leaned in. "Oh, my goodness – look at how beautiful it is. See the reflection in the black granite? Where's the protective golden grills that surround the tomb?"

"We don't know."

James interrupted them, "What's the guy saying now?"

Mo sounded almost disinterested. "Oh, he's telling them they've moved away from the true Word of God, and he's going to show them how to get back on track. He says it wasn't their fault and that for hundreds of years, all religions have made the same mistake. His words are not only for the ears of his Islamic brothers and sisters but for everyone. So they're preparing for some kind of announcement."

"That could bring about global mayhem," Carrie noted.

"Look at the detail in those ancient mosaics," Mo exclaimed again.

"Do you know who he is?" Carrie referred to the man in yellow. "The old man up front is Abdul Aziz."

"Yeah, I recognize the Grand Mufti. The guy in yellow, giving the lecture … that's anybody's guess. They've had plenty of lunatics claiming to be prophets before. This guy is good; I'll say that for him. Very convincing."

James slapped two frustrated arms against his sides. "Senior Saudi religious leaders are told they're doing it wrong, and they haven't killed him by now?"

"Believe it," Mo replied, taking more interest in Medina. "These are the Imams – Islam's highest clerics. It's a very selective audience. He did tell them he's the new Prophet."

"That could spark a holy war, or worse," Carrie gasped.

"Let's hope the guy has faded from view within a few days," James added.

"How did he manage all the lightning strikes?" Carrie thought aloud.

"Oh, you guys haven't figured that out yet?" Mo sounded surprised. His question received blank expressions. "The guy in yellow said something like … the lightning strikes were a sign from God. Are we recording this?"

"Yes," James snapped.

"Chief, you need to come and see this," Theo called out. "We tapped into their database. We've sourced their recordings. Their digital feeds are nice and clear. We've looked at this video clip half a dozen times – we don't know how to explain it. We just asked one of our tech guys to break it down and check for authenticity, but the video feed looks genuine," Theo beckoned them to join him.

James, Carrie, and Mo gathered around Theo's workstation. He pointed to the split-screen view. "This is what the two live feeds inside the mosque recorded earlier. As far as I can tell, nobody messed with them. I'll play it in slow motion for you. These two angles cover everything inside the tomb." Theo pressed play, and the images slowly edged forward. "We've confirmed that the lightning strikes at all six locations were simultaneous. In fact, they weren't 'about' the same time - they were exactly the same time."

"It's coordinated," James grimly confirmed.

"That sounds like something God could manage," Mo jovially pronounced.

"We're seeing the footage from inside the Green Dome," Theo explained.

The security footage showed no movement until a brilliant flash occurred in the top right of the screen. "There! That's the lightning strike hitting the dome," Carrie pointed.

Both feeds showed a powerful, brilliant white flash of light drowning out all visibility for a short period. Theo paused it. "Watch the time on the feeds. When the lightning hits, we can't see anything for 1.2 seconds – then this happens." Theo continued playing the feed, showing the yellow-robed man sitting cross-legged on the tiles in front of the Prophet's tomb. Pieces of the shattered roof drifted slowly down to the floor, and huge sections of the protective golden grill had vanished.

"Whoa. Stop it there! Go back a second," James cried out. "Impossible."

"I think I saw this trick performed in Vegas one time," Mo unhelpfully said.

"Rewind, please," James asked.

"Sure thing." Theo followed James' instructions. "We've done this over and over. It doesn't appear edited. The clocks on each feed never stop running. That guy just appeared like a Genie from a lamp."

"How long before tech can tell us if these recordings have been tampered with?" Carrie asked.

"To be certain – a couple of hours. They'll take it apart, but their initial verdict is that the footage is genuine." Theo straightened in his chair and loudly expelled air from his lungs. "If it's a magic trick, it's the best. If it ain't, then I don't know what to tell you, except we should say a prayer or something."

James patted his trusted assistant on the shoulder. "You can say a prayer or two for me. Let's see that again." James ran his hands over his head. "Think about this for a second: this guy just appeared inside the tomb of the Prophet Muhammad; lightning hit six religious sites across the world at the same time;

39

two hours later, he's lecturing Islamic leaders. It's so damned theatrical; it has to be a jest. They're going to tear him apart."

Carrie's doubtful expression suggested otherwise. "If he's a con man, we still have to explain how he did it."

They repeatedly watched the footage, exchanging theories about the spectacle. They watched the rest, showing the security guards as they put down their weapons and began to pray.

"We should prepare for all possible outcomes," Carrie said.

"Like what?" James snorted.

"What is his end goal, and the ramifications? If it's all a trick, and he's gone within a week, how do we ensure there are no religious fractures? What if he continues and escalates the theatrics? Or worse, what if he's authentic?" Carrie theorized, "you'll have a global hysteria on a scale you can't even imagine."

James inspected her. "And how do we prepare for all of those things? You're our experts! You're here to figure this out and make suggestions!" His delivery was testy.

Carrie disliked James' unnecessary provocation, straining to hold her tongue.

Mo quickly intervened. "It's early. Listen, religious believers will tip one way or another once the word gets out. We need to prepare a message that delivers a calm response. Nobody wants a war – I hope." He eyeballed James.

"Wars are expensive and something we want to avoid," James reiterated.

Mo continued, "If we can't show how this was done, then good luck explaining that to the people you report to," he told James. He tapped Theo on the shoulder. "Can you get me a laptop with the full recording and somewhere I can sit in peace to watch it? I'll need internet access."

Theo looked at James for confirmation and received a special nod. "Coming right up."

"I suggest we get to work," Mo said.

A young woman with short brown hair in a dark navy-blue suit entered the office without knocking on the door. She glanced with disinterest at the visiting Carrie and Mo. "James, the Senator is on line two. He wants to talk to you right now. Should I tell him you're busy?"

James shook his head. "I'll take it to the office next door." He looked at Carrie and Mo. "And I tell him what?"

"Tell him that you've got someone in Medina preaching to people of great influence, and we'll have a summary in the next hour," Carrie advised.

Mo quickly pointed out, "Whoever he is, he hasn't called for any violence. So make sure they know that."

"Could be some clever trick, but who knows. I'll get to work," Carrie agreed with Mo.

"We ran a facial recognition on the preacher, but we've got nothing on him," Theo said.

James slapped his hands against his sides again. "Great! Let's meet back here at noon. I'll need a full picture of what's happening and any recommendations you have," he fumed.

"We'll try to come up with something to keep us all in one piece," Mo sarcastically replied.

"You do that!" James hurried from the office.

"Welcome aboard. Follow me," Carrie gestured for Mo to come with her.

"I'll have you hooked up in fifteen minutes," Theo called after Mo.

Carrie took Mo to the office they'd allocated to her. She closed the door, and her eyes darted around the office. Her expression indicated there was no privacy. "Government spies," she shrugged. "There's this whole thing going on, and before I know it, I'm here – now, you're here …"

Mo cut her off, "Carrie, they didn't tell me you'd be here."

"Same here. Is that going to be an issue?"

"I hope not. The last couple of times we crossed paths, it was … a little prickly. I never meant to be pushy or to back you into a corner. I'm sorry it got out of control."

"Let's forget it, shall we?"

"I can't forget it, but I am sorry."

"Me too."

"I know you said that for you it was just casual, but I couldn't help the way I felt. I got caught up in … well, I'm sorry," Mo stated with sincerity. "It looks like we have plenty of other things to focus on."

"Mo, you're a great guy, but as I'd said, I didn't have the time or inclination for something serious – no more than I do now. I didn't intend for either of us to get hurt, so we've both got things to be sorry about."

"It's fine, it really is," he blurted unconvincingly.

"Good, I'm busy here in Washington, and you've got your stuff going on at Harvard. It would be great if we could be friends and get this thing done – whatever it is."

"Sounds good. Let's see what we can do, and I'll behave myself. You still look great. I can't believe it's been two years."

41

"Thank you. You look fairly good yourself." Carrie admired Mo and respected him as an academic and as a man, but their past had become a tangled mess. She knew their fling had caused him pain. She didn't intend it, and Carrie had abruptly cut him off when it ended.

Carrie was all about her career, and Washington had called to her. She could have easily become an established professor at Harvard, and she and Mo would have led comfortable lives together. But, for Carrie, settling down and playing the happy family felt like she would miss her chance to contribute something bigger to society. The two year gap seemed like only two months.

Carrie continually questioned the exact details of her contribution and how to measure her success, and the answers weren't obvious. Moreover, the idea plagued her that she might be better off as part of an elite academic couple. The two of them could be teaching the next generations how to assess centuries of material and apply them in a modern-day context for the greater good.

Carrie snapped out of it. "So, what do you make of all this?"

Mo scanned the activity surrounding them. He rubbed his chin hard enough to make an audible sound. "Do you want my academic summary or what I really think might be happening?"

"Give me what you really think because I know your brilliant scholarly mind will be too detailed for me to keep up."

"I doubt that's true. Based on my thirty minutes of exposure, it looks like God has sent his representative back to earth, and he's in the Al-Masjid an-Nabawi preaching to some of the most respected Muslim leaders on the planet."

He paused as he thought about it. "Saying that aloud makes me think I've lost my mind."

"You and me both," Carrie agreed. "They're setting you up in the little office over there," she pointed. "We can coordinate what we find and present it to James. I think we'll be speaking with Senator Garofalo in a short while. It's gotten complicated – fast."

"No kidding." Mo extended his hand to shake with hers. "Friends … and now colleagues."

"Oh, come here, and let's do it properly." She checked that the door was closed, and they hugged. For a brief moment, his arms felt good around her, comforting. A flicker of possibility ignited like a flame struck from a match but quickly died again. "I'll see you in an hour. I'm waiting on a dozen interpreters to arrive. I asked them to listen to all the places hit by lightning."

"You move fast, Miss Carter." Mo pushed his lips to one side of his face and raised a pair of impressed eyebrows before leaving her office.

The door clicked shut. Carrie blew out the air from her lungs and looked around. *Oh, Carrie, you'd better get on this girl.*

The main office was somehow busier, like a hybrid-human beehive, with a buzzing intensity of sound and motion. The scope was unclear – the situation even less so, but they all understood that danger lurked in every outcome. As Carrie thought about her recommendations reaching the President himself, her stomach performed an internal somersault. "I'm good at this," she grated her teeth.

Carrie didn't say it aloud, but she secretly hoped this phenomenon was rooted in truth and that it turned out to be something miraculous. God knows the world could use some universal hope, and it would be even better if she could assist. She'd always considered herself a realist, with a healthy sprinkling of optimism. If God worked in mysterious ways, mankind's intervention was useless anyway.

If this display came from an organization, it would spell disaster. Carrie felt obliged to sift through the data and make sense of it. But, for now, she would continue trying to predict the outcomes.

Most perplexing was the familiarity of the man in the yellow robe. He knew they watched him. Carrie's gut told her not to ignore the signs. "Signs of what?" she asked. Carrie subdued her spiritual desire for something extraordinary to occur. "Deal solely with the stone-cold facts." She tapped her fingers to the sides of her head, "Let's get to work."

CHAPTER FIVE

Abdul Aziz left the Prophet's tomb and gave instructions to his closest advisors. The Grand Mufti's words were second only to the King, and immediately obeyed.

With a flick of his wizened hands, his religious leaders scattered to prepare international news agencies to enter the sacred space of the Al-Masjid. Outside the gates, hundreds of reporters eagerly awaited an update on information about the precious resting place of Muhammad. More than that, they wished to know more about the rumors that someone had broken into the complex and why the Imams were attending meetings inside the Green Dome.

Abdul Aziz took himself into an adjacent mosque and sat quietly by himself in contemplation. His head was dizzy, and his heart filled with a bursting love. The old man had waited his entire life for such a moment, and he took his time enjoying it. His biological clock ticked ever closer to striking midnight, and there would be no alarm call to wake him from eternal slumber. He'd given himself to the service of God and his people. He bathed in the stillness, satisfied with getting this far and honored to partake in the next phase. He thanked God for granting him the longevity to see this glorious day and prayed that he would be able to see it through.

He sat for a couple more moments in the beautiful silence of the ornately decorated building. He marveled at the architecture and how those who had dreamed of its design had boldly displayed their genius in pulling the soul towards heaven in its upward-curving spirals. Abdul Aziz thought its designers' visions of ascension captured the spirit of something deemed untouchable and cleverly formed it into the remarkable monument.

He placed a call directly to the King – the reigning monarch of Saudi Arabia must be present. The King was technically the custodian of Al-Masjid an-Nabawi in Medina and Masjid Al-Haram in Mecca, the two holiest sites in the Muslim world. Abdul Aziz would update the King and prepare the ruler for what was to come. He walked outside into one of the many gleaming courtyards and paused in the central courtyard to gaze up at the Green Dome. He brought his hands together in thanks to Allah. The elderly Grand Mufti had dreamed that he would be part of something to change the fortunes of Islam, but now, he was allowed to influence the way all people lived together on the planet. His mission was to bring the Word of God to the world, but he never imagined it would be so direct.

The words he'd just witnessed filled him with excitable reservations. Newness always faced pushback. The ultimate message was as yet unheard, which caused a nervous flutter. His esteemed colleagues had expressed their concerns, which he shared. Doubt was inevitable, but he felt an undeniable persuasion in his soul. The vivid dreams that had bothered him so much in recent weeks had magnificently revealed their truth. Abdul Aziz would do everything required of him to unite the people in service to God.

General Salah positioned over a thousand men at the site and nervously awaited more to arrive. He'd asked for five thousand ground troops and air support, and he had organized artillery to be set up on the surrounding hills to protect the holy site. His immediate commanding officer, the General of the entire Saudi armed forces, was on his way to Mecca to secure the other holy mosque for fear it might come under attack by a stampede of anxious believers. The Grand Mufti supported the moves, recognizing that people would congregate at both holy sites in unprecedented numbers. Extremists looking to take advantage could disguise themselves within the swelling observers.

The General was busier than he'd ever been. He promised his wife he would give more attention to her and his family, but now this calamity had manifested itself and undone that promise. The man in yellow had stirred the General's thoughts. Before they'd ever met, the man knew the General and said they'd soon meet again. Subconsciously he knew it to be true. General Salah was a man who used data and facts to build strategic plans. This sudden spiritual vitality threatened to blow his world apart. "I am built for war, not sermons."

He asked Allah for guidance. No reply came. The General did not like to stumble about blindly. It was God's way of punishing him for living a life where prayer had taken a back seat to his military career. The same could be said for his long-suffering family, who rightfully resented the time he devoted to duty.

General Salah went to the restroom and called his wife, telling her to stay at home with their children. He arranged for his brother and family to stay with her. The compound they lived in was secure, and his brother, a former Lieutenant in the armed forces, would protect them. General Salah's wife spoke of riots and looting, but he assured her it was only a rumor. "I have to go because the old man wants me. Be safe and stay in the gated community." There were other things he wished to say, but the words deserted him for some reason. It was a perfect time to be a better husband, but his good intentions remained frozen. Surely, she would know.

He stared at his phone and hung his head in disappointment. He splashed water on his face, but it did little to cool the fires. He gathered his senior officers to inspect the complex with his own eyes to ensure his men did as he commanded.

He headed across the courtyard, where the Grand Mufti greeted him. Before he could ask a question, the old man was already chattering.

"General Salah, I've just spoken with the King – the royal family will be here within the hour, via helicopter. We'll escort them inside the north gate, and then the King, the Imams, and I, along with the TV cameras, will go inside the dome. There, we'll listen to the word of the Prophet Jesus. He has asked that you be there, too."

General Salah's nerves twitched. "Why me?"

"He says that you'll understand why, and he will need your help. What more do you need?" the old man asked with a glint.

"I'm a mere soldier. How can I help this man?" General Salah looked around the courtyard to make sure they were alone. "Is he the Prophet?"

The Grand Mufti grinned. "He is. You don't yet feel it? Confusion and hesitation rule long before our hearts intervene. We've much to do. Meet me inside the tomb in half an hour, and we'll make ready."

"I hope I can do what is required," the General said, his narrow gaze filled with distress.

"Do not worry. The eyes of the world will be upon us, and the words from heaven will soon be in our ears. No pressure," the Grand Mufti insinuated the opposite. "Praise be my brother, praise be!"

The General bowed. "Praise be to Allah." He hesitated before adding, "I am not a good Muslim. There are many things I have questioned."

Abdul Aziz placed a steady hand on the General's arm. "Who hasn't?" He gave him a friendly shake. "Now, ready yourself and your men. We go to speak with God!"

CHAPTER SIX

James Gordon wiped his sweaty brow after another blast from Senator Garofalo and facing the prospect of having little to offer when briefing the President. The pains in his chest were real. The White House wanted the President on national news to give the nation some assurance. James' team was doing all they could to make sure international partners kept open lines of communication. At least the Russians and Chinese were on board, despite accusing the U.S. of wishing to start a Middle Eastern war as an excuse to put boots on the ground. James was painfully aware of the miserable time this presented for anyone in the government office, and he was in the thick of it. It was impossible to comfort anyone. He grabbed a fresh coffee, wishing it were good bourbon, gulped it down, and poured himself a second cup. "No wonder I'm having palpitations," he murmured. It was only forty-five minutes before his White House briefing.

He dashed across the main office and slammed the door. "Talk to me, Theo. What's the latest?"

Theo's face was a mass of deep concentration lines. "Chief, all indications are that this guy appeared out of nowhere. Tech confirmed no one else tapped into the video feeds in the Prophet's tomb. The man in yellow is sitting there like he's meditating."

"A guy can't just appear from nowhere. There must be a trapdoor, or he's not there at all. We're watching a projection," James suggested.

"Sorry, but we've tried that, and he's there. We know that nobody can appear from nothing, but he did exactly that. There's a chance there is some trickery in the 1.2 seconds of blinding light." Theo pulled his lips tight and widened his eyes, knowing this wasn't helping. "We've given the footage to several professional magicians to see what they make of it. They have no idea the footage is from Medina or why we're asking. They've all signed disclosure agreements."

"That's the best we've got, collaborating with magicians? Really? C'mon, guys. I'm briefing the goddamn White House! I can't tell them we have the Arabic equivalent of David Copperfield yanking our chain. I'll be the one made to disappear faster than you can say, Alakazam! I need something concrete," James raged.

Theo pointed an extended index finger at the still shots from the floor in the Green Dome. "The bad news is that the floors are solid. There are no trapdoors or such. I wish I could say otherwise." Theo's lanky figure leaped from his chair to the other desk and returned with more images.

"Any chance he came in through the hole in the roof?"

"Nope. We checked other external feeds. He'd have broken to pieces on impact. It's over a hundred-foot drop onto pure marble." Theo threw his hands up in the air and waved the photographs around. "For now, it's simply magic."

"Keep me updated on anything you get. I'll take any theory right now."

"We already have one." Theo mumbled, "But you won't like it."

"What's that?"

"You're not a church-going man, are you, Chief?"

James' jawline tightened harder than the one Theo presented. "No. At least, not yet," he replied, heading for the door. His cell lit up with a call from Senator Garofalo. He signaled with his hand that he'd follow up with Theo. "Hey, Bob, if you're going to start yelling again, save it. We're doing all we can."

Senator Garofalo fumed, "James, we just got word that the state-run TV in Saudi has reached out to all of our major TV networks and will provide a live feed at 3:00 pm, our time. Everyone's showing it: CBS, NBC, CNN, Fox, ABC, and the rest – plus the internet – YouTube, Facebook. They're going global. I need to know what they're going to say. The President's going ape-shit – he wants to brief the American people before the Saudis go live. What the fuck, James?"

"We've done as much as we can. You're not going to like it, Bob, but we think there's a new religious voice in the region. We don't know the message, but the President can assure the nation not to panic or pay credence to whatever they broadcast until we verify the facts. Their religious leaders are talking with an unknown source. In the meantime, life goes on as normal."

"Normal?" The Senator mocked. "I'm told the Saudi Royal family are already en route to Medina. They'll be there shortly. So do your damn job and get me something I can tell the President. Call me in fifteen minutes with a plan, or don't call me again."

James sank his head into his chest. This was not the way to get permanently into the White House. "Good grief." Mr. Grey never indicated this would be what it took. He considered whether this was what he wanted, knowing the trajectory's vicious path. James wanted to leave the shadows and have his place at the main table despite all the aggravation. Mr. Grey assured him he'd get what he wanted, and Mr. Grey had proven accurate with his predictions. The game was in motion. James must continue for his success and for his family.

James needed more time. This was Washington, and it never stood still. He called his assistant. "Get Carrie, Mo, and Theo with the tech team in my office – in less than two minutes."

James listened to their unsatisfactory reports. He took what little he could use and dismissed them. He watched the President's stony-faced live broadcast, asking for understanding for whatever came out of the Middle East. American citizens in Saudi Arabia were warned to stay indoors. Ten seconds after the Presidential speech ended, Senator Garofalo called him back. "James – get me something usable or get another job."

Carrie entered Mo's office. "It smells musty in here. Hey, you got a minute?" Before he could respond, she took a seat opposite him and carried on, "The more I look at this mess, the less I understand the motives behind it. I understand the details well enough. It's like someone has studied what you'd expect a modern-day Prophet to do, how to look and act. It's as if someone modeled the perfect, holy representative and placed him in Medina. Too good to be true. This might be the greatest hoax of all time, or it might not be. Whatever we're about to hear, this will create a massive stir. Our President wasn't happy. They reckon over half of the world's population will watch the Medina broadcast."

"You remember I'm a Muslim, right?"

"Yeah, of course."

Mo walked around the desk. "I take my religion seriously – all religions. I'm what you might call a decent Muslim. Not a great one, but good enough. Carrie, I am scared for my faith, the safety of people I know and love, and all those in the Middle East. This feels dangerous, and not just for Muslims. You know as well as I do the whole region is permanently in a state of waving a

50

naked flame over dry gunpowder. There's no predictability, and especially not with this damned live broadcast. So I agree with you – the greatest hoax or not."

Carrie looked at him with suspicion.

"I know," he exclaimed with his hands up in surrender. "I actually agree with you on something!"

"What makes you say that?'

"Because it's too perfect. If you're going to put on a grand show, this would be the way to do it. Muhammad delivered the basis of the Koran to Muslims, and his predecessor, Jesus, delivered the Word of God to the Jews. They were humble men. They had to fight and struggle to spread their message. They didn't suddenly show up one day in a lightning storm, but they lived a normal life for their respective time until their lives became fully dedicated to the work of God. This doesn't fit the profile of what we know. If God was sending a messenger, why do it with such a spectacular entrance? This is all fireworks and marching bands. You know what I mean?"

"I get that, but then again, why not? The attention span in the modern world calls for the spectacular. If you're going to impress today's society, you need some fireworks. Unfortunately, even now, conspiracy theories are running amok all over social media before we've heard what he has to say!" Carrie studied Mo's face with dark eyes, stressed jowls, and tight neck.

His flickering brown eyes grabbed her attention. "What have you found?" Carrie poked a finger in his direction. "I've seen that look before, Mr. Twinkly Eyes." No sooner had the words left her mouth than Carrie flushed red for rekindling some familiarity.

"Nothing, I swear!"

Carrie quickly regrouped, "Bullshit, Mo. What is it? Tell me. We're supposed to be partnering on this."

Mo closed the door. "I just listened to the recordings of what that guy said to the Grand Mufti and clerical leaders. He's claiming to be the Prophet of God. He said God sent him to deliver us all from the mess we've created."

"Isn't that a good thing?"

"Carrie, this man is calling himself a prophet! He claims to be speaking on behalf of his Father. He said that he's the brother of Muhammad and Jesus Christ. He's already told the highest-ranking Muslim leaders that their methods of worshipping God are incorrect! He told them right to their faces. And he told them everyone else got it wrong, too! Do you know what that means? More than 1.5 billion Muslims will hear they got it wrong. That's just Islam! Muslims everywhere will not be happy about this. I'm not happy."

"You're never happy," Carrie interjected.

Mo rolled his eyes. "They're letting him broadcast, with Royal and clerical blessing. They've sanctioned his message! Global religions are going to flip out. The whole planet could be in flames by midnight."

"Maybe nothing will happen?" Carrie thoughtfully observed.

"Your optimism sounds naïve."

"He said everybody got it wrong. No exceptions. If his message was good enough for the Grand Mufti and the King to let him go global, I'm assuming the message isn't destructive. It could be the opposite. Isn't it better if there is a unifying link to the divine where we all get the same message? Something for the greater good."

"Ultra-religious people typically don't like change. This sounds like potential anarchy. Yet, by this time tomorrow, ninety-five percent of anyone with access to a cell phone, laptop, or TV will hear his message. As a Muslim, a believer in God, and as a human being – I'm afraid," he said, unable to prevent the tears from forming in his eyes.

Carrie stuttered, "Let's think positive. We'll find out soon enough." She offered a comforting hand on his forearm.

"Carrie, he said he's the third coming. The final messenger."

CHAPTER SEVEN

The Al-Masjid an-Nabawi had been the focus of attention since its first construction in 622 AD. As a place of worship and subsequently the resting place for the Prophet Muhammad, it maintained its focal point in the Islamic world. Medina was a bustling metropolis that grew around it. The six lightning strikes gripped the world in apprehension, and many believers feared this signaled something apocalyptic. Religious and political leaders everywhere called for restraint. Rumors circulated that Medina held the key. Every news agency on the planet was featuring this story as their main headline. People gathered in front of TV screens, laptops, tablets, and mobile phones, awaiting the broadcast.

As Carrie predicted, numerous sections of the global internet system failed under the strain of simultaneous usage. Companies scrambled to get everyone connected, especially as the paid advertisers salivated at the prospect of viewership statistics.

The TV and internet media were carefully orchestrated inside the ancient burial chamber. They huddled close to one another to get everybody inside the space. Photojournalists had strict instructions that they could not take any flash photography inside the building and no pictures until instructed to do so. Everyone nervously waited in complete silence – a rarity for the media. The atmosphere built to a thick crescendo as the chosen time approached. Many of those gathered nervously fidgeted. Inside the Green Dome, two hundred heavily armed uniformed men lined the walls, their eyes hidden behind sunglasses. General Salah made a final inspection of his men, and his officers confirmed the plans.

The General positioned himself at the end of the front row of elderly scholars. He felt the shared pressure, and the unknown played with his fractured nerves. Following strict orders was much easier than what was currently asked of him.

The Grand Mufti, Abdul Aziz, stood before them and signaled for the media to begin. He bid them a good evening and kindly reminded them of their instructions. The old man presented a brief overview. A talk would take place – no questions were allowed: the instructions were simple – record the event, say nothing, and leave.

"For those watching around the globe, we welcome you to our magnificent holy tomb of the Prophet Muhammad. We wish you all peace and goodwill." Then, Abdul Aziz moved to one side and joined the line of clerics.

The Saudi King sat to one side, surrounded by most of his family and personal bodyguards. Before the event, General Salah had witnessed the King telling Abdul Aziz, "If this is anything less than spectacular, I will not be pleased. The outcome will mean your retirement." Upon hearing the king's words, Abdul Aziz politely smiled and wished the King a long life and peace. General Salah liked the old man's unflinching attitude.

"What can he do to me at my age that would not bring relief?" the old man slyly whispered to the General.

A signal came from one of the senior clerics that it was about to begin. Then, from the back of the Prophet's tomb, the man dressed in yellow serenely approached from the shadows. The eerie silence deepened the abyss of anticipation.

The man in yellow stood centrally in front of the tomb. Abdul Aziz got down on his knees. Everyone, except the camera operators, followed suit without a word or thought.

In Washington, DC, Carrie, Mo, and James sat shoulder-to-shoulder around a monitor. A tech assistant whispered, "Estimated live global audience is climbing over three billion. Live in every country – except North Korea."

"Nearly half the world's population," Carrie said. "If you want all of us to be able to work tomorrow, you'd better have an alternative secure internet connection. The global web could collapse within hours."

James nodded towards Theo. "Good call," he whispered. An assistant took the instruction and rushed from the room.

Carrie's faith in the Bible was strong. Her nerves were on full alert, like when she had set herself in the blocks before a race. She hoped this sprint to the line would have a better outcome. Her latest dreams were a reality and gave rise to shallow breaths as if the gun were about to sound. Instinctively, she lowered her hand under the desk and felt for Mo's fingers, who, without flinching, gripped hers tight.

News presenters finished their introductions. The stage was firmly set. The translations were ready to roll on the screens that came live from Medina.

Inside the White House, the presidential advisors were in constant touch with their military advisors and the National Guard, and reserves were called to standby status. James Gordon let the immediate team know that, as a precaution, the President, and his close team, had taken residence deep underground, along with the Presidential family. James took no chances in case the live broadcast was simply a distraction for something else to unfold.

The man in the yellow folded his hands together in front of his body. He slowly looked along the line of cameras, the clerics, scholars, security guards, and other religious representatives. His expression was impassive. After an agonizing silence, he opened his arms and raised his palms.

"God is great. Welcome." He waited again. Some of the religious leader's heads began to move around nervously. The man in yellow saw their mild agitation. "I am Jesus. That is the name my spiritual Father has given me: There is but one true God. I am sent here to deliver what you require. Despair no longer – God is love, and God will show you the way. God does not divide you under different banners. You are all God's children. There is but one religion – to live in service of God. God's word is final. His word is peace, it is love, and it is understanding. Listen without bias, and act through kindness. This is God's plan for you."

The man claiming to be the prophet stared into the cameras.

"Why should you listen to me?" He moved a few feet to his right, and the media followed him. He pointed up at the hole in the Green Dome, where the stars were visible in the night sky.

"Listen to my master's calling. I am the vessel by which God will show you how to live in peace, love, and harmony with each other and the planet. You are each in God's grace and favor. I am the Prophet – I carry the true word." His eyes briefly looked up at the six-foot hole in the tiles, and a smirk came across his face. "You will look for answers as to who I am, but you cannot explain my presence. Only my spiritual Father can account for my being."

Jesus paused and once more looked at the rows of cameras. "Pay heed to what I have to say. You are all sons and daughters of our Father. You are all brothers and sisters in God. These times make it hard for you to comprehend, but there is no complexity in the Word of God. Your open hearts will be all you need – your willingness to change your path will alter humankind's destiny. Change is inevitable. You will all be tested. God knows this is the time, and God has faith for the collective consciousness to embrace change. It was always your destiny to be as one. God's words apply to those of all faiths and non-believers. God has no vanity and gives you free will to choose, and free will remains. Judge no one for exercising their individual choice; it is God's will that each of you chooses your relationship to the divine. God's gift is the divinity within each of you. Let it blossom so that beauty fills the world."

The faces of the learned Muslim men furrowed, nervously sweating, and full of anxiety.

Jesus saw their distress and stepped closer to them. "Do not be troubled, good men of Medina, or those watching with fearful hearts. Act in accordance with God's love, and all will be well. I will be with you for forty days and nights on this earth, and I will return from where I came. Modernity requires validation, and God understands. Your six primary temples are blessed in God's light, and you've witnessed his first great miracle. The lightning was a sign from my Master. A capability beyond any of your governments. It is a sign of God's love that strikes equally across all faiths and welcomes those who are lost. You have all been chosen—now you must choose. Conjurers and false prophets will seek to deceive and destroy, but God will show you his true power and mercy. God is merciful, and God is great."

The temperature in the Prophet's tomb had become unbearably hot with the people packed tightly together. Many wiped their brows with a cloth. Jesus approached the front row of scholars and reached down to Abdul Aziz, taking the old man's handkerchief, and he gently wiped the old man's forehead as he smiled upon the wizened teary face.

Jesus raised his head and addressed them all. "A Prophet was promised. Rejoice in God's commitment to his people." He gave the handkerchief back to the old man.

Jesus moved back towards the tomb. "Men of the Ulema, your God does not want you to suffer to hear his words." He raised his arms and opened his palms. "Find comfort in the power of God."

A strong cool breeze rushed through the mosque and into the tomb, circling and cooling those gathered. The strength was enough to flap their clothing and ruffle their hair. They looked around in confusion, frightened at first, as the cool breeze came from everywhere. They could not hide their astonishment as the night's heat dispersed, and their sweat-glistened skin was chilled. The lights inside the tomb became brighter, forcing them to shield their eyes momentarily.

Jesus knelt in front of them. "As God's children, you shall now find your hearts driven by God's love. A love to share. These good men here will be my keepers for my time on this earth." Jesus gestured to the gathered clerics and scholars of Medina.

His gaze moved along the line. "You were chosen, not for what you presently believe, but for the beliefs you have yet to realize. I am the return of my brother Muhammad and Jesus before him. This is my final coming. Take care to follow your heart. Today, you are born again in God's eyes, like newborn children seeing the world for the first time. Be wise in how you use God's word. Our Father does not see color, creed, race, religion, persuasion, sex, origin, or political belief. There are no exceptions – God loves everyone and everything. Be the light and be the keepers of this world – and keep sacred his word. People of the world – this is your time to unite in friendship, understanding, peace, and eternal love. Cast aside your fears and listen to your neighbors. It is your fear that holds you back. Let it go like an autumn tree casting a dead leaf to the ground. New growth is promised, and a bountiful earth will rise."

Jesus got back to his feet. "My brothers and sisters, God has instructed me to move among his people, to help you see that you are as one; equal in your fears, anxieties, and misguided thoughts, but equally united, uplifted, and loved as one, by our Father. The time for division and old quarrels is over. Our Father will show you this truth, and you learned people will lead the way."

He turned and faced the Saudi King. "All leaders will embrace the words of our Father in peace, unity, and inclusion. It will require bravery, innovation, great risk, and trust in God to bring people together. Taking your first steps here on earth will assure you of walking with God for all time. The world needs the guiding hands of courageous brothers and sisters who listen to God's peace. Be the change that God wants you to be."

Jesus turned his back on them, walked towards the tomb of Muhammad, and rested both his hands on the tomb. He stood in silent prayer for a full minute. Some of the TV crew's lights exploded, showering sparks across the tiled floor. The armed guards, particularly those by the royal family, became animated, but the senior clerics signaled for calm.

Abdul Aziz and the King nodded to one another. Then, the King signaled the guards, including his bodyguards, to place their weapons on the floor.

Jesus faced them once more. "My brother Muhammad dreamed of a better world. His brother Jesus Christ wished for the same. My brothers and sisters in

God's love, we will deliver on their dreams and heed the messages of hope they gave to us. Doubt is part of your free will, and doubt is part of the conditioning from years of misguided advice in the hands of men. Now you must question what you believe and challenge yourselves to build a better world."

Jesus came back to a central position and pointed to Muhammed's tomb. "The words God gave to my brother have been changed, twisted, and fabricated and no longer represent our Father's intentions. The same is true of all texts: The Quran, The Bible, The Tanakh, Buddhavacana, Sri Guru Granth Sahib, and the Vedas. The hand of man shall not interfere again."

Those seated nearby shuffled uncomfortably.

"This is hard for you to hear, but you are not surprised. You must hear it. God tells you that these ancient texts no longer contain the pure divine word. God will provide the one true word, as originally given and intended. Our Father's voice should not be used to invoke violence, suppression, oppression, prejudice, or force. God invites you to peacefully join his loving teachings. God's love is not a tool to compare one man's standing to another. The true word equalizes and uplifts the same in every open heart. When you are ready, he will deliver. God is great."

Jesus slowly joined his hands together. "Pray with me; be joyful and thankful that God chooses you." He waited a moment until sure they had all joined their hands in prayer. "God Almighty, we give thanks for all you freely share with us. We gladly give our love to you and those around us. God is great." Jesus raised his head.

"Tomorrow, I will share more of Our Father's true meaning. Hear my words. The absolute power of God will be brought to bear. God is loving and merciful. God is great."

The building filled with a brilliant white light, and everyone watching was forced to close their eyes. In less than two seconds, the light returned to normal.

General Salah looked anxiously around and radioed his men. The Royal family, their guards, and the holy men chattered excitedly and looked for the Prophet. Some clerics rushed forward, searching around the tomb, but the Prophet had vanished. The General's team radioed one another – confirming there was no trace of the prophet. Around the world, reporters in television and podcast studios ignited into action, busily talking, speculating into the mics.

In the commotion, Abdul Aziz waved General Salah to him. "Your men will not find the Prophet until he wishes to return. He wants your help."

"How can I look after someone I can't even find?"

"He told me you'd protest. If Jesus says you're ready, then you're ready. You do know you're in the presence of God."

"I feel something that I can't explain. My mind and body feel disconnected, yet I feel better than I ever have. I don't understand."

"Then don't try to understand – just be." Abdul Aziz looked around at the commotion. "General Salah, if you could please get your men to move everyone out of the building quietly, I will escort the King back to his helicopter. A sea of people will fall on Medina. We must prepare for it and make sure everyone is safe. They are coming in their hundreds of thousands to feel God's presence."

The General nodded. "When will he be back?"

"Six days from now. Much bigger things are coming to shake the fabric of what men understand about our world. Be ready, General. I will speak with you tomorrow." The old man walked away.

General Salah ordered his men to clear the media from the mosque.

Carrie let go of Mo's hand, not before giving it an appreciative squeeze, and one that he returned. Finally, the live feeds stopped rolling, and the network screens changed to their studios for commentary.

James Gordon barked orders for double checks on translations, a replay of the Prophet's disappearance, and anything else that might be useful. Theo had already rewound the last few seconds. "Look at their reactions – they have no idea. They're freaking out."

"Theo's right," Carrie said, sucking in the air. "This guy's good."

Mo's hands were clenched together, showing the whites of his knuckles. "This will get pretty interesting, one way or another." He held out two shaking hands for everyone to see. "Look at my adrenalin right now!"

"He didn't give us God's word yet." Carrie thought aloud.

"Find out how he disappeared so that we can bring this to an end." James sighed as his phone lit up. "The President," he explained, leaving the office.

Carrie whispered for Mo to join her, and they quickly moved to her office. Carrie referenced her notes. "Lightning hit six of the most significant religious sites around the world. Nobody knows how or why. This guy said it was God – and declared himself the Prophet, and now he's just vanished."

"I got all that," Mo scrunched his face in agitation.

Carrie pulled up a world map on the screen. "He just said all are equal and are one religion, one God. So why appear in Medina?"

"Your point being?" Mo enquired.

"I'll bet if you were going to demonstrate your power, given to you by God, and convince a cynical modern world you love everyone, then you'd be heading next to one of the other five sites. It's the most compelling way to spread the word equally and show all faiths you mean what you say."

"Muslims won't trust Christians, and the Christians won't trust Hindus, and they won't trust Judaism, and so on." Mo rubbed furiously at the stubble on his chin. "To get inclusion in a digital and divided world, you have to prove that you're for everyone!"

He thought about it and snapped his fingers in the air as he looked intently at Carrie. "You're either a genius or good at guessing."

"Both," she replied. "He said he's only here forty days and nights," Carrie nudged Mo out of her way as she paced up and down on the worn-out carpet tiles. Mo quizzically observed her. "I think better when I'm moving around," she explained, with a fire blazing in her eyes. "Everyone knows the significance of forty days. It's in everyone's religious stories, over and over again."

"We heard the Grand Mufti telling his clerics that this man is a prophet for a new age. They're bought in."

"Who could blame them. Theo told me the phrase 'New Age Prophet' is being used in social media. Catchy."

"What now?" Mo asked.

Carrie tapped her left fist into the palm of her right hand. "You're better on computers than I am," she pointed at the chair. Mo jumped into the seat.

"Can you use Google Maps and plot the six locations? We'll look at the nearest one and go for that. I guess that would make sense?" she theorized. "You can drive from Medina to Jerusalem in less than a day. Of course, he might already be on a flight or in a car by now."

"If you were put here by God, you wouldn't need transportation," Mo provoked.

Carrie's look suggested Mo should shut up.

He shrugged and plotted the locations. "I guess if you were uniting the religions and the world, I agree that the Temple Mount would be an obvious choice."

Carrie checked the news feeds on her cell phone. "There are already a hundred thousand people gathered outside Medina, and Mecca is the same. The pilgrims are on the move." She made various groans as she reviewed the updates on her phone. "This thing's going off the charts. They'll need basic supplies and medical care on standby."

"Looks like Medina to Jerusalem is a fifteen-hour ride. So, if our guy turns up at the Wailing Wall in that timeframe, we can hazard a reasonable guess that he drove there. But a questionable way to show God's power; he'd have to pass through checkpoints, no matter how he got there."

Carrie was still pacing. "If this is a fake, the perpetrators would realize that. So we should have James' team check for flights or helicopter movement leaving Saudi Arabia and heading anywhere near the other sites. All passengers will go through facial recognition scanning; we could see if we can pick up the Prophet's face! I assume James' hackers could get that data."

Mo jumped out of the chair. "I'll go see James." Carrie stopped him at the door, "Mo, what's your gut telling you?"

"That I'm starving," he nervously answered. Carrie's sneer prevented him from any more levity. "Honestly, I think it could be real. My subconscious wants it to be so we can all join hands. But I have to trust what I see, hear, and can measure. What about you?"

"I'm torn between wanting it to be true, like you, and not knowing what to believe. We have to rule out every possibility." Carrie felt relieved and added, "Good to get that out of my system and know it's not just me."

She paused, noting the hesitancy in Mo's body language. They shared a knowing look of recognition – a look only former intimate partners could share.

Carrie offered, "There's something in that man's eyes and voice that makes me believe him, even though I know he could simply be a good stage magician. Our tech guys can't explain it yet, but that doesn't mean what we saw was real. My instincts are fighting with my logic.

"This is hard, isn't it?"

"Imagine how the religious leaders around the world are feeling right now. They'll all have to give official statements." Mo took hold of the door handle and said, "I'll tell James they need to get the feeds for the other five sites hacked so we can see what's happening."

Mo looked uneasy with his suggestion.

"I'll come with you. I bet those guys have already done it." She followed him out of the door. As they headed to James' office, Carrie stated, "If I were the Prophet, I don't think I would go to the closest location – I'd go to the one with the biggest impact – Rome."

"It's for that kind of reason they brought you here!" Mo replied.

A minute later, they bombarded a flustered James with their ideas and requests. Carrie suggested they get access to all immigration checks on all passports going in and out of the lightning-affected countries. Theo listened and then assigned work to his team to get on it.

Carrie returned, alone, to her office. She began to watch news feeds from around the U.S. to assess the immediate impact. So far, no riots or demonstrations by anyone, and no calls of blasphemy from religious groups. James gave her two hours to get back to him with an educated guess on what might come next. It was already 4:00 pm in the Capital, and time seemed like it had stopped when the man called Jesus spoke. Suddenly – time seemed to move faster than ever.

CHAPTER EIGHT

On the outskirts of Montgomery, Alabama, Pastor Wally Radford stared at the conference room wall. His church leadership team was gathered around the teak conference table, consumed in a loud noise of disbelief, anger, outrage, and despondency.

The Radford Ministries of Christ had steadily developed over forty years around the Southern states of the U.S. – a proud nineteen locations, their own cable show, and a growing base developing around the country. Wally's savvy investment in social media marketing and live church webinars had helped spread the word and the brand, and it kept a modern audience in touch with their fervent pastoral base. The Radford Ministries worked hard and struck a nice balance of living better lives through the Bible's teachings and finding abundance. The mixture of old and new meant that the Radford Ministries had blossomed. There was no more fire and brimstone delivered from the pulpit, but messages of serving Christ so that earthly and celestial abundance would surely follow.

Wally Radford recently turned sixty-two. His youth had faded, but his determination remained as strong as ever. He'd built this mini empire from the ground up with his wife, Cheryl. Cheryl was his earthly rock, and she was ahead of the curve in publicizing and seizing growth opportunities. Wally wanted a legacy for his family to enjoy and for his name to be remembered. There was conceit in the latter notion, but Wally had given everything he had to the teachings of the Bible, and he figured some recognition wasn't asking too much. Wally's guiding light held true to the stories within the Bible. Wally would not idly stand by and watch it be extinguished with a few slick words from some foreign imposter. The prophet's words put everything at risk, including the souls of his congregation and his eternal place at God's glorious side.

He and Cheryl had plenty of investment money tucked away for a rainy day. They enjoyed three luxury homes, a collection of expensive cars, and their private jet for inter-state travel. The Radford's lived a spiritually and financially prosperous life.

He had advised his closest friends and colleagues to invest wisely. They had all done well. He and his ministry leaders held cash in personal offshore accounts. A wrenching in his gut, along with other recent visions, told Wally they would need those resources. The Medina Prophet was a distinct threat.

God's word was brought into question, and that was more than he could tolerate. Wally couldn't care less about Islam, Judaism, or any other belief, so long as it didn't interfere with his choice of worship. Everything was on the line. He felt lost within himself as the arguments raged around him. This foreigner's ramblings signified a much bigger threat than solely to his church – this was a threat to Christianity itself. His mind drifted as he conjured up images of how the Crusaders must have felt when they believed their entire faith and its geographical center faced annihilation. The man in yellow said the messages practiced by all faiths were corrupted. An audacious statement from a man that Wally felt he recognized.

His recent dreams were remarkably lucid, and what he'd witnessed brought to bear the culmination of the things that plagued his sleep. Dreams so disturbing that he kept them from his beloved Cheryl. Wally and Cheryl shared all their thoughts, feelings, sins, and worries – more than most couples would ever dare by laying themselves open, and each saw both the ugliness and the great in the other. They thoroughly understood one another like nobody else. Wally realized he must tell her about the terrible visionary dangers. Cheryl would understand - that's how Cheryl was designed – ferocious when needed and forgiving to move forward. Those were the attributes he loved in his dear wife. Battling through their imperfections had only made them stronger and bonded them together in Christ's teachings. Wally considered their partnership unbreakable.

Wally calculated the dangers. If the guy in Medina were a fake, execution would come quickly. In a high-speed information world, Wally knew there'd be thousands of determined people already shooting down the false prophet's credibility. He'd received warnings this would come to life in his dreams, and now it was growing like a poisonous seedling. Warnings required action. Why else would God have shown him those dreadful visions?

News stations continued to sensationalize the mysterious disappearing act from the tomb in Medina. Every pundit on TV salivated to give their unwanted opinion. This was the only news anywhere in the world.

Wally heard God's word. His dreams were not simply his subconscious toying with his faith – they'd manifested themselves into the real world. God compelled him to act. His blood pressure rocketed, causing him to sweat, and his heart rate elevated. His core was rattled. But not his faith. This was Wally's moment to follow the example of the Lord. Wally would answer.

He took a deep breath, rubbed his sweaty palms together, and observed the surrounding squabbles. Cheryl nervously glanced at him, which he returned with a gentle smile. As well as being a devout Christian, Wally was a savvy businessman, and, as such, he could already taste the potential damage. Their dedicated base would never consider equality with other religions. It wasn't a hatred of other people's beliefs but a steadfast belief in the Bible. If people fell for the Medina Prophet's words, his Christian followers would give their hard-earned offerings elsewhere.

Wally needed to open himself up to his inner circle. His friends and followers trusted him. They would know his explanation came forged in God's truth. God told him the False Prophet would gather momentum in his dreams – a frightening prospect. He dreamt of this false prophet with the exact features they had watched on the big screen – the long reddish-brown hair, the short beard, and the yellow robe. Wally fought in his dreams with the devil, but the devil got the better of him each time, and the world turned dark. This was not some cruel joke. He would now battle Satan in what promised to be an ugly war. God had shown him this for a reason. No longer the young buck, Wally wasn't afraid to turn his hand to God's calling. God would protect him in his pursuit of the righteous. Even if he lay down his life, Wally would serve his family, friends, congregation, and Christ our Lord.

He took the Bible from the table in front of him and clutched it in his right hand as though some invisible specter were trying to prise it from his grasp. He tightened his grip and prayed. Flames of eternal damnation threatened the words by which he'd lived his life. *I will not allow it*, he silently vowed.

He stood at the head of the table and checked the time, now 3:00 in the afternoon. Before commencing, Wally winked at Cheryl. "Guys, guys, let's have some quiet for a minute." He paused to let the noise subside. "Okay, here's what we're going to do, and here's the order in which we're going to do them. Bob, you, and your team will contact each of the Ministries and advise them not to release any individual statements. We'll provide a single response from here. Gracie, put out something on social media, letting everyone know that we'll be giving our thoughts soon enough. Make sure none of our Pastors or anyone in a leadership position is posting anything without my direct approval.

We all heard the pernicious preaching, and it festers like an open wound. We'll apply a unified response. Cheryl, can you set up a broadcast for 9:00am tomorrow? We need to get out in front of everyone to deliver our message."

Bob looked blankly at him. "Wally, what's the message gonna be?"

"I don't know yet. Cheryl, I, and Lydia will get hold of Tom down in Houston, and we'll get something out for the websites and our main page in the next hour. In the meantime, I don't want anyone saying anything. Is that clear?" Wally observed a bunch of nods and yeses. "I mean it, guys. Not a word of speculation from anyone who's public facing. If asked, the response will be 'No comment until we have further information.' Okay, let's get to it." He motioned for them all to get out of the room with his hands.

Cheryl stayed behind. Her round cheeks were flushed with concern.

"I need to call Chuck and John," Wally grimaced.

Cheryl's lip quivered at his open thought. "Darlin,' I ain't seen that look on your face since they told us your momma passed away. What's going through there right now?" She stroked a loving hand through his thinning gray hair.

Wally sat her down next to him and held her hand. "I have doubts in my mind as to why God put me here on this good earth. But never once have I doubted why he put you and me on the same path together. This thing from Medina is ... well, we either just saw the cruelest practical joke ever played on mankind, or we just witnessed something that could bring an end to all of us. I, Wally Radford, am actually lost for words!" He sighed heavily. "But ... I do believe it's something else entirely."

Cheryl's mouth fell open as she saw the fear in her husband's stare. "Wally, please!"

"There are things I've seen. We need to talk. The demon walks among us."

"Oh, my." Cheryl sucked in air as she teared up and asked, "What do we do?"

"Whichever way it falls, we could all fall with it," he predicted.

"Surely not." She took Wally's face in both her hands and kissed his cheek. "Will this kill our expansion plans?"

Wally stared at the floor; his gaze distant. "I believe it will, my angel. Who wants to listen to Wally Radford and his pastors when they think they can listen to God directly through Jesus? We face the unknown. Evil takes many forms to deceive the masses. We will not be fooled."

Cheryl moved a hand over her mouth, and the tears flooded. "If it's true, surely God will save us." Her sorrowful expression begged for his words of comfort.

"We trust in the Lord." Wally pointed at the crucifix hanging on the conference room wall. "More evil has been committed in the world, under the guise of compassion and mercy, than all other twisted reasons combined. Since man first began to record the troubles we've inflicted on one another with intolerable cruelty and vicious subjugation, it has often been subtly disguised virtue that brought forth the dormant malice within each heart. And we have managed, oh, so well, to show what vile and terrible creatures we are. I have witnessed the same today in Medina. My heart felt it long before my ears and eyes made sense of it. This is a war for the ages, my love. We must be angels trumpeting God's good graces and pulverize those in league with the devil."

Wally tightened his grip on her hand and gathered himself. "Maybe God put you and me here to do something more than have a family and perform our ministries. He's spoken to me." He smiled as best he could and returned a sweet kiss to the side of Cheryl's face. "I'll tell the leadership they all need to be here by the weekend. We've worked our whole lives to build what we have in God's glory. If God were here on this good earth in the form of Jesus, then I'd feel it, and I ain't feeling it. Unfortunately, other forces are at work."

He passed Cheryl a paper tissue to dab her eyes and held her hand as they walked from the conference room. "The Lord will give us the strength we need."

In the brightly lit hallway, Cheryl let go of his hand. She wiped clear her eyes, smoothed out her hair, groaned loudly, and pushed her shoulders back. "I'm fine," she insisted and strode ahead.

Wally recognized that purpose in her step. She was the most loyal partner any man could ever have. He was mightily proud to have her as his wife. Wally knew that she would need all of that strength.

He would call his old friends and gauge their reactions. Then, under God's guidance, he would do whatever it took to protect the word of the Bible. He looked back into the conference room at the crucifix on the wall. He released a singular resigned laugh and stated, "I, Wally Radford, am finally about to become a true soldier of Christ."

CHAPTER NINE

Theo Wallace had worked for James Gordon from the moment he'd graduated from Stanford, CA. He'd obtained his Ph.D. in computer science, and James had approached him after watching Theo win an online cyber security hacking contest. Theo learned that the government security service had organized and sponsored the contest. At the age of thirty-two, he'd been at the right-hand side of James Gordon for the last eight years, and he had traveled the world, enjoying every minute of his work. The sights and situations he experienced were a hacker's dream. He loved his work, and something that he genuinely believed benefited the American people and their allies. They'd successfully eradicated cyber-attacks and real-world threats. Theo's worldly education led him to form quick solutions and insights to assist James in their ongoing pursuit of national security. Theo had no explanations for this Prophet phenomena despite the plethora of remarkable things under his belt. He didn't care about the messages he'd heard as long as they didn't endanger the safety of U.S. citizens. He remained focused on the tasks, but the intrigue provided a deep fascination. Within James' safety-first approach, Theo could apply a broad spectrum of tactics and utilize the latest technical equipment to access information, so long as they remained invisible. Their most significant challenge came from a single man in Saudi Arabia. Theo's determination to figure it out simmered below the surface – he kept his thoughts as covert as his work.

Theo had moved a section of his team from the noisy main office to maintain absolute focus on gaining access to the security camera feeds from the other affected sites. In the unlikely event of discovery, they used digital signatures that appeared to originate from northeastern China. There were no digital traces to the U.S., especially not Washington, DC. That would be too scandalous for the American public to take and too difficult for James to explain. The rest of his team monitored the foreign security agency emails and phones in each affected five countries. Each tech team had assigned translators for all digital audio and transcripts.

There was a light tap on the office door he occupied, and one of his new recruits, Jessica Cortez, entered, chewing a mouthful of gum. "Hey, Boss, you should look at what I'm seeing. We got something," her voice hummed. She'd already turned and gone before he could get out of his seat. Theo followed her through the maze of cubicles. Jessica flopped into her chair, called over her translator, and moved her screen around so Theo could see it. "Here, we found this in Rome," she fiercely slapped her fingers over the keys and wiggled the mouse to adjust the resolution of the camera feed. "This is outside of St. Peter's Basilica, in Vatican City. There's a big crowd in St. Peter's Square. The crowd's been growing fast within the last hour." Her husky tones sounded like she'd smoked forty cigarettes a day since birth.

"Has the Pope made a declaration?"

"No, he hasn't said anything. All's quiet on the Catholic front. It's coming from sources we were tracking on Italian social media, so we followed it. They talk a lot, those Italians. Anyway, the focus is on the Basilica." Jessica switched views. "This is inside the Basilica. You see how bright it is."

Theo took a good look. "Have we checked all resolutions, angles, and camera issues?"

"Of course." Jessica switched to a different internal view. "We've only had eyes in there since about half an hour ago. They're encrypted up the wazoo. Crafty Italians," she laughed, even though it wasn't funny. "The brightness keeps increasing. It got the attention of the Papal guards, and they called in a load of the clergymen. There are at least fifty Bishops or Archbishops in there right now. There's no sound from their cameras, so we're trying to access the mics used by the Swiss guards. Local traffic cameras show the whole place is buzzing – police, clergy, and the army is coming in. More and more people are heading that way – word is spreading like wildfire on social media."

"Is it from the light shining in through the hole in the roof?"

"No, definitely not. That's what's so weird. The light is going the opposite way, inside to outside."

"Go back to the previous shot. How come this is out on social media?" Theo asked.

Jessica tapped the end of her pen on the screen. "Geo, my interpreter, found that since St. Peter's Basilica got hit by lightning, people have set up live feeds on social media focused solely on the hole in the roof. People started to comment that the light from within was getting brighter, and word spread. So Geo's been keeping an eye on it." She twisted her head and looked up at him. "Super-confusing working with a Theo and Geo simultaneously," she hoarsely cackled.

"Really," Theo frowned.

"You bet ya. Their internet bandwidth is collapsing. That's not the only thing. Two hours ago, a couple of thousand people were in the square – now there's over twenty thousand. Traffic is gridlocked all around Rome."

Theo took the tablet that Geo handed him and reviewed the climbing numbers on the media feeds. "Facebook's going to implode. How many other views do you have inside St. Peter's?"

"I have seven so far. There should be the eighth one, but it looks offline," Jessica said, tapping her notepad. "I'm working on getting all seven views into one screen. Another ten minutes, and I can improve the crappy resolutions they've got."

"Nice work. Don't move any of their cameras or do anything to let them know you are in there." He passed the tablet back. "Thanks, Geo."

"You're welcome, Theo," came the reply.

Jessica laughed aloud.

Geo scrambled to the other desk and bent forward over the screen. "Jessy, go to the external feed on the roof. Something is happening. Now!"

"Holy cow!" Theo moved to her shoulder. "It's the same cloud formations we saw before the lightning strikes hit our hot locations."

"The skies are getting dark!" She chewed extra hard on her gum. "Darker than you," she said, pointing at his ebony forearm.

"You're darker than me, Senorita." Theo's testy reply made Jessica laugh so hard that she accidentally spat her gum onto her keyboard.

She picked it off with her fingers and dropped it back into her mouth.

Theo darted out of the door. "I'll be back … keep watching!" He ran down the corridor and checked with the other groups, individually focused on separate locations. They had no activity. He called Carrie. "You need to come, quick. Vatican City!"

Carrie raced across the main office, waving at Mo to join her. They crammed into Jessica's space, who gave the intruders a dirty look. She pointed to the left-hand side of her monitor with the end of a severely chewed pen.

"This is the best view we have from outside of St. Peter's Basilica – a powerful light source coming from inside and shining through the hole in the dome. It looks like Batman's searchlight." She pointed to her other screen. "The interior view shows people from Vatican City running around like headless chickens trying to find the light source. Some of them are wearing sunglasses inside," she laughed hoarsely.

"What are they doing?" Carrie asked.

"Like us, they're trying to figure out why it keeps getting brighter in there. We've looked at the electric lights and measured their output, and that's not the source."

"Then what is it?'

"Not sure, but Geo says it's all over the Italian news. The dome's getting brighter, and the skies are getting darker. The Pope must be shitting himself," Jessica speculated. She leaned back to tighten the band on her ponytail and frowned at the group to make clear she didn't like them crowding around her.

"Social media has exploded, and half of Rome is heading on foot to St. Peter's Square," Theo added. "We don't have any ears on the ground yet. We're trying to access the Papal guards' comms system."

"Have you told James yet?" Carrie asked. Theo worriedly shook his head. "Call him!" she ordered.

Mo squeezed in to get a better view. "How long have they been in there?"

"Thirty minutes ago, there were three clergy and six Papal guards – now there's fifty of each," Jessica added.

Mo rasped hard at his chin. "This is it. That's where he's going."

Carrie checked the time. "It's only two hours since our Prophet spoke live from Al-Masjid, in Medina. How fast could you get to Rome from Medina?"

"Five and half hours if you were flying non-stop and had a fast jet," Jessica said. Everyone in the room stared at her. "Seemed like an obvious thing to check," she explained.

"So, it's physically impossible for our guy to be there," Mo reiterated.

Carrie tapped Theo on his arm. "Make sure your teams are tracking all these times. They're going to be key going forward."

Jessica's translator, Geo, whispered something in her ear. She pulled up a different video feed from outside of the dome. "Look! The light from the dome just significantly increased. The internet's going bananas!" As she spoke, the camera feeds in St. Peter's Basilica turned brilliant white, forcing them to look away. "What the hell!"

71

Carrie rubbed the sting from her eyes and looked at Theo. "You'd better tell your boss it's happening again."

"Are you sure?"

"Yep."

Theo left the office with his phone to his ear.

"I can feel it." Carrie clutched her stomach.

"Oh boy!" Mo fretted. He looked back at the screens as the light inside St. Peter's Basilica faded to normal levels. "Oh, shit – that's the same guy, right there!" Mo shouted, his finger pointing at the figure in the yellow robe. The man was standing in front of the great papal altar, underneath the Baldacchino, by Bernini. "It's him!"

"Make sure you guys are recording everything!" Carrie shouted.

The papal guards and some of the clergy rushed towards the man, and they all stopped twenty feet away. Jesus held out his arms as the priests, bishops, nuns, and guards fell to their knees.

"Can we get a close-up of the altar?" Mo asked. Jessica hit the keyboard, and the main view switched over. "There you go."

Mo observed, "It sure looks like our guy from Medina. Same clothes, hair, facial structure, and physical build. But how?"

Theo entered the room, his face contorted with deep stress lines spiraling in all directions. "Is that who I think it is?"

"You mean Santa Claus?" Jessica cackled.

"It looks like the Prophet, but we can't be sure," Carrie said. The cameras showed people kneeling on the ground, bowing, praying, and some raising their hands to the sky. Jessica split the screen so they could view from both sides, and within seconds they could see that those gathered had started to sing. It was impossible to tell what it was without sound, but they gave it their all in their exaltation. A handful of Cardinals were laying prostrate on the floor, with their arms outstretched and their heads facing the Prophet.

A breathless James Gordon arrived. "Is it him?"

"We think so," came the unified response, except for Jessica, who rolled her eyes in annoyance at repeatedly hearing the same question.

"Get me the facial recognition software to confirm."

"Already on it, Chief," Theo confirmed. "It's impossible to get from Medina to Rome in two hours unless you own a rocket ship."

"It could be a double, or twin, or whatever. So let's keep an open mind." James turned away and yelled into his phone. "Senator, it's me. We're on again." James immediately ended the call.

One of Theo's team poked his head around the door frame. "Hey, guys, the Italian army's just been put on red alert, and they're sending ten thousand troops into Rome. The overhead satellite view of the city is insane. A quarter of a million vehicles are trying to get to the Vatican. The Italian Prime Minister is about to go live to ask people to stay at home."

Carrie's mind worked at a frantic pace. "James, I'm not sure what circle of influence your group has overseas, but they will need toilets, first aid, water, and food – like now. If people think this is Jesus, they're not leaving anytime soon. Rome will grind to a halt in the next hour, and they'll need help. This will be like an appetizer compared to what Medina will look like in a few days – the Prophet said he would return there in six days."

James nodded. "I'll see what I can do. What else?"

"We need audio inside the Basilica; schematics for the building; secret passages etc. We need all the passport data in and out of Italy in the last few hours and beyond! We need someone from your organization in Rome who is close by. Every terrorist cell you've ever tracked should be located right now – in case there's a link. We need ears and eyes inside Palazzo Apostolico to know what's being said."

"What's that?" James asked.

"It's where the Pope lives – his house," Carrie replied like it was obvious. "We need the same access at the remaining four sites: Cambodia, Jerusalem, and the two sites in India. He's going to visit all of them."

"Anything else?" James asked, chewing on his lower lip.

"James, genuine or not, whoever's driving this has done their homework. It will keep going. I suggest you prepare for forty days. We'll have fanatics of every kind trying to take this guy down," Carrie warned. "The President and his leaders will need added protection. Hard to narrow down the outcomes just yet but be ready for an end-of-the-world type mentality. People get scared and aggressive before they get reasonable."

James began barking instructions to his team.

CHAPTER TEN

Senator Jim Crowley's supporters considered him a pious man. A label he appreciated. He checked the messages on the specially acquired, untraceable cellphone, telling him the seriousness of the New Age Prophet situation. Senator Crowley despised that label applied to what he regarded as an imposter.

His informant from the U.S. intelligence service sent evidence that showed the time for action had arrived. Senator Crowley had recently spoken with an old friend, who assured him this would happen. They faced an apocalyptic scenario. As a devout Christian and a man of standing within his constituency and the government, Jim Crowley would not shirk his moral responsibilities. He could not broadcast what he'd learned, or it would jeopardize any chance of successfully restoring balance in a world that teetered on the brink of disaster. He immediately returned the call to his old friend, asking for a plan and what resources he could assist in gathering. The world faced its greatest danger, and most people couldn't see the threat before them. Senator Crowley was grateful for the good, honest God-fearing people prepared to sacrifice their lives for the greater good. He thanked his informant and asked that he be kept updated on the information flowing through James Gordon's enterprise.

As much as Crowley disliked James Gordon, he knew that the power of Gordon's reach and insight could be useful in these difficult times. Senator Crowley would enjoy using James Gordon to his advantage and, if possible, reduce Gordon's apparent ambitions. "Parasite," he thought aloud.

He made the call: "Ah, my old friend – I wish I could tell you differently, but you were right. God calls us to do his bidding. We must strike hard and fast. What do you have for me?"

"Let me tell you my plan."

News spread fast that the New Age Prophet had appeared in Rome, although the reports were unconfirmed by official sources. Communication networks were overloaded with the weight of dialogue circling the earth. Millions foolishly argued over which religion the Prophet came to support and why their particular interpretation of God's word was correct. People had already clipped parts of the Prophet's initial appearance and used it to support their online viewpoint. Religious places of worship were a mixture of celebrations and demonstrations. Security at holy sites increased, and some locations became fortified. Calls for peace rained down like a verbal monsoon. Religious leaders did not commit one way or the other but simply asked that their followers behave peacefully, no matter what. Some saw this as a power play from the Middle East and refused to pay it any attention. In contrast, others admired the bravery of the leaders in Medina in showing an openness to new religious dialogue and ideas. Bewilderment and ambiguity reigned supreme.

Armies patrolled major cities as fear of riots and demonstrations increased.

At Al-Masjid in Medina, General Salah and his men neared exhaustion. Chaos had become his private Master since the Prophet appeared. Thankfully, there was no violence. Instead, a peaceful madness resonated from outside the walls of the religious center. General Salah found himself wearing many different hats at once. He worried about his family. Guilt reminded him he should have cared more for them. Everything escalated. People's nerves stirred into restlessness, and a shared sense of uncertainty was breathable. It only took one person, one overheated argument, or someone in a state of anxiety to spark something. The entire region and country felt balanced on the edge of a finely curved blade, and a slip in any direction would draw blood.

General Salah performed another walk-through of the entire facility with his officers. It eased his mind that they had prepared for the worst. His men looked frazzled but so far had withstood the initial challenge. If one man pulled his weapon, a carnage would break loose.

Medina never rested, but this was unparalleled, with even more visitors heading to the Green Dome. Early counts showed over eighty thousand people surrounded the complex – more arriving by the minute. The faithful came to pay their respects and to give thanks to God. Thousands were here, on their knees or sitting in quiet prayer. There reigned a curious reverence, considering the challenges laid before each religious following. The views from the control office captured every angle around the entire complex, and those views both inspired and terrified. General Salah joked to his senior officers, "We are under a siege." Reinforcements arrived, but the general did not know these men. Maintaining tight discipline was increasingly difficult. He checked with his officers that his orders were repeated with clear precision, but that did not account for the possibility of the frontline coming across something unexpected.

General Salah went into his private office. He needed five minutes to himself, to drink a strong coffee, and think ahead. He'd not slept for over a day. The speed of reports coming in from text, radio, email, and voicemail was impossible to manage. Tasked with the safety of the holy site was continually overtaken by the Prophet's voice entering his ears and speaking directly to his soul. Thinking about it made him hot as if his cardiovascular system had been injected with a magical serum, and his skin broke into a light sweat. He rubbed his hands over his lower arms, wiped away the moisture, and hoped to erase his worry. This New Age Prophet punctured through layers of the general's spirit that he thought were impenetrable. It had instantly changed him, like a pleasant virus invading every cell. General Salah was not, by nature, an expressive, loving man nor the affectionate husband or father he wished to be. The experience with the Prophet hit harder than the first time he saw his newborn children. Something went beyond his physical being, as though the Prophet touched parts of his consciousness yet to fully awake. Until a few hours ago, the general hadn't been sure he possessed a soul. He'd always been cold, calculating, and stern like his own father. He liked battle. Somehow, though, without any doubt and beyond his comprehension, he'd been in the presence of a higher power. It was all around him and inside of him. It had its own vibrancy, and he was permanently aware of its presence.

General Salah's entire adult life revolved around the military, a disciplined existence in which he excelled. The Prophet had caused him to question all he knew and gave him a sudden longing to be with his wife, hold his children close, and give them comfort – and in return, receive some back. The more the general thought about the Prophet's words of world unity, the less he cared about his loyalty to a questionable cause that now flickered like a candle's flame fighting an unrelenting breeze.

General Salah's instincts suggested that he was reborn in God's grace. He slapped his hands loudly on his desk and snapped himself into focus. "There is work to do and people to protect." If he allowed himself to drift, he'd surely walk away from his duties and sit with the ecstatic crowd outside the walls.

Instead, he texted his wife that all was okay and that he loved her. She immediately texted him back, asking if he was okay. He simply replied, 'yes.'

Abdul Aziz knocked and entered the general's office. The old man signaled for him to remain seated. The Grand Mufti lowered himself into the spare seat. "We should talk. Billions saw the broadcast, but you and I have been privy to something few have witnessed." A faint smirk came over his thick dry lips. "I see the change it has left on you. Your heart has awoken."

"I am questioning my sanity. I don't know what I have seen or felt." General Salah nervously played with the ends of his mustache.

"Yes, you know," the old man firmly stated. He held up his hands in front of the general. "These used to be curled over and useless," he said, wiggling his fingers. "This man has taken away my pain. I have retained my walking cane for appearances only. It's merely an ornament I carry around with me, where once it carried me. Your heart tells you that God has spoken to you. You will answer."

"I don't know what I'm supposed to do or what to think."

"Stop thinking." Abdul Aziz advised. "The Prophet enlightened your true heart. People will arrive here like wide-eyed infants seeing the ocean for the first time. They won't know why they came or what they want, but only to be close to God. There will be much bigger things yet to come."

"What does the Prophet expect of me?"

Abdul Aziz ruefully shook his head. "He expects you to do what is right. My sleep is illuminated with the joys of partaking in God's work. It will reveal itself to you at the proper time. You will do it well. That is why you were chosen."

General Salah offered the Grand Mufti a coffee, to which he shook his head. "I hope I am worthy. But, unfortunately, I have not been the man … the man that I wished to be."

"Nobody has. You are now Allah's General."

General Salah could no longer hold the old man's stare. His head dipped. He had many questions, most of which he could not comprehend, and others he was afraid to ask. The general's pride wrestled with his newfound senses, as he did not wish to appear frail or to humiliate himself. Overwhelm seized tightly at his throat. Any speech attempt would force him to crumple into a ball on the cold floor.

The old man rose from his chair. "It will be as God wills, my friend." Abdul Aziz looked at the general as if he was a favored grandson. "To be chosen is something to rejoice. Have no fear, general; if it were me looking for protection, I would choose a warrior such as you. Allah be praised."

CHAPTER ELEVEN

Inside St. Peter's Basilica, a hundred high-ranking clergy, three dozen Nuns, and a hundred Swiss guards forgot about the light they had come to investigate. The outside world ceased to exist. Instead, they prayed and stared at the beautiful man before them. The guards called for reinforcements, but they dared not share that the New Age Prophet was inside.

"Bring me the shepherd," Jesus asked the clergy. He sat on the altar's steps and crossed his legs. "Pray with me, my brothers and sisters." He lowered his head and prayed. Those gathered clasped their fingers tightly, with hands shaking, and despite the Prophet's lips being closed, they heard aloud his prayers.

Word went immediately to the Pope. He and his closest advisors watched the internal cameras from the Basilica. Then, he prayed with his inner circle of holy men. "Let us go meet the Prophet from Medina. Quickly now. We do not want to keep God waiting."

"Holy Father, how can you be sure this man is from God?" one of his Cardinals asked.

"You think I do not know divinity when I see it. We have met in my dreams. Now we shall meet soul to soul. So gather your nerve – God is with us."

A few minutes later, the Pope exited his vehicle and made his way inside the magnificent church, stopping at the top of the steps to wave to the massed crowds outside. It looked like the whole of Rome had made its way to St. Peter's. The Holy Father's sermons never produced audiences on such a scale. He passed the word to his guards, "Protect the church and the people." He waved again to the crowds.

Jesus rose to his feet and declared, "My shepherd is here. Brothers and sisters, I ask you that you move to the edges of the church so that I may speak alone with him."

They looked around in confusion until the great bronze Filarete door opened seconds later, and the Holy Father of Rome arrived. As they moved to the peripherals of the church, they blessed themselves and watched the Pope walk alone down the central knave, where he stood a few feet away from the Prophet.

The Pope's two personal bodyguards stayed back a hundred feet – seventy feet further apart than they'd ever been from the Holy Father's side in public.

The Pope bowed his head, moved forward, took the hand of the Prophet, and kissed the fingers of the man in the yellow robe. The Holy Father of the Catholic church looked into the reddish pupils filled with gray speckles of the man called Jesus. The Holy Father wailed aloud as if in pain, muttering in ancient Latin, holding his hands to his face as he collapsed to the marble floor. Jesus crouched beside the fallen Pope and embraced the elderly man, cradling him and rocking him in his arms like a mother with her newborn. The Pope's shoulders heaved as he yielded a lifetime of dedication and hope from within. His lifelong prayers were answered.

Jesus quietly said to him, "You will be the conduit that divinity intended you to be. You are to bring people of all faiths together as one. I have left specific instructions with the Grand Mufti in Medina. He will contact you this very day, and you will answer. Together, you'll spearhead a new age of understanding and show the world how to receive God's love. Others will soon join you. Some will not. Love them all regardless. Release your worries, my good shepherd."

The Holy Father managed to whimper, "Yes, my Lord." He repeatedly kissed Jesus' hand.

Jesus held the shepherd for several minutes until he regained his strength and sat him on the altar's steps, speaking to him in whispers. When they had finished talking, the Pope gathered all of his people in attendance and told them to prepare for a worldwide media audience from the Basilica.

Carrie made calls, rushed from office to office, checked data, gathered updates, and reminded herself to breathe. Prevalent in the back of her mind, multiple questions nagged at her, for which she had no answers. Was this it? If so, how would it progress? Could mankind save itself? Would the planet survive? Would she make it through? The list went on and on, raising more questions than solutions. She had wept as she watched the Pope meet with the Prophet. The Holy Father's reaction was much how she imagined it would be if she were cradled in the arms of the Prophet. Carrie told James to alert his high command to expect the next broadcast at 3:00 pm, Washington time.

The activity inside the Basilica was frantic, with cameras, lights, and cables spread in all directions. The New Age Prophet stayed motionless by the altar in a trance-like state. Carrie discovered a U.S. Cardinal was at the center of the action, but they'd been unable to reach him directly. "Keep trying his phone until we speak with him in person," Carrie told Jessica.

The Prophet stayed deep in concentrated prayer. He seemed oblivious to the activity as Rome prepared for what promised to be the single largest worldwide broadcast mankind had ever known.

Carrie Carter was always of a curious nature, relying heavily on her instincts as much as her intellect. A hunch nibbled at her. She privately discussed her idea with Theo, to which he said absolutely not, but Carrie persisted. Theo considered this whole Prophet business was a highly orchestrated and elaborate religious coup, and he would soon expose it. He wanted no part in her meddling. Carrie's tenacity matched her brilliance, and she kept chipping away at him, eventually convincing Theo to give her what she'd asked for. "I'll take full responsibility for the outcome. I'll say I acted alone."

Theo didn't like it, but his curiosity led him to give her access to the Basilica cameras. "If James finds out I did this, against his direct orders, he'll have my head."

"Then I guess I won't tell him if you don't," she earnestly replied. "It's only one tiny fraction of a movement on one camera. The Italians are working on so many things that they think it's one of their guys inside the church, and I'll finish it before they know it. We use the camera directly, looking at Jesus – we go in ten feet. You pull the facial recognition you need, and before anyone suspects, we reset."

Theo looked at her like she was crazy. "And we lose everything!"

"A risk worth taking. I'll do it so that you can stay clean. Then, turn your back so you don't see me do it. That way, you can pass a lie detector test."

"Do you steal cars and rob banks, too?" he asked, marginally impressed by her devious thinking. "The mouse is your controller. Don't zoom in too far, and don't tell me what you're doing. It gives me plausible deniability."

"It seems everyone else around here has secrets."

"Like what?"

81

"Like, why your boss visits the restricted floors below ground," Carrie said. "How do you know?"

"He takes the elevator down and never leaves the building – I can see the front entrance from my office, so I know he doesn't go outside." Carrie paused for a moment. "What's he doing down there, and who's down there?'

"I have no idea. Honestly," Theo replied. "Hurry up."

She clicked on the zoom button, and the camera over the altar rapidly rushed in, closely viewing Jesus' face. "You can look now."

"You're too close!" Theo exclaimed.

"It moved faster than I thought. Get to work," she advised. Theo took control of the keyboard and collected the Prophet's facial data. When Theo's software took the first image, Jesus stared at the camera. Carrie and Theo leaned back in their seats. "Uh oh! Keep going," Carrie encouraged him.

"You see that! He knows!"

"Keep going. A coincidence," she unconvincingly said.

Jesus tilted his head inquisitively and went back to his prayers.

Carrie's hands were over her mouth. "Three times that's happened. I told you! I knew it," she whispered triumphantly. "C'mon, Theo, or they'll be on to us."

"No shit," he snorted and took the last image before restoring the camera to its original setting. "This prophet could have a team tapped into the camera system and receive messages."

"Where's his receiver?" she asked. "Your guys confirmed nothing was in his ears. Did you get the close-up?"

"Yes. Plugging it into the database now. We'll see if it matches the guy in Medina. This software has a one hundred percent success rate in telling identical twins apart. Just a few seconds, and we'll know." They watched the program run through its checks and balances, and a window popped up on the screen. Theo ran his hands rapidly over his head. "It's complete. The guy sitting in Rome is the same guy from Saudi Arabia. It's him!"

Carrie clapped her hands. "Looks like we have a miracle on our hands."

"No way. I'm going to change some parameters and rerun it."

"Good luck. I'm going to get Mo. We've less than an hour until the next live broadcast."

"I was never part of this," he reminded her.

"Part of what?" she replied.

At 3:00 pm in Washington, DC, James Gordon's teams fixed on their monitors, checking multiple communications, scans, and audits. Everyone confirmed their readiness.

CHAPTER TWELVE

Commentators conservatively estimated in excess of a hundred and fifty thousand in and around St. Peter's Square. Mo Yousaf ran his data and suggested, "They're wrong, by some margin. There's at least a quarter of a million people in those streets." He passed his data to James' team for confirmation.

Jesus stood before the massed ranks of the clergy inside St. Peter's Basilica. Outside, the live broadcasts were on big screens, erected for the thousands of people packed into St. Peter's Square and the side streets of Rome.

A hush fell over the vast crowds.

Jesus bowed toward the ancient altar, carved from a single block of Greek marble consecrated in 1594. Above the revered altar, the Baldacchino canopy rose a hundred feet towards the dome. This sacred spot was where centuries of Papal Masters of Rome had performed Mass. The New Age Prophet paid his respects to the ornate Masterpiece and faced those before him.

"God is great. Welcome. I am Jesus. That is the name I have been given by my spiritual Father. There is but one true God. The true path to serving God can only arrive when you serve all others in absolute love and kindness. Evil persists. Good cannot exist without evil. Love is your armor. Power, greed, and adulation are easy corrupters. You will feel its presence, and it will not fool you. Your voice of togetherness in God's love will render you invincible. Violence answers nothing. Lay down your weapons, take the hand of who was once your enemy, and swear your unyielding love for them. God has never asked you to fight wars in his name. Mistrust and hate have been your masters for too long with twisted teachings to willfully blind you. No one is your enemy. Act in accordance with God's word – as one people, under one religion, without war, without violence, and without prejudice. That is God's word. Neither fear nor scorn anyone who does not believe in God's word – it is their choice. God asks you to love them like your children. God desires you to be instruments of harmonious change. These are his words."

Jesus observed those immediately before him. He stepped closer to the cameras, and the close-up showed his perfectly-formed eyebrows and his unusually colored eyes. The camera's zoom found perfection in his face. Shouts of massed adulation rose from St. Peter's Square.

The Prophet continued, "God is love. Through his ultimate wisdom and mercy, he will show humankind true love this very day. Let the eyes of the world fall upon Jerusalem in one hour. A new symbol of hope and peace. Behold a second unifying miracle. These are the words of God." Jesus opened his arms to all those watching. "Brothers and sisters around the world, pray with me: God Almighty, we give thanks for all you have given to us and all you provide for us. We gladly give our love to you, those beside us, and those we've yet to meet. Through your love and guidance, we will create Eden here on earth. God is great."

The lights within the Basilica shone brightly, forcing everyone to close their eyes. Within two seconds, the light returned to normal. The Prophet Jesus was gone. Those inside St. Peter's Basilica immediately looked around, with many of the Cardinals clambering around the altar. There was no sign of the Prophet. The faithful packed inside the ancient church could not help themselves as they began to grab each other, wildly celebrating, as elderly robed men danced like children – they laughed, cried, and shook each other in joyous rapture. They'd witnessed a divine miracle. The Pope and his leading Cardinals were on their knees, singing the praises of the Almighty. From the streets of Rome, hundreds of thousands cheered and screamed until their throats burned with a joy that provided a wall of sound that wrapped around the ancient church in a vast, audible reverence.

Carrie crossed her fingers as she witnessed the celebratory hysteria in Rome. Massed gatherings from around the world showed similar reactions from all temples. Mo Yousaf's teary eyes stared in disbelief as the images from around the globe displayed millions of all faiths rising to their feet to praise the heavens.

James Gordon asked, "Theo, what do we have?"

"Only that it's the same guy," came the resigned reply.

"Okay, back to work," James instructed. "Let's find some answers."

Instantly, rapid activity increased inside the offices of the nondescript building on Wisconsin Avenue, and the noise level of the shared space jumped as teams went into action. Then, the machinery of Washington, DC, went about its business.

"That was short and sweet," Carrie said, hiding a loose tear from the corner of her eye.

"Not so sweet if you live in Jerusalem. Israel should be on full alert," Mo advised. "I guess it should be something good, but we've been wrong before."

Carrie struggled to contain the excitement inside her body – she wanted to dance and sing like the millions on TV. Every word from the Prophet resonated. Her internal worlds of personal versus professional collided, and she needed to think fast. She grabbed Mo and headed out of James' office.

"We only have an hour – what do we do about Jerusalem?" James called after them.

"You tell all American diplomats, or whoever you have out there, to stay inside and off the streets. Have the military work with the Israeli government, and get eyes on every inch of the city, especially Temple Mount! Make sure your people talk with Egypt, Jordan, Lebanon, and Saudi Arabia to stay calm."

"And then what?"

"Check every holy site in the city to make sure nothing goes bang," she replied. Then, Carrie closed the door, taking Mo with her.

"Do you think that's what's going to happen?" Mo asked as she rushed him towards the elevator.

"I hope not. The Prophet indicated something positive. Lightning struck six places at the same time – miracle number one. I can't even think what the second one looks like. It's unpredictable." Carrie hit the button for the ground floor.

"Where are we going? Your office is back there."

"You're going to buy me a drink at the Irish bar across the street! Time for Muslims and Christians to come together. We're making a start right now." She dragged Mo from the elevator and headed onto the street.

"I don't drink alcohol," he said as he straightened some of his tangled hair.

"Good. I'll have your share." Carrie held out two shaking hands. "See that – same as you had earlier. I need something to kick down my adrenalin."

"The world is excited but nervous, the White House is in crisis – James Gordon and the President of the United States want answers, and you're pulling me into an Irish bar?"

"Damn right. If all goes well, we can make some reasonable predictions. If it all goes wrong, I may as well die with a drink in my hands," she replied. They jay-walked across the street and into the bar. "You know what? We need to stop running around, clear our heads, and figure out where this may be going. The next hour will give us an indication. If this is the Prophet of the third coming, what's the use in two theologians versus the Word of God? Could be the shortest consulting gig we ever do."

"Or the last."

"What sign would you give to Jerusalem if you were God? We've already had lightning. That's very biblical and hard to beat," Carrie suggested.

"Better not be a flood or plague."

"No, he indicated peace, understanding, unity, and love."

"And if it's a giant hoax?" Mo asked.

"Let's remain positive. Wait and see."

They took a seat in the far corner, facing the TV screens over the bar. Carrie ordered a martini for herself and an iced tea for Mo. There were only a handful of customers scattered inside the dimly lit interior. The fabric inside the booth was worn out, and parts were torn away. The other patrons quietly chattered and pointed at the TV screens. Mo clinked his glass against hers, and they sipped at their drinks.

"So, what did we just learn in the last few minutes that might help us?" Mo played with his tall glass like he might find the answers in the moisture on the outer rim.

Carrie used her plastic pen to slowly stir the contents of her drink. "For those paying attention, we learned it's the same guy," she looked sideways at Mo. "Theo did some facial recognition mapping. We learned he speaks fluent Italian, as well as Arabic. Beyond that – I'm all out of predictions. I'm trying not to simply say it's God's will." She ran her fingers down the side of the glass and loudly yawned.

Mo slumped his body into the seat and stared straight ahead. "Some sleep would be good."

"I hit a wall hours ago. Running around makes your body forget it needs rest until the second you stop. I feel like I could sleep for twelve hours straight, right here." Carrie leaned sideways and rested her head against his shoulder. She knew Mo wouldn't care.

She did not see Mo's look of confused contentment. Instead, he said, "All that stuff we sent James to get supplies to Medina … it never moved."

"Didn't the President sign it?"

"I didn't leave James' office, according to Jessica."

"Well, maybe they found a different way?" Carrie guessed.

"I hope so. Do you still think this is real?"

"I'm so tired; I don't know." She yawned again. "But, I'd say yes, based on what I've seen. We're witnessing something historic."

"What have you done?" Mo asked.

Carrie explained about moving the security camera inside the Basilica and the reaction she got.

"No more risks," Mo urged.

Carrie adjusted her head against him to get comfortable. "What do you think James Gordon wants? I mean, what is it they're doing in that building? What are we doing? Is our government leveraging this, or are they interested in protecting the American people's interests? You know what I mean?"

Mo gave it some thought and quickly gave up. "They have more resources at their fingertips than I've been able to get my hands on in the last five years of asking. These guys are serious. I'm guessing James Gordon is too well connected to the Senate and the President to have a secret agenda. Surely, they would have had him fired or shot by now."

"Hmm. A part of me feels like we're working for shadows and being asked to provide the light," was all Carrie could be bothered to say, yawning loudly again. Their tired bodies melted into the comfortably tattered seats. Lazily they covered possibilities until, after twenty minutes of tiring speculation, the TV screens over the bar were all focused on Jerusalem.

Mo said, "We should get back. Do you have a report for James?"

"I'll think of one when I move my arms and legs," Carrie replied. She stretched her limbs and then growled like she was about to start a fight. "I want to see if Theo can get us a satellite shot of Temple Mount." She slurped down the last of her martini and jumped out of the bench seat. "Don't forget to pay for the drinks," she smiled at Mo.

"You're a bad Christian," he shouted after her. He dropped cash onto the table and caught up with her. "The U.S. has a big military presence in the gulf. James can get some aircraft to film whatever happens from the skies?"

"How do you know that?"

"I saw it on one of the news segments."

"Nice. Jesus will come back to Rome," Carrie blurted. "I can feel it. I'll tell James to expect it."

"Don't tell him it's a gut feeling."

"Never."

CHAPTER THIRTEEN

The city of Jerusalem was a maze of mostly deserted streets as the majority of people stayed inside their homes, fearing the city could erupt. The police and military patrolled all sectors. The primary religious sites had squads sweeping them clean for explosives, but the city was too large, too complex to cover everything.

Carrie sat between James Gordon and Mo Yousaf, with Theo on her extended right. They had a dozen different views of Jerusalem, including the overhead satellite. The sporadic movement on the ground showed the people who'd gone out to worship and protect their sacred monuments.

"Are you sure about this?" James asked her.

"Nope," Carrie said, pulling her lips to one side of her face.

Mo switched his attention away from the monitors on Jerusalem. "Look at St. Peter's in Rome. The lights are increasing again."

A blinding flash occurred, and the yellow-robed Prophet appeared again by the altar. Some of the Catholic clergy fell to their knees, and others threw up their arms as if they were at a rock concert. The Prophet declared, "God is great. People of Jerusalem and the world - God shows you pure love."

After less than a few seconds, Jesus fell into silent prayer and raised his head. "The time is now. For the watching world, behold a demonstration of divine power. The good people of the city will suffer no more. They will soon return – cleansed of ancient woes that plague them. This is God's will."

The satellite and multiple views of Jerusalem turned white. James Gordon yelled for people on the ground to relay updates. The message was the same; they'd lost all contact with their colleagues in Jerusalem. He groaned and used his cell phone to speak directly with a U.S. military attaché within the city walls. The line was dead. "Let's get our communications back up and see what everything looks like. Our satellites are being blocked."

"Our satellites are fully operational," Jessica said, chewing rapidly on her gum.

James glared angrily at her. "Why can't we get hold of anyone?"

A dense shiver ran down Carrie's spine. This was more than the cutting of communication lines. The Prophet remained perfectly still inside the Basilica. "He's not finished," she said.

"How do you know?" James asked.

"I can tell, but I don't know how I can tell," she replied.

Jesus raised his head. "It is done. Our Father has given you an undeniable sign of his love. God will restore everyone and everything back to where it was in one day. Your loved ones are safe with God. They will tell of his magnificence and his infinite glory. All will be reborn in God's true light. God is great."

The Basilica lights went white. When normality returned, the Prophet was gone.

"I am sick of these magic tricks," James raged. "Find him!"

Mo screamed aloud, "Oh, my God!! Look!" He pointed to the online satellite shots of Jerusalem. "It's gone! The city's gone!" Theo and his team scrambled, but all feeds showed the Holy City had vanished.

James was on his feet, "Get me the President – now! Call Tel Aviv and order them to stand by. Do not let anyone fire a missile anywhere!" James walked around in a tight circle chewing on the back of his hand, with beads of sweat formed on his thick brow.

Theo shook his head in disbelief. "This can't be right. Check how they're jamming us," he yelled at the two guys next to him. "Our feeds show real-time, but we can't see anything." He moved left and grabbed another laptop. "Let me try this." He searched online.

Carrie asked Jessica, "Can you randomly call some home phone numbers in Jerusalem and see who picks up?"

"Sure." She pulled up some numbers and began dialing.

Theo held up his laptop. "All live feeds are operational, but there's nothing at the end. Nobody's jamming us. They've made it look like the entire city has gone."

Carrie whispered to James. "Can you get jets to fly over the city without starting a war?"

"No, we can't do that, but we can get the Israeli air force to do it and see what they're looking at." He looked at Theo. "Did you get that?"

"On it, Chief!" Came the reply.

One of James' assistants announced, "Israel's on red alert. Mobilizing their aircraft and all military vehicles to their borders. Nukes are armed!"

"I need to see what they're looking at when they fly over the city," James yelled. He heard the voice at the end of the phone and walked from the room. "Mr. President, I need your help to make sure Israel's neighbors remain calm." James left the office.

Through the glass, Carrie watched James pace around, arms waving, and his face a deep red, making his lips look pale. "He's wasting his time," she assured Mo.

He returned a moment later, slamming the door, almost breaking it from its hinges. "Yes, Sir. I'll call you back." The office was a flurry of excited voices and activity. "Somebody give me a goddamn update!"

Carrie spoke quietly and methodically. "James, you're going to find Jerusalem is gone."

"A whole city with a million people can't just disappear!" He barked.

"It just did."

An hour of mayhem followed. Reports confirmed Jerusalem had vanished.

James Gordon and the team watched the Israeli air force flyover where Jerusalem was supposed to be but saw only desert. Israeli ground forces sent in teams from nearby Bethlehem and reported the entire city, its walls, houses, temples, streets, and people had vanished, with no physical traces left behind. The thermal scans and heat scans showed the same. It was as though Jerusalem never existed.

Frantic relatives, friends, and concerned citizens deluged the Israeli government offices. The Prime Minister appealed for calm from his Tel Aviv conference, swearing all resources were engaged to ascertain if this was an act of war. The American President made calls to Egypt, Lebanon, Jordan, and Syria, asking them to remain in control of their reactions. The surrounding countries feared it was some kind of laser weapon the Americans or Russians deployed. World leaders quickly connected. Nobody admitted to possessing the capability for what they'd seen, let alone carry it out.

Once confirmed that Jerusalem was gone, the neighboring countries, who had plenty of Muslim, Jewish, and Christian friends and relatives missing, asked what they could do to help. Israel asked that they wait for further news and stand down their militaries.

James excused himself and returned to his private office. His phone was red hot with calls from the Senate, especially those with close ties to the many influential Jewish connections. There was no logic to these events, and he struggled to explain. Trying to get people to be reasonable proved impossible. James called his wife, telling her to take the family down to their place in Florida for a while. He told his sobbing wife they'd be okay. In truth, his stomach lurched with the strangest feeling that he'd never see his family again. He steadied himself and stared at the ceiling, taking deep breaths. "C'mon, James, get a grip," he thought. The dull ache inside his chest worsened as the pressure mounted. "I am not dying today," he assured himself.

Carrie theorized that other world centers of power could be targets for the unexplained, and James believed she might be right.

Mo's anxiety spilled from his mouth in a high-pitched rant. "Carrie, millions of people are celebrating and millions are in meltdown. Including me! The finger-pointing of governments and religions will get worse before it gets better. The Prophet said there's still another day. I'm freaking out over here." He raked his clawed fingers through his tangled hair.

"We should have stayed in the bar," she replied. "You should tell James this could get worse?"

"Why me?"

"He likes you. Let's go to my office."

Mo collapsed on the two-seater couch opposite her untidy desk. "I need some sleep!" he said, ragging at his head.

"Everyone does. What comes next and from where?" Carrie asked herself. "If I were the prophet Jesus – what would I do?"

"What would you do, my Lord?" Mo sarcastically played along.

"I'd show up in another country. Return Jerusalem to where it was, and the world will undoubtedly proclaim that I am the Prophet, sent by God."

"Plenty of people will think it's some amazing magic trick. CGI or some other Hollywood bullshit."

"Well, he said God would show us more than one thing, seeing as we don't believe shit these days." Carrie looked into Mo's soft brown eyes. "You look awful. Get some rest. I'm going to do a bit more here. I'll keep you posted if I find anything, and then I'll go to the hotel and try to get a few hours of sleep."

"Sleep!" he indignantly laughed. "I'll leave you to it. Don't overdo it," he sarcastically remarked and wearily left the office.

Carrie rubbed her face. Even if she could predict where the Prophet would show, she couldn't predict what he'd do. There wasn't the time to go through all of those computations in her head. She thought it odd that if God and his Prophet were looking for peace, they'd created something as volatile as the Cuban missile crisis. "How does this unite us?" she questioned. "Faith!" The answer was simple. Carrie needed to find a way to predict the next moves, or the peace might not hold.

Wally Radford finished with the conference call and considered his limited options. His oldest ministry associates from the southern states informed Wally of revenue decreases. "You need to do something about this false Prophet," was their combined plea. Wally gave an impassioned speech to his old friends about holding their nerve and believing in Christ the Redeemer. Time was against them. Wally never said it outright, but he strongly intimated this prophet must go.

Wally received a frosty reception from his church leaders. Still, once he'd extrapolated the inevitable problems brought about by the False Prophet, including declining monetary projections, his church leaders bought in. To those with remaining doubt, he would reach out individually to work his charm. Another thirty-nine nights like this one, and they'd all be scraping for a living. Even the Holy Father of Rome fell for the theatrical nonsense. Not Wally!

Money was a good motivator for many, but Wally was focused on something much more important.

His church partners would fund the necessary endeavor with cash, so they'd agreed. It was time for them to dig into their personal reserves – money they had all made, thanks to Wally's advice. Wally knew people who would conduct the Lord's work alongside him. Good people that supported Christ, and Wally, for the right price. The path forward was radical, drastic, and borderline suicidal, but Wally was not afraid for himself. His concern was primarily for Christianity, his family, and the repose of his soul.

He fervently prayed. The New Age Prophet had already caused enough waves, and Wally intended to drain that ocean dry.

Dangerous endeavors required men brave enough in their faith to see it through. Wally's options were few and difficult. He needed detailed planning and a way to know where the jokester would be. But, no matter what happened, this conjurer calling himself Jesus wasn't going to destroy his ministries.

Cheryl looked at the furrowed brow of her husband. "I can see the wheels turning. My Wally Radford will undertake what no one else dares." She admired his convictions, and she would do what he asked of her. "Darlin,' should I move some money from one of our personal accounts and have it ready in cash? We'll need liquid assets to purchase what's necessary to do the Lord's bidding."

Wally smiled at his faithful wife. "The Lord blessed me when he brought you into my life. Unfortunately, not everyone would understand what's at stake. Sometimes I think I don't deserve you, my sweet lady." He stared lovingly at Cheryl, soaking in her goodness. "Go ahead and move the money. We'll do what God commands us to do."

"Amen," she replied, blessing herself.

CHAPTER FOURTEEN

James Gordon awoke at his desk. It was 4:30 am. He'd fallen asleep for two hours. In the main office, people were working; some were slumped, with their heads next to their keyboards. He sifted through his messages and emails. If it didn't come from Senator Garofalo, the President, or one of his immediate team, he simply deleted the voicemail or email. But it was the text message from Carrie Carter that got his full attention. It read: READ MY EMAIL!!!!!

James looked at the note she sent. Carrie predicted the Prophet would appear in the Hanuman Temple, Prayagraj, India. She reasoned that capturing the three most significant religious followings on the planet would be the obvious choice. Jesus had already visited Medina and Rome, covering the core of Islam and Christianity. Jerusalem's mysterious disappearance continued to dominate world news, although no one had come close to figuring out how. Her advice contained Mo's data on visibility, safety, and resource requirements. James gathered those that were in the office and got to work. After a few hours' sleep, he engaged them in figuring out supply lines when the rest rolled in.

James' dialogue with their agents in India was non-stop. At least he might be one step ahead of where they'd been a couple of days ago. If Carrie's advice proved accurate, the Prophet would appear at 3:00 pm Washington time. He gulped down the cold coffee and found the half-asleep Theo busy working. The bags under Theo's eyes suggested he'd not slept for more than a day. "I see you read Carrie's email. What can we do differently?" James asked.

"I have some cameras heading to Prayagraj. We will use some high-speed cameras to capture all angles inside the temple. If the Prophet appears, we'll get a resolution that nobody can cheat, even if they're using some funky white-light source."

"Foolproof?"

"Exactly!" Theo replied, never once looking away from his screen. "The cameras I've got going in there record over two thousand frames per second – they can also see in any light spectrum. So, we can replay it in super-slow motion at 23,000 frames per second. No matter what happens, we'll know how it's done."

"To clarify – when the Senator asks me, I can assure him we'll have the answer, and I can walk him through video evidence."

"Yes, Chief, that's it. It'll show that, too, if it's not a trick." The stony silence from James was enough to prompt Theo to add, "I'm just saying."

"Don't. Even the U.S. government isn't capable of striking a deal with God."

James called the team in India and explained what he wanted. Then, after several more calls, he went to Carrie's office to see if she'd arrived. Upon opening the door, he found her curled up on the small couch, fast asleep. His phone showed it was approaching 6:00 am. James quietly took her jacket from the back of the chair and carefully draped it over her. There was nothing new from any news feeds, so he figured she could remain undisturbed for a short while.

At his desk, he looked at the data from the Pentagon. Despite all the detailed reports coming from various sources in Israel, there was no evidence of what happened to Jerusalem. Over a million residents and visitors had vanished without a trace. The guys behind this show proved their abilities. Impressive in some respects. Although if Jerusalem failed to reappear, then the shit would hit the fan.

Mo Yousaf looked barely awake as he stepped out of the elevator into the sparsely populated office space – a stark contrast to the previous day and a half. The jaded faces showed a bleary-eyed focus on flat screens, with barely a sound anywhere. For over a day, information was ebbing and flowing at a furious pace. The power of government was evident with the number of people, equipment, and communications they engaged. He thought Carrie made a fair point about who they were working for. James Gordon's broad-brush statement about saving U.S. lives sounded fine, but everything he saw around him showed a high-resolution covert substructure.

Mo found himself in a building with no signage, no departments, no names on doors – something like an unnoticeable eclipse during broad daylight. Mo looked up the address of their building on Wisconsin Avenue, and the best he could find stated that it contained a nondescript government accounts center.

Everything Mo had seen suggested peaceful solutions were the primary concern, but this entire operation was designed to hide in plain sight. The juxtaposition worried him.

"Good morning. Did you get some sleep?" James asked.

"Not enough. Anything new?"

"Not really. Jerusalem and its people are missing. The Middle East remains on full alert, but at least they're holding firm." James sat by Mo's desk. "NATO's declared a state of emergency, and the Mediterranean Sea has more warships in it than fish. Surprisingly, the Russians have said they are willing to send in aircraft carriers and submarines to support. Everyone is helping but cautiously looking over their shoulders. The situation gets more bizarre and complex by the hour. This Prophet could have found an easier way to bring peace."

Mo nodded. "The Middle East is playing nice and we should foster it and enjoy it."

"And?"

"Middle Eastern people are passionate and fiercely proud of their heritage. What they believe in makes little sense to us, but a threat to their culture is like trying to supersede thousands of years of what you might call a generationally shared psyche. You can't control something embedded in their DNA. We have to get their leaders and influencers to make rational decisions. The Middle East reacts from the gut and despairs afterward – this is where your networks have to supply guidance. Trying to defeat something by using common sense won't work against what's biologically wired throughout hundreds of generations."

"Trying to get the Pope at a table with the Imams and clerics is easier said than done, but the Prophet seems to have managed it," James replied.

"Bigger problems face us in India and Cambodia," Mo advised. "India has up to forty million people in a single day who turn up for the Kumbh Mela festival near Prayagraj. That's on the edge of a city of two million residents. If Carrie's correct, can you imagine the stampede the Indian authorities will be facing if the Prophet goes there?"

"I hear people in India are already en route. We can't send troops to help in India – it's politically and religiously too sensitive. We've offered, but the Indian authorities declined. American boots in any country arouse suspicion. So we'll have to advise from a distance." James said.

"That's the issue right there," Mo pointed at him. "This is a time for new thinking and new ways of doing. We have to make friends and be ready to help – or millions could die. We should send aid and people to support – not people who are wearing AR-15s around their necks or have hand grenades hanging from their belts. Try that! We have the opportunity for change, but it won't take much to derail it."

James and Mo went deeper into their conversation despite some objective differences and covered beneficial ground on what James could propose to Senator Garofalo and the President.

Carrie awoke feeling groggy and disgusting. She went to the hotel, showered, changed, and returned. She spent part of her morning looking at the potential disaster that could befall Prayagraj in India. The Bade Hanuman Ji Temple took the lightning strike, but the geographical point nearby where the Ganges and Yamuna River met was the focal point for millions of Hindus. She submitted her reports and recommendations before joining the others before 3:00 pm. They viewed the live feeds from inside the Hanuman Temple and watched the live news feeds around the densely packed Indian city.

The view over the two rivers from their banks provided a breathtaking spectacle. Carrie saw the estimated five million people sitting quietly and attentively where the rivers merged. A mile away, helicopters circled the temple. Big screens had been erected all over the grounds where the festivals usually took place. "That's unbelievable," she observed.

Mo cautioned, "The crowd will triple within a day or two and triple again if the Prophet appears."

"The people are showing the way as governments fall behind," Carrie said.

Mo looked at her but said nothing.

Right at the stroke of 3:00 pm, bright lights blazed within the temple, and when the haze cleared, the Prophet stood at the foot of Hanuman's statue. The noise that came through the speakers created by five million ecstatic people threatened to blow out the sound systems in the office as the walls vibrated with the cheers from the throngs.

Inside the temple, the handful of Swamis selected to greet the Prophet kissed his feet as they screamed in celebration. It took a while for Jesus to gather them close, and he spoke to them in whispers. He asked everyone to pray, and he remained motionless for an hour until the time approached when he promised the return of Jerusalem.

Jesus rose to address the learned scholars and the live broadcasts. "God is great. Welcome. I am Jesus. That is the name my spiritual Father has given me. There is but one true God. Today, our Father will restore Jerusalem and show

98

you another miracle. Those who return to us will tell of great things – Muslim, Christian, Jew, Hindu, Buddhist, Sikh, Taoist, and all faiths within the city will be as one, united with God. The disabled walk, the blind see, the deaf hear, the hateful will love. They have felt God's embrace. People of the world - pray with me as we welcome back those reborn under God's grace."

Jesus adopted the same hands clasped stance, and the feeds from Israel turned blindingly white. When visibility returned, the city of Jerusalem was back.

The satellite images showed people looking bemused, stopping to chat with those nearest to them, and checking their limbs as though they'd awoken from a strange dream. James told his people to call the U.S. consulate. Word came straight back that they were alive and well, asking what had happened. The residents of Jerusalem couldn't recall anything meaningful. The people massed by the intersecting rivers in India were chanting and wildly dancing at God's miracle. Millions of feet created a dust cloud four miles wide and five miles deep until half the city of Prayagraj became lost from sight.

"He did it," Mo gasped.

James scratched his head.

Carrie smiled. James glanced at her. She stifled a laugh, but her look was a clear 'I told you so.'

Jesus proclaimed, "Thank you, Father. Let this be the beginning of a new age. Brothers and sisters of India, God our Father will show you his love and provide a re-awakening."

The light became impossibly bright as the celebrating millions suddenly cowered, covering their eyes. The river Ganges and Yamuna were bone dry when they dared to look! Not a drop of water. No fish, no mud, no plants, no crocodiles, or signs of life. It defied the senses, and a shared silence prevailed. Reports from India confirmed that the two great rivers, reaching a combined two and a half thousand miles, were dry.

"Good people do not despair – God will provide for the millions of those who rely on its waters and its bounty." Jesus walked along the edge of the Hanuman's statue and placed his hands on the effigy. "Our Father, who is the giver of life to all things in the Universe, will bring life back to the rivers in one hour. It will be reborn, just as your brothers and sisters in Jerusalem have been. It is God's gift to you, his beloved people."

Jesus kissed the effigy of Hanuman. "God wishes you to understand for yourselves that you are not separated by colors, borders, languages, or flags. Look to the newborn children of Jerusalem – they know the way. Three weeks from now, God will give you the written templates to live as one. God is great."

The lights brightened inside the holy temple, and the Prophet departed.

James Gordon inquired about the timing to get from Rome to Prayagraj in India. Theo confirmed that the timing was impossible. No border patrol in the world had picked up any sign of the Prophet Jesus, no street camera, no airport, train station, or radar, or private planes – simply nothing.

James cleared the room allowing Carrie, Mo, and Theo to stay behind. "Thanks for everything you guys have done so far. It's too big to ask for such a small group but thank you." He asked Theo, "Can you show us what those fancy cameras of yours picked up?"

"I'd love to." Theo pulled the review from the secure internet line and fast-forwarded the recording from the Hanuman Temple. "This little technological miracle will show us exactly how he's doing it. We'll watch the recording in infrared in case we've been dealing with some cool holographic imaging in previous locations, and people in attendance were pretending to kiss his hands and feet."

"You mean like the Pope was acting," Carrie sighed.

Theo ignored her sarcasm and began the super-slow-motion. "This goes beyond the flashing white light. If you look down here at the bottom of the screen, you can see the Indian Holy men sitting on the floor, their heartbeats, brain activity, etc." The figure of Jesus slowly appeared out of thin air and formed into the person by the statue of Hanuman.

"Impossible!" James barked. "Rewind it. It has to be a trick."

Theo shook his head. "Chief, I'm sorry to tell you, but this is real. This dude appears from nowhere. Our view picks up everything. We've already run it in ultra-violet, and it's the same story. I replayed his exit from the temple, and it's the same thing. He fizzles from view. We know he's there, as flesh and blood. We can see his heartbeat, skin temperature, and the electromagnetic pulse from his body. There was nothing, and then he became real."

James looked helplessly at Carrie and Mo. "You're coming with me to meet Senator Garofalo. I have to explain this crap. I'm going to need expert backup.

Theo, get me that on a thumb drive to show the Senator." James phoned his assistant. "Get me a car; we're going to the big house across the street."

"We're going to the White House?" Carrie stuttered.

"Yep. Too late to change your mind now," James retorted.

They found themselves sitting in a large office with views across the rear White House lawns ten minutes later.

Carrie whispered to Mo, "Can you believe how beautiful this building is?" She tapped her feet on the floor, wishing she could find something to do with her hands, as nerves pushed her entire system into overdrive. James asked her to take the lead on the overall discussion points, and if the Senator got antsy, James would take over.

The side doors opened, and Senator Garofalo introduced himself. He approached Carrie. "Carrie, good to see you again," he said with a little extra enthusiasm. Once courtesies were complete, he asked, "Show me what you have and what comes next."

Carrie began walking the Senator and his advisors through the video.

James Gordon carefully studied Carrie Carter. She barely missed a beat in her observations. She was wearing a black trouser suit with a plain white shirt underneath and black slip-on flat shoes. Carrie had her hair tied tight to her head with some dangling wispy strands hanging on either side of her face, softening her angular features. Her large oval eyes soaked in the feedback as she went through her presentation. Her powerful delivery looked effortless. The strong physicality she possessed oozed formidable sexuality. Her shapely thighs and glutes showed through the clinging material of her trousers, making it impossible not to follow her every movement. James thought Senator Garofalo observed more than the brilliance of her mind when he supported her move into the political arena. Their earlier embrace and eye contact were held for a fraction too long. James decided he would delve further into their shared backgrounds to discover whether the Senator shared more than just his political experience with her. Knowledge wasn't the key to power in Washington, DC, but it helped.

Three minutes into the presentation, the side doors opened, and in walked the President. His reddened jowls rolled like silent thunder. He headed straight towards Carrie. The President shook all their hands, took a seat at the table, and asked them to continue.

Carrie's body boiled. Typically she was well prepared and knew her subject matter, back to front, but this was new, full of pitfalls, and riddled with educated guesswork. She coughed and stumbled initially but quickly recovered her rhythm. Two days ago, she talked with professors and low-level government advisors – today, the President himself. She found it impossible to lock out his presence. A few minutes later, Carrie felt relieved when she asked, "Questions, anybody?" She took a seat to ease the shakiness in her legs. Mo and James kept quiet, and their expressions gave nothing away about her performance.

The President half raised his hand. "Carrie, based on what you guys are saying, I'm hearing this is very likely divine intervention or something we just don't understand? So I want to make sure I'm getting that right."

"Yes, Mr. President, that's correct – could be either. Unfortunately, we cannot find any biological or metaphysical answers for what we're seeing."

"Which do you think it is? I won't hold you to it," he asked, noting her hesitation.

Carrie glanced at Mo, who raised his eyebrows and lifted one shoulder to say, 'go for it.'

"Mr. President, based on what we have so far, it appears real. By that, I mean a Prophet of God. Whether you believe in divinity or not is immaterial. We're dealing with something we cannot explain. We're facing the possibility this is a Prophet sent by God the Almighty or some universal force we've yet to identify."

The President gave her an appreciative nod. "Nobody mentioned this at the inauguration," he joked. He motioned to his security escort, and they opened the double doors. He thanked them as he left the room, adding, "Do all you can to keep us one step ahead. Our great nation's safety and the world has many variables." The double doors closed, and he was gone.

"That's the guy who has to address the nation – think you've got it bad?" Senator Garofalo inferred to James. "I know this is rough. James, get me a briefing from India. Thanks, everybody, and keep doing what you're doing."

James, Carrie, and Mo took the limousine back to HQ. At Wisconsin Avenue, they gathered in the small conference room with Theo, Jessica, and their immediate team.

The one-hour timeframe the Prophet had spoken of was about to end.

"What can we expect?" James asked them.

"Nobody can find a drop of water or life in those rivers. So we've advised the Indian authorities to clear people away. There are no dams or ways to drain its millions of gallons. It's dry, like there was never anything in it," Theo confirmed.

Carrie paced behind the row of chairs.

"She thinks better on her feet," Mo explained.

The team observed multiple views of Prayagraj and its surrounding areas up the river. "The Ganges River is one of the most polluted and dangerous waters in the world. Mankind has poisoned it to the point that you can't eat anything you pull from it for over a thousand miles," Carrie explained. "We've accessed the test data for the water pollutants. When the Prophet comes back, and, hopefully, the water, too, we can analyze the water to see if it's the same. If the chemical compounds and concentrates are the same – it must be a trick."

"If not – a miracle. They have the testing kits ready," Mo said.

Carrie looked at her colleague's grimaces. The unbearable tension lay thick throughout the room. "Can we talk to the people we have nearby who are watching?"

"Sure," Theo confirmed, and James gave the okay. Theo tapped some keys on his laptop. "Brett, do you copy?"

"Copy, Theo – how's it going, you crazy bastard? Are you still banging that girl from the European spyware division?"

"Got you on speaker, with an audience," Theo quickly replied. "We have views of the two empty riverbeds, the edge of the city, and the festival areas filled with people. We want you to describe what's happening; can you do that?"

"I can describe anything from the earth to the stars," Brett replied in a thick Indian accent. "It will be my honor to give words to what your ears and eyes cannot explain. There is a miracle waiting to happen. It is in the air. I swear you can taste it."

"He's a little eccentric," Theo explained to the immediate group.

"There's been a lot of chanting from the crowds, but they have settled down," Brett shouted. "The clock is ticking toward the hour, and it's gotten incredibly quiet. I'm right where the rivers meet, in old Fort Allahabad. We are set up on the walls of the fort. We can see if anything happens. It's very exciting, like when a baby is born or when India wins a cricket match." Brett gave a countdown over the final ten seconds as the giant clock ticked down. "It's getting very bright like the sun is exploding. The crowds are … hang on; we can't see – too bright. Bloody hell! Hang on. Extremely hot! Light is coming back to normal. I nearly shit my pants!" Brett began chattering rapidly in Indian to his assistant on the ground. "We are looking with binoculars, but nothing is happening yet. The riverbeds are dry, like an old lady's thirsty lips."

"I like this guy," Jessica said, chewing her gum.

The group in Washington waited, unable to see any changes. Brett exchanged words with his assistants. "Hang on, Theo, you crazy bastard, I think we have something." More excitable Indian chattering followed with multiple voices firing back and forth. "To the northwest, there's a noise coming from the Ganges! Now it's from the west! We have a rumbling from the Yamuna! Car horns are sounding in the distance, from the far side of the city." There was a moment of silence. "Give me those binoculars, you bloody fool," Brett scolded someone. "Let me see!" Another short silence followed. "Hang on to your horses."

Those in Washington eyeballed each other. "Brett? Brett? What's happening?" Theo called out.

"Theo, if you have a satellite, look from above. There's water coming from both sides," Brett shouted loud over the raised voices in the background. "It's coming fast from everywhere, like a bloody big tidal wave!" He shouted something in his native tongue and switched back to English. "Sorry – sorry – very crazy here! We are most excited." He shrieked as if he stumbled and reappeared. "It's here. It's here!" Brett's shouting melted away as the background noise of millions of raised voices came from the grounds of the Mela. Masses of exalted cheers filled the conference room that rattled the ceiling tiles.

Mo pointed at the overhead view from the southeast corner of the city. "Water's flowing – fast." They observed as millions of gallons of water rushed from two sides, combining into one and creating a surge of white water at its apex that tumbled, swirled, and surged in a spitting torrent that rushed southeast through the city. Brett screamed down the line, but his voice was unintelligible over the background racket. The news cameras on the riverbanks showed millions of people chanting, their voices raised in unison, as a state of mass euphoria took over Prayagraj.

"That's six million people dancing, right there," Mo explained as the dust rose from their stamping feet.

"Say thanks to Brett," James told Theo, signaling him to cut the communication. "The Prophet did it," James sighed in disbelief. "You think Amritsar, next? So the Prophet stays in India?"

"To cover the highest religious attendances, then yes," Carrie replied, and Mo nodded his agreement. "It's the spiritual home of the Sikh religion, accounting for over forty million believers. So as a unifying gesture, it makes sense for the Prophet to go there."

"The global internet's crashing again," Theo announced.

"Keep an eye on the news," James instructed. "Let's get ready for what's next and for potential impacts. The Middle Eastern countries have ceased their military red alerts. Something good – at last." The news resulted in whoops and high-fives all around, and the message transferred into the main office, causing some short celebrations.

Carrie enjoyed seeing everyone's reaction to the military stand-down. It gave her cause to believe the branch of National Security James Gordon represented sought peaceful solutions.

Carrie and Mo revised their projections, suggestions, and theories, plus potential impacts, and submitted them to James.

In the early evening, Mo suggested, "Let's duck out of here, eat and get some sleep. The Prophet hasn't come back, and I think we've got until 3:00 pm our time tomorrow."

"Our recommendations get bigger each time," Carrie puffed. Their exchanged glance contained a realization that the expectations became incomprehensible.

"All we can do is estimate, advise, and let the big boys do their bit." Mo's face looked like he'd aged ten years.

"Are you okay?"

"Fine." His shoulders dipped. "I'm worried about these mass gatherings and if the people will be okay? The potential for disaster from something that size is too large. Presently, it all looks good, but the law of probability suggests it can't stay that way. I know that sounds pessimistic, but a realistic viewpoint matters."

"Our government has pledged to collaborate with the Red Cross and other agencies to make sure food, water, and shelter gets there – that's a good thing. The Russians and Chinese are helping!"

"I guess," he replied, but with little satisfaction.

"Can I choose where we go for dinner?"

"I already know what that means." He rolled his eyes as they entered the elevator. Five minutes later, they were sitting in the same Irish bar and booth as the previous day. "I can tell by your face and your tone that there's something else going on in there besides the need for Irish bars," Mo suggested, "I get the feeling there's more to this than me watching you eat a corned beef sandwich with fries."

Carrie made a face at him and checked that no one was close by, "I'll tell you what's on my mind, but it stays here."

"Agreed."

"Sure you don't want some corned beef?"

Mo shook his head, giving her a friendly sneer. "I'll stick with my potato wedges, thanks."

"I've had the same dreams three consecutive nights." She saw Mo switch off and nudged him. "Listen, you numbnut, this is serious. Every single detail is the same. It's all relevant. Prophets galore." Mo tried not to laugh as she playfully punched him in the ribs. "You want to hear this, or not?"

"Go for it," he mocked.

"Each time, in my dream, the Prophet's here in the U.S., and you and I are talking with him."

"What's he saying – something magical, like they're going to pay us for our time here?"

Carrie ignored his sarcasm. "He's saying that it's okay – he's in the hands he was meant to be in, and it will end as his Master has ordained."

"Jesus? Right here in Washington?" Mo asked, raising his inquisitive eyebrows.

"Yep. Right here. Jesus delivers the templates with God's word, and the world gets the same message so that no one can dispute or manipulate the word. That's the abbreviated version of the repeating dream I've had."

"It's natural for you to be dreaming about this kind of stuff, given what we're doing here."

"You're right, but three in a row? All the same? Word for word? Come on, Mo!" Carrie checked around the corner to make sure they had privacy. "That's not all! Jesus told us we must help the men from Medina. I don't know what that means. Something bad happens to the Prophet. He gets taken away."

"By whom?"

"I don't know, but it's not good."

Mo gave it some thought. "I think I need a shave," he said, feeling his face. "Sounds like your brain is feeding you parts of what we've seen and heard, mixing it with the Bible. No offense if I'm over-simplifying it."

"It's all too specific not to mean something. The Grand Mufti, Abdul Aziz, from Medina, is in it, too, and he's over here. There's a tall military man – fierce-looking. I can't figure it out. I wouldn't say it if I didn't think it was significant."

"True, very true. In the meantime, I need some more ranch dressing."

Carrie slapped his leg. "I'm telling you – I can feel it."

Mo called the waitress over. "Can I get more ranch, please, and a Miller High Life?" Carrie stopped eating and stared at him. Mo interjected by raising his hand toward her astonished face, "Not a word from you on the beer, or I'll tell your mother about you having sex before marriage."

"At my age, I think she's pretty aware."

They returned to the business at hand, and Mo suggested she get Theo to pull the details on the Medina gathering and study them. She liked the idea. "We can't tell Theo it stemmed from a dream," Carrie insisted.

"Definitely not."

The TV screens behind the bar were full of people from Jerusalem telling their stories of feeling God's presence, and since their return to Israel, all of their previous medical ailments were gone. Each testimony from people of different ages, religions, and backgrounds came loaded with their story's emotion and transformation.

"If that's a mass hypnosis, it's quite brilliant," Carrie observed. "If nothing else, it's achieved something already."

"What's that?"

"There are people of every denomination sharing their experiences and supporting one another. They're together on the streets of Jerusalem. When have you seen that before?"

"I looked at the initial data from Jerusalem. Those who previously had symptoms of diseases or physical impairments, are healthy. It's early days and only a small sample, but the story's the same – people are out of their wheelchairs, they're off life-support, and the hospital beds are empty. Maybe we'll find a reason."

"Maybe we find God," Carrie replied.

"That's what I'm afraid of."

"James needs rationale to report to the President. And he is duty bound to keep looking. At what point do we finally acknowledge this is divinity?"

"I don't disagree," Mo said. "But we have to be sure."

"Do we?"

Their phones simultaneously beeped with a text from Theo. Carrie scrolled through and summarized. "It's confirmed – the Ganges is pollution-free! Loaded with fish and life. For all our sakes, this better be God at work."

"If it turns out to be anything else, I'm having the corned beef sandwich before I die," Mo affirmed.

CHAPTER FIFTEEN

As Carrie predicted, Jesus appeared the following day at the Darbar Sahib in the Golden Temple of Amritsar. Over two million ecstatic worshippers greeted him from outside the holy site. James Gordon was absent as the team watched the live events. Carrie watched him locked in his office in a series of long, animated discussions.

Jesus made his way through the gathering of the Sikh elders. The Granthi and Gyani touched his robe as he passed through them, placing his hands on their heads. Old men and women openly sobbed.

"God is great. Welcome. I am Jesus. That is the name my spiritual Father has given me. There is but one true God. Faith is to accept certainty without rational explanation. The newborn of Jerusalem have bathed in God's mercy. The great rivers in India have new life. God asks that you respect what you have. The earth is not for wealth and profit. Be the caretakers of life on the planet. Rejoice in God's majesty and have empathy for those who do not."

Jesus stepped forward among the elders seated on the floor. "My brothers and sisters pray with me – let us give thanks for this beautiful earth. Father, forgive our doubts, our frailty, and, though you speak clearly, forgive those of us who still do not hear. We give thanks for the opportunities of each new dawn in which to make amends." Jesus turned to face the world's media, "People of the world, God has told me you should look to this great continent's jungles and the plains of Africa. His divinity will once more reveal itself. God is great."

Carrie pointed out, "Blinding flash, and he's gone. Watch." Right on cue, as she said it – it happened.

"You know the trigger point, don't you?" Mo said.

Carrie half-smiled. "There's a slight motion of his hands toward his body, and he's gone."

Theo looked at the slow-motion. "You're right. There's a faint hand motion and vamoose. Bet you'd be useful on a baseball field," he inferred of Carrie's observational skills. "Our cameras show the same as before – the dude comes from nowhere. We can't work it out."

"Maybe you're not supposed to," Mo suggested.

Jessica Cortez called them over to her screen, chewing her gum like she was angry with it. "You guys – look. I hooked into some live feeds in Africa as soon as he mentioned it. This footage is from Tanzania, the Serengeti National Park. Watch." Jessica switched to a full-screen view. In the foreground were several highly animated reserve wardens jumping up and down, talking excitedly, and filming a massive herd of elephants. Jessica read the translation. "They're saying this large herd isn't tagged – they came from nowhere." She flipped over to another screen. "This is a live feed from Kenya." They watched the shaky video of the pride of lions walking into view with similarly excitable chatter. Jessica split the screen and read the alerts. "It's happening all over Africa: Elephants, lions, rhinos – all kinds of animals appearing in large numbers."

She paused to observe her second screen. "The same is happening in Nepal, Bangladesh, and India, too: They are saying there are Bengal tigers. We'll get verification."

"Based on what we've seen, I'd suggest it will be true," Mo predicted.

"Lions, tigers, and bears, oh my," Jessica dryly cackled.

Carrie and Mo didn't laugh.

Jessica shrugged in disappointment. "I'll keep you posted."

"Thank you," Carrie said as she and Mo returned to their think tank. James would want to know what came next and from where.

Cheryl Radford confirmed to Wally, "The money transferred. Half a million dollars in cash will be available within two days."

Wally ruefully replied, "The Lord's work begins. Thank you, Jesus Christ, our Lord, and Savior."

"Amen."

Wally stood at the front window of their home, taking in the view of half of Montgomery. The light faded on the horizon, giving a dazzling color spectrum over the foliage and lawns. "My darling,' the good Lord has smiled upon us. I'm thankful for everything you've done to nurture our children, share your love with me, and follow our walk together in Christ. One last time, I ask you to have faith in me as I go to do the Lord's bidding. We both know where this will likely end."

Cheryl's eyes hung heavy with tears, and she slid her arm around his waist, resting her head against his sturdy shoulder. "I'm honored by your bravery. I know the Lord will call you to his bosom, no matter what happens. I pray you'll return. You're a good man, Wally Radford, the best of men. I will keep our house, our family, and our congregation in a manner to make you proud."

Wally pulled her closer, kissing her forehead. "Thank you for your undivided love and loyalty. Gary's coming around here tomorrow with all the papers. I will sign everything over in your name. I'll have no ownership of any assets, no partnership, so they can't touch you. I know you'll do the right thing."

Cheryl straightened her head. "Do you have the right men? They'll need your strength and conviction. This is no time for you to be in the careless hands of rednecks." She wiped the first trails of salty drops from the ends of her face.

"No rednecks. Chuck and John believe in the power of Jesus Christ and the teachings of the Bible. Men who know the False Prophet for what he is. They seek no reward on this earth – only that of eternal life. I've assured the men that their families will financially be taken care of." He took a long deep breath.

Cheryl observed Wally's strained posture. The burden of continuation fell on her, and she needed all her strength to keep the ministries together.

"Once the money is here, we leave for Saudi Arabia. We've more than enough to buy what we need and bring an end to this. I've booked the flights. I'll send word to you, as we talked about. Once we're set up, you'll tell the local police I've gone missing and follow the plan. That'll be the end of our direct communication. Our contacts assured us that this so-called New Age Prophet will return to Medina, and when he does, we'll be waiting for him."

Cheryl gripped him tight. "Can you get close enough in that God-forsaken country?"

Wally patted the back of her hand. "Half a dozen men of Christ are providing half a million dollars in cash – it buys us a way to the heart of Medina. Arrangements are in place. Twenty-five percent upfront to our Arabic support, and the rest when the False Prophet is dead. Plenty left over to see us home."

"I pray for your return?"

"That's in God's hands. If our purpose is true, we'll find salvation in the Lord. Your faith in me will not be unplaced."

Cheryl ran a hand across his face. "You look strange with a beard. Please come back to us."

CHAPTER SIXTEEN

Carrie browsed the details on the men from the Al-Masjid Medina. The list read like a who's who of Muslim scholars who'd attended the Prophet's first appearance. In her dreams, she'd seen a couple of these men – Abdul Aziz and the fierce military man with a piercing stare and square jaw – General Salah. The Saudi military man was responsible for the holy site at Medina. Carrie read his biography, a man who fought in the Gulf War, having been wounded twice before rejoining his battalion to conclude the conflict. He had the look and history of the warrior mentality.

Shivers passed through her as if she already knew him. A handsome man, fifteen years her senior, but nonetheless striking. She copied his file and emailed it to herself. Carrie thought their destinies inevitably meant they'd play a role together in upcoming events – a scarily exciting prospect, given his reputation. From a scholarly standpoint, and infinitely more mouthwatering, was the opportunity to connect with the Grand Mufti – a man Carrie much admired for his logical approach, in a realm where the application of logic seemed forgotten. She wanted to hear Abdul Aziz's thoughts on the future of religion since the arrival of the New Age Prophet.

Carrie left the dreary building on Wisconsin Avenue early and went to the hotel, where she ate dinner and took a bath. By the time she finished, it was 9:00 pm. She sent James Gordon and his team her predictions that the Prophet would be in Cambodia tomorrow, and hopefully, James' contacts ably supported logistical supply lines for people's basic needs. The Prophet's enduring symbols of unity gave Carrie a list of a dozen key places she thought he would visit. Picking the correct order was hard, but Carrie added the caveat of updating her theoretical guesswork as new data became available.

She lay on the bed reading Mo's data on the divided reactions to the New Age Prophet's words and deeds. Millions argued for their faith, but they were easily outnumbered by multiple millions who believed in the miracles the Prophet had brought forth on God's behalf. Nevertheless, the tide was moving in favor of religious unity, and open discussions had formed across the globe. Ordinary people hoped for a better world, and the messages and miracles they'd seen convinced them this was the way. Open-minded religious leaders had followed suit. Momentum built rapidly, giving Carrie chills. "Maybe we can do this," she dared to believe.

In other parts of the world, a minority of fanatics became increasingly isolated and vociferous in their fundamental beliefs. They called for the head of the blasphemous Prophet, declaring Holy Wars aimed at anyone who followed his teachings. This vitriol came mainly from a tiny minority of Islamic extremists and a handful of deep-rooted Christian believers from the U.S., Brazil, the Philippines, and Spain. The extremists surprisingly swore to merge their efforts to remove the Prophet. Carrie despaired that such uncompromising violence could not see the irony of their idiotic unification to pursue destruction. "Power-seeking crusaders," she sighed.

These extremists represented only a microcosm of the reactions, but the media gave it their full attention. Mo's report compiled the surveyed data in over seventy countries and extrapolated the results based on ethnic and religious origins. A staggering 78% of all religious followers believed the Prophet Jesus was the true representative of God. When they projected those numbers to a global scale, it suggested that around four billion people would listen and talk about a new way. It was those who protested that screamed the loudest. Mo took the data before the Indian rivers returned or the African plains filled with herds of wild animals. Mo also indicated the data needed bolstering but figured the positive incline would increase with other miracles. There was no other way to describe what unfolded.

Theo's team and all their hi-tech gadgetry couldn't explain how the Prophet came and went, let alone the lightning strikes, Jerusalem's cured inhabitants, the unpolluted rivers in India, and now the African savannahs and other countries filled with millions of wild animals. Carrie felt her eyelids drooping as her body urged her to sleep. Her heart's expectancy bristled with excitement at what the next day would bring. She'd never imagined she would feel unbridled joy like this, yet here it was.

When she awoke, the laptop rested on her stomach as her arms and legs flipped wildly, trying to ascertain her whereabouts. The realism of her dreams shook her awake in panic-stricken disorientation. Carrie pulled on the hotel robe and called Mo. "Hey, can you come over to my room?"

"Why?" he groggily answered.

"I have to tell you what I've seen. You're going to say I'm crazy," Carrie excitedly said.

"I already know you're crazy."

"Just get over here."

Minutes later, Mo sat on the end of her bed, doing his best to absorb what she said. Mo assured her that if things fell in the order, she'd predicted, she could slip them into her work, and he'd support them. But, if she told James, that part of her work was based on dreams, "We'll be sent back to our day jobs, or we'll spend the rest of our days wearing straitjackets."

The following day, the New Age Prophet made his fifth appearance in Angkor Wat, Cambodia. James Gordon cursed at everyone in the building because they couldn't understand how the Prophet appeared and disappeared. The team in Washington watched, discussed, argued, and came no closer to an answer.

The Prophet's speech assured all those listening, faithful or not, that God would provide the templates for mankind to follow. His Holy Father would remove barriers placed upon man as easily as he'd placed endangered animals back on the earth.

One hour after Jesus spoke, the thirty-eighth parallel between North and South Korea lost its physical barriers. The military installments, the landmines, and the weapons were gone. Korean citizens from both sides of the border ignored the weaponless security forces and, in the thousands, wandered across in both directions, exchanging gifts, sharing food, and looking for long-lost relatives. Thousands of military personnel from each side stood by and watched. Some eventually joined the citizens, exchanging handshakes and supplies with their former adversaries. Within three hours of the border's disintegration, fifty thousand citizens were in the former no man's land. Threats from their respective leaders went ignored when they instructed citizens to return home. The governmental powers looked on helplessly as the people of Korea began to explore.

James Gordon gave Carrie plaudits for her level of accuracy. The Korean border was one of the top three places she'd highlighted in her last submission as a place of high interest.

Carrie told James, "Your team needs to be ready for the Prophet to arrive on U.S. soil." She argued that the U.S. contained such a diverse spectrum of faiths and a high percentage of worshippers that the Prophet would make an appearance. However, she did not mention that her summation held its foundation in her dreams.

James asked Mo to gather together the top religious leaders of all faiths within the U.S. and bring them to Washington. He wanted the world to see a united front of religious influencers alongside representatives from the White House. Carrie and Mo prepared the list of people they thought should be invited. It would be an invitation to Washington under the guise of a theological/political conference. The actual expectation would create a media frenzy they could all do without.

Carrie and Mo predicted that the Prophet would go to Jerusalem tomorrow, the last of the original six places from the lightning strikes. Israeli news reported that over a million people from all over the Middle East had crossed the border and surrounded the Temple Mount area. The U.S. government assisted the Israeli forces in securing the safe passage of travelers, checking for any potential threats. James pushed his government contacts for Israel to accept the offers of support from Jordan and Egypt. They conceded only when the Israeli government saw the swelling numbers of pilgrims. Finally, it allowed a coalition of four nations to provide troops to support travelers on the desert roads. The troops worked under Israeli guidance as eager civilians traveled to Jerusalem.

"If only we could have found a way to do this a thousand years ago," Carrie confided to Mo. "Imagine how the world might look today."

"Utopia is only a state of mind," he warned. "As individuals, we're too warped ever to allow ourselves to be at peace."

Carrie mocked him for his dismal outlook on humanity, although she admitted his reasoning had historical evidence on his side. Mo added, "A wicked minority will tear apart everything good to find personal elevation and inflict hurt. We have no idea how to eradicate the fractional insanity that resides within all of us. A handful of people allow it to permeate and fester to bring about chaos." Carrie hated the fact he was right. Mankind had proven its reluctance to control its spiteful tendencies. It saddened Carrie. "We have no gratitude for anything anymore," she told Mo. "I don't believe we ever did," he replied.

On the sixth day since his arrival, the Prophet appeared in Jerusalem. The crowds around the city went delightedly berserk when the Prophet appeared outside the Dome of the Rock. The Temple Mount boomed with the chorus of wailing, happy voices, raised as one, in praise to God. Jews, Muslims, Christians, Sikhs, Hindus, and more, stood shoulder to shoulder, forgetting former troubles, as they focused their delight on the yellow-robed man who they believed had come to save them.

The local authorities decreed the usual religiously segregated sectors unworkable, and the people mixed freely with one another. It quickly became impossible to decipher who was who as people cried out in dozens of languages, screaming for blessings and salvation.

Jesus walked alongside the mosaic walls of the Dome of the Rock, gently waving his arms to welcome the baying crowds. From beyond the outer walls, the deafening noise sounded like something from ancient stories that reduced the walls of Jericho to rubble. Inherited belief systems meant nothing in the presence of the living embodiment of the undeniable force. Their genuine outpouring of love to those around them instantly washed away centuries of bitterness, hatred, and bloodshed. They wished only to hear God's word from his chosen Prophet. They'd seen the miracles God had already brought to the world and had cried out for more. For many, it was too much, and they could not contain themselves, yelling, chanting, shouting, and singing until their voices gave out. The city residents swore they'd already been in God's arms and gave thanks.

Carrie observed, "Jerusalem is something it's never been before – it's unified in celebration." The city shook to the frequency of consummate love.

Jesus waited for the noise to subside, then lowered his hands, calling them to attention. It took some time to ease the ecstatic crowds into a hush. Then, patiently, he brought them to hear his words.

"God is great. Welcome. I am Jesus. That is the name my spiritual Father has given me. There is but one true God. God loves all his children. The believers and lightworkers shall lead the way and show love for those who seek solace in mere distractions." Jesus raised his arms high and spoke a language nobody recognized. The translations on the screens in Washington, DC, didn't register his words.

"Find out what he said!" James Gordon ordered as people immediately scrambled.

The New Age Prophet remained perfectly still. Then, a lightning bolt from the clear blue sky drew a loud crack as it struck the top of the dome, sending sparks showering in all directions. The adoring crowds ducked low, fearful at first until they realized it to be a miracle, and immediately their gasps turned to jubilant cheers.

Five more strikes in rapid succession thrashed the dome. "God is universal power for all his many creatures. Our redeeming Father retains a sense of humor," Jesus confirmed. "His message of love and peace is with you this day and for all days. Rejoice, Jerusalem, rejoice all united peoples of the world." The crowds could not contain themselves, and their praises rang out: some in songs, some in screams, and all combined in a resounding ear-shattering chorus.

The Prophet waited patiently.

"God provided the earth, the sun, all the stars you see in the universe, and what you've yet to discover. What took billions of years to form is part of God's plan. God will show you that he is the universe – he's all there has ever been and is all there will ever be, and you are privileged to partake in its wonders. Partake, you must. God will not wipe away what you must contend with. Life comes with suffering. Free will demands effort. Please make the most of what is offered and help nourish those who need it. Profit is gained only when you've given away everything you have."

Jesus turned around and moved a few paces toward the dome, gesturing toward the building. "For centuries, these lands have been the focal point of intolerance. God asks you to put aside old differences, customs, books, and fears – join hands and hearts with those next to you. Be patient, as God has been with you. Flesh and blood share the same fate. Through God's love, you can share the same joy. As his messenger, I ask you to make Jerusalem a symbol of hope. You cannot change history, but you can create what is yet to come. Be worthy of the responsibility of life and be a worthy representative of humankind."

Jesus faced the hills to the north. "Here, one of my brothers was condemned to death. My brother came back to you centuries later and lies at peace within Medina. I am the final flesh and blood messenger. I am content with my destiny. Man will show his frailty, his corruption of purpose, and you are all charged with following God's word and not to be distracted by the actions of a few misguided men. Take heart – God blesses you. Together your love can overcome adversity. Your mistakes will help you discover your true purpose – part of everyone's journey. Banish fear - choose love. God is great. Pray with me."

"Your dream," Mo whispered to Carrie. Her face was gaunt as the Prophet's words hinted at what she'd described to Mo in the early hours.

Those gathered and billions watching got to their knees and listened as the Prophet blessed them with the courage to remain steadfast in kindness and love. Then, within seconds of him pausing and to rapturous praise from what looked like the whole of Jerusalem, the light grew too strong for them to see. When they opened their eyes, only the Dome of the Rock remained.

CHAPTER SEVENTEEN

"He changed the light outside!" Theo exclaimed, checking all his equipment.

"Something did," James skeptically added.

Carrie took her scribbled notes and headed toward her office. James Gordon angrily pulled her aside before she was across the shared space. "What's he talking about, frailty and corruption? Does he mean fanatics?"

Carrie scowled at his hand on her arm, but he ignored her. "Could be religious extremists or power-hungry politicians," she offered accusingly. James guided her into her office. His out-of-character approach took her by surprise as he slammed the door shut.

"In sixty seconds, my phone blows up – what now?" His downturned mouth wrinkled as he snorted through flared nostrils.

"Well, I … um …" Carrie found herself stammering, seriously wondering if he were going to lash out. Suggestions escaped her.

"Well?"

His manhandling and attitude flipped her from shock to aggression. "Read my damn reports! Tell the Senator and President you should already be combing the airwaves for those seeking to harm. It's coming."

"We're way beyond that. Do you believe someone will take him out?"

"Of course, they will! People are dangerous! He warned us that something bad would happen to test everyone. History repeats itself. Previous prophets met with stiff resistance."

"We can't cover every inch of the planet," James snapped.

"What about here? If he comes to the U.S., and something happens, you'll all be in the world spotlight," Carrie hissed. Her natural defiance prevailed. James' grab incensed her, and she wanted to smash him in the face. Carrie jabbed her finger into his barrel chest. "I've already advised your sections to track the internet and airwaves for ghosts in the machine. Have you? Where are the results? Why don't we see any of it? It's like you want everything but won't give anything in return. I don't trust relationships where it's a one-way street." Carrie's sudden hostility had her square up to him. "You don't want it going wrong over here, James – we're not exactly popular around the world these days, and you will have to face the difficult questions," Carrie warned him away with a dismissive hand. "You've got my reports – fucking use them! I'm finding it hard to tell who's my friend or enemy around here!"

James raised his hands in surrender and dropped onto the couch opposite her desk. He offered Carrie to sit at her workstation. Her fists clenched, and she seriously considered giving him a personal demonstration of her kickboxing skills.

"Please," he said, gesturing for her to sit a second time. Carrie lowered herself behind the desk, with her steely gaze locked onto him. James calmly offered, "If anything happens to him, we'd all better strap on our tin hats and burrow deep. Mo's data shows we're approaching five billion people who are already pretty impressed by him."

"And no wonder. Watch the news. What more do you need to be convinced, James?" She continued to shout. "You should be ready. What are you doing?" She began to rise.

"We don't know if he is coming here." James motioned his hands for her to stay put.

"I'm telling you, he'll come." Carrie was brewing for a fight. "Our government has to be open with us. We don't want this to be some kind of Roswell on steroids. It's our only chance for meaningful and lasting change."

James stood, and straightened the lapels on his jacket, his face flushed deep red as he headed out the door. "We'll be ready – will you?"

"I'll have that report for you within the hour," Carrie shouted at him. "Asshole."

She made sure he heard it as she slammed the door after him. Carrie growled like a wounded animal. She didn't want anything to spoil the tentative relationship they'd established, but the pressure was building. Carrie felt a double knot in her stomach as James stuck his head inside her doorway.

"What happens in an hour?" he gently asked, forcing a smile as a peace offering.

She pursed her lips, giving him the death stare. "He mentioned nourishing those in need. I'd guess something like crops, central Asia, Africa, like Bangladesh, Ethiopia, or similar. I'll get you something soon."

"Thanks." His tone lacked gratitude. "If you're right about all of this, we can't win." James closed her door.

"There is nothing to be won," she reminded him. "You're still an asshole," she mumbled.

Carrie referenced the Prophet's words alongside ancient texts for her report and forty minutes later sent it to James and the team. The room held a staleness in the air, and it felt smaller like the dingy walls had closed in on her. Some of Carrie's excitement evaporated, and she didn't like it.

Mo came into her office and cautiously sat opposite. "Are you okay?"

"I'm fine. James had better stay the fuck away from me. What do you have? You're hiding something."

Mo looked disappointed that she could instantly read him. He tutted and slipped a scribbled piece of paper across the table. "A colleague of mine at Harvard reached out. When the Prophet spoke the strange words (before the lightning struck) and nobody knew what it was – my friend does. She's an expert in ancient Sumerian written texts. Nobody has heard these words in their spoken form for more than five thousand years."

"What did he say?"

"Master, show them what they came to see. Something close to that."

"Master? Why that choice of words? He called in lightning strikes from a clear blue sky."

"Somebody heard him. Thought you'd like to know," Mo offered.

"Aren't you going to give this to James?' Carrie asked.

"No. He's got two hundred people running around this building – they can figure it out for themselves."

"You're still a rebel," Carrie managed to raise a smile.

"Only when I think I won't get caught. I'll catch you later."

Because of that, Carrie reviewed other ancient texts after receiving access to everything in the Washington library. She stopped when the latest news report showed thousands of acres of deserts filled with lush vegetation, forests, and clear-water lakes appeared from nowhere. Overhead satellite images showed that once-decimated Brazilian rainforests were a solid jungle.

Similar findings from Australia, Central Asia, South America, and the Southern parts of Africa. Estimates were over two and half million square miles of desert, or once destroyed landscape, was green and blue.

Carrie's next report recommended that the respective governments should commit to preserving the new forests and lakes and prove it with declarations.

Carrie read the text from James; *Save me a tin hat and a space under the desk! Sorry about earlier.* She felt a fractional release of tension in her gut. She did not respond and deleted his message.

CHAPTER EIGHTEEN

The short walk through the damp lower passageways sparked an unpleasant hesitancy. Everything the eyes and senses received triggered an automated disgust. This forgotten underworld slowly rotted as if threatening to drag everything from above down into its filthy clutches and render what it touched into an immediate state of crumbling decay. James Gordon imagined this must be how condemned men felt as they shuffled through dark passageways to meet certain death. The impending gloom pushed heavily down on him.

His dislike for this place had turned to hate. He picked his way through the rusted junk and stagnant puddles to the dimly lit room, where a single bulb struggled against the dark. He found Mr. Grey leaning on an old step ladder, with his bare feet on the bottom rung and his body suspended at an angle that suggested he should topple into the murky water.

"Jim – ahoy! Welcome aboard."

"Mr. Grey," he cautiously reciprocated. "Your ship is in danger of sinking."

Mr. Grey looked at the stagnant water and shrugged. "In a few weeks, we'll make Washington, DC, look like the second coming of the Titanic. People are waving, cheering, and dancing to some awful live music as they strike an invisible iceberg and sink without knowing they're drowning. It will be beautiful – history repeating itself, but with much more style and class. Don't you think so?"

"Not really. People survived the Titanic."

James' provocation forced a singular laugh from Mr. Grey's long thin lips. "They did survive and had a lifetime of nightmares to prove it. Drowning repeatedly in frozen water every night in your dreams is no picnic. The sound of children screaming in your nightmares is way louder than the real thing – operatically unbeatable."

"Better that than nothing at all."

"Why so pessimistic, Jim? All is going to plan."

"It seems that way," James flatly responded. "Religions have come aboard quickly, with the majority believing they can be as one, except for some hardliners. Non-believers are becoming believers in the tens of millions. Countries supporting one another and providing relief for these gatherings, so I'd say it's working."

"I love a good Kumbaya, especially around a roaring fire in the dark." Mr. Grey climbed up a rung on the ladder. "You don't look happy, even though you're getting one step closer to your goal."

"Seeing the trajectory makes me think the world is a better place when it plays together."

Mr. Grey hopped from the ladder, skipped delicately through the rancid pools of water to the old chair, and swung his arms dismissively at James. "You're becoming ever so dull. You know what they say about making omelets?" He waited expectantly for James to reply. Mr. Grey pulled his knees to his chest, his bare feet dangling off the edge of the fractured leather. His long face turned grim; the smirk inverted into a sneer.

"You tease," he accused James. "Omelets have nothing to do with breaking eggs, Jim – any fool can crack an egg. It's about how you corral and feed the chickens. They need to believe they're safe from predators, but that nagging doubt keeps them fresh and on their toes. It makes them tasty." He licked his lips with a strangely long tongue. "All it takes is one sly fox, and the cozy coop becomes a flapping frenzy."

"Did you ask me here to talk about chickens?" James responded with agitation.

"So touchy," Mr. Grey pulled his hands to his chest as though clutching an imaginary dagger in his heart. "When will your President declare this is real?"

"He can't, at least not yet. He'll stall for at least another few days. Some world leaders have already decreed the Prophet as real."

"I hope you're advising him to concede."

"Of course. How about your end?"

"I got me some of them good old boys, all fired up and ready to go. Gotta luv some of that southern spirit," Mr. Grey roared in mock southern tones. "They is all full of the li'l old spirit of Jesus Christ, our Lord, and Savior." Mr. Grey's impersonation gave him pause to celebrate his triumphant attempt.

"Will they get it done?"

"When it counts. The first go-round is just an illusion. To keep the chickens running …" He made clucking noises and bobbed his head forward like he was pecking at the ground. "Once finished, I'm disbanding them."

"I want to make sure my team is kept intact – they're good people," James insisted.

"Jim, are you sure? Are you getting sentimental on me? You've got so many – you could afford to lose a few. What about your outside consultants? No?"

"NO," James firmly replied.

"Bad boy. I bet you'd like a piece of Carrie Carter's ass, eh? Yes, you would. We both know her trousers don't need to be that figure-hugging. I'd do her myself if I weren't so damned busy!" Mr. Grey pulled out the blackened pipe from inside his jacket. "Mind if I smoke?"

James gestured for him to go ahead. "I love my wife and family."

"Still … bet you've thought about having your hands all over that soft light-brown skin. Who wouldn't? I like your old-fashioned values, Jim – doing it for the family. Something noble to believe in." Mr. Grey jabbed the pipe appreciatively in his direction like it had significant meaning. "A good family man."

"My family stays out of this. We had an agreement!" James snarled.

Mr. Grey lit his pipe and puffed clouds of smoke across the damp room. "I'm not interested in your family. I'm busy. Don't look so angry; you have my word. You don't believe me?" He postured as if he were offended.

"My team said the Prophet will be in the U.S. soon."

"He will – such a showman. Lights, camera, action, and all that. I'll keep you informed as we get closer. This requires detailed attention for maximum effect. I know I make this look easy, but I can tell you that it's hours of pure tedium to produce the right effect. A bit like rehearsing for an opening night. The encore will be spectacular."

"Anything else?" James asked.

Mr. Grey shook his head and pumped his thin lips on the pipe, watching the smoke drift to the ceiling. As James walked out the doors, Mr. Grey shouted after him. "God is great, isn't he?"

James did not respond to the laughter that followed him to the elevator. As he rose a dozen floors back into the main office, he thought about the road ahead and wondered if it was worth the effort to have himself a permanent presence in the White House. He believed he'd invested wisely for himself and for those he loved. But, like all good investments, the markets could crash.

Abdul Aziz spent several hours contemplating the power of God and the miracles from around the world. He stared at the tomb of Muhammad and wondered what God's second Prophet would have made of it. Proud, he hoped. Deserts became oases on a scale defying human intervention: Animals near extinction roamed in the thousands; families fished from once polluted rivers, and people bathed in clean waters. Jerusalem's people came together as one. Miracles beyond miracles. Allah's mercy tickled his flesh – a benevolent Father beyond what he'd ever dreamt possible.

That first look into the eyes of the Prophet Jesus convinced him of the truth, and the rest was simply layers of sumptuous icing upon the purest cake. Undoubtedly God's third messenger walked among them. He stretched out his legs and chuckled at being able to sit on the hard floor for so long – a miracle in itself. It was past midnight and six days since Jesus first appeared before them. Abdul asked the four most learned Muslim scholars and General Salah to join him. God's messenger said he'd come. A lifetime of prayer, hard work, sacrifice, and skillful maneuvering had brought the Grand Mufti to this glorious dawn of something he imagined would forge humanity closer together and closer to God. The rising of a new age was taking shape, showing a delicate form no different than a seedling growing into a brilliant flower.

It would be any moment now, and once more, he'd be privy to the words of God. A comforting thought and one for which he gave thanks. Abdul Aziz wasn't aware that one of his colleagues transmitted the events on a hidden cell phone, relaying live information to some high-ranking friends. A promise of great reward came for his disclosures. The informant thought the broadcast went only as far as Egypt, unaware that the eyes and ears of Washington, DC, pulled the strings. The Americans were silent puppeteers of the highest quality.

U.S. Senator Crowley agonized at the continuing audacious magic show, fooling the world. It disgusted him that billions of decent people were easily cajoled by the elaborate hoax. Senator Crowley believed only in the teachings of Christ. Defending his beliefs meant everything to him, not just in this life. He received the latest updates from his informant within James Gordon's team and his sources in the Arabic world. Senator Crowley passed the information anonymously into the hands of the good men who were not afraid to pursue righteousness. He admired these men of great purpose who had made it into Saudi Arabia. He prayed with a vigor that they could serve the Lord.

Senator Crowley knew all about James Gordon's team monitoring the interior of the Al-Masjid complex. They expected the New Age Prophet to appear. If the Prophet showed himself, he would send word to Christ's soldiers. A perilous undertaking but a worthy sacrifice. Restoring order to the world must come soon. This False Prophet had already undermined religious foundations, and if it didn't stop, all would descend into bedlam. The Senator could not bear losing control of the human spirit into the hands of the common man. Peace in the world meant that munitions and the military would become obsolete, and control for people like him would cease to exist. The Prophet's hoax assaulted religion as much as it did governance. Jim Crowley understood that the world needed a little chaos and distrust. For all nations – separation meant safety, division meant order, fear meant control, and control equaled power. Jim Crowley and his colleagues needed to ensure the machine operated and thrived.

As carefully as he and his colleagues had manipulated their flow of information, he'd been surprised when James Gordon privately approached him and disclosed that he knew every detail about Crowley's association with Wally Radford. It was more surprising that he had no interest in stopping it. James Gordon admitted he knew a mole existed inside his operation but had no care for who gave Crowley his information or how they passed it along. James Gordon never said why he wasn't interested, nor did he infer the direction of his ultimate goal. Jim Crowley had asked what James Gordon required from him, and the answer had been, "Simply nothing. Do whatever you're doing. I have bigger things to focus on. Stay the fuck out of my way."

He wondered about the exact meaning of Gordon's remark. Gordon assured him he wasn't waiting for things to come crashing down to expose the Senator as a traitor. In fact, he'd wished him good luck. Crowley despised James Gordon, seeing him as a low-life desperate to be noticed by senior White House staff. But Jim Crowley had to trust the low-life who could ruin him. The game's momentum moved fast, and nothing could stop it until it played itself out.

Senator Crowley assured James Gordon, "if anything happens to me and you betray me, I'll take you down." James Gordon laughed at the idea and said, "Senator, never speak to me about this again."

Nevertheless, Crowley wished to know James Gordon's angle and on whose behalf he operated. He considered James Gordon an ambitious miscreant. The Senator's informant spoke of clandestine meetings that James Gordon would attend deep below the building on Wisconsin Avenue. "Find out who he's meeting with, or I'll go down there myself!" Crowley insisted.

CHAPTER NINETEEN

Outside the Medina complex, hundreds of thousands of pilgrims slept in make-shift tents, happy to be near the source of miracles. Four weary travelers made their way through the sea of canvas – one from Saudi Arabia and three from the U.S. Each wore a traditional thaub covering the length of their bodies—a ghutrah, with a scarf wrapped over the face, and sunglasses on their heads. The group looked like any of the tens of thousands of pilgrims making their way across the sands. The sophisticated armaments they carried were concealed inside the camping equipment slung over their aching shoulders.

The surrounding military presence that handed out supplies to the peaceful crowd paid no attention to the four men.

Wally Radford had spent four years of his youth in the U.S. military and had done his duty for his country. Every step towards Medina brought him one step closer to God. He'd been overseas before, but not like this. Underneath the ghutrah, Wally's clothing was soaked in sweat. His heart boomed loud enough to wonder if his body could take the strain. Less than a quarter of a mile ahead, he saw the beautiful minarets of the mosque containing the Prophet's tomb. Their Saudi guide arranged for them to set up in the Gulnab Hotel, opposite the south gate. Unfortunately, they could not gain access to the Al-Masjid complex.

Wally felt buoyed that the False Prophet had shown himself outside the mosque's walls in Jerusalem and figured the Prophet's vanity would give Wally's team the shot they needed. Wally's internal quiet could only manifest when the imposter's life had ended. The closer they came to their destination, the more Wally had reconciled with the prospect that their mission meant certain death, but his life paled into insignificance compared to the survival of Christianity. The New Age Prophet grew bolder on each appearance, walking among people, waving, and lapping up the attention like some foolish Hollywood celebrity. Wally counted on it.

He checked his phone. The fact that there were no further updates from Senator Crowley worried him.

Carrie slept on the small couch in her office, refusing to go to the hotel. She predicted the Prophet would show in Medina, and Abdul Aziz and his small group were sitting by the tomb of Muhammad for hours on end, giving her additional hope. Theo integrated their access from inside the tomb, and Carrie spent a while listening to the melodic sound of the Grand Mufti's voice. His humming prayers soothed her so that she nodded off several times. She considered the Grand Mufti to be an extraordinary man.

Her desk phone startled her, and she slid from the couch. "Hey, it's Jessica. The Prophet's back; see ya." The line went dead. Carrie straightened her legs, steadied herself, and for once appreciated Jessica being a woman of few words. She joined Jessica and two other analysts watching the live feeds and pulled on a pair of headphones.

"Who's translating this?" she asked.

Jessica pointed to the older man at the end of the desk. Carrie hadn't seen him before, but no matter. The Prophet sat on the mosque floor, talking with the four Muslim scholars.

"There is much burden on you. You understand that God has chosen you to lead your brothers and sisters through changes. Some will refuse to hear you. People will try to force you to stay with the old ways. Mankind will not survive in its current state. People such as you are required to do exceptional things to spread the Word of God. This will challenge you like nothing you have witnessed before. Follow the guidance. You are all about to embark upon a journey towards changing earth's destiny and yours with God. Have courage in yourself and one another. Learned men of other faiths will come to your side when you call upon them. I must leave here to do my master's bidding. I will return to you before I return home. Stand with me."

They gathered in a small circle. "There's good and bad in everyone. Trust your judgment. Feed this habit, and it will nourish you. My Master put you on this hallowed ground for this." He looked at the Grand Mufti, saying, "My friend in God, you will go to the United States and take the General. He will be my protector and the one who lays me to rest with my brother Muhammad here in the Al-Masjid. Death is only a doorway to something greater. So do not fear my death or your own. It is a stepping-stone to walking beside God."

Carrie shook Jessica's arm. "Get James Gordon in here right away. Tell him we have confirmation that the New Age Prophet is coming, and soon."

"He's sleeping at the hotel," Jessica said, chewing rapidly.

"Wake him up, now!" Carrie forcefully instructed.

Jessica stood with her arms raised in surrender. "Whatever."

Abdul Aziz could not prevent his voice from cracking, "Master, what am I to do in America? I know nothing of their world, language, and strange customs."

Jesus smiled at the old man. "Everything you've learned will be all you need. You will be the voice of reason in a place where vitriol and status take precedence. People will hear your voice, even though some will oppose you. You will know what to say and what to do. The General will be your support, and you will be his."

Abdul Aziz fell to his knees and kissed the feet of God's Holy messenger. "Master, I will do as you ask."

"Rise up, my friend," Jesus helped the old man to his feet. "It is I who thank you for what you've yet to achieve." Jesus dusted down the Grand Mufti's thaub. "Find the woman who sees the future when you get to the U.S. You will know her as soon as you see her. When you dream tonight, the plan will be revealed. Your royal King will provide the earthly resources you need, and he will send representatives to join you on your pilgrimage, not as kings, but to follow you like a foal does to a mare."

Jesus called General Salah to one side. "I will speak alone with the General. His destiny is for his ears only. My brothers, go now and prepare to change the world. Before I leave here, gather all your holy men and women in the complex courtyard so that I may speak with them. No cameras or media. I will be there in fifteen minutes."

The four men bowed and left the tomb. General Salah stood with the Prophet.

Jesus asked him, "What is on your mind?"

"I am terrified of the Americans. They are reckless cowboys. I'm also scared for my family."

"You only fear what you don't know. I shall remove those fears for you." Jesus raised his hands towards the nearest cameras and spoke with the General.

"We've lost the audio," the translator said. One of the tech assistants began adjusting controls. Carrie removed her headphones. "Don't bother; he knows we're listening. It must be fun having a higher power working on your side. Let me know if you get the sound back and what he says. It won't happen until he's finished with the General." The New Age Prophet had confirmed that she would meet these men from Medina.

A dark-eyed, groggy James Gordon came into the office, and Carrie showed him a part of the recording. "He's coming to the States, James – he confirmed it. He'll come to Washington DC. You might want the National Guard on standby. Mo, Theo, and I will need access to every building and office in this city, no questions asked. Can you do that?"

James rubbed his eyeballs. "I can do that. I'll call Senator Garofalo – he's going to have kittens."

"I bet Jesus could make that happen," Jessica remarked, laughing at her joke.

James rolled his eyes and walked away with his phone to his ear. "Bob, it's me — you need to get the President. It's happening."

CHAPTER TWENTY

Wally Radford's team had split up over two floors of the Gulnab Hotel. From the fortieth floor, Wally saw the Green Dome containing the prophet's tomb.

His colleague, John Waterford, adjusted the sights on the high-powered rifle.

"John, how much of that courtyard have you got?"

John stayed focused, with his eyes on the target area. "Just over half of it ... the east side, and the middle.

Wally radioed to the room above, where Wally's other colleague readied himself along with a third Saudi guide. "Chuck, what about you? What do you have?"

There was a short delay until Chuck replied. "I have most of the west side, thirty percent of the entire courtyard. We have no coverage on the mid-section – the minaret on the southwest corner is blocking the line of sight."

"Okay, guys, we have about sixty percent of the outdoor area. Let's stay focused. The Lord is with us." Wally wiped the sweat from his brow and checked the news feeds.

"John, I'll be back soon. Keep the guide here with you in case anyone comes to the door." Wally pulled the Saudi clothing back on, telling Salem to join him, and he went to perform a physical check on the hotel layout. Once they fired shots, it would be only minutes before the hotel would become surrounded, giving them only a slim chance of escape.

He walked the stairwells, dripping in sweat and breathing hard, but he found a back route leading to an atrium on the south side and across the street to a large café area. He told the nervous Salem that he was to say they were lost if anyone stopped them. They checked beyond the atrium, finding a multi-story parking lot attached to a mall. Wally kept one eye on his cellphone in case Jim Crowley's contact fed them more intel. He had Salem move one of their rental cars over to the lot by the mall and left the keys under the front seat.

Riding in the elevator back to the room, Wally thought about Cheryl and his family. "Pray for me," he muttered.

In the hotel room, John remained motionless, hunched over the rifle, with his eye trained through the sights.

Wally's cell beeped, and he read the message from their contact. "Guys, he's there. Get ready."

Chuck radioed, "Hey, guys, I've got movement on the west side door of the mosque. Four men headed south. They're calling other men to join them. They're all wearing white or black robes – there's no one in yellow."

"John, you see any of this?" Wally asked.

"Negative. Out of my scope."

"Chuck, keep your eye on that door. Let me know if you see him."

"Copy that. Hey, John, are you seeing activity at the southeast gate? I have people producing IDs and rushing through," Chuck asked.

"Yeah, it just started. A single line of people. Time to pray to Allah?"

"Not at this hour. The complex is locked down to the public," Wally confirmed. "Guys, watch closely!"

Wally grabbed a pair of binoculars and stood at the window. Hundreds of people were steadily filing into the inner courtyard and forming lines that faced the prophet's tomb. "He's coming. Christ confirms our divine mission." The hotel room door slammed, and Wally spun around. Fahad had fled the room. Wally grabbed hold of Salem. "He'd better not talk."

Salem shook his head. "No, sir. He's afraid that we will all die here."

Wally glared into Salem's jittery eyes. "I knew he was a pussy! Call him, and tell him that if he talks, my people will find his family, and he'll be sorry." Salem nodded and made the call. Wally radioed upstairs, "Chuck, is Mohammed still with you?"

"Affirmative. Looks nervous as all hell." Chuck gave Mohammed a look of disgust as if he considered him to be less than a man.

"Tell him that he can leave if he wants, but he won't get paid. If he talks, he knows what will happen. The Lord has no time for the faint-hearted."

"Amen." Chuck and John unanimously replied.

Wally clutched the phone tightly. His source in Washington had done well. It was now down to him and his guys.

Inside the Green Dome, General Salah had his best men escort the New Age Prophet into the courtyard. He worried that the crowd's passion might get the better of them, causing them to surge forward with the risk of people getting hurt. He arranged for two hundred armed men to be outside and for his immediate group of twelve to form a barrier around the prophet. The General gave his last-minute orders.

Jesus positioned himself within the guards' escort. His face was a picture of serenity, as though they were taking a stroll in the park.

Yasser Al-Temyat stood tall and was excited to be one of the private guards to support the New Age Prophet. General Salah had personally told him he'd selected him due to his alertness, discipline, and devotion to the cause. Yasser felt prouder than he'd ever been before. His friend and colleague, Saeed, stood on the opposite side, head held high, shoulders straight, just like Yasser instructed. Yasser was thrilled that the prophet Jesus stood between him and Saeed. He couldn't help turning his head and sneaking a sideways glance. The prophet faced him and looked directly into his eyes. Yasser froze.

Jesus said to him, "My brother, Yasser, walking with me today will lead you to walk with God for all eternity. Rejoice."

Yasser's legs started shaking, and he wanted to cry. The prophet turned away, and they slowly moved as a cohesive unit towards the mosque's south door. God's Holy Prophet had spoken to him – what an honor! What a story he would have to tell his sister and her family when he got home! They would all be blessed! The pride swelled in his chest, making him invincible.

The General commanded, "Eyes front!" as he walked alongside. Two thousand people were seated on the ground in the courtyard. Suddenly, they spontaneously jumped to their feet, cheering wildly, chanting the name of Jesus, and proclaiming, "God is great." General Salah spoke quietly into his mic, telling his snipers and the guards to be alert.

On the fortieth floor of the Gulnab Hotel, Wally Radford saw the yellow-robed figure appear, closely flanked by a dozen armed guards moving slowly towards the courtyard's center. "Are either of you guys seeing this? Chuck – he's on your side."

"Not yet," Chuck replied.

"Nothing for me," John confirmed.

Wally saw their direction meant that the prophet and his entourage would soon disappear from view as they headed south and eastward. "Chuck, you might get a shot. I'm heading up to you. Tell Mohammed to open the door for me. If you get a shot, take it."

"Copy that."

Wally raced for the door. "John, stay alert in case he moves around and comes back this way."

John never flinched. "Copy." As Wally disappeared out the door, John shouted after him. "The Lord is with you!"

Wally found the heat, the tension, and the entire undertaking dragging on every ounce of his resolve. He gasped for breath as he entered the elevator. He prayed aloud. "Lord Jesus Christ, my Savior, help me. I have held your words to my heart my entire life – give me the strength to finish this." He leaned his back on the elevator and used the edge of the headscarf to wipe his brow and stop the sweat from stinging his eyes.

As the doors opened, he ran around the corner, where he spotted Mohammed standing halfway in the corridor, frantically waving his hand for Wally to speed up and get inside the room. Wally sprinted the last fifty feet, staggered through the doorway, and dropped to one knee at Chuck's side. "What you got?" he gasped.

Chuck stayed resolute. "Like waiting for a buck in the forest. Be patient, and he'll walk right up to you."

Wally reached out his hand towards Mohammed, who handed him the binoculars. Wally could barely keep them steady to his face. Thirty seconds went by, and then he saw the military guard coming into view. "He's here," Wally whispered.

General Salah helped relieve some of the grasping fingers and hands, reaching over to touch the prophet's clothes as they moved along the front of the crowd. The learned scholars forgot their status, overtaken by happiness and exhilaration. Their proximity to Jesus turned them into something akin to teenagers at a rock concert. The crowds remained in their lines. The noisy jostling kept the General and his team on their toes. He worried that the noise created in the vast courtyard would quickly alert those spreading beyond the walls, where over half a million people camped outside the gates. If they surged, the masjid would fall under the strain. No sooner had the General considered the danger than, from outside the walls, the cheers began to rise. General Salah hoped the prophet would be quick. The hysteria he injected was evidenced in the high emotion etched on the crowd's faces. It was an unprecedented exaltation as their unified spirits lifted into a trance-like fervor.

The New Age Prophet asked the General to stop at a central point in the courtyard. General Salah signaled his men to halt. The front line of spiritual leaders gestured for the rest to sit down and be silent, but they could not curtail their excitement. As fast as the crowd would settle in one area, another would rise, clapping with chants of "God is great" ringing through the inner yard, and on it went.

General Salah told the bodyguards, "Remain firm. Do not move."

Carrie Carter, Mo Yousaf, and James Gordon watched the live feed from the overhead satellite.

"Why is he doing this without the world media?" James asked.

Carrie's eyes never left the screen. "If I had to guess, it's the same personal touch his predecessors used long before we used the media or internet. Face-to-face gives a better feel for what he's about. It's smart, like saying, I can use the modern media if I choose to, but I'd rather use the hearts and minds of you guys in front of me. They'll deliver his message with personal feelings to millions. More impactful than watching a news clip."

James looked at the crowds outside the complex. "Hells Bells, if he comes to Washington, we'll need the entire army."

"When he comes – not if," Carrie corrected him.

Chuck Ramsey was a devout Baptist from just outside Ozark in Arkansas. His Bible-thumping grandparents had raised him with a love for all things Jesus and the Razorbacks. A part-time preacher in the church, Wally Radford kept him gratefully employed. For the last thirty years, his faith in the Lord, the Bible, and Wally, never wavered. In his early twenties, he met Wally in the armed forces, and their friendship has remained solid ever since. If Wally said it was Christ's work to rid the world of this demon Prophet, then it was so. At age seven, Chuck Ramsey had witnessed the devil's work when his drunken daddy murdered his sweet momma. His daddy died of heart failure after serving twenty-four years of a life sentence. Chuck swore he'd be a good man and walk with Christ to deliver the world from such evil.

That opportunity slowly came into his sights. Chuck had enough daylight between the crowds of excitable Arabs and the armed escort surrounding the False Prophet, but there was still no chance of a body. With a microscopic adjustment, he saw a partial view of the head, just two inches. "I have a partial shot. It's tight."

"Take it," Wally replied, holding his breath.

Chuck's finger nestled around the trigger, and he gently eased back, ready to unleash. There'd be a slight drift in trajectory with the light breeze, but the rifle's velocity should be enough to hit within a quarter of an inch. His right index finger felt the weapon's resistance, and with a smooth, swift action, Chuck squeezed through the trigger.

He re-loaded as soon as he'd released, preparing to take another shot. The glass window splintered in tandem with the fizz of the bullet going through the silencer.

The bullet grazed across Jesus' right eyebrow, removing the top layers of skin, and blood instantly seeped from the flesh wound. A groan sounded next to him, and the young officer collapsed to the floor, his left temple blown wide open from the bullet.

General Salah and his team heard only the sound of their guard's body hitting the ground. He saw the blood over the prophet's eye. "Cover the Prophet!" His men huddled tight around Jesus, pushing his head down, and moved as a unit back to the Green Dome. The delighted screams of the clerics suddenly changed to horror. General Salah bellowed in agony at Yasser Al-Temyat's lifeless body lying on the polished tiles.

"Godammit!" Chuck sighed as he re-aimed. He let fly another round and re-loaded again with a third. A second guard clutched his shoulder and fell away from the leading group. General Salah dragged the soldier across the ground. The group moved at pace through the door and went out of sight.

General Salah radioed, "Return fire only if you can find the source. It must be from one of the hotels outside the southern gates. "Storm the buildings. Marksmen in the minarets look for anyone on the balconies or with the windows open. If you see a muzzle flash, return fire."

One of the General's men fell to the ground with a deathly groan. They hustled the prophet away from danger. General Salah hauled his injured soldier through the doorway. Another bullet splintered the doorframe an inch from his face as he closed the doors.

The prophet stood beside Muhammad's tomb.

"Are you okay?" the General asked.

"I am unharmed. Let the people know this straight away," Jesus instructed and dropped to one knee to help the guard who'd taken a bullet in the shoulder.

The General ordered the people in the courtyard to be ushered safely outside the gates.

"Did you get him?" Wally asked.

"No. It wasn't clean. We need to leave!" Chuck replied.

"All of those bodies in the way!" Wally's agonized groan sent his body rigid.

Salem and Mohammed were at the door, backpacks in hand, screaming at the two Americans to leave. Wally and Chuck grabbed their bags and followed the two Saudis.

"John, get the hell out of there. I'll meet you in the southeast stairwell," Wally instructed.

"No, Wally." John calmly replied. "We've got dozens of armed men heading this way. Get yourselves out of here. I'll keep them occupied." John fired a shot at one of the minarets that exploded the tiles an inch above the head of two soldiers.

"John, c'mon, we gotta go," Wally shouted.

"I'll buy you a few minutes," John replied as he took the rifle and ran next door into the bedroom. Shots riddled the room he'd just left. "Go home, my old friend. I'm staying here. Say a prayer for me."

Wally and his three companions moved at high speed down the back of the hotel. There was no time to argue. Wally's gratitude for the bravery of John Waterford increased his determination to survive.

"Ditch your radios," John advised. "May God be with you." He removed his radio communication device and threw it from the fortieth-floor window. John Waterford knew he would die here. He hadn't told Wally or Chuck, but his recent cancer diagnosis gave him only several months to a year at best. Doing God's work seemed like a fitting end. He fired a couple more shots toward the towers, aiming high to ensure he did not kill any innocents. John had no reason for the blood of ordinary men to be on his hands. He paused for a moment, listening to the screams of despair from over half a million people below. The sound brought tears to his eyes, like the rising terror of hell beckoning for his destruction.

He ducked low and dragged some of the furniture to barricade the doorway as a couple more shots blew shards of plaster off the wall above his head. He dived to the floor and raced back to his rifle. On the way, he grabbed his pack with his sidearm and ammunition. He'd hold out as long as he could, making a good show of it, and take his own life if need be. He would not risk compromising Wally and Chuck.

Sirens blasted from every direction. Wally and his group were already down the fire escape and moving across the walkway to the atrium. Not far to get to the mall and beyond to the parking lot. Once in the mall, they were in the clear. From there, it was a stone's throw into the desert. Beyond that, their fate rested in God's hands.

General Salah organized an additional hundred armed guards outside the outer doors of the mosque. Half of the courtyard had emptied as his soldiers forced the scholars from the complex. The General and two men went outside and picked up Yasser Al-Temyat's body. They quickly carried his corpse inside the safety of the tomb. The General radioed for his officers to spread the word that the prophet lived. He called Abdul Aziz to confirm. The old man said he would have the King make a TV announcement.

Majed Abdullah groaned in the middle of the mosque, clutching his bloodied fingers where the bullet had smashed his collarbone. Blood from his wound soaked the floor.

Jesus knelt beside him and said, "Be silent." He placed his hands on the injured shoulder. Majed Abdullah passed out.

"Your brother is sleeping. Let him rest," Jesus told the worried guards.

The soldiers saw that the wound no longer bled, and the signs of trauma had vanished. Without words exchanged between them, they got to their knees and gave thanks to Almighty God.

Jesus walked over to where General Salah knelt by the bodies of his two fallen comrades. The General looked up at the prophet, unable to hide the pain on his face. Jesus closed the eyes of Yasser Al-Temyat. "Our brother is gone. God has called him to a better place. Do not be sad, General; this man's soul is eternal."

The General said nothing as he prayed over Yasser's body. Then, he would have to call Yasser's sister and deliver the awful news.

Carrie and James frantically made calls, asking for updates as the chaos unfolded. James instructed U.S. embassy staff and citizens in Saudi Arabia to lockdown. Theo reviewed the video, and as far he could tell, the prophet made it back inside the Green Dome.

Mo calmly pointed at the live feeds from inside the Green Dome. "Look, he's walking around. He's fine."

Carrie breathed a massive sigh of relief. "The Prophet said that he was flesh and blood."

Theo read out the news feeds from Saudi Arabia. "They've got an active shooter in Medina. The military has surrounded a nearby hotel. The Gulnab."

"Why?" Carrie shouted, taking the room by surprise. "Somebody finally does some good, and now somebody's shooting at him?" The whole office stopped what they were doing. "I swear it's a shame on humanity and all of us."

"How do you really feel?" Mo said, holding his palms downward to get her to ease back.

"Shut up." Carrie snapped. "If he dies, everything could fall apart and we'll have a war to make all others look like a picnic in the park. Do you even read your own data? Close to five billion follow his every word, and the numbers keep climbing. His death will leave billions of bodies stacked higher than the tallest mountains." She angrily pointed at Mo like he was the one who'd fired the shots.

"Hey, take it easy, Carrie; I was just saying."

"The vast majority of all religious believers listen to every word from this man. He's the one – this isn't a joke!" Carrie paused, suddenly realizing her outburst had halted all activity in the room.

"It's not a joke," she repeated as she stormed from the room.

"I was only kidding," Mo explained.

"I guess she didn't find it funny," James said, puffing out his cheeks. "She does have a point. Okay, everybody – back to work."

"Well, the data also indicates non-believers are converting in large numbers, and more and more people are waiting for the new Word of God. If my numbers are right, somewhere close to 5.2 billion are already on board with this." Mo realized all eyes were on him. "And yes, I read my own data."

"Carrie said he's coming here. Let's get ready. I don't need a dead prophet on our watch," James instructed. "I'll get the word out that the Prophet is alive."

CHAPTER TWENTY-ONE

Jesus briefly spoke to the world's media. Over ninety percent of the world's population watched the two-minute segment. He spoke of peace and forgiveness and reminded everyone that God wanted no violence in his name under any circumstances. He asked people to pray for the two guards killed during the incident. Jesus reiterated that the pursuit of truth, love and common sense must prevail and banish anger and resentment. "I will soon face my would-be executioners, and I will show them the error of their ways. Pray for their souls."

The news reported the body of a Caucasian male was recovered from a barricaded room in the Gulnab hotel. The Saudi armed forces shot him three times. He had ended his own life with a single shot under his chin. His falsified documents meant that his real identity had yet to be verified. Local Saudi authorities said they'd release information as soon it became available. Rumors spread that the dead man wore a silver cross around his neck.

James Gordon's team pulled information on every single passport scanned at every major airport in the Middle East. They discovered three men from the US entered Dubai in the UAE and had since gone missing. James suspected they'd slipped into Saudi Arabia. All three were ex-military and were devout Christians. Saudi police checked the whereabouts of all western visitors in the region, but no one could locate Chuck Ramsey of Arkansas, Wally Radford of Alabama, and John Waterford of Louisiana.

Carrie and James studied their profiles. Two were preachers from the same church network, while John Waterford was a significant financial contributor. "James, these are our guys," Carrie assured. "Can we get financial information for the Radford Ministries of Christ?"

"We can," James replied. "The guy who killed himself blew off half his face, but Theo thinks he'll have a picture within the hour, and we can match it against the passport. We need to find these other two guys before anyone else does. We can't risk a beheading or something on foreign soil – still too sensitive." James then closed the office door and said, "Carrie, you look like shit … no offense. You've barely slept a dozen hours in a week." James lifted his hand to stop her attempt to protest. "I want you to get some rest. We're all asking so much from you, including me. Your insight is driving this whole team. Take a few hours. If anything happens, I promise we'll call you."

Exhaustion removed her instinct to fight. This government assignment proved to be the most exhilarating thing she'd ever done. "I'm sorry about earlier. I'll speak with Mo; he'll be okay. More extremists will try to get to the Prophet. People have a lot to lose. We've had seven of his forty days – imagine what day forty-one will look like. Every government should be ready to support one another."

"And that's why we need you in optimum condition. No one else sees what you can." James pulled his hands together as though he were praying. "Please, go and rest. Sleeping on that couch in your office doesn't count. I know more than you think I do."

"Like, whatever goes on in the rest of this building that we don't have access to?" she challenged. James' friendly disposition rapidly faded as he folded his arms across his broad chest, his lips sealed tightly, and his eyes narrowed. Carrie didn't care to push it. Reluctantly she nodded. "Okay, but I'm taking the laptop with me."

"See you back here in the morning," he frostily replied.

"Early morning," she affirmed.

James watched her leave. She'd already proven why she had come so highly recommended, and she enhanced her reputation with each passing day. James needed her sharp and ready.

How did she know he went to other parts of the building? She was too smart for her own good! Mr. grey was right about Carrie. When the New Age Prophet arrived in the U.S., James didn't know of anyone better than Carrie Carter who could estimate the outcomes.

Wally Radford awoke with a start, surprised that he'd nodded off, especially given the high state of alert his body was experiencing. Next to him, Salem and Mohammed remained fast asleep. It was twelve hours since they'd fled Medina, and the entire planet was scouring every nook and cranny in pursuit of them. They had temporarily camped in a dry ditch, away from the desert roads underneath a rocky crag. Wally sneaked from the cramped tent and crawled along the gully. He found Chuck propped against a pile of rocks, looking out to the horizon under a camouflage net. "Seen anything?"

"A few hours ago, lots of military vehicles headed towards Medina. A couple of helicopters have gone over those hills to the north, taking their time looking around. Quiet since then." Chuck's gaze remained fixed through the binoculars. "They haven't seen us yet, or we'd be dogmeat by now."

Wally angled himself on the rocks. "Didn't think we'd ever be doing this again."

"The Lord works in mysterious ways, a bit like these thermal blankets, huh? Good idea to purchase those and keep the overhead eyes from finding us."

"Amen. The authorities think that we are still somewhere in the city—a good idea from Mohammed that we ditch both rentals and take that SUV. For the police and army to comb through all the pilgrims, it will take at least a week. Nothing on the internet with our names on it yet."

"They'll know soon enough," Chuck said. He pointed to the tent containing the two Saudi guides. "If they can get us close to the airfield in Yanbu, we might get out by tomorrow night. Do your high-place friends still have a plane waiting for us?"

"They'd better. We paid a lot of money for a private jet to Istanbul. Then, we'll have new identities and be back on US soil." Wally scanned the desert. "Yanbu is full of westerners so we can ditch this clothing. I want to feel normal again."

"Whatever normal may be. We might get to the US, but we can never go home. We both know that."

"I know," a resigned Wally agreed.

"What do we do with those two guys?" Chuck motioned in the direction of the tent.

"When we get to Yanbu, I'll take care of them. The Lord told me to leave no loose ends."

Chuck nodded. "They've served Christ's purpose."

"Let's get to Yanbu first. We're only thirty miles out. Staying on these back roads, it's about an hour away. We'll stop five miles out on the north side and I'll do what needs to be done; then, we'll make our way to the private airfield."

"Let me know what you need me to do." Chuck pulled his chin tight; his mouth arched downturned. "Wally, I'm sorry I didn't get the shot to count. The wind must have been slightly stronger than I thought. The False Prophet lives because of me."

"Chuck, you did all you could and then some." Wally patted him on the back. "If the good Lord gets us back home, we won't stop. You and I still have a part to play in this game. We're not bowing down to the devil, and we'll not let him desecrate the Word of God. We'll fight on," he decreed.

"Amen, brother … Amen," Chuck rallied. "You're a good man, Wally Radford. The Lord brought you into the world for this purpose."

"Go get an hour's sleep; I'll keep a lookout, and then we move," Wally offered.

Carrie awoke at 3:00 am, fully clothed on top of the bed. She took a quick shower, cut off the tags from the pajamas that the government provided. Not only were they much better labels than she bought for herself, but all of them were a perfect fit. The fact they knew her style, size, and one or two of her brand choices was scary. Given what she'd witnessed about her government's spying capabilities, she figured her nightwear and underwear measurements came easy. She dried her hair and fired up the laptop, nibbling at the leftovers of her room service chicken salad.

Four hours wasn't enough sleep for her body to recover, and her jaw hurt with the constant yawning. Carrie replayed the last message that Jesus delivered, knowing the detail in his words carried more weight than people realized. Something he said that she'd missed the first time around caused her to leap off the bed, stuff the laptop in her bag, and run down the hallway and bang on Mo's door. She hammered a third time loudly until he wearily opened the door. His wild hair stuck out in all directions; his sleepy eyes were two slits centered in the puffiness of his sockets.

"Hi, you won't believe what I found," she said, breezing past him into his room, talking fast and loud.

Mo staggered, unable to catch what she said. Finally, he shouted at her, "Time out!" He motioned for quiet with his hands. "What time is it?"

"Four am," she replied, as if perfectly normal. "I have to tell you that …"

144

"Why do you have to tell me anything at this time? You're impossible," he cut her off and staggered back to bed. He climbed under the sheets, pulling the covers over his head. "Go away."

"No, no! You don't understand. His speeches are coded with what is yet to come." Carrie followed him, still talking, "You have to see this."

"I'm exhausted, go away, please."

Carrie looked at the lump hiding under the covers. She gently grabbed the top of the duvet and peeled it back. "Mo, I'm sorry about what I said to you at the office. I was out of order, but I need you to listen. I admit I'm an asshole, not as much as James Gordon, but an asshole, nevertheless. Can you listen to me?"

He tried again to cover his tousled hair under the covers. Carrie wrestled them away again. "Oh my God, you never give up, do you?" he grunted. "I accept your apology, and you were right, as usual. There – issue resolved. Whatever it is, can you make it quick? I'm trying to sleep. I'm not some human-vampire hybrid like you." He blinked hard and glanced at her solemn face. His familiarity with her expression immediately told him she wouldn't stop. He pulled back the covers with an exaggerated sigh. "If you're going to keep waffling, then get in."

Carrie was comfortable with their physical proximity; their brief affair gave them plenty of opportunities to know each other's bodies. She slid her legs underneath the sheets. "I know what's going to happen next."

"You shut up, and we get some sleep?" he suggested.

"I replayed the video of Jesus telling everyone he's unharmed," she continued, ignoring Mo's sarcasm. "I listened carefully to what he said. The clues are there."

Mo dropped his head onto the pillow and feigned that he was already asleep. "So what?"

Her voice lowered. "So, Jesus said he'd soon face the people who tried to kill him. The guys taking shots at him are from the US."

"You don't know that's the case," Mo replied, wagging an accusatory limp finger.

"I do. The assassins have disappeared. Data and dreams confirmed it; besides, they're Christian radicals out of the south. Jesus will go to the south, and they'll try again. They believe in what they're doing – radical, rich, crazy Christian extremists."

"Sounds like a Kevin Hart movie," Mo complained. "We have security everywhere. You'd think the prophet would be safe," Mo added, sliding further down the bed and taking his pillow.

"Everything is building. Nothing is safe." Carrie slid down, following him, and gave him a gentle kick. She pushed the laptop in front of Mo as she typed. "Look here," she said, accessing the shared folder. "Just a second."

"Only you could bring a laptop into bed with you. I can't believe you're still single," Mo scoffed.

"Whatever," she replied. "Here, listen. Theo's night shift team added this a couple of hours ago. Chuck Ramsey and Wally Radford boarded a private plane in Turkey from Istanbul, heading to the US – we believe it'll land somewhere in the south. Location unknown. They've got some nerve. We don't know who organized it, but somebody paid for it. It's believed they used the same methodology leaving Yanbu to escape Saudi Arabia to Turkey. Anyway, it's an eleven-hour flight back to the US. Their colleague, who arrived with them in the UAE, is missing. I'll bet you your entire paycheck the dead faceless guy in the Medina morgue is John Waterford."

Mo groaned. "Some southern preachers arrive back in the US, somewhere, and so what? They'll soon be in jail. If not, they can't go anywhere. They'll need to spend their lives holed up in motels with cheap hookers and a crack pipe. They're finished."

"They've shown incredible resourcefulness; we shouldn't underestimate them." She paused, noting a file had dropped in from Theo. Immediately she opened it. "Oh my God. Here we are; Theo just confirmed it; John Waterford is the dead shooter in the Medina morgue. We have to find those two other guys. I'll call everyone."

"Good luck," Mo replied, turning his back on her. "You can't arrest two guys for traveling to the UAE, taking a sneaky stop in Saudi Arabia, and coming home via Turkey without evidence of any wrong doing. Even I know that. They could be held for questioning and quickly released with a decent lawyer because there's no direct evidence." He shuffled his body, agitated at getting no sleep.

Carrie flexed her feet as she thought. "I bet James can hold them for a while if we know where they will land. After that, something will turn up."

"John Waterford could have acted alone."

"No way. They'll ignite a holy war if we don't stop them." Carrie suddenly realized she was body-to-body with Mo. Her concentration broke, and momentarily it felt weird. She sneaked a look, noting he still slept in his boxers, and his body looked lean. She liked his narrow waist. "I need to get into the office and alert James. It's starting." Mo didn't flinch. "Would you like a blowjob?" she asked.

Mo sat up. "What!??"

"Thought that might work. Potential wars between old and new religions – it's on top of us. I need to go – so do you." She had a sudden injection of energy and started across the room.

Mo rubbed his eyes and shouted. "Good grief! I'll get dressed and meet you in the lobby in twenty minutes."

"Make it fifteen!" She replied.

"You owe me a BJ," he shouted as the door shut.

Carrie was in the lobby ten minutes later, texting Mo to hurry. There was an enormous church Carrie had seen in her dreams that required investigating.

James Gordon met them in the office; his scraggly gray hair swarmed in all directions over his head. His heavy eyelids looked like his lashes had turned to lead. He sipped on a giant-sized coffee. "This better be good," he moaned. He shuffled past Carrie and Mo, beckoning them to join him in the conference room.

"Good morning to you, too," Carrie chirpily replied to annoy him.

James dropped himself into a chair and waited. Jessica moved from one workstation to another, tapping away on keyboards and moving to the next, readying what Carrie asked for. Carrie walked James down the line of monitors, showing him the storyline she and Mo had put together, although ninety percent of it was her work.

James listened, asking some pointed questions. "We have alerts all over the south to pick up Ramsey and Radford for questioning. There are private airfields all over, so we can't cover all of them. Nothing we can charge them with yet. No evidence. They'll walk. We'll tail them and approach like we would any homegrown terror cell."

Before Carrie could respond, Jessica called their attention. "Guys, I just picked this up from Saudi Arabia. The bodies of two Saudi males were discovered seven miles outside of Yanbu. We know Ramsey and Radford came into Turkey from a private airfield in Yanbu late yesterday. Our records indicate the two dead men were Saudi guns for hire. Both shot in the back of the head."

"An execution." James put his drink on the table. "Looks like our two friends Radford and Ramsey cleaned house. Did we get any fingerprints from the shooter's hotel in Medina?"

"No, sir. The two rooms were free of any fingerprints. The Saudi police found two rental cars nearby, paid for by the two dead men found murdered in

147

the desert. Financial transactions put both Saudi nationals in Medina on the day of the shooting." Jessica chewed harder on her gum. "Guess they won't be getting their deposit back on those rentals." She scooted her chair along to the next keyboard.

"Okay, thanks. Keep looking. Try to find something concrete where we can tie Radford and Ramsey to Medina to hold them longer. Assuming we can find them." James asked Carrie and Mo to follow him to his office to cover US government preparations for the Prophet's potential arrival.

Mo presented a who's who of the most respected clerics, priests, rabbis, and other holy representatives. "We have to get these people in a room together today. They bring all of the major faiths to the table. We should brief them on what is happening and tell them the Prophet is in great danger. Then, they can share a unified message."

James told him, "Do it. I want to speak personally with the religious leaders."

Carrie reminded them, "The Prophet makes his appearances in new places at 3:00 pm, our time. So, we have less than nine hours to get these people together. I'm certain he's coming to DC. Besides which, who will turn down a front row seat to Jesus? I bet they'll come running."

"I'm on it," Mo said.

"Tell Jessica what you need, like vehicles and a meeting point, and then give me a time when you can have them all here. Let's say midday. It gives you five hours," James said. "Bring them on helicopters to avoid traffic congestion. Jessica and Theo will get you what you need."

Mo gave him the thumbs up and exited.

James asked Carrie. "What else do we need to do? I know you're holding something back from me. Tell me what it is; I can help."

Carrie didn't want to go there, but the time constraint and the lingering threat gave her no option. "You're going to think I'm crazy but hear me out." She told James about the repeating dreams and added confirming details as each segment had come to fruition. "I know it all sounds nuts, but I am sure the Prophet is coming to Washington, DC. In my dreams, I've seen this huge church with two great towers on its front and another towards the rear, looking like something you'd imagine from a Tolkien novel. Unfortunately, I haven't had a chance to research it. So that's the first thing on my list."

"Recently, I've seen many things that defy explanation, so your dreams and theories are tepid by comparison." James typed something into his laptop and spun it around to show her. "Does this look like what you described?"

"That's it. Where is it?"

"I thought you were the theologian. It's the Washington National Cathedral. Two miles away from here. I can't believe you didn't know. I'll have Theo get his team in there right away. We can set this up on our doorstep." James dialed Theo's cell. "Some of our team, including us, should be there before 3:00 this afternoon."

Carrie pulled the laptop closer and explored different views of the magnificent building. "That's it," she confirmed.

Staring at the Washington Cathedral and knowing she would be in there and face-to-face with the New Age Prophet brought a quick drain on her brain's ability to connect to her body, and she fell into the nearby chair. James had exited the room. There was no one to see her shaking as she dropped her head between her knees and sucked in air. She would meet with God's chosen representative. "Jesus!" A being of flesh and blood, but one who came and went across the globe at will that defied explanation. She tipped her bottle and poured some water from it into her hand and wiped her face. The curious little girl from the outskirts of Detroit, who had forced her way through everything in life, would meet the personification of God himself. She almost burst into uncontrollable tears, thinking of how proud her adoptive parents would be. She could see their teary eyes glistening with a prideful substantiation of what they'd always instilled into her. You can do anything you set my mind to. She sipped some water and hauled herself from the chair. "It's all coming together."

CHAPTER TWENTY-TWO

Wally Radford and Chuck Ramsey perfected their unlikely story of traveling the Saudi desert in the hopes of seeing the New Age Prophet until their friend, John Waterford, had gone crazy and then disappeared. Their cover story consisted of having completed their illegal tour through the desert as planned and returning home, unaware they were wanted men.

The rough landing on a narrow strip of land in the swamps of Florida meant that they walked off the aircraft, into a waiting car, with false IDs, and headed toward Montgomery, Alabama. They knew their families and friends would be under surveillance, but Wally had confidence he could find a way past it. Both men were pleasantly surprised not to be in custody. They needed to re-group and re-set. Wally desperately wanted to see his family before orchestrating another attempt to stop the false Prophet.

The two men were all over the news. Chuck enjoyed the attention. He laughed at the authorities' failures to track them down. He wanted to taunt their accusers and ram their blind observations down their throats. The pressure seeped from his pores, and he became increasingly vocally combative. "They ain't seen nothing yet! I won't miss next time."

Their dim motel room did nothing to lift Wally's spirits. Finally, Wally had heard enough and whispered to his trusted friend, "Quiet now, Chuck. We say nothing to no one. Pray with me. We'll keep going. Christ, our Savior, has shown me the way." Wally got down on his knees and beckoned Chuck to join him. Wally began to pray, "Surely, He shall deliver you from the snare of the fowler and from the destructive pestilence …"

In Washington, DC, James Gordon watched old footage of Radford and Ramsey preaching in their ministries. "Look at these two," he exclaimed. "Pious assassins." He turned his attention to Theo's team. "Do we have the wiretaps and all their communication channels covered?" Theo confirmed.

Carrie watched the same footage. "Chuck Ramsey is their weak link. You should focus your surveillance on his connections. Radford won't give anything away. The hotels in Medina were paid for by the two guides that they killed. Surveillance cameras show a bunch of guys dressed in thaubs and ghutrah running out the back of the Gulnab hotel. It could be anyone, even if we know it's them. They kept their faces hidden when they checked in."

"We need to find them. These guys are well funded." James looked almost unconcerned. He caught Carrie's observation of his indifference. "We have two hours until the Eagle lands." James pulled on his overcoat and called his assistant. "Get us a car outside, please." James looked to Carrie, "Come and walk the cathedral with me. This could be a once-in-a-lifetime opportunity to talk with a Prophet."

"Sure," Carrie replied; her body felt boiling at the prospect. "Mo is already in there talking with religious leaders."

"Cool," said James, although his tone indicated otherwise.

"Mo's good at rallying people to a common cause. I'm sure he's weaving his magic. Our religious leaders have equal amounts to lose or gain, so it's in their interests to ride along," Carrie explained. James stayed unusually quiet. She considered the pressure from the White House had subdued him over the last couple of days. James' cantankerous mood soured as each day went by.

Dozens of government agents set up sensors, cameras, and communication lines inside Washington Cathedral. The cathedral more than lived up to Carrie's anticipation. Every corner, joint, column, and stairway were carefully crafted to display the ornate Neo-Gothic structure and filter light through the mixture of stone and glass, illuminating a path towards divinity. The rising columns supporting the arches extended so high it gave the impression the building sent prayers from the faithful straight to God.

At the central spine within the cathedral, near the main altar, Mo had gathered the clerical leaders. Mo made the introductions to Carrie and James, who shook hands with the twelve men and women. James said a few words to them about the importance of national safety, hoping they would be respectful of the Prophet's words – should he arrive. "The government doesn't want to control your narrative but let me be clear – I expect you all to be constructive so that a peaceful outcome prevails."

151

Carrie laughed internally as James gave with one hand and took away with the other. The religious leaders agreed they wanted peace and unity, despite some reservations about whether the Prophet genuinely represented what he claimed. Mo briefly explained the content of their discussions, and, as Carrie listened, she wondered what it would take for people to wake up and realize the truth. She wanted to bop the disbelievers over the head and ask them to explain Jerusalem, India, Korea, Africa, and how several of the world's deserts were now lush with vegetation. The world had witnessed events on a grand scale, proving they were no conjuring trick.

A troubled James asked Carrie to walk with him through the cathedral.

"Our religious leaders seem mostly on board. What do you believe, James? I won't hold you to your answer."

James mumbled. "It's a world full of CGI film tricks and deception, so people have a hard time believing in something they can't touch or feel for themselves. I get why the religious leaders are skeptical. They've dedicated their lives to a specific set of beliefs, and now one man claims to know better. How would you feel?"

"Pretty stupid," Carrie succinctly replied. "James, you didn't answer my question. What do you think about it?"

He made sure they were alone and hushed his voice. "I know good and evil coexist. As for the rest – I'll tell you in the next hour. I might just get on my knees and repent. I've instigated things to keep this country safe that would give most people nightmares. The New Age Prophet brings the unexplainable into the world of reality. It's hard for a man like me to make sense of it. But, I know that nobody can get in or out of this cathedral without my say. If he appears, maybe I can give you a better answer. The continuation of American democracy is my priority, and anything that stands in the way I consider a threat."

Carrie's twisted face showed her disappointing surprise. "You think the Prophet Jesus might be a threat?"

"Not directly. His actions and stunts indicate otherwise, but his words, and what he brings, present all kinds of dangers. People get spooked. We've already seen that. Armies mobilized, missiles primed, governments arguing. I know that isn't the full story, but danger seems to hang in the air."

Carrie clenched her lips sideways. This wasn't the time or place for her to lose it and create another commotion.

They met with Theo in the back of the cathedral. "We have every single angle and all possibilities covered. You couldn't squeeze an ant inside this building without us hearing its heartbeat," Theo explained.

James made one last perimeter check. The outside world saw a cathedral closed for repairs. On the inside, it was a hotbed of the world's most technologically advanced monitoring systems. James updated Senator Garofalo and the President, who watched proceedings from deep beneath the White House. James sealed off the entire area around Capitol hill; it was on unofficial lockdown, with thousands of hidden troops on standby.

Carrie and James took a seat behind the clerical leaders and waited. Her left leg quivered with anticipation, and hot sweat formed on her skin. James leaned over and said, "Relax. You've nothing to explain – unless the lake by the Lincoln memorial is suddenly full of elephants and hippos. Then you're on your own."

It was one minute before 3:00 pm. Mo swiveled around. "Here we go." Carrie patted his shoulder and straightened his tangled hair from his collar.

At exactly 3:00 pm, an intense light filled the cathedral. Suddenly, they were staring at the man in the yellow robe.

Jesus looked upon them with affection.

James listened to the chatter through his earpiece. Theo confirmed that no doors, windows, nor sewer system triggered security beams. His team was rechecking each piece of apparatus, camera, audio, thermal infrared, and spectrometers. "We don't know how he got in here," were Theo's frustrated words.

Carrie heard the same audio messages in her ear device, but it quickly became white noise as she stared at the beautiful man before her. Her senses told her to weep, but no tears formed. She edged as far forward as she could without sliding off the bench, and she placed a hand on Mo's shoulder. He bent his arm upwards and held the back of her hand. Carrie removed the useless earpiece. Only one voice mattered, and she was about to hear it.

Jesus didn't look around the cathedral as if he knew the layout. His poise showed his perfect comfort, unbothered by the people on the edges scurrying to gather data on his appearance.

"God is great. Welcome. I am Jesus. That is the name my spiritual Father has given me. There is but one true God." He looked through the line of clerics, straight at Carrie and James. "Seek what is in your hearts. You will save millions of lives worldwide, but you will not save mine. Be at ease with my words – as I am."

He beckoned Carrie and James to join the others on the front row. "As much as you've waited for me, I've waited to see you. My brothers and sisters, the world's focus is upon you. Act in accordance with your hearts – your heads won't help you. I do not need to persuade you of who or what I am – my Master shows you the truth and the way."

Through her awestruck disposition, Carrie noticed his speech had no foreign accent and sounded genuinely American, despite her having heard him fluently speak several other languages. Each time, his words were perfect in pronunciation and form. It should be impossible, and yet it matched her expectations.

Jesus approached them and placed a hand on their heads one by one. "You are all leaders of the people – chosen by the divine before ever you were born. Your President will need to act fast when God shows his power today. Our heavenly Father abhors violence. Tell your earthly masters that what happens next is God's plan. To live with one another, you do not have to destroy one another. God shines his brilliant light of peace upon the earth this blessed day. A handful of men will become nervous as billions of others rejoice."

He continued to move along the line, blessing them with his hands. "Some of you have seen me in your dreams. You are here by design to fulfill my Father's work. You will know what to do when called upon." Jesus continued along the line of clerics until he arrived at Mo. Jesus smiled at him and placed both hands on his head. "Eliminate your fears. All is well. Tyrants will fall. Guide those who are lost."

He came next to James. "Make wise choices. Be wary of those in the depths. All contracts can be broken if you have the will."

Carrie was the very last. Jesus took hold of her hands and kissed each one before placing his hand on her forehead. "When I return to my Master, you'll talk new languages to people you've never met. Bind the world in harmony, and it will respond."

Jesus stood back and raised his hands. "Bring light to the world." He looked upward. Outside the grim weather in Washington, DC, was a heavy blanket of thick dark clouds. The Prophet's words resulted in bright shards of light piercing through the high stained-glass windows. Light rained down from every side of the cathedral as if the earth had four suns. The recipients in the front row felt the warmth of the intense color spectrum. Then, after a few seconds, it subsided. Jesus stepped back six paces and continued: "God gave each of you a specific task. Next, I will be with our brothers and sisters in Africa, and then I will return here tomorrow to address the world. Then we shall hear the guiding words of God. God is great."

Jesus knelt before them and looked down the line of mesmerized faces. "It is alright to question your purpose and understanding. God has never demanded fealty. Know this, my learned brothers and sisters: God wishes you to hear his new words, share them without alteration, and find true hearts. Those who spread his word without misrepresentation or personal gain will find reward with eternal bliss. When God created the universe, he sowed the seeds that formed this planet and others, allowing them to develop as they would. It takes billions of years for nature to find its way, but not long for over-developed primates to interfere. God understands his guidance is needed so that life can move forward. You are made from the same building blocks that exist throughout the universe. One day mankind will recognize the earth's unique signatures but know you are not alone. Brothers and sisters, I ask that you pray with me." Jesus lowered his head.

Without hesitation, they all slid off the front bench and knelt. Carrie noted Mo's arms were shaking, and James Gordon's hands were clasped tight enough to show the whites of his knuckles.

"Your children here have opened their hearts, and now for the first time, they see. Make their daily distractions fade like a mist. Each of them will use their gifts to do your bidding." Jesus beckoned them to stand. "I will remain here until the turn of the next hour. I will pray on my own. Go in peace and God's grace."

The clerics filed into the central aisle, bowing as they whispered excitedly amongst themselves. James and Carrie were the last ones to pass by the Prophet. He raised a hand for them to stop. He looked purposefully at James Gordon. "Your earthly masters will need your guidance. Be ready, James Gordon. All advanced nations will require calm. God will equalize them all – make sure they know it." He turned his attention to Carrie. "You've been ahead of the story so far – be ahead of this piece, too." He turned around, headed to the altar, and knelt before the highly decorated cross.

Carrie and James followed the group towards the front doors of the cathedral. Carrie's light heart made her feel like she was floating along the central walkway. Those in front of her chattered furiously. Outside, the clouds and the drizzle were as thick as they'd been all day.

James tapped Carrie's arm and signaled that she should replace her earpiece. Then, he got on his mic. "Theo, what did you get?"

"Same as before – I've got sensors for every spectrum we know about, and each one shows the same darn thing. If this is a magic trick, then we can't explain it."

James beckoned Carrie and Mo to ride with him back to their headquarters. "What comes next?"

Carrie and Mo looked expectantly at the other. A thick reluctance bounced between them. "Reading between the lines, I'd say he's going bigger than ever before – he talked about your intervention and advanced nations requiring calm," Carrie said.

"He's here for peace, though," James hopefully suggested.

"If not he would have annihilated us all by now," she replied.

"Nuclear armaments came to mind," Mo said. "That's as far as I got."

"Mo's right. Seventy percent of ordinary people want worldwide nuclear disarmament, although the Russians poll lower, at around fifty percent. So I agree that's the direction he's taking."

"So, you think we'll have marches in every major city, like back in the seventies? People demanding no nukes," James said.

Carrie stifled a single laugh. "No, that's too easy. Based on the unexplainable things we've seen; I'd say that our nuclear arms won't launch? I'd also say it will be the same for everyone. He intimated that the President would get busy – how? Make your attack and defense system inoperable?"

"I hope you're wrong," James groaned and immediately dialed.

Carrie shook her head. "You've got forty-five minutes to give all nuclear-armed countries a heads up. If we're right, then at least they can't obliterate one another."

"And if we're wrong, we'll be ashes and memories by nightfall," Mo added.

CHAPTER TWENTY-THREE

The day after the Prophet's appearance in Washington, Carrie observed the manic activity within the government building. James Gordon was locked away in his office on one call after another. Theo confided to Carrie that the government kept a lid on the fact that at 4:00 pm the previous day, their full nuclear capabilities and reserve stockpiles were gone. Every base, submarine, warhead, missile, launch code, and fusion equipment had disappeared. America wasn't on red alert because they had discovered that the Russians, Chinese, Europeans, North Koreans, and sub-continent countries were all in the same position.

Russia sent thousands of troops to their western front, worried that NATO might invade, and NATO ramped up its presence, fearing the Russians might push into Europe. James Gordon advised the President to tell those countries which had formerly maintained nuclear capabilities that they should hold their positions. International tensions ran at all-time highs, and no one publicly admitted that they'd lost their nuclear arsenals.

Carrie shook her head at the governments failures to recognize a chance for lasting peace, although she kept quiet on the subject. Secretly, Carrie was delighted that disarmament was forced on them. She'd always imagined herself at the front of the nuclear demonstrations and marches back in the day.

She fed information via Theo to James, reminding them that dealing with the reality of an unexplainable power did not mean the end of the world. In the blink of an eye, a power disarmed every nuclear nation. Carrie believed that if the Prophet meant them harm, they'd know by now. She theorized that their nuclear arms would not return and that it would be futile to try to build them back up. Carrie advised that world leaders should spend their time figuring out how to live in peace. Mo's data showed the costliness of nuclear arms and given that nobody had used any of them since 1945, they were, in effect, an expensive and defunct system of attack or defense. The money could be spent elsewhere, like on clean water and education.

Carrie confided her belief to Mo, "Nobody will go into a ground war with tanks, rockets, guns, and grenades. It's a game nobody could ever win, and the modern powers have run that data, and they know it. It would be perpetual trench warfare into infinity at an expense no one could afford. So the New Age Prophet may have taken war off the table."

The Prophet appeared eight hours later in Ethiopia, and within two hours, the rains came and kept coming. Two hours later, in Nigeria, he denounced persecution against people for their sexual persuasion, stating God loved everyone, directing his remarks to religious hardliners in the African nations with intolerance towards homosexuality. The Prophet encouraged acceptance, and increasingly his messages became more specific.

Carrie liked the humanist approach, even if it created some controversy. The Prophet's challenges needed to be addressed.

Mo, working from the comfort of the couch in Carrie's office, told her, "James messaged me – the guys from Medina are arriving here this afternoon."

"Is General Salah coming with them? The guy who looks after the Al-Masjid?"

Mo scanned the names on the list. "Yeah, his name is on here. They're supposed to be here to exchange ideas on theology with the US group from the cathedral."

Carrie slurped on her hot tea. "Any Saudi Royal family?"

Mo scanned again. "Yeah, two princes and a cousin to the Saudi King. It's a bit risky sending out some of the Royals, don't you think?"

"Yes and no." She reached out to get the list from him. "The King only trusts those related to him – he's afraid religious upheaval could destroy his power base. For public appearance's sake, the royals have to play along. I'm interested in meeting the Grand Mufti, Abdul Aziz. He seems remarkably reasonable, given the pressure he's been under. The group could provide a sensible path forward."

"We can hope, but I wouldn't hold my breath." Mo dropped his butt back onto the couch.

"You're such a pessimist."

"No, I'm a realist," he countered and half lay down. "Oh yeah, I see why you like it on here – surprisingly comfortable."

Carrie glanced up from reading the list. "Don't get too comfortable there; that's my space … has James asked for anything specific concerning this list?"

Mo adjusted his position and snuggled down into the cushions. "He didn't give any instruction, except that these guys are coming today. 'Figure it out,' he said."

"Cool. Free reign to talk about whatever we want. So where are they staying?"

"In the same hotel as you and me. Convenient, huh," Mo hinted, as though he suspected it'd been arranged for some time. "Theo told me they can't allow them into this building. Hotel only."

"What about the cathedral?"

"They didn't mention that."

"We should use that, too. It's a good setting for this kind of thing. I can help you if you want to put a quick agenda together."

"Thanks. You read my mind or saw it in one of your dreams."

Carrie thought about throwing something at him, but he looked so peaceful on the couch that she dropped the pen she had planned to use as a missile. Suddenly, an alert popped up on her screen: "Jesus is in Kenya." She changed her mind, rolled up some paper, and launched it across the room, bouncing perfectly off the top of Mo's head.

"I hate you," Mo wearily yawned.

"No, you don't. Next time, I'll throw the paperweight." She referenced the list of names coming from Saudi Arabia and began making notes. When she looked up, Mo was fast asleep. Carrie prepared the meeting agenda.

Wally Radford was covered in mud, leaves, and brush; his face was cut, and his clothes stank. Days of living rough in the woods were compounded by Wally crawling the last five hundred yards to his house through the old sewer pipe. He alerted Cheryl by using the flashlight against the rear kitchen window. Wally waited until she returned their secret signal. Undercover of dark, on the back porch, they embraced. Wally's condition brought Cheryl to tears as he squeezed her tight.

"I never thought I'd see you again?" she gasped.

"I can't stay long. We received word that the demon was in the US and that he will return."

"Let me get you something to eat," Cheryl said, dragging him to sit at the dining table. "They're out front in the street. Watching the house."

Wally dimmed the internal lights and checked out the front of the house. He spotted three cars that had no business being there. Cheryl fixed him a plate and sat next to him. She tried to groom his unruly thinning hair and kept her hands on him despite his disgusting state. "Wally Radford," she softly cooed.

"My love. You are an angel," he gushed with absolute love for her. He wanted to tell Cheryl much more, but time won the battle. He ravenously devoured the homemade meatloaf.

Earlier in the day, Wally had arranged for one of his associates to sweep the inside of the house for listening devices. Those found in the living room and Master bedroom were destroyed. Wally briefly explained what happened in Saudi Arabia, and in less than two minutes, they caught up on the family and the church, and they exchanged their love for each other. Wally put down his silverware, holding his satisfied stomach. "Darlin,' you make the best meatloaf I ever tasted. I'm a lucky man."

"You've lost twenty pounds," Cheryl noted. "I've been worried sick. Look at what they've done to you."

"I'm fine," Wally assured.

"Where's Chuck?"

"Chuck is being Chuck and keeping an eye out in the woods. I have to see John's wife, Nora. He sacrificed himself so we could get home."

"How could they make my Wally the most wanted man in the US? How could they? Those …" she held back from unleashing a string of profanity.

Wally looked down at his shoes, sighed heavily, and took Cheryl's hands into his. "Listen, honey; you can't tell anyone that I've been here, not even the kids. It will put you all in danger, and I can't have that. So we have to try again until we succeed. We missed the devil by less than a quarter of an inch."

Cheryl stroked his dirty face. "John Waterford is with God. You have to finish this, Wally Radford. Christ and his church are counting on you!" Cheryl's sadness rapidly switched to grim determination, seeing the awful condition of her husband and his good name slandered across the globe. "The money from our savings accounts was processed two days ago. The cash will be at the pick-up point by Friday. The Lord gives us a second opportunity. Have you heard anything else from Washington?"

Wally shook his head. "Assume every call, text, and email you send is compromised. Zero communication to me or about me. You can't talk about our special mission within these walls – they'll come back and listen again."

"Those rotten people are welcoming an apocalypse," Cheryl angrily replied.

"Assume the churches are bugged as well. I've tasked Aaron with getting me the phones. I sent him over to Columbus." Wally saw the look of surrender in her gaze. "It will be for the greater good."

"Amen," Cheryl affirmed. "How long will you be here?"

"In the area for another day. They'll keep watching the house."

"I should appeal to our governor – it isn't right."

Wally stroked both her arms. "They'll keep looking for me. I'll be taking the trail bike from the old horse sheds and leaving via the woods." They hugged each other, and Wally tenderly kissed her full lips. "I'll love you in all things, Mrs. Radford."

"You'd better," she said, faking a smile, but her face showed she was ready to crumble.

"Once we get some more information, we'll complete our mission. To keep you safe and from any repercussions, I'm sending you a note saying that I can't take it anymore, and I decided to take my own life. No trace of me will exist. Chuck will do the same to his wife." Wally took a step back and admired every inch of the woman he loved. "My wife and my best friend. Tell Aaron if those reporters try to get on the property, and he'll sort it."

"I don't care about those gutter rats." Cheryl toppled into his arms and grabbed him, her fingers digging into his flesh. "I have to lose you all over again. Wally, you're the instrument of Christ to save us. I want to let you know …" her voice faded, and her head dropped onto his filthy neck.

"I know. The Lord hasn't finished with us yet."

"Amen to that."

Wally slipped out through the cellar to the end of the patio and dipped over the wall, then skirted down the lawn to crawl back inside the old sewer pipe. Cheryl watched, almost unable to feel anything less than pure anger that her husband, a man dedicated to lifting himself and those around him into God's grace, had been reduced to crawling underground up to his neck in waste. It showed the determination of the man. Neither she nor Wally would buckle. Cheryl prayed she'd see him again.

Wally came through the end of the shit-laden pipe to the fence line and sniped his way back into the fields. He stopped at the old horse sheds and took the motorbike. He missed his wife and kids. God had shown him the way through the darkness, and he would follow through. He glanced back at the faint lights from his beloved house and blew a tender kiss to Cheryl, vowing he'd see her on the other side. He quietly said goodbye to what he had once called home.

161

Carrie and Mo entered the hotel's top floor, where the Saudi guards frisked them and escorted them into the penthouse suite.

"How have they got guns? They just got off the plane," Carrie whispered to Mo.

"Diplomatic immunity? Saudi Royals and all that," Mo guessed. He checked out the view across the city, and they emptied the laptops and translation devices from their backpacks. "This is some cool shit they've put together for us."

Carrie had already positioned hers and smiled triumphantly. "I know – talk in here, and Arabic spits out here. So, finally, technology is working for us."

"How did you get that set up …" Mo didn't finish the thought.

The side door opened, and the half dozen men from Medina entered. They made introductions. One of the armed guards brought in hot tea, and another presented a tray full of snacks. Carrie said hello and welcomed them, with her lips almost touching the microphone. The machine translated through the laptop speakers. The Medina group smiled and nodded. She pointed to where they should speak.

Abdul Aziz said, "We are pleased to be in the US and looking forward to exchanging information. We want to help."

The talks slowly picked up speed into something fast, friendly, and productive. Carrie and Mo waited until the end of the conversation before letting the Medina entourage know, "Jesus said he's coming back to Washington." Mo showed the group footage from the cathedral, explaining how Jesus had spoken with US clerics, and other world religious leaders would arrive within twenty-four hours. Jesus wished to share God's plan.

"I have spoken with my brother in Rome, the Papal Father. We are aligned," Abdul Aziz told the group. "Worldwide governments are slow to react favorably, but peace prevails. This makes sense. They will come around with some persuasion."

Mo thanked them on behalf of the American government for taking the time to visit the US. "Tomorrow, you'll meet with James Gordon and walk through our security procedures."

"I will walk with this James Gordon," General Salah said. "We have learned a lot in Medina."

Carrie had no opportunity to speak with the General one-to-one, but she noticed him sizing her up. His intense gaze never held back. The two-hour meeting concluded, and they wished their guests a good night's sleep after their long journey. Carrie shook the general's hand. His grip was warm and solid.

Carrie wrote a quick summary of the meeting and sent it to James for review.

CHAPTER TWENTY-FOUR

Mr. Grey sat on the edge of the metal table, his legs dangling over the side, swinging them back and forth. "Jim, there you are. Always on time. Do they give out medals for that? Government efficiency at its best."

"You should put something on your feet. You might catch something." James suggested as he splashed through the fetid puddles. "It gets worse down here."

"Oh, I've seen worse," Mr. Grey assured. "Footwear is unnatural. Being barefoot makes me like a tuning fork. As soon as I touch down, I can hear the hopes and dreams of everyone above; they're mostly predictable, and the noise is very distracting. All that searching for a better tomorrow, for their inner self, for a brave new world, and on it goes – I can't hear myself think. An unwelcome gift from the man upstairs," he pointed above with a knowing grin. "Still, we all have our cross to bear – pain lets us know we are alive."

"If you say so," James sounded bored. "The Saudi entourage arrived. They met with my team. I've denied them the access they wanted to all things Washington."

"Good man, Jimmy, good man. Keep an eye on those guys. You might think they're a bunch of backward sand-rats, but they're craftier than a coyote trailing a rabbit. Passionate to a fault, and that passion makes them unpredictable."

"My security will escort them to the meetings, and we won't let them leave the hotel floor they're assigned to."

"Is anyone pushing back?"

"Only the Saudis. I told my people we couldn't rely on the Saudis, especially after the assassination attempt. Although Carrie Carter wasn't happy. She said if we punished everyone who'd made a mistake, we'd all be in jail."

"She's a feisty provocateur. I like her. How did you pacify her? A spanking?"

"I told her the Saudis are an unknown quantity, and their security status was unconfirmed."

"Jim! You have an imagination! I'm so happy for you."

"What's so special about the Saudis?"

Mr. Grey swiveled from the table into the armchair, his toes barely touching the filthy water. "Pure hearts – completely misguided, but pure. They've got thousands of years' head start in their cultural sophistication, and it is rooted deep. It took me a while to loosen them up. Their beliefs and instincts make them dangerous, but a part of me likes a challenge – after all, that's why we're here."

Mr. Grey swiftly pushed an arm downward, faster than a professional boxer's jab, and swooped up the giant rat by its tail. It swayed upside down and squealed. He observed it for a second and flung it over his shoulder, splattering it against the wall with a dull crack, leaving a bloodstain on the jaded paintwork. "God's awful invention," he sighed.

"One of my team is having lucid dreams about the Prophet and things that might happen. They've proven decidedly accurate. Should I be worried?" James asked.

"You should only be worried if her skirts get tighter, and you can see every sinew flexing in that ass. She moves those hips side to side like she's performing to a conductor's baton guiding her across the room," Mr. Grey snickered at his imagery. "C'mon, Jim, we've all wished to get lucky with that. It must be so tempting – your wife and kids so far away, and Carrie Carter looking at you with those big smoky eyes – you a man of power – her a mere consultant looking to hit the big time. Late nights in the office together, all that tension. C'mon, Jim? Just us guys here."

"She's a good kid. Bright, just as you said she would be. Should I be worried?"

"Only if your wife finds out what's really on your mind. Miss Carter's tempting every time she's near you. I bet she tastes like maple syrup – sweet and sticky – yum!"

"Did you bring me here to talk about Carrie Carter's pussy, or something useful?"

"I'm just saying. We're guys – we can share, you know? Lighten up. It's our private club down here without the secret handshakes. We should be friends."

"We're not friends. This is a business transaction, that's it." James firmly replied with a crimson complexion. "I believe we're clear on that."

Mr. Grey rose menacingly from the chair. His bare feet swished the water aside as he moved within two feet of James. His tall, slender body usually appeared wiry and weak, but now it seemed more prominent. His eyes widened, his pale lips tightened through the clenched jaw; he scanned the length of James Gordon and smilingly sneered, "I'll say what this is and what it's going to be. Do what we agreed, or we'll find ourselves a new arrangement. I believe we're clear."

Mr. Grey patted James on the top pocket of his jacket, back-stepped, and dropped into the dirty chair. Once again, he appeared boney, but there was an overriding indifference in his stare. He pulled out the short pipe and lit the contents. Smoke sailed upwards, and one side of his lips curled towards his forehead. "My invention," he said, waving the pipe with satisfaction. "Now, back to business. Don't worry about Carrie Carter. She's entertaining, and I like being entertained."

"What if the Saudis present an issue?"

"Kill them, but not on U.S. soil. Their plane goes down over the ocean or close to home! Or how about one of those drone strikes you like so much? You don't want that blood on your hands when you're making progress with worldwide relations. You need to be careful, Jim, or you're gonna make America popular. The main action will be on U.S. soil. Be ready."

Mr. Grey motioned for James to leave, his long boney hand waving him away through the stale air. James walked away but stopped when Mr. Grey called, "Jim – check your top pocket. There's a cell number and instructions. Text that number and tell them that's where the Prophet will be."

James looked at the scribbled note. "What?"

"Just do it."

"If you say so." James headed through the stinking hallway.

"Do it when you get to Texas."

"Texas?"

"More than one of us works in mysterious ways, Jim – we're counting on you," Mr. Grey tauntingly sang the last few words.

James wanted out, but now he had the President's ear, as promised. Finally, he was within touching distance of getting what he wanted. He convinced himself that once this business was finished, his commitments would solely be to his family, the President, and the safety of the American people. He would be rid of Mr. Grey's tumorous influence and could do what he always thought himself capable of. However, as he ascended in the elevator, James could not extinguish the burning sensation in his gut.

Washington, DC became surrounded by highly trained troops without raising any media attention. The cathedral remained closed to the public for 'sewer repairs.' James' advice, via Senator Garofalo and Senator Crowley to the President, had been readily accepted and acted upon. The more of Carrie's briefings he read, the more nervous he became. He called in consultants who specialized in securing large open spaces if the Prophet decided to go walkabout. Radford and Ramsey remained on the loose.

James' briefing to the small group of Senators and the President was uncomfortable. Senator Jim Crowley came down particularly hard on him, accusing James and his team of incompetence and lack of foresight that almost got the prophet killed. James explained that the Prophet didn't provide a timetable and map of his intentions. Crowley pushed for more intel and called for James to be stepped down, with Senator Crowley taking over. It took Senator Garofalo's intervention and a word from the President to keep James in his position.

A ballsy move from Crowley, especially as James knew all his secrets, or at least he believed he did. Crowley's bravado worried him, thinking he may have missed something. He'd yet to find Crowley's mole within his department. James disliked Crowley. He would circle back and eventually hammer that douchebag. James already told Crowley he knew of his association with Wally Radford, yet the man called for James' head. James suspected that it could be something initiated by Mr. Grey to double-cross or antagonize him. So far, Mr. Grey had kept his word, but James didn't trust him. He would save Crowley's downfall for another time.

James Gordon could see the light at the end of this long, dark, and twisted tunnel. He needed to push through. Getting what he wanted teased, as if within the palms of his hands. He pulled his team together at the cathedral. The Prophet would speak soon.

167

From inside the cathedral, Jesus spoke to the gathered religious leaders and then live to the world's media. The armed forces secured a one-mile perimeter outside, preventing large crowds of cheering worshippers from forming. Three hundred dignitaries lined the cathedral's seats.

The New Age Prophet took them all by surprise when he announced God had removed all nuclear arms from the earth. "Do not see yourselves as defenseless, but open for opportunity." Jesus invited the world's leading nations to find a peaceful way forward. "Nuclear weapons are unnecessary. They won't save you from anything. I encourage your chosen leaders to find amicable solutions to establish understanding." His revelation sent shockwaves and celebrations around the globe. He concluded, "God wants unity, peace, and love, and has provided a perfect base from which to build."

His speech was short. After a few minutes, the Prophet disappeared. One hour later, he appeared in Rio De Janeiro, Brazil, to mass celebrations as millions gathered below the Corcovado mountain in the capital city. Brazilian news showed images where the world-famous statue of Christ the Redeemer was gone, and in its place, a statue of two gigantic angel wings wrapped around the kneeling figures of small children. The new sculpture towered twice the size of its predecessor and was covered in brilliant gold that glistened from every angle. The figures of the children represented kids from all ethnicities under the protection of the angels. The new statue was quickly given the name 'Christ the Liberator.'

When the Prophet returned to Washington, DC, he told the religious elders he'd come back every other day and help guide them on how they could influence the world's opinion and drive towards unity. He appeared across the globe on the days between, performing miracles of unexplainable proportions. For two and a half weeks, he followed the same pattern. Carrie and the team were present at each mesmerizing gathering inside the cathedral.

Carrie's spirit told her from the first moment she'd seen the Prophet that he was the genuine article. His words provided an overwhelming glow that grew stronger, and for the first time in her life, she felt completely loved. The truth she saw in Jesus directly reflected God showering his love on mankind. It was a personal receipt alongside the collectively immersive gift. The world changed and kept changing. Everything she experienced proved it. To be in his immediate presence and to hear his voice wrapped her inside a heavenly womb. I was a place of warmth, nourishment, and an eagerness to push into the world and share the glowing effect. Carrie considered it a rebirthing of her soul.

People, previously of different faiths, were now united under one cause, touched by the same powerful inspiration. There was a collective shift in the physical, verbal, and unspoken surge of people coming together in all parts of the world, hands being shaken, where previously blood was spilled, and a euphoric overriding desire for people to listen and understand and help their fellow human beings. The political vitriol faded as the public demanded peace and equal opportunity for all in all things. People saw it – they felt it. Going to bed each night, Carrie's exhaustion increased, as did her toe-curling feeling a child gets on Christmas Eve, wondering what the morning would bring.

Carrie was continually frustrated that world leaders showed a stubbornness to fully accept what was clearly a worldwide transition. The ordinary people were leading the way. "We have to keep pushing and we can do this."

Carrie finished her reports and walked James through her conclusions. He thanked her for the high level of accuracy with which she'd predicted the movement of the Prophet. So far, she'd correctly predicted twenty-five of the twenty-seven countries he'd been to. Within those, she'd predicted the right location twenty-three of twenty-five times. Nevertheless, her predictions worried him – as world unity grew, so did the extremist threats. There'd been no more attempts on the Prophet's life since Medina, but the end of his forty days was fast approaching, increasing the likelihood of something happening.

Outside of Washington, DC, the Prophet made only one other appearance within the U.S. when he appeared at the site of the former twin towers in New York City. Jesus addressed the world, asking that that level of atrocious hate never be repeated. He implored for similar compassion when he'd appeared in Halabja, Kurdistan, where thousands of innocent civilians were slaughtered in a gas attack. After the Prophet visited New York, lower Manhattan was gridlocked for four days as millions of people lined up to place their hands on the ground and walls that the Prophet had touched as he toured the 9/11 memorial.

Carrie discussed the remaining USA options, where she identified three sites in Texas. She highlighted the three locations: "The Hindu Shri Swaminarayan Mandir in Houston, The Alamo in San Antonio, and the Prestonwood Baptist Church in Plano. The Hindu Temple was the most likely of the three as a symbol of unity." James set up their security at all three sites, and if the timeline she'd indicated was correct, there were only three days to prepare.

There was the ever-present threat of Wally Radford and Chuck Ramsey. They'd been spotted in Shreveport, Louisiana, but managed to evade the authorities, slipping away into the bayous. Rumors surfaced that they'd come to Washington without any foundation to support the idea.

James had noted in his reports how well-protected and funded Radford and Ramsey were. However, he neglected to report he also knew exactly who was one of their primary benefactors. Despite that, he increased the size and scope of the manhunt. He didn't buy the suicide notes from the two men, claiming that the government tarnished their reputations.

The following day, Jesus went to Australia and then to Beijing, China, where he spoke to over ten million people. After more than half the nation protested their right to religious freedom, the Chinese authorities did not attempt to intervene, and amazingly the citizens won the argument. The appearances increased in size and scope. Mo's data showed increasing worldwide belief in the Prophet, with more and more people abandoning their regular places of worship.

James flew half his team down to Texas and set up on the outskirts of Dallas, including Carrie, Mo, Theo, Jessica, and three of the men from Medina, one of them being General Salah.

Equipment tests were conducted from each of the three locations, and logistical components were confirmed. James called the immediate team to a meeting in the hotel conference room.

"Thanks for coming here on short notice. We have support from the local police, the National Guard, and a section of the Marine Corps stationed in the Gulf of Mexico. We've got help in getting supplies of water, food, and sanitation needs to the areas where we believe the Prophet may appear." He faced Carrie. "I appreciate what you've done to prepare us for such events." She wrapped her bottom lip under the top and reservedly smiled. James addressed Theo, "Who's leading the sweepstakes right now?"

Theo nervously glanced at the small group. "Chief?"

"Oh, I'm sorry," James observed Theo's shock. "Based on Carrie's predictions, Theo's team and their support techs have been running sweepstakes on when and where the Prophet will appear. Am I right?"

Theo and Jessica sheepishly nodded. James continued. "Last I heard, our friend Theo was up over five hundred dollars?"

"I just used Carrie's data and made an educated guess. I'm only up three hundred dollars," he qualified. A faint ripple of laughter went around the room, including the Medina team listening on their headphones.

"You guys are running a Jesus fantasy league and didn't invite the rest of us to play?" Mo complained.

170

"Hey, I'm sorry, man. It was just something within the comms teams. They get weird about letting in outsiders, especially those with inside information."

James made sure he used the translator mic. "You guys getting this?"

General Salah spoke into his mic. "We got it. Miss Carter is the betting man's source of gold," he suggested, as another trickle of light relief passed around the room.

James explained the game plan, asking each member of the group for their input, and to raise security or communication concerns. After three hours, they'd agreed on deployment, resources, and how to react, based on which location the Prophet appeared.

When the room cleared, James texted the message given to him by Mr. Grey. He did not know who the recipient was, nor could he use his team to trace the number that Mr. Grey provided. He sent the location for the Prophet's next appearance. It was not a place that his team was considering.

After dinner, Carrie moved into a secluded corner of the hotel bar, where she had a translating device, and spent some time with General Salah. They talked about their backgrounds and tried to determine why the Prophet made particular references to them.

They both understood their day jobs, but neither could pinpoint the end game. The General confided he worried he was not the right man and in the wrong place – having little influence on American soil. He explained that in Medina, at the Al-Masjid, he played an important role with a level of control, but he was a passenger in America. Carrie told her story, and they talked long into the night – two intelligent, dedicated individuals sharing the same self-doubt. Carrie thanked him, and they briefly hugged. Her physical contact surprised the General, but he assumed it was normal for Americans. He smiled at her and immediately glanced away, shuffling his papers before retiring to his room. They trusted in the Prophet's claim that they would do what was necessary to fulfill what was needed.

CHAPTER TWENTY-FIVE

Wally Radford and Chuck Ramsey used their connections and cash to increase their dedicated fold from two to eight. First, one of Wally's old associates provided a neat two-story house on the outskirts of Austin. The men gathered in the dining room, drank beer, and finished a grilled steak dinner as if they were old friends at a reunion. Then, with the cash provided, Chuck purchased the weapons via the Cooley brothers, getting the arsenal of automatic weapons the team requested.

The inside information from their Washington source gave them the three potential locations of the False Prophet's next appearance. The men cleared away their plates. Wally spread out the map of Texas on the dining room table to finalize their approach. "I've marked out the three sites we've been given. I'll take Bobby and Steve up to Houston. Chuck, you'll take Garvey and head for San Antonio, and Rocky will take the Cooley brothers to Plano. You've all got your assigned addresses set up, and each one of you knows what to do. We've been over this as much as possible, but time is not our friend. I pray that the Lord is. All it takes is one good shot."

Wally became distracted by Chuck fiddling with his tablet. "Chuck, are you good with all this? You seem preoccupied," he said with some exasperation.

Chuck pressed his fingers twice more on the touch screen. "Wally, I apologize, but I tell you, this just doesn't look right. I received a random message on the burner phone you gave me. It came from an unknown number, and I haven't given the number to anyone except you. Looking at what the message says, I can't help thinking we're heading the wrong way."

"What do you mean? Our contact in Washington has been good up to now? They gave us the three sites."

"I know." Chuck's heavy eyebrows frowned so deep that they almost covered his eyes. "Look!" He pushed the phone in front of Wally, saying, "Something ain't right."

Chuck placed the tablet on the map. "I'm good with our plans if we got the right locations, but … something's been bugging me since I got this new information."

"Why didn't you say anything before?"

"I was busy researching it. Just hear me out?" He looked for Wally's approval and was met with a sweeping hand gesture that gave him the floor. "Back in the corps, when we were doing our bit for our country, I spent a few months working intel, searching for patterns in our enemies' communications."

"This ain't the corps," one of the Cooleys interrupted.

"I hear ya," Chuck noted. "Looking at the coordinates that I received it suddenly makes sense. I used the data to compare with the records I've been keeping." He moved the tablet around, hoping they could all see it. "Every time this demon preacher has been somewhere, I've plotted the places he's visited. There's a very distinct pattern." Chuck scrolled through the graphs and spreadsheets he'd put together.

Wally stared at Chuck's data. "What's all this telling us, Chuck? Pie charts are no good to me."

Chuck pulled up a digital map of the globe. "The False Prophet makes his big crowd appearances in places with open space nearby, good roads, transportation access, and a significant religious center point, where it's always easy to get supplies in and out of the area. The three sites our contact in Washington gave us also fit that model."

"And where's that leave us?" Wally asked, straining to hold his frustration.

"The message told me to look at the patterns, and it gave me some coordinates. If you look at the pattern of where the demon should go next, the data tells me he'll turn up at one of the Muslim places — not Christian, Hindu, Buddhist, or whatever. He started at a mosque, and every sixth place he goes is always a mosque. The list we got from Washington doesn't have a mosque on it. They got it wrong, and I was sent coordinates for a mosque."

"Have you tried finding out who sent you the text?"

"The number isn't listed anywhere," Chuck replied.

"Turn the phone off and take out the battery," Wally instructed. "Walk us through each step." Chuck did as Wally asked. After listening for a while, Wally asked. "Why would our Washington insider take the trouble to give us what their teams are using, and now someone wants to send us off on a wild goose chase?"

"But that's just it, Wally; I think Washington has messed up. Whoever sent us this message gave us the key. The pattern is so simple that it's virtually undetectable. Follow me to the end, and it makes sense."

Chuck went through the three locations where James Gordon's government teams prepared. Chuck pointed out the flaws in the infrastructure with each one. "The Washington group has a high accuracy, but they will miss this one." Chuck moved the tablet and pointed to the map, "I believe the next site he visits will be Muslim, and looking at demographics, accessibility, and all that, this is where he's gonna be. It's right where the text coordinates suggest." Next, Chuck pointed to the northwest side of Dallas. "Here … Irving, Texas. Specifically, he's gonna be at the Islamic Center of Irving. They have a sizable masjid there."

"A what?" one of the Cooleys asked distastefully like someone insulted his momma.

"It means a mosque, where the Muslims do their praying," Chuck replied, motioning with his hands on either side of his head like he was bowing towards Mecca. "I think the government boys are setting up in the wrong places."

Wally scratched the back of his head and pulled the tablet in front of him to study the compelling argument. "Is there any place the government teams are preparing, based on the data, that you think we could rule out?"

Chuck pointed to the map. "For sure, San Antonio. The demographics and population density doesn't fit." He poked his finger on the other side of the map. "If you look at Irving, it's got almost four hundred thousand Muslims …"

"What in hell?" One of the Cooley's cut him off. "Damn, near half a million of those mongrels are in our backyard. You're kidding me?"

"They're right here, and if we don't stop this demon, they'll be taking over," Chuck suggested. "You got all of them Muslims in the surrounding cities, and there's damn near twelve million gullible Christians, too, just waiting to give the demon an audience. So I think he'll go for this." Chuck tapped a firm finger on Irving, Texas.

Wally pulled up one of the chairs, wiped his sticky brow, and took a seat. "Some monkey wrench we've been thrown. It could be a trap to lure us out there, and we get shot to pieces."

"If it was someone wanting to stop us, knowing I've got the phone, then by now, they could have triangulated our location, and we'd all be dead or in jail." Chuck shook his head. "This is a friend. Somebody wants us to finish Christ's work."

"The Lord works in mysterious ways," Garvey said.

Wally studied the data, asking Chuck about layout, buildings, and surroundings. Once they'd exhausted every possibility, Wally took Chuck to one side and whispered in his ear. "I should have never doubted you," he affirmed with a friendly pat. "You're right. If it were a trap, we'd already be dead."

Wally called the room to attention. "Here's what we've decided to do to cover the two most likely locations. The Cooley brothers, Rocky, Bobby, and Steve, will come with me to Irving. We'll set up close by the mosque and be in position sometime tomorrow night. Chuck and Garvey will go to Plano, just in case. Let's say a prayer together so that Jesus Christ our Savior may give us the strength needed to do his bidding."

They gathered around the table, and Wally led the prayer. "Lord Jesus, our true Savior, shed your infinite light of strength on these, your dedicated soldiers. We ask that you forgive all those fooled by this imposter. We ask that you give courage to the hearts of your humble servants. Bless us all, keep us safe. We ask this through Christ, our Lord, Amen."

His words met with a resounding Amen from his team of Christian mercenaries. Another weapons check, and they headed to their respective locations thirty minutes later. Wally insisted they take four different vehicles in case either he or Chuck were recognized, in which case the others might have an opportunity to complete the mission.

Wally left them with his final battle cry: "The world thinks we're just some dumb bunch of southern hicks running barefoot through the backwoods thumping Bibles to our chests, but little do they know – we see the demon for what he is. Now, let us do the Lord's work."

Mr. Grey tapped his pipe on the table's edge, emptying the ash into the murky water. He motioned with his long index finger for the man to approach. He put away his pipe, carefully slid it inside his jacket, and stepped onto the floor. His teeth pleasurably grated together as he listened and slowly rolled his eyes. "Ah, such sweet songs of hope," he hissed with satisfaction. He gazed into the man's pupils with affection and placed a soft hand over his face. "The effort to create you was worth it. Are you ready?"

"I am."

Mr. Grey moved close as if approaching a lover and fixed himself an inch away from the man. He slowly placed his hands around the man's jawline and sweetly kissed either cheek. "My beautiful child. It is time. My old friend upstairs has become careless and complacent. I despise negligence; it's so unnecessary. Very soon, mankind will be deliriously happy, and then it'll be just like the good old days."

The man smiled at the thought. "All this adulation from millions of people I thought would give me a sense of belonging, but I still find myself empty."

Mr. Grey ran his fingers through the man's reddish hair. "That's because God is a liar. There is no finding oneself, inner peace, or happiness. There is no Holy Grail. There's just me and you and the love I give to you." Mr. Grey sighed with satisfaction. "Through me, your emptiness will overflow with the intimacy you deserve."

"I've never had a mother's love before. Will I get …"

"Oh, yes, you will," Mr. Grey assured. "You are so loved, my beautiful boy." Mr. Grey frowned with empathy and gently kissed the man's lips. He smiled adoringly at his creation. "You have my eyes. I know what it's like – all those lives, those voices, those prayers, and nobody to care for you. Finally, you shall have the mother you wish for, and I will be your eternal father." He forcefully pulled down on the man's head and delicately kissed his forehead. "Show them the rapture they so eagerly desire. The pain they bring to you will be brief. Your reward will be eternity with your mother and me."

Mr. Grey turned his creation around and patted him firmly on the rear. "Go now. Shine bright."

CHAPTER TWENTY-SIX

A beautiful early evening blue sky nestled over the bustling suburbs of Irving, Texas. Outside the small hotel on the city's outskirts, nobody paid any attention to the group of men, dressed like laborers, pulling their large bags from the two vehicles and checking in. The men, dressed in jeans, t-shirts, baseball caps, sunglasses, and unshaven faces, lined up to take the three rooms booked under assumed names. Rocky took one of the free apples from the basket by the reception desk, and Steve helped himself to the stale coffee that permeated the air in the tattered lobby.

The journey was uneventful. Wally noticed the heavy police presence closer to the entry points of Dallas. He figured the government agencies were watching for people traveling up to Plano. So he and his team diverted off the freeway and took the longer route. They slipped unnoticed into the city from the west, and as soon as it got dark, they would head to the Islamic center to scope it out.

Chuck provided them with the prayer times and advised Wally that the site closed down at 10:00 pm. The Cooley brothers would take care of the alarm systems while Rocky kept watch. Wally, Steve, and Bobby would enter the mosque to prepare and observe.

They intended to discover, in detail, the physical nature of the mosque, its proximity to main roads, police access, escape routes, visibility to the surrounding area, and, if necessary, how they could defend the site if anything went wrong. In addition, the mosque's proximity to Dallas International Airport accounted for a naturally heavy police presence, something to consider if they had an opportunity to get away from the area.

Wally Radford had long since made his peace with the Lord. He no longer feared death, but he feared for those he'd leave behind. The five men with him, and those heading to Plano, would fight to the very end without the need to be asked.

Three days earlier, Wally had visited the widow of John Waterford in Louisiana, arranging for her to meet him on the Red River trail. It had severely taxed Wally's emotions, and he took no comfort in learning that John had been hiding his terminal cancer diagnosis. John's widow, Nora, told Wally, "John was gonna stay behind, regardless of any silly old cancer. You should know that was his plan." Wally acknowledged that John Waterford was molded from the rock of Saint Peter. "I'm content in knowing he died for our sacred cause," she said. "Wally, you take vengeance on those who believe in the False Prophet. Show the world the serpent who presents them with a ripened orchard. Tell your boys that my prayers are with them." Wally vowed they'd do everything to make John's sacrifice worthwhile.

The team split up, each taking a five-block radius to explore the layout of the streets, checking for road works or anything that presented an obstacle. An hour later, the group of five gathered by the local Walmart next to the 183 Freeway and compared notes. They made revisions to their getaway plan and returned to the Islamic center, waiting for the last car to leave. Once it was deserted, it only took ten minutes to disable the alarms, pick the lock, and get their team inside the mosque. They hid their vehicles behind the main building, out of sight from the main road. The Cooley brothers and Rocky kept watch.

Wally and Steve headed for the central point of the main building. Bobby went around the perimeter walls, checking how best to secure the exits to keep the gathered worshippers under duress when the time came.

"It's a fine-looking building," Steve remarked, looking at the tilework.

Wally didn't want to admit it, but Steve was right; it was an incredible piece of architecture and as beautifully finished on the inside and the outside. "See if you can get up there." He pointed to the balcony. "It should give us eyes on the whole crowd."

Wally spoke via the radio. "Bobby, what do you think about securing the inner doors? How long will it take?"

"Five minutes, six maximum. So long as you guys have your sights on the crowd, and nobody moves."

"Alright, see if you can do it in less than four. We'll need to be quick. The Muslims will think we are here for them and begin to panic – they're a hysterical people anyways."

Steve called down from the upper balcony. "I can see everyone in the main room except anyone directly underneath me."

"We'll get everyone to lay down, throw out their cell phones," Wally replied. "Steve, if anyone moves, you take them out. No warning calls or warning shots. I'll make sure they understand that if they move, they die." He called Rocky on the radio. "Hey, what about their cameras? Do we have full control from one place?"

There was a slight delay before Rocky replied. "Yeah. The gatehouse has full control so that I can watch the parking lots and the internal building."

"Nice." Wally checked his watch. He didn't want to be in there any longer than necessary. Tomorrow they would quietly take over the building at 1:40 in the afternoon. If Chuck's information proved correct, it would give them twenty minutes to secure the people and the building and await the False Prophet's appearance. As soon as Wally was sure they'd killed him, they would lock all the people inside and make their escape. For now, they'd seen all they needed to.

"Okay, rendezvous in the rear lot in three minutes. Make this place look like we were never here." The affirmative responses came back over the radio.

Before Wally headed for the exit, the blinding light forced him to cover his eyes and instinctively he crouched. He assumed a flash grenade had gone off and the police were onto them. It took a couple of seconds before he could see anything. There was no sign of a raid, shouting, screaming, or heavily armed men rushing through the building. "Guys, are you okay?" Wally asked.

Steve hid between the benches on the balcony. "I'm good. What was it?"

"Not the police," Wally said. "Bobby, are you good?"

"Yeah."

"Outside team, are there any police?"

"Negative," Rocky replied. "Just us."

Stand by." Wally instructed. "We have a situation on the inside; hold your ground, stay low."

"Nothing out here," Rocky whispered from the gatehouse.

Wally crept toward where the prayers were offered, breathing fast and hard. He whispered into his mic. "Steve, you got anything?"

Steve slowly moved his head above the balcony's ledge and scanned the large space. Then, he quickly ducked back down. "You ain't gonna believe this. He's here. Sitting by the microphone stand – you're right there," he informed Wally. "He's on his own."

Wally's heart almost leaped into his mouth. There was no time to hang around; as his adrenalin carried him forward, rushing around the corner of the pillared walkway, Wally dropped to one knee, his sidearm pointed ahead at the man in the yellow robe. "Don't move!"

"Wally Radford. I was expecting you."

A shudder slammed through Wally's body. He steadied himself, breathing hard with sweat soaking his skin. Wally inched closer; his gun ready. Wally's eyes darted around so fast they looked like fireflies dancing inside his head. "Keep your hands where I can see them."

The man in yellow smiled at him.

"I'm here to end your games," Wally stammered.

"Do as you must."

Wally's arms shook as he got to within two feet of the demon. He looked closely at the false prophet, and he saw what was behind the reddish eyes that contained faint grey speckles. "Keep 'em up. Steve, get down here!" Wally pressed the mic. "Rocky, any movement outside?"

"Negative. What's going on in there?"

"Never mind. Hold your positions and stand by." Bobby entered through one of the fire exits and rushed alongside Wally. "I'll check to see he's not armed. Cover me." Bobby holstered his handgun and frisked the False Prophet. "He's clear."

"Tie his hands," Wally said. A couple of well-placed shots would have put an immediate end to this, but Wally knew this was a gift from the Lord.

Bobby froze and stared in disbelief at Wally. "Just shoot him!"

"Bobby, secure his hands. He's coming with us."

Bobby cut the cable to the prayer microphone and bound the prophet's hands.

"Wally, what in God's name? Shoot the guy!" a breathless Steve declared.

"God has spoken to me. Let's get him out of here. We'll prove his existence is pure evil."

Steve protested, but Wally shut him down. "We're making a new plan. Bobby, have you got him tight?"

"Yep."

"Okay, let's go." They moved quickly out of the exit. Wally got on the radio. "Be aware! We are bringing a passenger. Rendezvous in one minute."

Wally called Chuck on the prepaid disposable cell. "We got him. Forget going to Plano – turn around and meet me in Wichita Falls. Leave now! We're going to finish it together. Chuck, we have the False Prophet! We have him!"

"Hallelujah!" Chuck salivated. "On our way! Have you killed him already?"

"Not yet. The imposter will die soon enough."

Rocky wiped away evidence of their break-in and set the cameras to start recording in five minutes. He locked the gatehouse door and met with the highly agitated Cooley brothers. Both had their guns drawn and were gibbering like they'd learned a new language. Wally ignored the stunned observers and bundled the False Prophet into the back of the vehicle. "God's divine intervention! Back to the hotel to collect our gear, and we're heading west. God is with us; now move!"

"Wally, we oughta shoot him dead now," Rocky suggested.

"He isn't supposed to be here until 2:00 pm Central time tomorrow. Then the eyes of the world will await the beast. We'll provide a fitting finale. Did you wipe the security tapes?"

"Yeah, but …"

"But nothing – at 2:00 Central time, he will die in front of the world."

The highly animated group wanted to put a bullet in the False Prophet's head and be done with it. Instead, Steve told them, "Wally brought us this far. We go with him and go with God to the end."

At the hotel, they were in and out in ten minutes. Wally ordered them to head northwest on the 287 and then west for Groom on Interstate 40. He transferred the prophet into the trunk of Bobby's vehicle, telling the group he would stop in Wichita Falls and pick up a couple of things while the rest of them headed for Groom, Texas. "When we get there, we'll deliver God's justice," Wally preached.

Carrie awoke under the strain of the disturbingly detailed dream. She'd seen millions upon millions of people crying and a dark fear gripping the globe threatening permanence. She disliked the contrast compared to her recent euphoric dreams.

The bedside phone rang. "Hello?"

The voice at the end of the line was electronic. "This is General Salah. I am using one of your laptop translators to speak. Can you hear me?"

"I hear you." She sat bolt upright. "It's 6 am. Are you okay?"

"I need to talk with you. You know why. Allah has made it so that we share the same visions."

Carrie started to pull on some jeans. "Can you come down here?"

"I will be there in five minutes." The General slipped down the back stairs to her floor.

Carrie answered the door, still trying to make her thick hair neat. She gestured for the General to come in. He nodded and, in a thick accent, said, "Hello." She responded, "As-salam alaykom." It brought a faint smile to his stout lips.

The General opened the laptop and pushed his face close to the mic. "Since I first met the prophet, he has shown me signs that have come true. I saw the world mourning his death. You saw it, too."

"I did. How do you know?"

"You were also in my dream," he said. "I fear the Prophet is lost, like a piece of my soul is cut away."

"Lost, how?" she asked.

"I don't know," he replied with a saddened expression. "The Prophet told me, when he first came to Medina, that I would meet you – the woman who sees the future, and you would help us find him. He also instructed me that I must place him beside the tomb of Muhammad in Medina. He spoke those words to me. So you are here, and I am here."

Carrie held her breath as he spoke. She leaned to the mic so that their heads almost touched. The General's semi-sweet body odor was strong, something unfamiliar but evocative. Carrie didn't speak, and she looked into his large brown eyes. They silently held each other's attention. Then, a slight movement of his head spurred her to say, "When Jesus appeared in Washington Cathedral, he told me I'd be speaking a new language to people I've never met." The shared recognition pulsed between them.

"I have faith in God's plan," she muttered. Her words carried a heaviness that barely spilled from her lips. She tried to smile at the fierce General, but her face scrunched tight, and her gaze narrowed. "I'm not sure what it means."

General Salah's sharp gaze showed the dilation of his intense pupils. He reached out, patting her shoulder. "We'll find a way." The general leaned back into the mic. "I don't believe he will come to the sites we've identified. Abdul Aziz told me to trust in God. Our dreams confirmed it. Can you look at other possibilities – something unusual?"

"I'll get my laptop." Carrie became increasingly aware of his strong presence. Up close, his brown eyes were soft, almost pleading, but his firm jawline matched the sternness of his gaze. His presence commanded the warrior beneath his khaki shirt, and his proximity unnerved her. She wanted to give him some comfort, some words, or a touch. She caught herself staring, so she rose sharply and switched on the little coffee maker. She held a cup towards the General, to which he graciously nodded, and they ran through the options. Carrie contacted Theo's team, asking for anything unusual reported from a place of worship in Texas.

Jessica was the one holding the fort at headquarters. "I'll get back to you after scanning police reports, and I'll forward the results."

General Salah studied the first handful of reports while Carrie worked directly with Jessica to narrow the search criteria. The General focused on a broken window at a church in Austin, a small fire at a rural church in Cumby, some stolen chalices at a church in Harper, and a break-in at the Islamic center in Irving. The General took a closer look at the last one. The early morning security guard reported someone broke in, wiped their videotapes clean, and left again. There was no sign of any damage or theft. The guard only noticed it as an issue because he always left his chair facing east toward Mecca and had found it facing the opposite way. He was the last one out and the first one in as his shift changed. He looked at the video footage, fully expecting to see the mosque being robbed, but instead, there was nothing except three hours of recordings wiped blank. The only indication someone went inside was that the cable for the microphone in the main prayer room was cut, and a piece of it was missing. All doors were locked and secure. The police came out, but with nothing missing nor any real damage, nobody pursued it. General Salah searched the internet for the center's details and phoned the mosque. "This must be something. The other reports are thievery and drunken childishness. Nobody breaks in for no reason," the General theorized.

Carrie liked the simplicity of his perspective.

He called the mosque and found one of the scholars who spoke Arabic. The General asked him about the break-in. After twenty minutes of small talk, General Salah thanked the cleric and wished him a blessed day. Using the translator, he told Carrie. "This is the place. Somebody took the time to break in, pick the locks, and then close the building and gates as though nothing had happened. There is a determined method to this. Can your team look at the surveillance from nearby buildings? There's a police training academy next door; they must have cameras."

"Are you sure? But why?"

"I cannot explain in words." He touched a large hand over his heart. "It is here. In my dream, I saw the crescent moon with the star. It is over the masjid."

Carrie explained to Jessica what they were looking for. It only took her a few minutes to return the call. "Hey, Carrie, it's me. I looked at the layout of the Islamic center and checked their system. Security was right that someone wiped a bunch of their footage. However, the Islamic center has a new extension with a bookstore attached to the back of the mosque. It has its own CCTV system – newly installed last year. The recordings are held on a separate server from the gatehouse. I'm sending you a link to access it right now. Take a close look at 11:30 last night. You can see the break-in."

"Jessica, you're awesome!"

"I know," came the reply.

Carrie and the General accessed the link. "Here it is," Carrie pointed. "Three guys are picking the lock at the back of the mosque, just like you said." The men wore masks and gloves. General Salah pointed out the speed at which they entered the building, suggesting a level of expertise. "They do not appear to carry explosives or anything with intent to destroy." After fast-forwarding for a bit, Carrie stopped at the General's request to go back. They observed the cameras picking up an intense light coming from the direction of the mosque. The camera angle showed the surge in the brightness coming from the door where the men had broken in.

"It is him, the prophet. God's light!" the General said.

"Oh, my goodness. You're right." Carrie held a hand over her heart. She continued to fast forward until they saw the first men emerge from the back door.

General Salah pointed. "The first man carries a handgun." They watched the rest of the security tape unfold. "The first man is talking into a mic – looks like they're waiting for a confirmation until it's clear to move." There was a short gap, and then the next man emerged, followed by a third. The General and Carrie jumped from their seats, witnessing the fourth man in the bright yellow robe, with his familiar long red hair and matching short-cropped beard. "Allah help us. They have the prophet!" The General cried out. "His hands are bound behind his back!"

"The cable from the speaker system!" Carrie suggested. She ran around the bed, called James Gordon, told him what they were looking at, and sent him the link. "Irving, Texas," she cried out. "We are in the wrong place. James, I'm sorry!"

"I'll contact Theo. Then, I'll get everyone in the meeting room," James informed them.

Carrie called Mo to come right away.

When James, Theo, and Mo watched the footage, they listened as General Salah explained that they should source all nearby footage in the area and see if they could track the movement of the vehicles. The car headlight's movements suggested three vehicles. Theo relayed instructions to his team, making sure anyone in bed, at home, or out sick got themselves online and helping to pull what he needed. Nobody had any idea how or why the prophet would go to Irving.

"It was a day early," Mo said, scratching at his chin.

Carrie didn't say it, but she felt personally responsible for not having Irving as an option.

James called Senator Garofalo, and alerts were put on all freeways and roads in the Irving area.

Carrie explained, "The footage is seven hours old; you'll need alerts widely spread."

Road checks on major freeways yielded nothing. It took two hours before they found footage from the small hotel in Irving that showed the six men and the prophet leaving in the middle of the night.

James Gordon dispatched his team to secure evidence from the hotel. They found internal footage showing Wally Radford and five unidentified men entering the hotel and a few minutes later checking out before midnight. Theo spoke directly with the hotel and learned the men were supposed to be there for two nights. They checked out early, paid in cash, and said their work had taken them somewhere else.

James kept all the teams in Texas on standby. "Theo, have we got anything from the freeway cameras?"

"Not yet. Working on it now." His phone rang. "Hold on," he said. "Thanks, Jessica! Keep looking." Theo pulled his laptop close. "Coming up on the screen now. Jessica found the three vehicles getting gas in Melody Hills, just north of Fort Worth. They took I-35 north at 1:00 am this morning. That's the last sighting we have of them. The I-35 goes up through Denton and eventually to Oklahoma City."

"Radford has a ministry in Oklahoma City. He also has one in Fort Smith, over in Arkansas. So are they heading back to a place they know?" James added.

"You think for ransom?" Mo asked and stopped himself. "Why not just kill him; they tried it in Saudi Arabia."

"I doubt it's for ransom," Carrie shrugged.

James nodded toward Theo. "Get some teams at those locations and have eyes on those routes so that we can intercept these vehicles. Put up more roadblocks and search every damn vehicle."

One of Theo's team shouted across the room. "Hey, guys, take a look at this. When they stopped to get gas, they switched the prophet from one car to another. They put him in the trunk of the silver-colored Chevy."

"It doesn't make sense," Mo persisted. "Radford has the man in his possession that he went to Saudi Arabia to try to kill. Where the hell is the other guy, Chuck Ramsey? Why would they go to all that trouble only to take him alive?"

"I don't know. Ramsey could be used as a decoy somewhere else. We need to find him, too," Carrie said.

"Radford is highly recognizable, and he knows we're looking for him, so if he gets pulled, he doesn't want his plan to fall apart. We need to know who these other guys are!" James shouted around the room. "Put out an alert for the kidnapping, but don't say it's the prophet Jesus, or we'll have a million cars out on the damn roads. I want every cop in Texas looking for those vehicles."

"We run the risk they might panic, and the Prophet gets killed," Mo shouted.

"We have no choice," James suggested. "He may already be dead. They can finish him at any given moment."

Carrie was tired of looking at screens and endless data streams. "Hang on a second. We know they have the prophet, but how in the hell did they know where he'd be? Even we didn't guess Irving, Texas … and a day early! It wasn't on any shortlist we ever had. So how did they get it right?"

"Maybe they got lucky," James said.

Carrie's face turned crimson, and she found her fists clenching tight. "I'm not being funny, but a preacher and his southern buddies didn't just get lucky. They were in the right place at exactly the right time. They have help, and from a source even we couldn't get to." She gave James an accusatory stare.

His grimace showed his dislike for her hostility. "All our resources are at the three sites you recommended. So why would we be looking elsewhere or telling some homegrown radical extremists where to find the man claiming to save the world? And how could we know? We're using your damned data!"

"Why indeed?" Carrie inferred.

"How about we make better predictions and find the people we're looking for. We have to preserve the safety of the American people!" James snapped.

His stinging rebuke alerted the rest of the office. He became aware of the elongated pause and added, "Everyone, do your fucking job! Now!"

Theo pulled up a digital map. "Look at places seven hours away from Irving and presume they're not stopping for a leisurely breakfast at Denny's along the way. Those guys could already be in Oklahoma City or Arkansas by now. We've got the alerts going out to those places and all across northwest Texas."

Mo called Carrie off to one side and squared up to her reddened face. "Fuck James. Ignore him. You've brought us all this far. Focus on what we need to do. Something's wrong with this whole picture. Radford and Ramsey must have something else in mind, or they would have executed him inside the Irving mosque. These guys are hardcore – they want to make a statement," he suggested.

Carrie forced herself to push aside her urge to pounce on James Gordon and rip out his eyeballs. "You're right, but what?" she agreed, furiously tapping the sides of her head with her fingers. She began to pace in a small circle. "Why risk getting caught with the world's most recognizable face in the trunk of your car?"

Mo perched himself on a chair in the corner of the room and stared blankly as she passed by every few seconds. Carrie lightly clapped her hands together to help stimulate some thoughts. "They're religious fanatics – we know this. If you were going to make a statement, and now you have the prophet in your hands – what would you do?"

"Something of Biblical proportions!" Mo snapped his fingers, and his eyes expanded.

"Exactly!" she replied, "Radford believes he's protecting Christianity. If they wipe out their biggest threat, then they'll become martyrs. A win for Christianity as they see it."

"Radford is looking for martyrdom! But what's the delivery method and where?"

Carrie tapped the soles of her feet on the carpet to support the frantic pace at which her mind worked. "Let's walk through what else we know: Jesus appears to the world at 3:00 pm Eastern time. Eighty percent of the global population will be glued to TVs or digital devices. Radford and Ramsey know that. Nobody will be visiting theme parks, cinemas, or whatever else you can think of.

"If you're going to do something crazy, then tomorrow afternoon is the perfect time. Jesus told us he'd be laid to rest next to his brother Muhammad." She couldn't stop her eyes filling with tears at the dreadful thought of losing the prophet.

Mo rubbed her arm as she passed him by. "You're right. Like executing someone outside a church, or a video cutting off somebody's head."

"Exactly that. Although I wouldn't use my church because that would mean it would be shut down forever, making my other places of business a target. They'll stay away from their network – plus which, they know we're watching those places. They won't go home – they can't. We shouldn't waste our time looking at Radford's ministries," Carrie said. She stopped pacing and poked her finger into Mo's chest. "I'd use someone else's place of worship that had meaning to me. It has to be Christian to get the impact they're looking for."

"Yes – a place of religious significance. Something to make people sit up and take notice." Mo sprang out of his seat, paced a few feet, and returned. "They'd want to show their faith is beyond reproach, even if it gets them all killed. We need some resources to find a good place for an execution. You and I can provide some key indicators to initiate the search."

"I missed this one completely. I should have seen it!" she croaked, and her head dipped toward the floor. People in the next office were too busy tapping at their keyboards to notice her and Mo.

Mo placed a hand on Carrie's shoulder. "If it weren't for you, millions of people would have been at risk. You've done an amazing job second-guessing stuff. Nobody else could have come close to getting it right. You can't be expected to be a hundred percent accurate. Nobody except you thinks that. You've brought us here – take us the last few miles. C'mon, we need you." He pulled at her arm.

"What if I can't," she sniffed, harshly wiping her face, and removing the salty distraction with her sleeve. She turned her back to the others, not wishing to appear like she couldn't handle it, especially not wanting General Salah to see her crying.

Mo reminded her, "You're the only one who can find out where they've taken him. Nobody else, just you."

"No pressure then," she groaned.

"Not unless you consider God's final messenger or the fate of mankind as pressure," he succinctly replied. Mo pointed the way to the arguing crowd across the other side of the office. "They don't know where to begin. Move," he ordered.

Carrie took a deep breath, wiped her face, straightened her skirt, and headed in Theo's direction. She whispered to Mo from the side of her mouth. "I hope we find him in time."

Carrie explained to James and Theo, telling them to eliminate any place connected to Wally Radford. "He's too smart and too fixated to walk into a trap of his own making. Find something big, a church, a cathedral, or something like that. They want to make a statement." Carrie and Mo set the parameters, and Theo's team set to work on finding the place of intended execution.

CHAPTER TWENTY-SEVEN

Wally Radford's team took shifts throughout the day to watch the small, steady trickle of visitors to the Cross of Our Lord Jesus Christ. The small town of Groom in west Texas saw regular groups of curious onlookers touring the local attraction. Set on a small hill just outside the town, a towering steel cross stood two hundred feet high that could be seen for miles across the flat landscape. The cross shimmered in the sunlight and dominated the skyline. At the base of the gigantic symbol ran a circular walkway, where a dozen bronze sculptures represented the journey of Christ through the stages of the crucifixion. Each scene was life-sized and carefully crafted in fine detail to represent agony, betrayal, and sacrifice. Alongside was a small chapel and a well-stocked gift store. At the base of the steel cross, on a slight concrete rise, sat three life-sized crosses, showing the crucified figures of Jesus Christ and the two condemned criminals next to him. The shading of the bronze figures heightened the portrayal of agony, with the perpetual pain unavoidable to the gaze.

Groom was set in the middle of farmland, forty miles east of Amarillo, and consisted of only a thousand residents. Most of them went about their daily business and paid no attention to those taking photos at the attraction. Wally's guys alternated turns to the local grill and blended with other visitors. They took pictures of each other at the site, enjoying its splendor.

The town's residents would soon be indoors, fixed on their TV sets. These were good Christian people, and at 2:00 pm Central time, they expected to see miracles. Wally understood their desire, although he pitied their blindness. He and his men would show the true word of Christ in God's name. They'd begin their work early to ensure they were ready for the 2:00 pm Central deadline.

They'd stopped in Wichita Falls earlier in the day and purchased a small extendable ladder, ropes, barbed wire, cuts of 2x4 timber, paint, and a nail gun. Wally sent Bobby to another store to pay cash for a digital video camera so that they could provide a fitting end to the masquerade. Steve also paid cash for an air card to live stream the end of the False Prophet. After that, it was time to set the record straight with their live broadcast.

Rocky's voice came over the radio. "The last car of visitors just left the parking lot – it's just us. The lady in the gift store says she's closing up and will be back around 4:00 this afternoon. So we told her we don't need anything, and we'd be forming a prayer circle."

"Bring the asset over and let's get this done," Wally ordered.

The eight men stood in the empty lot and looked up at the majestic steel cross. "This is what it's all about. Serving a higher purpose, no matter what the cost to ourselves."

They stood beside the three life-sized crosses and joined hands to form a circle. "Our blessed Lord Jesus Christ, our true Savior, Son of Almighty God; we die here today for God's glory and pray you will grant us a seat with you for all eternity. In Christ, our Lord, Amen."

"Amen." They chorused.

Wally declared. "God has spoken through me. If the demon wants to be like our Savior Jesus Christ, we'll grant him that experience." The faces of his men showed their understanding.

"Every cop and government agent will come for us. We won't make it out of Texas," Garvey observed.

Wally solemnly nodded. "This is our final destination as mortal souls."

"We'll go down with a fight," Chuck said, patting the pistol strapped to his body.

"If any man doesn't have the stomach for this, he can leave now without judgment." Wally waited. They all remained steadfast. "Get the camera ready and tell me when you have it live on the internet. Don't show any part of the big cross, or it'll bring every cop within a hundred miles. And, put on your masks."

Steve and the others followed suit. "Okay, guys, you heard the man. Let's go!"

The group split up, unloading the tools from Wally's vehicle, while the Cooleys marched the False Prophet towards Wally.

"I got him," said Bobby.

The Cooleys headed to assist with constructing the makeshift cross.

191

Jesus looked at Wally Radford and Chuck Ramsey with deep sadness. "Thank you for serving a higher purpose."

Without warning, Chuck lashed out and smashed his fist into the face of Jesus, sending a spurt of blood onto the concrete. It took Wally by surprise. He instinctively stepped between the enraged Chuck and the False Prophet.

"Easy, brother, easy," he said while preventing Chuck from taking another shot.

Jesus spat the blood from his mouth to the floor and raised his head. He smiled at them. "My Father sent me to bring unity. You will play your part. I forgive you for what you're about to do."

"Screw you!" Chuck snarled as Wally held him back.

"My Father has set forth my destiny, not the hand of man," Jesus replied.

"Let's see how forgiving you are when you're begging for your life!" Chuck snarled, with spit flying from his angry mouth.

Wally glared at the demon. "Your magic tricks won't save you."

"The magic is yet to happen," Jesus replied.

Wally disbelievingly snorted, "You're a fool."

He nodded towards Bobby. "Strip him of that robe. I want no doubt about his death." Wally pushed Chuck away. "Come with me, my friend. We need a special sign for a special occasion."

Carrie glanced outside. Six army helicopters waited on the open grounds of the hotel. The outskirts of Dallas hadn't seen this level of government activity since the Kennedy assassination. Twenty of their best government agents and four dozen Marines waited on the patio, sipping coffee, checking weapons, and carrying enough arms to invade a small country.

Mo relayed messages through Jessica and her team, while Carrie did the same via Theo. Communications flowed back and forth faster than ever before – so many people talking, shouting, passing messages, running across the room, talking on cell phones, making notes, typing on keyboards, and everything channeled by James Gordon. Yet, James somehow found time to pacify the numerous incoming calls from Washington.

It was 1:45 pm in Texas, only fifteen minutes away from when everyone expected the Prophet to make his daily appearance. Carrie prayed that everything would come together, and they'd find the New Age Prophet. Time cruelly ticked by. The number of religious sites throughout Texas meant that narrowing the field of possibilities was excruciating.

Carrie reminded the research teams. "Look for something old or significant! Leave the little chapels and churches." She tried to hide the desperation in her voice.

"Keep going!" Theo shouted encouragingly to his exhausted team. "We'll find them!"

Mo searched the internet, and General Salah used the translator to pinpoint a target as more agonizing minutes slipped by.

Theo raised his fist in the air: "Just got this from Jessica!" They assembled around his screen. "Facial recognition mining sent us this – Home Depot from Wichita Falls, in west Texas. When they opened right at 6:00 am, Wally Radford and one of the other men from the hotel, making a cash purchase."

He turned his head and shouted, "Jessica – what items?"

"Gimme one minute!" she shouted back.

Theo continued. "Cameras show them loading all their stuff into two cars and heading northwesterly. It's a lot of shit they got there. Still no names on these other guys – c'mon, you guys, we need names!"

"Sent you the list of items," Jessica called across the room.

Theo rewound the video and froze it on the two carts they pushed across the parking lot. "Timber, nail-gun, hammers, rope, and stepladders."

"Are they going to barricade themselves somewhere and make a last stand?" James speculated.

Carrie exchanged a knowing glance with the General. "They're going to crucify him!"

"What? Are you kidding me?" James barked.

Carrie held out her hands in front of her. "It's the embodiment of Christian belief."

"These guys are frickin' nuts!" Mo agonized.

"They headed west on the I-40," Jessica added.

General Salah listened carefully to the translations through his earpiece. He pulled up the history of what he'd studied and found the place he recalled wasn't too far from Wichita Falls. "Here! Take a look at this!" he shouted into the mic.

The team converged around him. He used Google Maps to show Groom, Texas. He spoke slowly and deliberately into the mic. "This is a nineteen-story-high cross by the highway. The Cross of Our Lord Jesus Christ." He angled the screen so that they could see. "This is significant, yes? It is two hundred miles northwest of Wichita Falls. It is next to the I-40 freeway."

Mo leaned on the General's shoulder. "He's got it. That's it! Do we have any eyes in that area?"

"On it!" Theo replied.

Carrie squeezed the General's shoulders. "He's right!' He tapped his warm fingers on the back of her hand.

James was already on his phone. "Choppers in the air in less than two minutes." He pointed at Carrie, Mo, and the General. "Come on! Everybody … bring your gear with you; we're going!"

CHAPTER TWENTY-EIGHT

Wally had the Cooley brothers angle the wooden cross beam at forty-five degrees. The final construction appeared more like a winged wooden bird. "The False Prophet isn't worthy of the pure cross. The different angle will ensure a quicker death," he explained.

Chuck and Bobby tied the false Prophet's hands, arms, and legs to the frame. Next, the Cooleys and Rocky prepared the ropes beneath the 15 ft bronze statue that would be used to raise the demon off the ground. Rocky signaled Chuck that they were ready. Wally approached, wearing a thick pair of specially made gloves for dealing with the barbed wire that he'd pre-cut into smaller pieces and then wrapped to form a crown. Chuck smiled. "A fitting crown for a false king."

Steve secured the last rope around the False Prophet's arms; each piece lashed tightly with no room to maneuver. "Once we get him up, he ain't going nowhere. You want this yet?" he asked, holding up the nail gun.

"Not yet," Wally replied. "I'll give the signal." He radioed Garvey. "What you got, Eagle Eyes?"

Garvey scanned the horizon through the binoculars. "Not another living soul within sight. Barely a car on the freeway."

"Good." Wally checked the time. "Eight minutes before 2:00. The world's waiting to see something spectacular – let's not disappoint them. Make sure you keep your ski masks on." He looked over at Steve. "Let me know when you're ready to start broadcasting. YouTube, Facebook, and whatever else you got."

"Ready in one minute," Steve responded.

"Only start when I say go. Guys – don't use anyone's name. God bless all of you."

"Amen," came the resounding response.

Wally got on one knee next to the man, bound helplessly to the cross. "Let's see if your God comes to save you."

"My reward is already assured. Can you say the same?" Jesus asked.

Wally jammed the coil of barbed wire onto Jesus' skull. The prophet screamed in agony as the spikes punctured fine holes, causing him to shake his head in a vain attempt to dislodge it. Chuck and Bobby laughed at the False Prophet's cries. The Cooleys and Rocky stopped what they were doing to watch.

Streams of blood trickled down the Prophet's face.

"Any regrets?" Wally sarcastically remarked. Jesus moaned in agony.

Wally signaled a thumbs-up to Steve, and the live streaming began. Wally secured his mask, said a silent prayer, checked to confirm it was two minutes to 2:00, faced the camera, and began his opening comments. "The world will see this False Prophet for what he really is. Jesus Christ, our Savior, has tasked these good men and me to bring this demon to justice. There's only ever been one Son of God – there will only ever be one Son of God … this is not him," Wally pointed to the figure tied to the cross.

Steve moved the camera back to capture Wally and the writhing figure on the ground.

Wally Radford delivered sermons as good as any preacher and knowing this would be his last; he would make it count. "This False Prophet mocks God. Feel no pity for him – this creature is in league with pure evil."

Wally walked around the wooden cross and picked up the nail gun. "This demon, this deceiver, wishes to be like Our Lord and Savior. This is a vile creature. No miracle can save him. His words are lies."

Wally crouched, took a tight hold of Jesus' wrist and fired a nail through the false prophet's right palm. Jesus groaned loudly and his body arched upward, but he could do nothing as the ropes and nail held him firm.

Wally marched to the other side and repeated the same, nailing the left hand into the structure. "This vile spawn of Satan came to perform the devil's work!"

Wally moved to Jesus' feet and fired two nails above the metatarsals, causing shrill screams from Jesus, who called out in a foreign language.

Wally turned to face the camera. "These are the cries of hell and damnation … remember them. This is no prophet."

Wally gave the signal, and his guys pulled on the ropes from behind the bronze statue. Slowly the wooden cross rose, along with Jesus. The Prophet rapidly gasped, bloodied spit flying from his open mouth and screaming in agony. His rib cage heaved as he fought to control his air intake, and blood poured from the open wounds through his hands and feet. Once he was hoisted in the air, the sun's rays caught the barbed wire crown, sending shards of light in all directions. Wally's team secured the ropes. Chuck, Bobby, and the Cooleys walked to the front of the cross to form a semi-circle. Rocky tied the final knot and joined them.

Chuck eyed the swiftly advancing dark weather front.

Wally beckoned Steve to point the camera to the five heavily armed men standing before the cross of the true Christ as they witnessed the demise of the False Prophet.

Pride swelled inside Wally, utterly sure that he had fulfilled his true purpose. The semi-naked demon jabbered in some devilish tongue. Wally showed no fear.

He looked up at the skies. Swirls of dark clouds rapidly formed overhead, squeezing away the natural sunlight. Wally raised his battle cry to all true believers. "Lord Jesus, we thank you for allowing us to see through the veil of evil and hear beyond the cries of this self-indulgent devil's creation. We will not stray from the path of righteousness." He unclipped his automatic and pulled the carbine rifle from his shoulder. "Let the hordes of evil come! Bring them all!" He brandished the weapons.

Aboard the second helicopter, James Gordon alerted the team. "This is from our communication techs in Washington – it's live. Not pretty," he groaned.

The team accessed the link, and a chorus of disgust resounded in the back of the helicopter. The New Age Prophet helplessly hung from the make-shift cross, blood trickling from every part of him. The Prophet's stillness indicated his poor condition.

Theo confirmed. "Live footage. We've zoomed in and can see he's breathing – he's alive." The announcement brought cheers from the armed troops and security teams.

"How many people are watching?" James asked.

"Over three hundred thousand and growing fast. As soon as the media gets it, it'll explode."

"Is there any way we can cut the feed?" James asked.

"They're streaming over six different mediums, including foreign networks. We can't shut it down. It's too late," Theo replied.

Carrie watched the split views that Jessica provided. "Oh, my God, they nailed him to it!" she moaned, as though she felt the pain in her own body. Guilt grabbed her dry throat as though powerful fingers were squeezing it. She endlessly thought about her inability to predict the right location, feeling as though she might as well have nailed him there herself.

"God help him," Mo muttered as he chewed on his knuckles.

General Salah nudged Carrie and pointed at the weaponry on the ground next to the masked men. He pointed for her to alert James Gordon. "James, they've got weapons next to their feet," Carrie called.

"Theo, can you get in closer?"

"Coming to you in ten seconds."

James observed, "Sniper rifles, automatics, and that's just what we can see. The ground teams need to be ready for a firefight. These guys are making their last stand."

Mo watched a review of Wally Radford's speech. "This is it. Martyrdom."

James radioed the pilots. "How long until we get there?"

"Forty-five minutes. Local weather shows a massive storm coming in."

James screamed, "We need to go over or under any weather … we can't slow down!"

"Copy that."

Wally Radford felt inspired by God's command. He dreamed of one day having this kind of moment. Then, the world would remember his name. But, more than that, he hoped God would not forget him. Steve indicated over one million viewers. At two minutes past 2:00, the word spread quickly.

"The Bible tells us an eye for an eye is God's command. The demon will bear witness that evil cannot lure us away from God's grace." Wally was free from other worries despite his inevitable death as he poured forth combinations of all the most fantastic inspirational phrases he had used over the years.

Once satisfied that his message was clear, he joined his friends to watch the life draining from the False Prophet. Wally prayed, "Thank you, God, for granting me this opportunity. I pray that Cheryl and I will reunite with you and serve you for all time."

Wally had no idea Cheryl was on her knees, watching live and crying uncontrollably, knowing that her brave husband would be dead within the hour.

Wally's attention was caught as Jesus stopped whimpering, and the False Prophet's head dipped onto his chest. Blood steadily oozed from his wounds, further weakening him.

"The demon is coming to an end. Praise the Lord!" Chuck observed.

Overhead the dark clouds covered the entire sky. A sudden crash of thunder rolled loud and long; the sonic boom's strength rattled the ground. Wally's men stood firm under the deteriorating thick, blackening sky.

"Steady boys – the devil's playing with our resolve. God loves us," Wally announced.

Rocky asked. "Is he dead yet?"

Without hesitation, Chuck aimed the nail gun and fired a nail into the right side of Jesus' abdomen. He reared his head, crying aloud.

"I guess not," Chuck casually observed.

Jesus strained to keep his head upright and looked down at the group in ski masks. He tilted his head to the man at the end and focused on Wally. "My Master thanks you, as do I."

Wally didn't know why those words profoundly touched him. He stepped forward as if some invisible force were pulling him closer to the foot of the cross. He removed his ski mask and stared into the face of the man he'd crucified. He studied the man's eyes as the thunder boomed for several ear-shattering seconds. "Those eyes … I've seen them before."

Wally's team anxiously observed, unable to understand why he had revealed himself.

They looked around for the lightning, but nothing came. Standing a few feet away from a 200 ft. metal cross was the last place to be in an electric storm. Chuck aimed again with the nail gun, but Bobby pulled his arm down and shook his head. Chuck unhappily tossed the nail gun onto the concrete.

Wally was surprised by his sudden remorse. He signaled to Steve that it was okay to capture his face on the video. "They'll be coming, boys. Take your positions." The Cooley brothers sprinted away, carrying their high-powered rifles over the grass, and set up facing the road that arched in from the freeway. Chuck took his M4 carbine and Bobby to the opposite side. Rocky turned and jogged to his position. The rumbling from the tormented skies angrily sounded.

Jesus tilted his head towards Wally. "Mankind's abandonment of God has diminished his divine power," he weakly suggested. His voice barely had enough strength for Wally to hear, and the harsh breeze kept their conversation from being picked up on the live broadcast. "Even you have been deceived."

The Prophet coughed hard as the pain ravaged his body. "I am merely a messenger … a messenger from my Father."

The thunder rolled hard, and then forked lightning crashed on the open plains. Brilliant white streaks snapped angrily, like the flashing jaws of a mythical beast. For miles around, the lightning pulverized the earth. Then, to Wally's immediate right, the colossal steel cross took a direct hit, sending sparks flying hundreds of feet into the darkened air.

The cacophony of noise continued. Wally looked at the False Prophet, and they exchanged a long stare. Then Wally pointed his sidearm at the demon.

The False Prophet's lips curled upward. "God was once great."

"What?" Wally cupped a hand over his ear. Surely, he meant God is great – the False Prophet's signature sign-on and sign-off. "What did you say?" Wally screamed.

The crucified man's head dipped back into his chest; his ribcage barely moved.

"What do you mean?" Wally demanded.

No response came from the False Prophet – only faint laughter on the swirling breeze. Wally whipped around to find the source. Nobody was there. He wasn't dreaming. Laughter surrounded him. "Show yourself," Wally cursed as he spun in circles, pointing his sidearm. Whispers inside the breeze goaded Wally, telling him he was deceived.

Wally radioed his faithful friends, "Be ready. The devil is here!"

The noise inside the helicopter, combined with the powerful storm, made it impossible to hear the words exchanged between the Prophet and Wally Radford. "We're not going to make it in time," Carrie called out. "He's losing too much blood. He told us he was flesh and blood." The shiny metal of the nail sticking from his side made her want to vomit. "How could they do this? Please, God, let him live," she openly prayed.

Theo announced. "We've got a drone overhead. It might not last in the storm. It's on your screen, marked SKYLARK479,"

They all switched over to get the view from the drone. It was overhead, a mile off the ground. The image flickered, and resolution stuttered through the raging storm.

General Salah quickly made his assessment, shouting into his mic. "They have a kill zone at the entrance. Do not let your police enter. Come in from the other sides," he advised.

200

James Gordon ordered the local authorities to stay back with at least a one-mile perimeter; no sirens or alarms to be used. "How long, Captain?" James asked.

"Twenty minutes," came the reply.

"It'll be too late. They have to go in now," Carrie shouted at James.

James shook his head, refusing to give the order. "It's certain death … No!"

Theo looked at the data coming from the live feeds. "It's officially global. It's everywhere. The whole planet is watching!"

"James! Please?" Carrie implored him.

James shook his head. "We can't order the local police into a slaughter. We wait."

"We can't wait!" She screamed at him.

James gave Carrie a dirty look and focused back on the live feed.

CHAPTER TWENTY-NINE

Steve followed Wally's sly hand signal and mounted the camera on the tripod.

Wally heard the light whispers passing by his ears. He whipped his head around, pointing his gun at nothing. He briefly looked at the dying figure hung above him. Wally pulled the small Bible from his back pocket and stood tall, holding it over his heart. "I am the way, the truth, and the life. This is our path to salvation," he shouted and held the book up high, expecting to see the crucified demon recoil. Instead, the man's eyelids flickered open, and his dulled gray speckled eyes laughingly mocked the furious Wally.

The False Prophet breathed in fits. "You've saved no one."

Thank you, came the whisper in the wind. Wally spun around, confused. The words were as clear as his own. "Who are you?" he growled at the man above him.

There was no reply from the man called Jesus.

Snickering jibes filled Wally's head, yet the crucified man's lips were shut. The cackling danced around him. *Thank you,* the invisible voice repeated.

Wally held out his Bible. "I am the soldier of Christ. You cannot defeat me!"

Before he could utter further defiance, a lightning bolt struck the top of the giant metal cross with such a crack that Wally's eardrums almost blew apart. He instinctively cowered. Then, another strike hit squarely between the vertical and horizontal intersections. The ferocious thwack produced the whining strain of metal. Wally dared to look up, seeing the giant cross split apart. The shriek of tearing steel grew until the vertical section ripped in half and the cross was split cleanly in two.

Wally and his team danced on their feet, waiting to see which way each side would fall. Two hundred feet of metal screamed along with the thunder as each side plunged in opposite directions, crashing to the dirt and violently shaking the earth. Wally came out from under the hands he'd wrapped over his head to see two dust clouds rising fifty feet in the air. Voices quickly came over the radio as each man confirmed he was alive.

Wally saw a flash of someone skulking under the life-sized cross where he'd crucified the False Prophet. Thunder and lightning crashed through the air and streaking white bolts struck ground. Wally's team reorganized their defenses around the twisted tons of metal wreckage.

"Who's there?" Wally glimpsed a man in a light gray suit. Wally slipped between the bronze statues to get a better look, but there was no sign of anyone. He shook his head and drilled a finger in each ear in the hopes of clearing them.

Another glimpse, this time from the opposite side, of the same slender man, with long, dark hair. "Show yourself," Wally demanded, his gun readied.

Wally heard the whispers; *I have you now – you're mine.* Wally took a knee, aimed forward, rolled over twice, and came upright on the other side of the cross, ready to fire. *Cheryl too;* the voice hissed. Malicious intentions cackled a vile chorus that echoed inside his head. The winds increased, blowing Wally's thin hair over his scalp and snatched his breath as flashes of forked lightning pierced the ground on all sides.

God loves a sinner, the whispers teased.

"Where are you?" Wally cried out, tired of Satan's games. The laughter trailed away, and the voice ceased, but the twisting sensation in Wally's gut grew painful. "Not my Cheryl!" he defiantly screamed at the howling wind.

The whispers confirmed that he'd been complicit in something more profound than crucifying this man. "You bastard! Show yourself!" Wally spluttered. The only sound was that of the raging storm.

Wally fell to his knees as lightning repeatedly struck the ground. Terrible visions reduced his soul to ashes. He lurched forward and puked beside the cross. "What have I done?" Wally spat the sour residue on the concrete and sobbed uncontrollably. "Oh God, help me!"

The False Prophet's slowing ribcage showed that death called him closer.

Wally suddenly recognized that he'd inadvertently fallen into the devil's perfect trap. The full extent of the deceit was wickedly revealed to him. He rolled forward with his head wrapped in his hands, screaming, "Don't take her. Please, not my Cheryl!" He was reduced to a mere shadow of the warrior, who minutes earlier called for a war on evil.

Billions watching the live stream couldn't tell why the man was wailing, screaming, and beating his fists into the ground as if possessed.

Chuck saw his friend's complete distress. He did not know what ailed Wally but rallied the guys to keep them focused. "Bring the vehicles over by the chapel to use them as cover," he shouted at Rocky.

"Bobby, round up the payphones and torch them all; make sure nothing's left," Chuck ordered. Bobby took Chuck's burner phone and then ran across the small hill to get the others. Chuck walked down the slope as Rocky pulled alongside one of the vehicles. He passed an automatic to Rocky. "Let them have it."

Wally straightened himself and wiped his face. It was too late now. The man on the cross was done. "I've defeated myself." His mumbled confession accompanied his blank stare. "I've defeated everyone."

The lightning ceased, and the rumbling thunder rolled away. The skies quickly lightened, with the dark gray fizzling to blue. The absolute stillness of the air caught Wally's attention – no sound of an insect, bird, a car, or anything beyond. For a few moments, there was perfect silence.

He looked around at the brave Christian men. Their eyes were fixed on different horizons, and their guns were at the ready. He could not tell them of the deceit they'd sacrificed their lives for. Their faith cut deep into him as he comprehended their deaths would be on his hands.

Wally strode down the hill with a false swagger in his step. He approached Chuck and Rocky. From close range, Wally raised his silencer and shot them both. They dropped to the ground, and he fired another shot through their skulls. Then he pulled their bodies out of sight from the rest of the team.

The other guys were positioned in a semi-circle perimeter. He opened the trunk of his vehicle and took out the two Uzi automatic machine guns, checked that they were both fully loaded, and got on the mic. "Guys, listen up. Slight change of plan. Gather with me by the bottom of the steps ASAP." Wally met the five remaining soldiers at the base of the three bronze crosses. "They'll be here soon," he said.

"Where's Chuck and Rocky?" one of the Cooleys asked.

"They're doing something for me around the back," Wally replied. "It has been an honor and a privilege to have spent time with you all. May God bless you, and may he forgive me."

Wally opened fire before they could flinch, striking Steve and Bobby within a split second from his right hand and the left, spraying bullets into the Cooley brothers and Garvey. Bobby fired off two rounds as he toppled over. Wally stood over his comrades, took out his handgun, and finished them with a shot through the head. Wally's sorrowful tears burned his skin.

Wally knelt beside the dead bodies of his colleagues. "Thank you, my brothers, in Christ." His prayer was interrupted by the loud droning of the helicopters. He looked east, where six military helicopters rushed through the clouds. Their formation split into three pairs, two heading south, two to the west, and two circling wide before landing somewhere behind him where the steel cross had collapsed in two halves. The two helicopters to the south spewed out heavily-armed men like ants pouring from a threatened anthill. The soldiers moved in crisscross patterns over the flat terrain.

Wally grabbed a high-powered assault rifle and aimed. He paused. A singular laugh released from his lips, and he dropped the weapon to the grass. He crouched low and skirted behind the two rental cars. Sitting with his back against a tire, the sun warmed his face. He observed the body of the man called Jesus hanging from the cross. He snorted, caught between laughter and despair. He stared at the bronzed statue of Christ. "I dedicated my life to your service. Why?"

The first shrill tones came from a bullhorn demanding weapons to be put down and hands raised in the air. Wally's tired face formed an ironic smile. Wally unclipped his sidearm, ensured the bullet was in the chamber, and placed the barrel tight under his chin. "God have mercy on my soul."

The approaching teams halted their progress, repeatedly calling for the men to come out.

Theo and James viewed the overhead feed. "Sir, no one's moving. Sending in a drone." Theo said.

"Hurry," James nodded, and he ordered all units to hold briefly. The three tiny drones flew around, sending back images of bloodied bodies on the ground, and scattered weapons.

"Approach with caution," James ordered.

CHAPTER THIRTY

Abdul Aziz stayed in constant communication with General Salah. The old man watched the awful proceedings from his hotel in Washington. He called the Saudi prince, who was permanently busy in his Washington hotel room. The Grand Mufti needed the prince's innumerable resources. He anxiously awaited the return of General Salah, who would lead their upcoming mission. The greatest of modern times.

Standing beside the cross as the medics lowered the lifeless body of Jesus to the ground, Carrie's hands were clasped tight to her face. Mo had buckled to his knees, crying hysterically and wailing an Arabic prayer. She wanted to put an arm around him and offer him comfort, but she knew that she wouldn't have the strength to get back up if she lowered herself beside him. His sickening grief pierced the humid air.

Billions watched the live transmission and learned that the New Age Prophet was dead.

James Gordon told his men to leave the cameras filming. He wanted people to see the Americans doing all that was possible. Theo's techs added two more live feeds, ensuring they filmed the multicultural efforts. "Make sure you get some shots of General Salah and the other Saudis," James instructed. James suspected full-scale riots would soon begin – quickly followed by finger-pointing, and most of it aimed his way. He rubbed a hand over his aching chest.

Drone footage established that Wally Radford had executed his entire group and killed himself. Carrie didn't care about that; Jesus' death hit hard. The world had come together, and these maniacs crucified the one man who brought hope and peace. She couldn't imagine how the world might recover. Finally, Carrie couldn't stand it any longer. She pulled Mo to his feet, and they paid their respects as the prophet's body was quickly transported into a helicopter.

James left part of his team behind to investigate the scene. He told Carrie, "We're heading straight to Washington. We need a plan for common sense. You and Mo get on it. The President is talking with world leaders as we speak, and then he'll go on live TV." James signaled everyone to get moving.

On their return to the dreary building on Wisconsin Avenue, a dark atmosphere hung heavily within. Carrie could barely get a smile or anything positive from anyone, nor could she offer anything in return. Carrie's only glimmer of hope was when Mo reminded her, "The Prophet clearly stated he'd be with us forty days and nights, and there are seven days left to go. So far, he's delivered on his word."

Carrie proposed the idea to Mo that it could mean a second resurrection. A final and undeniable demonstration of God's divinity. The entire populace of the planet was strangely quiet. Mo told her she should tell James her theory. Carrie refused. "I don't trust him," she said. Carrie didn't like the way he'd handled himself. He was government, through and through, but it manifested in how he'd carefully controlled the footage and the body's transportation. It was cold and business-like.

James organized the autopsy of Jesus to be shown to a small, select audience from around the world, but Carrie didn't like the idea of treating the Prophet as some political and medical circus act. James felt it was better to have an open book and remove the potential for conspiracy theories after the fact.

Carrie grumbled to Mo, "The President must tell the world to continue in the same spirit as if the Prophet were alive!"

"No way he can do that," Mo argued.

"He's a coward if he doesn't. There's zero harm in it. I can't watch the autopsy."

"I have to," Mo replied.

The autopsy was quick, and the body was moved to a secure government location. There were no surprises about the cause of death through blood loss and asphyxiation. The final declaration sent awful gooseflesh over Carrie's body.

Mo reminded her (again), "It'll only take one group or country to break down, and the rest could follow like dominoes."

He was right, but the glumness remained as she tried to predict the outcomes. Focus eluded Carrie, with constant visions of the Prophet's body being lowered from the cross.

It was midnight before she finished her report. Carrie took the short walk to their hotel. The fresh night air felt good on her skin. She swiped the card in her door and stumbled inside her room, where she found General Salah and one of his military advisors sitting in the chairs by her window. "How did you get in here?"

The two men looked at one another, not knowing what she'd said but taking an educated guess. The General leaned close to the translator. "We mean no harm. We're here to ask for your help. We need to take the body of the Prophet back to Medina."

Carrie dropped her stuff on the bed and leaned in between the soldiers to reply into the mic. "Even if we knew where they took the body and how to get it, you couldn't get it out of the country. So why would I help you?"

"The Prophet told us that the only way for him to receive life again is to be laid to rest next to his brother Muhammad," General Salah explained. "There's a tomb already awaiting him. It is the wish of the Prophet. The Grand Mufti wanted to explain to you in person, but he's too old for climbing across balconies in the night."

"Abdul Aziz told you this?"

"Jesus the Prophet told me. He said I was to bring him home. The Grand Mufti has seen it, too. You are to come with us."

Carrie laughed, partly through lack of sleep but also the suggestion of going to Medina with a dead Prophet. "Body snatching isn't my thing."

The General firmly replied, "We're returning him to where he wants to be. There, he'll show the world a power nobody can deny."

Carrie liked the General – an honest man, distinguished and sincere. He fully believed every word he said. "Only James Gordon, our President, and a handful of people know where they took the body. The chances of recovering it without being killed are slim."

The General's lips edged fractionally upward, and his Captain did the same. "We're a resourceful people. We know where he is and how to get him without a gunfight. The prince has a private plane waiting on the runway."

"Then what do you need me for?"

"You are supposed to come with us. You can speak sense to the people here and everywhere else. You influence those who think they're smart but could easily cause trouble."

"What makes you think I won't tell people what you're about to do and stop it all?" Carrie asked.

"Jesus said you'd help. You can walk out that door or come to Medina, where you'll witness the miracle of all miracles."

The spinning in her gut told her this was something she dared not miss. "What do you need me to do?"

"Put on some comfortable clothes. Get your passport if you have it. If you don't, we'll take care of it back home. We'll provide anything else you need." The General stood, and they shook hands.

"I want Mo Yousaf to come along. He's good at this, and I trust him," Carrie added.

"We know. He's already waiting upstairs."

Carrie raised her eyebrows and shook her head. "He's so sneaky!"

"Come up with your laptop, and they'll let you through."

"How long do I have?"

"Two minutes."

Twenty minutes later, Mo's face was pressed against the window of the prince's jet, tapping his feet so hard on the floor that Carrie felt the vibration. The noise from the engines hummed with a low menace. "I wonder how many years we'll get for taking a body and transporting it illegally overseas."

"You're not helping," was Mo's wavering response. "That's the body of the Prophet, sent by God and revered worldwide!"

"Look on the bright side. Jesus arrived illegally in Washington, so technically, we're simply repatriating him," she quipped.

Mo looked around; his eyes widened with worry. "If that's the bright side, don't say another word."

Carrie spotted the headlights of several fast-approaching vehicles. "There," she pointed over Mo's shoulder.

"Two cars and a truck coming this way. No sign of the police," he shouted, banging his fists against his thighs.

The vehicles sped across the tarmac of the private airfield. Mo lost sight of them as they went around to the back of the plane. Carrie jumped from her seat and stuck her face to the glass on the other side. "It's the General." The truck reversed. "They're unloading a casket!" Mo joined her, squeezing his face next to hers and his unruly hair getting in her eyes. "Move over," she huffed, sweeping aside his curls.

The plane's engines swiftly increased their rotation. The front cabin door closed. Seconds later, Abdul Aziz, General Salah, and a bunch of highly excited men came aboard from the plane's rear. Before they were seated or buckled in, the plane was in motion and speeding to the runway. Carrie's translator device was switched on, but the men from Medina spoke too fast, each voice drowning out the next.

"They got him - the Holy one," Mo translated for her.

Abdul Aziz signaled to them with a double thumbs up and was pushed back in his seat as the plane raced down the tarmac, which caused the old man to shriek with laughter. Within seconds the plane sharply lifted its nose off the ground.

"Oh my God, can you believe it?" Carrie excitedly grabbed Mo's arm, shaking it around.

"No! I hope we like it in Saudi Arabia."

"Why is that?"

"We might be there forever."

Carrie let go of his arm and dropped back into her seat. Her elation drained rapidly like the last inch of water going down the drain.

Once they were airborne and leveled off at altitude, General Salah got out of his seat and knelt on the seats in front of Carrie and Mo. He beckoned for her to move the translator closer to him. "The Prophet is coming home."

"How did you get him?" she asked.

"Money easily buys information in America. Our King owns the building where they stored his body and half the properties your government uses in Washington. The guards will be sleeping for a while. They are unharmed," he explained. "Enjoy the flight and get some rest." The General went back to his seat.

It was a few hours later when Carrie awoke. Mo was fast asleep, mouth open, leaning on a pillow against the glass. She switched on the screen in front, plugged in her headphones, and watched the news. The main story told of how a group of unidentified men broke into the 'secret' government facility and removed the body of the Prophet – no indication of who or why.

Carrie had no messages from James. It wouldn't be long before all hell would break loose, with conspiracy theories running wild on social media and the news.

When Mo came out of his slumber, she filled him in on the latest. Carrie composed an email to James to tell him they were part of it and the reasons behind it. Carrie figured it was better to explain now and take the heat afterward.

Abdul Aziz had advised them it was okay to tell James Gordon why the Saudi group had liberated the body of the Prophet, saying, "Tell James Gordon you've been invited to come along to ensure that the Prophet is appropriately looked after."

They thanked him for giving them a decent excuse not to be shot on sight by American forces. "At least they can't launch nukes against us," General Salah noted.

Abdul Aziz also told them that he'd spoken via an interpreter with James Gordon, telling him exactly where they were taking the body. The Grand Mufti agreed to send exclusive live feeds to James' team. "The Americans won't risk an invasion for one man – not even this one. They will settle their nerves soon enough."

Carrie and Mo sent James their email and promised to send regular updates. His response was instant and less than friendly, demanding full transparency and reminding them they reported to him. His reply stated their actions were a betrayal of the American people. He said he'd do what he could to keep them from federal prosecution, but at this point, they were the least of his worries.

"I think we're okay," Carrie cheerfully commented. Mo stayed silent.

Medina dazzled with its beauty and eclectic nature. The city was full of modern conveniences mixed with ancient relics and a respectful hustle of people throughout the streets.

General Salah provided Carrie and Mo with a hijab and thaub; the only permissible garments allowed within the Holy Site. They followed the casket containing the body of the Prophet and watched it being placed into the enormous marble tomb next to Muhammad's.

Carrie and Mo provided a teleconference update to James. "Many difficult questions will come your way. Keep the communication channels open," he advised.

Carrie assured James they'd continue their regular work from Medina. After much discussion with Mo and Abdul Aziz, she suggested that they should spread the word that the Prophet may return. She stressed the word MAY. The rumors that circulated the globe were already plentiful, so why not add to them.

Abdul Aziz provided Carrie and Mo with a private tour of the Al-Masjid. Carrie recognized a lot of the interior from Theo's security camera hacking. She guessed Theo's teams watched their every step as they walked through the highly polished stone floors.

Later, General Salah escorted Carrie and Mo to their nearby hotel. The top floor suites afforded fantastic views over the Holy Site. The General showed them around, told them the clothes in the closets were theirs, including personal care items in the bathrooms, and that they should send a text request for anything else they wanted.

Carrie arranged to have dinner with Mo, but first, she got busy on her laptop, sending updates to James and letting him know what she had heard from Abdul Aziz. The Grand Mufti told them Jesus would rise from the tomb on the third day. He assured them his visions were inevitable, and Jesus would deliver God's message to a world that suddenly didn't want to believe in anything.

"Three days seems like a cliché," Carrie suggested.

"Perhaps." Abdul Aziz gave it some thought and explained, "Everyone knows the story. It's symbolic. The world has seen this man die. American and Arabic experts have confirmed that the shared grief is global. Many religions hold the three-day rising in their belief systems. The Prophet promised the direct words of God, and he will deliver."

Carrie liked listening to the soothing voice of the elderly and wise cleric. His words and tone were a comfort in a time where she found little other peace. Carrie blended her report with Mo's data and submitted it to James.

Small religious splinter groups claimed the Prophet's death was caused by some other group, leading to a small number of extremist acts. Most happened in the southern states of the U.S.

On the world scale, all was much quieter. People remained in shock. Word spread that the Prophet would return, and every flight into Saudi Arabia, from every airline, was booked solid. The airlines took full advantage by putting on more flights. Carrie and Mo informed the Medina group that crowds would come, like nothing they'd seen before. They had two days to prepare for millions of visitors. Mo's early estimate was that it would be over twenty million people. Every border crossing into Saudi Arabia saw miles of bumper-to-bumper vehicles as pilgrims, desperate to see God at work and the Prophet restored to life, made their way through the desert.

CHAPTER THIRTY-ONE

James closed the elevator door and made his way through the stinky dark hallways. In the distance, he heard music coming from the basement's old infirmary. A few more echoing steps along the rotting tiles, and then he heard the raspy sound of an orchestra and a crooner singing a crackly version of "I've Got You Under My Skin." James stepped through the angled doors barely attached by decaying hinges and found Mr. Grey slowly drifting through the puddles of water as though he were waltzing with an imaginary partner in his arms.

The last few notes faded from the gramophone on the table. Mr. Grey spotted him, winked, and as he finished his last turn, bowed to his invisible partner, kissed an invisible hand, and turned his attention to James. "Ahoy, Jim lad," he said like a pirate on the high seas. "Did you like the music?"

"Not my thing," James replied.

"Al Bowlly sang this song more than a decade before Sinatra. I like originality. It resonates. I'm an original myself, and my genius is often overlooked. Al Bowlly's not making a comeback anytime soon. I've always been relevant."

"Seems like the odds are getting stacked against you. And by your own hand."

"I know – funny, isn't it. It's tiring having to do all the work yourself because the guy upstairs is half-asleep. How are you, James? You look tired."

"Busy," came the bland reply.

"We're about to get busier. Everything's looking good through my periscope. What about you?"

"Things are moving as planned, except the Saudis have the body."

"Don't worry about the Prophet's location," replied Mr. Grey, as he climbed into the tattered chair and swirled around like a dog settling on a rug.

"You gotta love free will, eh? That tricky Carrie Carter and her pet dog, Mo Yousaf. I can taste her anguish." He suggestively flicked his tongue in the air.

"They've put themselves in trouble."

"I know. The finale is going to be spectacular. It's like an encore at the end of a show. You have to give the audience something they're familiar with – send them home happy." He pulled the pipe from his pin-striped jacket. "Mind if I smoke?"

"It's your funeral."

Mr. Grey raised an appreciative eyebrow. "I like you, Jim. It's not easy to keep a sense of humor through these times." He lit the pipe and watched the smoke curling upward, like a child seeing snowflakes falling into its hand for the first time. "See if you can get your friends to let Carrie and Mo back into the U.S. I want to meet them."

"Why?"

"Why not?" He heavily frowned.

"Our deal is still good?" James enquired.

"Been good since we made it. You'll have your reward, and I'll have mine." Mr. Grey diverted his gaze from the smoke. "You ever hear people saying you have to change yourself before changing the world?"

"Sure."

"Proved them wrong," Mr. Grey proudly announced. "The world needed change, and I provided it in abundance. I'm maturing like a fine wine."

"And when will it all be done? I can't keep coming down here."

"When I say it's done!" Mr. Grey eyeballed him with contempt. "Every time I think you have potential; you display a disturbing lack of creativity."

"Your creation seems to be running away from you," James provoked.

"That's more like it," Mr. Grey jabbed the pipe in James' direction. "Let me tell you about creation, Jim lad."

"Millions of pilgrims are gathering in the driest desert in the world, singing their hearts out for their most earnest desires to be fulfilled. I shall deliver what they seek, and at the height of their exaltation, I shall remove, piece by piece, their pitiful wishes. The tears from the faithful will be enough to make the desert bloom, and when it does, it will harvest a poisonous crop of ripened despair from which I'll feast for a millennium. That is creation, dear boy."

"If you reap what you sow, I'd say you're fucked," James sounded unimpressed.

Mr. Grey tilted his head curiously, observing James as he puckered his lips over the end of his pipe. "Fascinating species." Mr. Grey puffed a heart-shaped plume of smoke towards James. "You continue to be so ordinary. Run along, Jim. Go hoist the mainsail, weigh the anchor, and all that …" Mr. Grey swiveled around in the chair and marveled at the smoke rings. "Rise, little ones," he gushed.

"I'm done here," James grunted and walked away.

"We're just getting started," Mr. Grey whispered.

General Salah briefly saw his family. "We prayed for your safe return and give thanks to Allah that now you are here," his wife said.

"Stay out of the city, and I will see you in another week." He wanted to say more. He held his wife in his arms, squeezed her hands, and hoped she'd understand. It seemed like she did.

"We are blessed," she cautiously suggested. He kissed her cheek and departed.

The General returned to the Al-Masjid an-Nabawi and walked the facility with his officers. He knew every stone, every tile, every lock, and where the shadows fell from the minarets. Thousands of troops were stationed around the walls. Cameras and motion sensors were upgraded. Any building nearby, within range of the complex, had their rooms and roofs vetted and, in some cases, shut down, much to the displeasure of the hotel owners, who claimed significant loss of revenues for their top-priced rooms.

The next two days in Medina followed the pattern of checks and re-checks. Around the city, camps containing millions of pilgrims littered the streets and desert. More descended and were given food and water sent in by charitable organizations. People from all nations of all prior faiths sat side by side at night around makeshift campfires, exchanging stories and speculating on what might be.

Carrie and Mo watched world leaders appealing for peace, and talks continued. They sent regular reports to James and conversed with Theo and Jessica via Zoom.

The time quickly approached. The world's media were lined up inside the Prophet's tomb. Each camera and piece of equipment was thoroughly inspected to ensure no concealed weapons came inside the Green Dome.

General Salah convinced Abdul Aziz and the Royal family that only two hundred observers should be allowed inside. Then, before nightfall, he walked through the Green Dome and out into the gardens, where he spotted Carrie.

She was taller than the other five females, one of only six women inside the complex.

She gave him a friendly wave and activated the software on her cell so they could talk. "Do you foresee any issues," she asked.

"Only two. The Prophet appears, or he doesn't." The faintest twitch of his heavy mustache signaled his mirth. "It is an honor to break with tradition that women are to be allowed inside the tomb. The Grand Mufti sees it as an opportunity to set new standards – one step at a time. But, unfortunately, he has met with some resistance to allow you here."

"I can see that by the cool reception the other women and I have received." Carrie gestured towards the angry sets of eyes from the guards surrounding the inner walls.

"It's still progress," the General quietly replied.

Carrie pulled up the view on her cell phone that showed the outside of the complex. "Look at all those people out there. Mo says approaching thirty million. A perfect mixture of those formerly identifying with separate religions – all together, actually at peace. If nothing else ever happens, then this shows we can do it. As you said, it's progress."

General Salah nodded in agreement. "Many more are still arriving. We have hundreds of trucks with water and basic supplies via our military partners." He looked a little flushed as he pulled his face away from her cellphone.

Carrie tugged at the veil in front of her mouth. "Darn thing keeps sticking to my lip balm."

"Don't take it off, or you may find your head doesn't stick to your neck anymore."

Carrie's concern manifested in fine wrinkles assembled at the corners of her eyes. The General walked away and began to laugh.

"Not funny," she called after him.

He swiveled around, bowed towards her, and moved away across the courtyard.

Carrie felt safe around the General — a man who wanted to make a difference in a humanist context. She found many of her predisposed notions were thankfully starting to unravel in her dealings with the men from Medina. All of those she'd met were smart, amiable, and funny. They loved their families and their traditions as much as anyone. They had interesting perspectives on life, but the base of what she'd found in these men was intrinsically the same as she'd found anywhere else; To live, love, and do their best. Carrie wasn't sure if her prejudices had led her to these discoveries or simple ignorance based on hearsay and years of sensationalist news reports.

She quietly considered what life on earth would be like if the Prophet did not return. Abdul Aziz assured her this would not happen. He reminded her, "Nuclear weapons are gone, so wars are doomed to failure."

The old man quickly changed subjects and told her of his plan to visit the new forests in southern Mongolia, once part of the Gobi Desert, and there he could taste the fruits provided by God's hand. Carrie liked the notion and said she would join him if her government didn't have her imprisoned.

It was the first time she'd seen the old man laugh, and it made her swell with pride. He used both of his paper-thin hands to tentatively shake hers, showing his embracing of the western custom. "I will look forward to our trip of discovery together," he enthused.

Carrie told him, "It's a date."

CHAPTER THIRTY-TWO

At 9:55 in the evening, on the third day, the atmosphere inside the Prophet's tomb held a tortuous weight. Abdul Aziz invited Carrie to sit in the front row, along with the scholars, clerics, and other religious leaders. The honored guests of previously different faiths formed three rows in a large semi-circle around the resting place of the two Prophets.

Mo sat behind Carrie, muttering, "My butt's numb from sitting on this marble floor."

"Deal with it," she whispered back.

The hijab covering Carrie's face stopped those nearby from seeing the enormous grin on her excited face.

A natural silence fell throughout the space as the last few minutes ticked down. She adjusted the tiny earpiece that received instant translations. Giant screens showed views from major cities worldwide, where hundreds of millions were gathered together. Another screen showed the packed pilgrims outside the masjid walls as millions more sat patiently on the sands. Mo's magical data indicated that more than 6.5 billion citizens were assembled in homes and businesses or watched the event outside.

There was a thickening sense of an untouchable layer that she and billions more could grasp and taste. Carrie could barely restrain herself from flexing her knees, feet, and fingers as the adrenalin made her fidgety. Abdul Aziz patted her upper arm on more than one occasion, a friendly gesture to get her to sit still.

Collectively the world held its breath. The digital clock on the wall counted down the seconds. Carrie folded her arms over her knotted stomach. Mo whispered the ten-second countdown in her ear, making her nerves explode.

General Salah sat next to Carrie at the end of the front row. He was motionless, and his eyes were locked on the tomb. Carrie wished she could be as sturdy as the pristine General.

Carrie's attention was caught by the change in light from above. At first, it was subtle, like a sunray pushing through dark clouds, and then it became brighter. A stir rose in the crowd, and some scholars moved for the first time in over an hour. The light changed from bright to brilliant white, forcing everyone to shield their eyes. Carrie squinted in a fearful panic when she cautiously glimpsed through her fingers - before her were the cold marble tombs.

Agitated clerics and VIPs began chattering.

Abdul Aziz raised his voice, "Be silent," he called out. He pointed to the black marble tomb. "You do not gossip to a pregnant woman's belly, thinking your words will bring forth new life! I beg you, be patient."

From the black marble, a faint mist began to rise. Its wispy spirals floated aimlessly at first, and within seconds the mist grew larger. The features gradually became evident with each passing second the mist formed into the shape of a man. In less than half a minute, the New Age Prophet stood before them, living, breathing, his palms outstretched, his eyes wide open. "God is great," he said.

The old men surrounding Carrie leaped to their feet like teenage boys when their team scored a goal, taking her by surprise, and it took her a moment to join their celebration.

The deafening roar of millions outside the walls of the complex simultaneously filled the masjid with a vibrating avalanche of sound. It was so ferocious that it felt like the dome's roof would be torn away. Those immediately around Carrie joined the chorus from the desert. The big screens rattled to the cheers of billions from every corner of the earth.

Carrie slapped her chest to remind herself to breathe. Then, she wildly clapped her hands. A profound stirring cleansed her spirit and renewed everyone surrounding her.

She wanted to hug General Salah, and have his powerful arms around her, but the general remained steadfast. They gazed at one another and he solemnly nodded.

The prophet was here. God was great. Carrie looked into the eyes of Jesus. His yellow robes dazzled, his red-tinted hair shone brightly as it flowed over his shoulders, and the familiar spark in his gaze touched everyone as they rose in delirium. The scars where the nails went through his hands and feet were visible, a further confirmation the prophet lived.

Abdul Aziz danced with joy, his arms held upward, his smile bright and wide across his old face, and the ecstatic clerics matched the infectious whoops he exuded. Their reserved holy selves were forgotten by the return of the New Age Prophet. The old man did the unthinkable, momentarily lifting Carrie off her feet as he whooped with joy. His strength took Carrie by surprise as she pumped her fist repeatedly in the air.

Behind her, Mo held hands with a circle of a dozen elderly scholars dancing an uncoordinated jig. Abdul Aziz put Carrie down. She glanced at the screens showing billions of waving hands, dancing swaths of millions of people jumping, cheering, and singing in unison. She was overcome and wanted to cry, but the excitement held back her tears.

The earth vibrated as one. This was mankind's turning point. "God is great!" she shouted in unison with everyone. The chant repeated over and over, with the earth-shaking in unanimous victory. "God is great! God is great!"

Jesus applauded their joyfulness. His smile lifted the hearts of everyone, and the noise of celebration increased. The hysteria surrounding the masjid went into overdrive.

He stepped forward, reaching out to those closest to him so they could confirm he was real. The religious leaders fell at his feet, touching the end of his robes, kissing the holes on his hands, crying tears of ecstasy as he lay his hands on their heads.

The prophet moved along the line of delirious scholars. He touched Carrie's hand and the same with Abdul Aziz. Jesus continued. Carrie and Abdul Aziz clutched their hands to the circle of happy clerics, skipping in circles as if they were children in a frantic ring of roses.

Millions of hands were raised skywards, rejoicing in the power of God's love. Previous religious allegiances were instantly wiped away. One belief, one God. A unified earth.

Jesus quickly addressed General Salah. "My Master thanks you." He returned to the middle of the tomb. Jesus gently held his palms face down, calling for quiet. It took some time for the earth to settle.

The room went quiet. Medina went quiet … and the world waited.

"My brothers and sisters in God Almighty, let it be known, now and forever, that God is great. What greater love and devotion could a father have for his children."

The noise of the living earth ignited so loudly that the volume from speakers and the adoring millions outside the walls forced Carrie to cover the mic in her ear and those nearby shoved their fingers into their ears as the decibels blistered the masjid.

Jesus waited patiently, again calling for quiet. "I am the messenger, like my brothers before me," he pointed to the tomb of Muhammad. "God neither commands nor demands but asks that you, his beloved children take his final words and follow them as best you can. Encourage your leaders to build from God's foundation." The prophet's gaze fixed the world's attention. "Hear my Father's words: Go about your daily lives in the service of three things: To love yourself, love others, and love all things God provides."

The cameras closed in to reveal the reddish pupils with brilliant gray speckles that dazzled the onlooker.

"All you undertake should be underpinned by one or more of these three things. They are bound together in your love for God. Loving God is the same the world over. Show kindness; show love and understanding to all you meet."

Jesus stepped back, placing a hand on the tomb's marble in which he'd been laid to rest. "Those who deny God and deny life deserve your prayers and understanding. Listen; do not judge. God's word is love, and love is your guide. Love is your unbreakable shield. You are as one under God. Hear God's words."

There was a pause as Jesus moved forward and knelt before them. Then, as he brought his fingers together, the light within the masjid began to change – not brilliantly blinding as before. Still, there was a noticeable increase in luminescence surrounding each part of the building. Millions of gasps came from outside as they marveled at the divine. The Green Dome illuminated the desert and surrounding skies, with the light penetrating beyond the earth's atmosphere into the vastness of space.

Jesus opened the palms of his hands, and the silence was instant. "God wishes that you respect and preserve this rich and beautiful earth. It is here to sustain and enjoy. Money cannot help you if you cannot breathe the air or drink the water. Pursue a richness of spirit and fulfillment of the soul. A life of service, truth, peace, and generosity will provide you with all the riches you'll need. God does not discriminate with his love – nor should you. Love, life, peace, and happiness are for everyone. Perfection does not exist; mistakes will be made. Recognize your frailties and try again. God made you from the same elements, so you are all divinely connected. Each of you will fall. Extend a hand to your brothers and sisters and trust in God – together; you will rise again. I shall rise again soon to be with my Master for all eternity. Do not look to build effigies, signs, and temples of the mind – God resides in your heart and your eternal soul. God is great."

Effortlessly Jesus rose from his knees and moved toward the center of the semi-circle. He cast his gaze on them, taking his time, showing the sincerity of the words he delivered.

"I am the messenger. Your relationship with God is for you to decide. His words are simple. You have gathered peacefully in your tens of millions, together in common purpose. God wishes you to follow this same path and let the world be a better place for it. Your goodwill and tolerance have already changed many divided hearts. Share in God's vision. The meaning of your existence is to be love. These are God's words. To know they are pure and to remain unaltered, God has provided them, through me – for you."

Jesus pointed to the inner walls of the masjid. "Behold." Those gathered saw the Prophet's words were carved all across the stone walls, etched in hundreds of languages. The gathered scholars stood on their feet, muttering and feeling the engraved words. "God's word is permanent," Jesus declared.

Great cheers resided from all parts of Medina. Jesus motioned for the gathering to retake their places. "God's words are etched on the walls of the six sites where he pronounced his love for mankind."

Once again, cheers rose from every country that blasted through the speakers. Jerusalem, Rome, Prayagraj, Angkor Wat, Amritsar, and Medina bore the words of God on their walls, and live broadcasts flashed views from each location.

Jesus continued, "Four days from now, I will rejoin my Master. God does not abandon you. God is great!" A mist formed around the Prophet, and his physical form melted away before their eyes.

Carrie was fifteen feet away, witnessing the impossible but knowing it was real. The noise from the millions of pilgrims created a palpable vibration through the walls of the Prophet's tomb. The scale of jubilation they heard from the live gatherings across the world was unimaginable.

As tears of pure joy flowed, the unified celebrations continued.

Abdul Aziz beckoned Carrie and Mo to follow him up the narrow winding steps to the top of one of the minarets. There, they observed an endless sea of people celebrating around infinite campfires. "The Prophet's return and the Word of God have ignited fires within the souls of mankind," the Grand Mufti explained.

They marveled at the multiple songs, chants, and stamping feet of the beautiful human choir humming across the sands.

Carrie placed an arm around the Grand Mufti's old shoulders. "God is great," she gasped, absorbing the spectacle.

CHAPTER THIRTY-THREE

The following day, the Prophet appeared in Rome, Morocco, and Sri Lanka. His words were brief. He used the native language fluently, effortlessly, and always to rapturous worldwide appreciation wherever he appeared. In each case, he left behind miracles to restore the native ecosystems.

Carrie spent hours going over their original notes, pulling apart sentences and phrases the Prophet had used to find clues or links as to what might come next. Carrie re-watched the footage from inside the masjid, paying close attention to something the New Age Prophet said that reminded her of something when he first appeared in Washington, DC. It was a crazy theory but worth pursuing. Carrie took some deep breaths and made the video call to James Gordon in Washington.

"Hi, James."

"There you are," he frostily answered.

"Not like Mo or I expect a warm reception."

"Your reception in Washington might be in silver bracelets. I'm working to prevent that, but you haven't made it easy for me," James warned. "What have you got for me?"

"Your help assuring our safe return is appreciated," Carrie said. "We did what we thought was right from a global perspective." She waited for James to respond, but nothing came, so she continued. "We wanted to call you personally and take you through this. Our next prediction is kind of out there. I don't want you or anyone else thinking I've had too much sun," Carrie politely laughed.

"Theo tells me you have a ninety-three-percent success ratio in your predictions. So the statistics are in your favor," James replied.

"When Jesus spoke to us in Washington DC, he said something that initially went relatively unnoticed. He said God did not interfere in the designs of life that developed here and elsewhere in the universe. The scientific community got extremely excited by that sentence, but Wally Radford's group subsequently took the prophet, and all the drama meant thing got pushed to one side. He said one-day mankind will realize we're not alone."

"Your point being?"

"We think these are related. God sends his messenger because we're either killing each other, killing the planet, or losing our human identity over petty squabbles. However, we are left with newfound growth as a species and abundant life where there used to be deserts. Jesus said he's the last messenger from God, but he said God hasn't abandoned us. To keep the momentum going, you'd send in expert help, no different than a business using a consultant. That's the basis of our next report," Carrie explained.

James cleared his throat. "Well, Carrie, perhaps the sun in Medina has gotten to you. If I hear you correctly, the prophet will leave a group of people to help. The ones in Medina?"

"Something like that. We're guessing some learned minds will be chosen to maintain the momentum and keep it on the right track. A world coalition."

Next to her, Mo sat silently, fingers crossed, trying to remain hopeful.

James did not look impressed. "Do you think we'll be left with some modern-day apostles in exchange?"

Carrie gave it some thought. Mo shrugged. "Something like that."

"Send me the report. It's going to piss off a lot of senior people. They're already nervous about who's running things."

James paused before asking, "Are you both part of the departure party heading out?"

"Yeah, we've been invited—twenty of us and half a dozen guys filming it. We drive to a secret location later today – only Abdul Aziz knows the destination. We've been told there's a three-hour hike to the final place. Theo and the team can start calculating sites."

"I'll ask him to get started. Just over twenty-four hours to go. It will be weird when this is over," James observed.

"Maybe it isn't over, just beginning," Carrie offered. "James, your profile has sky-rocketed in recent weeks. We hear you're being touted as a senior advisor within the White House."

"You believe the news?"

"I'd believe anything these days. You deserve it, James – you've kept it all together when others were."

"Less than rational might be a good way to put it," he suggested.

"Yeah – at the very least."

"We'll see what happens. Senator Crowley wants both your heads."

"Maybe we'll hang out here in Saudi Arabia for a while," Carrie suggested.

"I've got a meeting with the President later today. He knows the value you guys have brought to this thing, so maybe I can work it out. I'll keep you posted, but in the meantime, don't do anything without letting me know, or you'll need to become permanent Saudi residents."

"Will do. Thanks," Carrie replied. "We'll give you a couple more options and reach out soon."

The video call ended.

Mo sighed, "We'd better get our shit together."

Carrie prepared her things for an overnight stay. She sat on the edge of the bed, and a sudden dip in energy came over her. The Prophet's departure felt personal, as though a piece of her was being removed. She'd already considered the global effect; she had reported on it, and it was worrisome. Nevertheless, Carrie believed she'd personally experienced true divinity, and she knew without a doubt that she oozed pure love for the Prophet. His energy made a lasting impression on her entire being, and she was saddened to lose him. General Salah described it as, "We're preparing for a funeral of a loved one who hasn't yet passed away."

The thought of going back to an everyday life seemed dreary. She'd always loved her position on the education advisory council, but anything else would be mundane after this adventure.

There was a light tapping at her door, and the familiar stern face of General Salah waited to greet her. He tapped his wristwatch to show it was time to leave. He took her bag and escorted her down to the vehicle. He took Carrie's hand as she climbed into the battered vehicle, and Carrie politely smiled.

Mo was jittery and was conversing in Arabic with their driver.

"What's up?" she asked.

"This is it," he replied as he dramatically raised his arms and accidentally stubbed his fingers on the roof. "What comes next? The data and intelligence at our disposal do no good whatsoever, and I don't like it."

"Nobody likes the unknown," Carrie said.

"Precisely my point," he glumly replied. "It's like we're poised on the edge of a knife. We have the templates, but mankind's fate is completely in the hands of mankind – and we know what a problem that can be!"

Carrie puckered her lips as she chewed on the thought. "I think it will be fine. Too many people have seen and understood. People will do the right thing. We have God's words in all languages, so it will be difficult to manipulate them. And he said we would not be abandoned."

"You have more faith in people than I do."

"I guess I do."

The old minivan set off, joining a line of a dozen beat-up vehicles, and headed south out of Medina. Large crowds remained throughout Medina in hopeful expectation that the Prophet would appear once more. The drive into the desert was surprisingly easy, as their convoy went unnoticed through the millions camped out on the sands. Carrie realized why General Salah chose a convoy full of battered people carriers and small vans – it was a perfect camouflage as they escaped the city. After four hours, they turned off the main road and headed east into the hills. It was another thirty minutes before they arrived at the small town of Jabal Al-Nour.

On the approach, Carrie saw the sizeable rocky outcrop rising from the town. Mo used his cell to relay the facts, "The rock is over a two-thousand-foot climb that juts out north of the town." They were ushered from their vehicles amidst the usual shouting, pointing, and general chaos, into the small hotel.

Carrie confirmed with Abdul Aziz that they were okay to let James Gordon know their location. The old man suggested, "Do you think he doesn't know already?" he pointed to her phone.

From her hotel room, Carrie called James Gordon. He answered after a single ring. "Hi, Carrie, what do you have?"

"Just wanted to check in with you guys and let you know where we are."

"Thanks. It looks like the Prophet is going to be on the mountain, in Jabal Al-Nour."

"You can tell that from two seconds on a phone call?"

"No, we deployed drones that followed the convoy. Theo's team had eyes on you the whole time. Modern technology is as fascinating as it is intrusive. Jessica likes that long green robe with a black headscarf you've been wearing."

Carrie looked out of her hotel bathroom window. "Can you see me now?"

"No, but we saw you walking in. Tell Mo he needs to cut his hair – you can see it sticking out from his headscarf." James coughed, cleared his throat, and then added. "Don't worry; we can't see inside the hotel."

"Thank God for that." Carrie looked at her reflection in her underwear. "We have quite a hike tomorrow up that mountain. No sign of the Prophet yet. That's about all we know."

James asked for updates or any video they could take at the focal point on the mountain. He wished her and Mo good luck. "We'll call you as soon as possible," she confirmed.

Senator Jim Crowley pored over the reports on the overall outcome of the operation. He was part of the internal White House briefing on the fate of the Christian mercenaries, led by Wally Radford. After the death of the Prophet, rather than face capture by the authorities, Radford's execution of his team was a bizarre ending to their efforts. Senator Crowley's cash contribution to Wally Radford's cause was undiscovered. His source from inside James Gordon's group had proved most useful.

He couldn't understand why nobody on Gordon's team knew that the Prophet would appear at the Irving, Texas, mosque. Somehow Wally Radford knew. He considered it was the sneaky James Gordon, who played all sides for his personal benefit. Wally Radford's men were all dead, and there was nothing to tie Jim Crowley to any of them. He couldn't have written a better ending himself.

There was only one loose end left to close out. He received a text from his colleague that their informant was alone at home. Crowley alerted his associate to make the next move. He called the informant, and she instantly picked up.

"Hi."

"Thank you for your service to your country," Crowley stressed each word.

"You're welcome. There are still a few more things to get through before moving to the next phase."

"Jessica, I appreciate your commitment to our Christian cause and patriotism."

"You're welcome, Jim," she replied, chewing on her gum.

"The final cash payment will be with you any minute. I trust we can rely on you for any future endeavors."

"Absolutely. For God and my family. You know I love my Bible and would never allow anyone to steal its meaning."

"Good girl. Service to the true word will bring all of us our deserved reward."

"Hang on, Jim, someone's at my door."

Senator Crowley heard her accept the cash from his associate and the next sound was her body hitting the floor. Finally, a man's voice came over her phone. "It's done."

"Good. Make it look like a break-in. Take her phone and destroy it. I'll have my friends wipe the records."

"Yes, Sir."

"I'll contact you when Carrie Carter returns to the U.S. She's too bright for her own good," Crowley inferred.

As easily as that, Jim Crowley had removed his last exposure. The False Prophet may have somehow faked his death and resurrection, but Jim had people who would prove it wasn't real. He proudly looked forward to Sunday and the regular service at his local church. All this other nonsense was very distracting.

CHAPTER THIRTY-FOUR

Carrie's restful sleep came as a welcome surprise. She arose early, and met with Mo. He gave her the stats on the mountain's gradients that they were about to climb. She used his information at breakfast, stuffing herself with as much extra protein and carbs as possible.

The hike up the mountain was more strenuous than it looked from the view below in the town. Carrie's physical fitness came fully into play – the steep incline led to a severe burn on her thighs as she picked her way up the narrow track. She admired how Abdul Aziz set a strong pace. He confided to her that the Prophet had helped him by removing his pain like those in Jerusalem. The old man attacked the trail showing that his determination matched his impressive lung capacity.

Locals in the town of Jabal Al-Nour figured something was happening when a dozen heavily armed guards were stationed at the bottom of the mountain trail and closed off the route to all visitors.

The Grand Mufti led the group upwards for two straight hours until he raised a fist and called a halt. Carrie sat on a flat rock next to the heavily sweating Mo. She poured water into her hands and dunked her face in it. Mo dripped in perspiration and panted like he'd run a marathon.

"Are you gonna make it?" She made fun of him.

"Shut up, or I'll throw you off the track," he gasped, sucking in the hot air.

Carrie laughed at him, attracting the attention of the Saudi soldiers. She gestured a walking motion with her fingers and wiped her brow, pointing in Mo's direction. They understood and joined her laughter. They chattered in Arabic and pointed at Mo. Carrie liked how sign language could raise smiles and provide a common understanding. A fitting micro-moment reflecting the transformation of the last forty days and nights. People discovering common ground in the human experience and suspicion cast aside. The world had come together like never before in its history.

General Salah came along the line, asking his men if they were ok. He received affirmative responses. He got to Carrie, smiled at her, and passed Mo a piece of paper, which he read aloud. "Are you doing well? Can I get you anything?"

Mo gave the General a thumbs-up sign. Carrie said. "Ana bekhair, shokran."

The General bowed to her before he continued down the trail.

"I'm fine, thanks?" Mo quoted her. "Where do you get that from?"

"I've seen it several times with our translators."

"Show off," he said, chugging more water.

"You're the one who speaks fluent Arabic," she reminded him. Carrie looked over the trail's edge, where it looked like they were a mile directly above the town. One false step and it was a straight drop to certain death.

Carrie pointed ahead. "It gets steeper. We passed the cave of Hira an hour ago, where God initially contacted Muhammad. It's a fitting place for a Prophet to spend his last hours on earth."

"My glutes would argue that fact," Mo replied.

Five minutes later, the word came down the line to move, and they dutifully picked up their gear to continue the ascent. It took another leg-straining, sweat-inducing hour and a half. At the top, seats were carved into the rock, and metal barriers were firmly fixed on the cliff edge to safely view the valley below. Carrie took a few pictures on her cell of the spectacular surroundings. The media crews set up their equipment as Carrie and Mo unloaded their laptops with mics ready to receive the Prophet's final words.

Abdul Aziz called them together on the rocky outcrop where the stone seats formed a cozy natural amphitheater. The old man tested the mic and looked at Carrie to see if the translations came through, to which she gave an approving nod. "Thank you all for making the climb. And thanks to Allah, I've been given enough energy to make it up to the top. Let us say a prayer together. God has provided a prayer for all people, a new world, and a new understanding of a relationship with God. The Prophet gave these words to me."

The cameras rolled live, and the old man's prayer was heard worldwide.

Abdul Aziz sank to his knees and formed his fingers toward the heavens.

"Love from within and love those without.

Trust in God's words to remove all doubt.

Serving kindness will make you whole.

Eternal blessings for the brave, loving soul."

The Grand Mufti sighed with satisfaction as if the prayer gave him energy. "All temples and churches are for everyone. I have been guilty of thinking my way was the right way, but God has shown all of us that we are the same, under one God. His love and compassion are endless," the Grand Mufti exalted. "God's loving guidance is carved on our temples. So let us pay heed and live united under one religion."

His words cut to Carrie's core: simple, beautiful, and inclusive. Next to her, Mo sniffled quietly into his sleeve.

"And now we await our Prophet." Sudden frailty overcame the old man. General Salah stepped forward to help steady Abdul Aziz. He thanked the general as he asked those seated on the stone if they had any thoughts or questions. Carrie wanted to say something, but the strong knot in her throat balled tight and prevented any release.

"I have a question." From the middle of the group, a man rose from the stone steps, removed the ghutrah from his head, and revealed his distinctive long reddish hair. He dropped the traditional white thaub showing the bright yellow robe underneath. Those around gasped as to how he got there.

"How is it my Master is eternally benevolent?" Jesus asked.

Abdul Aziz steadied himself on the metal railing, his face wrinkled in joyous surprise.

Jesus came forward. "My brothers and sisters, God is great. Let us rejoice in the words we've heard from our learned friend and echo them in our deeds. New prayers are for a new time."

Carrie and Mo spontaneously started the applause that quickly gathered momentum. From way below in the town, they heard the echoes of the cheers rising from inhabitants.

Jesus came to the front of the small crowd, touching each of those he passed. Overwhelm doubled them over, weeping with gratitude, giving blessings, and uttering his name. They chanted, "God is great."

Jesus paused beside Carrie and, in perfect English, said. "My Master sends his thanks."

He moved past them and joined Abdul Aziz in the center of the stone circle. The old man was shaky. The Prophet approached, and the old man knelt. Jesus helped Abdul Aziz to his feet. "You shall kneel only to God. Your prayer will be used the world over." Jesus stood firm with a slender arm wrapped tightly around the old man's shoulders.

The group before him was unable to stop clapping and cheering. Jesus waited a while and finally motioned for them to sit. "My Master has given me this time to deliver his love. The miracles provided are for the benefit of all."

Jesus gestured with his arm in a circular motion. "My time here is at an end. Elsewhere, time will last forever." Jesus escorted the shaky Abdul Aziz to sit with those on the front row. "The Grand Mufti was right; God's words are inscribed in each of the temples that witness one God, one religion. Share them in love and peace – always and forever."

Jesus looked up at the skies. "This beautiful earth is a rare gift. Others, besides, you, have been close to extinction – you are not the first. God tells you to have no fear. Guiding hands come with love, kindness, learning, and support. Embrace those who come among you; they are here to help. This is the Word of God. I go to a better place and pray that you will join me one day. God is great."

The New Age Prophet fully extended his arms, tucked his head into his chest, and slowly folded his hands over his body as the clouds parted. The world watched in saddened awe as Jesus faded from view.

Carrie and Mo gripped one another. Abdul Aziz raised a trembling finger toward the skies to the east. His voice was frail. "Children of God, let us show peace and understanding. God is great." His arm dropped, and Abdul Aziz slumped sideways onto the stone.

Carrie and Mo rushed to his side as General Salah called over the military medic. They tried to make him comfortable, but their attentions were diverted as the others raised their voices, pointing to the distant skies. At first, the humming was low, like machinery in a factory, but within seconds it became a loud drone that filled the airspace, drowning out the cheers from the town below.

The General shook his head and closed Abdul Aziz's eyelids. Mo announced, "He's gone." The General covered the old man's face.

Carrie's heart was broken, but there was no time to mourn his passing as the thick clouds were pushed around like hordes of angels were riding across the skies. The swirling clouds indicated something of monumental proportions stretching two miles across. To her surprise, her cell phone started vibrating in her pocket. She answered. "James, are you seeing this?"

"I wish I weren't. But it's happening here in DC. It sounds like a giant swarm of invisible bees. Nothing shows on our radars, but we have word it's the same in Rome, London, Moscow, Beijing, Sydney, L.A., Mumbai, Berlin, and so on."

Mo excitedly pointed. "There! They're here!" The first glimpse of the enormous metallic craft came into view through the clouds.

James' frantically declared, "Oh God. We've got no defense!"

Carrie quickly reminded him. "Tell your friends in the Pentagon and elsewhere not to scramble jets. They're here to help! If they weren't, we'd already be history! This is the help we were promised. So tell them!" she shouted.

"The President's calling me!" James was gone.

Mo stood at her shoulder with a broad smile more suited to a child with ice cream on a hot summer's day. "I've only seen these in movies."

The dark metal reflected the light, and its formidable size cast a giant shadow over the mountain. Its trapezoid design was ten times the size of a luxury cruise liner with no apparent signs of propulsion or command deck as it gently coasted through the sky.

Carrie called Washington. "Theo, it's me. Tell James this is the help we were promised. I don't think he heard me. They come in peace."

"They're everywhere, Carrie," Theo anxiously groaned. "In every country."

"Jesus promised us help."

"Hey, not sure if you heard, but Jessica is dead. Someone broke into her place and killed her. Thought you should know."

"Oh, my God, no."

"Sorry. I have to go."

"Call me if those assholes in the Senate think about launching an attack – it'll be useless anyway." Carrie stared at the open-mouthed Mo, telling him, "Jessica's dead."

"That sucks," was all he could say. Mo's gaze never left the overhead behemoth. Mo's walked his fingers down Carrie's wrist and clenched her hand. "Don't let go," he pleaded.

Carrie gratefully gripped Mo's fingers. "The Prophet said we're not alone. Meet our galactic neighbors." Carrie watched the gigantic craft hovering over the town. Its scale forced her to release all the air from her lungs. "Jesus was right."

"About what?"

"God is great."

CHAPTER THIRTY-FIVE

The descent from Jabal Al-Nour was laden with uncertainty and sorrow at losing the Grand Mufti. They held a small ceremony in the hotel garden, said prayers for his soul, and gave gratitude for his inclusive leadership.

Carrie used video conferencing to speak at length with Theo in Washington. He relayed that the government was in a state of absolute panic. Carrie updated reports, calling for America to extend a hand of friendship and lead the way. But unfortunately, she was unable to connect with James.

Over the next ten days, the visitors from the Pinwheel Galaxy slowly introduced themselves. They originated from a series of planets on the edges of the system known as Messier 101 – M101. They inhabited two planets that shared orbit around a sun that was eight times the size of ours. They'd waged war from planet to planet for hundreds of thousands of years until most of their worlds became uninhabitable.

Divine intervention had occurred. War ceased, saving the four primary intelligent life-forms and millions of subsets of alien creatures, similar to our insects, mammals, and birds. By laying down their arms and following the path recently given to mankind, they'd peacefully prospered for close to a million years across thousands of generations. Their human-like form was more diminutive and flimsier in many ways, although their feet and hands were long and flexible, and their oversized heads quickly got them the nickname of The Pinheads from Pinwheel.

The twenty-one-million-light-year distance from the earth was considered easy via their technology, allowing them to bend space and time simultaneously. Divine intervention bid them not reveal the source of their power drives or technologies. Mankind wasn't sophisticated enough to venture into the far-flung reaches of the universe. If mankind could live peacefully for a couple of hundred more generations, sharing the technology might be a consideration. One thing at a time was their squeaky response. They had reiterated that they were here to observe and to help. They had rebuilt no differently than what mankind was undertaking. If the people of earth wished them to leave at any time, they'd go back to the Pinwheel Galaxy and would only return if called upon.

Their presence rattled nerves, but they kept a respectful distance, only setting foot on earth to attend advisory meetings. For ten days, they assisted with infrastructure initiatives to help support harvesting supplies from the millions of acres of new fruit and vegetation. Food and water soon reached those most in need.

Carrie and Mo said their goodbyes in Medina. Both were sorry to leave the majestic holy site, and the new friends they had made. As they flew back to the US, Carrie explained to Mo, "I miss Abdul Aziz and General Salah." Carrie fiddled with her necklace. Mo gave Carrie a cursory glance and remained quiet.

When they stepped onto the tarmac in Washington, DC, Carrie wore the necklace given to her by General Salah. She hoped to see him again soon. Carrie and Mo were escorted straight to the building on Wisconsin Avenue.

James Gordon met them at the elevator and walked them into Carrie's office. His manner was all business. "There's much we want from these visitors, and we need to find ways to get them to play ball," he said, rubbing a hand against his upper ribs. "We can't let the Russians or Chinese go interstellar before we do. Valuable mineral resources are everywhere."

"Is that the limit of our thinking? Really?" Carrie snarled with her hands jammed into her hips. "The world is healing, the visitors are helping and showing us how to develop better irrigation, solar energy systems, and wave power, but you guys want spaceships for minerals? It's like the government hasn't learned a damn thing! You're fucking unbelievable!"

"This is how revolutions start," Mo warned James. "People of all nations want our planet fixed before we think about flying off around the stars."

"You tell that to the President," James snapped. "I'm simply saying there's more I think we could be doing – should be doing. Where's your patriotism?"

"Patriotism, my ass," Carrie scolded him. "I wouldn't let you guys get your hands on their technology – you don't know how to handle the responsibility that comes with it. And why aren't the Russians or Chinese governments working with us, not against us? Screw you guys! You never listen!"

"To preserve our way of life, we need order," James insisted.

"Our way of life is as earthlings – not simply Americans. God sent his Prophet followed by goddamn aliens because we don't know how to preserve life. All you guys understand is a life dictated by aiming down the barrel of a gun!" she screamed.

The entire office stopped to observe.

James closed the door. "I've got everyone on my ass. We need to be proactive in our communication to learn, that's all. You guys have a proven track record in getting ahead of the curve."

"Yeah, when it comes to religious and social applications, we follow data combined with history. We're not fortune-tellers!" Mo clarified.

"So, use the same principles you used and do your stuff!" James ordered. "You've been pardoned by the President – which wasn't easy, and you've got the highest-paid government consulting gig anyone's ever been granted. Your country needs you to perform."

"Perform for who?" Carrie blasted. "It's like you're determined to start another cold war."

"We're trying to prevent war. I would've thought that was obvious by now," James argued.

"No, it isn't. I thought you'd be spending all your time in the Oval Office with your new advisory role to the President," she goaded.

"Our President is a man of detail, and he's highly demanding, so I need you guys to do your jobs. I've jumped through hoops to get you back here and get you these contracts," he sternly reminded them. "I need something by the end of today."

"And do what with it?" Carrie exclaimed.

"In case you hadn't noticed, over a hundred alien spacecraft are hovering around the planet. We've been invaded by the Pinheads from the Pinwheel Galaxy!" James barked.

"It's hardly an invasion. They're helping us."

"For now! Get me the report I asked for. We could use your talents. If not, give me your resignation letters." James slammed the door and almost brought the office crashing to the ground. He angrily flailed his arms through the air. "Everyone, get back to work!"

"Welcome home," Mo sarcastically smiled at Carrie.

Carrie stepped into the doorway and picked up James' security badge that had dropped from the clip on his top pocket. "We should burn this."

"Why?" Mo asked, with an exaggerated shake of his head.

"Just because he's an asshole," she said, throwing the badge on her desk. "Can you pull data on how the visitors have or have not interacted? In other words, what have they shown an interest in solving, or not? It might take away the conspiracy theories that they've come here to take over and eat us."

"I'll see what I can do. But, to be honest, I don't know if I want any part of this crap."

"Why not?"

"It doesn't feel right. Like I'm fueling an invisible futuristic war."

"Stop being such a pussy," Carrie firmly said and pushed him out of the door.

"Medina was easier!"

"Not from under a hijab," she replied.

His shoulders were sloped from travel fatigue and pushed down by the weight of expectation in impossible circumstances. Everybody wanted assurances. He'd be okay. It was Mo – he was always okay.

Carrie clawed her fingers through her hair, strongly resisting the urge to pull out every strand by its roots. The world had come so far in such a short time, yet those supposed to be leading from the front were only interested in furthering their interests. "Idiots!"

She emailed General Salah to let him know they were back in Washington and thanked him for the help. She let him know that she was wearing her treasured necklace. She added that she'd soon be back in Medina for the international peace conference if things went well and looked forward to seeing him soon. "International peace? As if world governments have any concept of the meaning," she scoffed.

Carrie saw James climb inside a limo from her office window, taking him to the Oval Office. He'd earned his place.

Carrie stared at his security badge on her desk.

Curiosity took over. Everyone whispered about James visiting the lower floors, reputedly full of powerful data compiling hardware and theories that important, unseen people worked there. She took her coffee and his badge and got in the elevator. She placed his badge in the scanner and pressed the button to the lowest level.

The carriage shook and disappeared down into the bowels of the building. When the doors opened, Carrie fully expected to have an armed guard stick a gun in her face and send her packing with her tail between her legs. Instead, the elevator stopped with a resounding clunk, and the doors opened. Instead of seeing armed guards, long, brightly lit tunnels, and men in white coats moving around in golf carts, she was met with only semi-darkness. The hallway was like the opening of a decaying mouth filled with loose rotten teeth threatening to swallow her into its festering internal organs.

Carrie tentatively stepped from the elevator. "Not a good idea," she hummed. The dank air was stale. The place was creepy.

Carrie turned the corner and received the faint whiff of smoke, something sweet, and light took her back to when she was a little girl. A familiar scent reminded her of her grandfather, a man always full of joy and big hugs.

"Hello?" she called out. The echoing of drips replied. Ceiling tiles were rotted away through years of moisture pulling them apart in the side rooms. It looked more like a haunted asylum than a hotbed of government systems. The scent of the sweet tobacco became stronger. She followed it to the room at the end of the hallway. Carrie tiptoed through the stagnant pools and strained her neck to find the source of the smoke. A janitor or caretaker, she told herself. "Hello!"

She edged inside the doorway. The smoke curled upwards from behind the oversized swivel chair. Facing her was the back of the chair. There was no sign of anyone's arms or legs.

"Carrie Carter, the fire starter," a voice melodically chimed from the chair.

"Who is it?"

"Your number one fan." The chair swiveled around to reveal the tall, slender man with long dark hair. His knees were tucked to his chest, and his bare feet were curled over the edge of the chair.

Carrie was taken aback and waited for him to explain himself. His sparkling eyes methodically consumed her essence as his lukewarm smile eagerly greeted her.

"Do you work here?"

"Not officially," he replied, tapping the contents of his pipe on the wooden arm of the chair. "You might say I'm a consultant – a bit like you and Mo, only on a grander scale." His grin looked too wide to fit on his long narrow face.

"Who are you?" she frostily asked.

"You can call me Levi, Levi D Grey at your service." He twisted sideways in the seat and refilled the pipe.

"What are you consulting on, Levi?"

"This whole Jesus thing, the same as you, but from a different angle."

"What angle would that be?"

"Making sure everyone does what they do best, so we all win." His reply made it sound obvious. "I like winning."

239

"Funny place to take a smoke break?" Carrie observed him. "Why are you down here?"

"I rarely make personal visits upstairs. It's too bright – too much going on – you know how that is. Everyone has problems with everything. Woe is me and all that jazz."

"Kind of." Carrie had no wish to explain herself. "How do you know my name?"

"So glad you asked." He placed the pipe inside his jacket and wiggled his fingers before cracking his knuckles. "I've been watching your career and figured you'd be perfect for getting things done – be part of a winning team. My first-round draft pick. And you just gotta love that Mo Yousaf with his crazy hair – he looks like Charlie Chaplin in a windstorm." His sly grin suggested he knew much more.

"You asked for me? I haven't heard of you – do you work for Senator Garofalo?"

He feigned disgust with a wrinkled frown. "No, I wouldn't work for that asshole – he's not to be trusted, you know. None of them." He tapped a secretive finger to the side of his long straight nose. "James Gordon, Jim Crowley - pah, liars – and a bunch of amateurs with no imagination!"

Carrie heard the distressed groan behind her. She swiveled around and screamed, having to stuff her hands inside her mouth to prevent herself from screeching.

Senator Jim Crowley's naked body hung from the wall, and his bloodied torso limply dangled from the crudely tied ropes. His feet were only two inches off the ground, and a dozen giant rats eagerly leaped at his legs, devouring pieces of his flesh. His purple, bloated face looked distorted, as though his jaw had come loose, and his eyeballs looked ready to burst from their sockets. Both hands were bound behind his back. The rats squealed with excitement as they fell away with bits of his skin and muscle in their sharp teeth. The Senator moaned again.

Mr. Grey explained, "Don't pity him, Carrie; he doesn't deserve it. He played everyone, and I caught him. He's in the naughty corner. You bad, Senator," Mr. Grey called across the room.

"Help him," Carrie pleaded.

"I am helping him," Mr. Grey casually replied. "If you knew what he had planned for you, you'd join the rat-pack. He's untrustworthy. You'll find out just what he did to poor little Jessica Cortez when you get back upstairs. Making it look like a violent burglary." Mr. Grey tutted. "Jim Crowley fed Wally Radford all his inside information. Now Jim Crowley is feeding these God-awful creatures. Believe me; they are God's creatures – the big man is not as squeaky clean as he'd have you all believe." Mr. Grey sneered at the ceiling.

"Who are you, and who do you work for?" Carrie demanded, wiping her face.

"Don't cry for him, Carrie. Lucky for you, I had your back." Mr. Grey gleefully pointed at himself, "As for me – I work for me and me only. Unlike those slack-jawed goons in the White House, I have a clear agenda, and I stick with it – and people call me the liar?"

"Working on what?"

"Not everything went to plan, but on the whole, I consider it a success. Some unforeseen last-minute interventions caused me to renegotiate. Senator Crowley can attest to that. Thinking he could come down here and take me to task – tut, tut."

"I don't understand. Are you CIA or Secret Service? Who are you exactly?"

"I'm the guy who makes things happen." He rolled his eyes. "This whole Prophet Jesus thing – my idea!" he boasted with great enthusiasm. "Just when I was starting to enjoy myself, you-know-who interfered." He looked upward with a shake of his head.

Carrie's face wrinkled in confusion. "Who interfered? I don't…"

"You're all the same – no imagination! C'mon, Carrie!" Mr. Grey bared suddenly sharp teeth, and his face twisted in annoyance. "God the Almighty interfered! He's always poking his celestial nose into other people's business. Do you think I invited those peace-loving pussies from the Pinwheel Galaxy? No ma'am. He surprised me with that little stunt. The Pinheads are no fun anymore."

"You're one of them?"

"Aaargh," Jim Crowley moaned.

Carrie cringed as one of the rats gnawed on his testicular sac.

"Oh, my God!" she pleaded. Carrie glared at Mr. Grey. "Are you an alien?"

He pretended to take offense. "How dare you, madam," he haughtily replied. "I almost had those bubble-headed pipsqueaks wiped out at one point. Interplanetary wars are so cool."

"Wars?"

"About a million years ago, they used to be meat eaters – they were terrifically exciting back in the day until your God intervened. He got everyone all Kumbaya. Fair play - I never saw that coming when he brought those guys here to the rescue. Of course, neither did my firstborn, so I've eternally grounded him. The little rascal," Mr. Grey affectionately chuckled.

"Your firstborn?" Carrie queried.

"Jesus is on a timeout." Mr. Grey puffed his cheeks out to show his disappointment at her lack of understanding. "I'm the one pulling the strings, Miss Carrie Carter, not James, not the President, not the Prophet nor your useless God. He doesn't have the imagination to bring everyone love, peace, and goodwill. He likes it when you're all cowering and begging for forgiveness. His ego is shocking."

Mr. Grey stealthily shuffled sideways from the chair. "Still don't recognize me?" He turned his head ninety degrees, giving her a profile view.

Carrie recoiled in horror as his face twisted, the features grew more prominent, his skin tone darkened, and his flickering tongue rasped in the foul air. She clasped her hands over her mouth and her thighs melted to jelly when she realized Mr. Grey was the one nobody wanted to meet.

Mr. Grey recognized her fear, smiled, and his face returned to its earlier sallow appearance. "That's my smart girl," he cooed. "One has to maintain appearances. Levi D Grey - saving the world, one miracle at a time."

"It doesn't make sense," Carrie stammered. "Why would you? The world's more united than it's ever been!"

"I was bored, for crying out loud!" He flung his wiry arms in the air and sprang forward, with his bare feet splashing into the feculent water. He rested on the edge of the metal table, fluttering his long eyelashes.

"I still don't get …" Carrie stalled. The heavy essence of death and decay emanated in his sparkling stare. A stare that wished to dominate. Carrie would not bow down. "It was real. I've seen the clean rivers, the new forests, and people cured," Carrie exclaimed.

"It was all real, you clever consultant, you. Do you have any idea how exhausting miracles are on such a scale? You try pleasing a cynical world inside forty days!" He stretched out on his side with one arm propped under his head on the table as if posing for a painting. "You have to admit it's a Masterpiece," he enthused.

"But you've united all of us," Carrie stuttered.

"Yes. A united world is exactly what I want." His laughter taunted Carrie. Mr. Grey's laugh lines grew thicker, his brow heavier, lips plumper and his body writhed like he was having an orgasm. "Yum, yum."

He sat upright, crossed his legs, and retrieved the pipe inside his jacket. "Mind if I smoke?" he asked. Carrie said nothing. He lit the tobacco and sent up plumes of smoke to the moldy ceiling. "So beautiful. Things on fire bring me joy – some old habits die hard," he admired the smoke. Then, he slithered effortlessly from the table to the stepladder and perched himself near the top.

His gaze penetrated her skin. "I told you; I was bored. People think I lie all the time, which I do, but not all the time, if you get what I mean? I didn't have a chance to get in the game – people were maiming and killing for the smallest reasons. You can only bring true chaos from order. I've given you order and purpose." He took a couple more puffs and pushed the heart-shaped smoke rings towards her. "The Jesus thing is genius, huh? Who's not going to believe that?"

Carrie ignored the groans from Senator Crowley as the rats devoured him.

"All the miracles, the one God, and my dreams?" Carrie shook her head. "It can't be."

"You think those dreams were given to you by God? Ha! I love it! Carrie, you were so amazing – so convincing! The dreams were my gift to you, the same as I gave to the General and Abdul Aziz– before I killed him – a fitting end for the old man on the mountain. He went out in style. You should thank me for that." Mr. Grey closed his eyes and sighed with immense satisfaction, "Ah, you beautiful dreamers."

Mr. Grey swung his feet around, stepping through the filthy water, as a dozen rats rushed away, giving momentary respite to Jim Crowley's dying body.

Carrie cringed at the scurrying creatures.

"I swear those are not my invention. Your friend from up on high is trying to give me a bad rap. They're always under your feet, pesky little critters." He looked with disgust at Senator Crowley and jabbed the end of his pipe in his direction. "Don't think you're getting off that easy, you naughty boy. They're just taking a break. It'll soon be feeding time again."

Mr. Grey glided closer to her; his lips threateningly curled upwards. "Don't think I don't know about the other dreams you've had. Getting all friendly with the handsome General. That necklace you treasure and constantly fiddle with. The General's enough to make any gal stand to attention, isn't he?" Mr. Grey's floaty tones mocked. "I give you hope in your dreams so that you may dream again. There is opportunity in dreams. I like a challenge – it makes it much more fun. So, not all plain sailing. The Pinheads from outer space are total killjoys, at least for now. I'd like to convince them to give up their vegetarian diet … then it'll get interesting."

"You're a monster," she scowled. Carrie's body shook, but she held her ground.

243

"Thanks for saying so," he smiled. "The Pinheads are virtually incorruptible. God's throwing down the gauntlet on this one. Finally, he awoke!"

Mr. Grey took a further spry step towards her. He pointed toward the gramophone, and it began to play, Goodnight sweetheart, all my prayers are for you. "Do you dance?" he asked.

"Not with you."

"Pity, I think we'd be good together." He faked an exaggerated pout. "Hey, what about Pastor Wally Radford and his merry men! You've got to give credit to those guys. They got it right! You were all wrong! I almost felt sorry for Wally."

Mr. Grey dreamily sighed. "I have Wally with me – he's a good Christian man but also a murderer, and his wife a willing accomplice. He became quite the crusader. The man upstairs is very unforgiving when it comes to killing. Whereas I, on the other hand, am very accommodating. Wally thought he was going to heaven. So it came as quite a shock when I greeted him, waltzing with Cheryl at the burning gates. She's surprisingly light on her feet! I love surprises, don't you?"

Carrie argued, "I looked into the Prophet's eyes and saw God. I heard it in his voice and witnessed it in his deeds." Carrie balled her fists in case Mr. Grey stepped closer.

"Deeds? Typical theologian babble. Have you heard yourself? I presented the Prophet Jesus exactly how everybody wanted to see him." Mr. Grey stuck his face towards her and fully opened his eyes. "Recognize those devilishly alluring red pupils with the pretty gray speckles, huh? Huh?" His cavernous smile looked like she could fall inside and never get back out.

Carrie sniffed hard, holding back tears. Her fighting nature kicked in, and she hissed, "You will fail. You always do."

Mr. Grey looked delighted. "And who are you to criticize me?" He pointed a limp accusatory finger at Carrie. "The poor little girl, who never fit in, boo hoo. So desperate to prove yourself to everyone – and especially to yourself. So drab," he cackled. His face twisted, "What have you achieved? Only what I gave to you. Your reputation is what I provided."

"I did that all for myself," Carrie protested.

"Ha! Your ego is priceless. I am the Master of deception. You've exchanged anonymity for fame – I offered and you willingly received. Quite delicious!" Mr. Grey licked his lips.

"I don't believe you."

"Join the back of the line my dear." Mr. Grey folded his hands together and bowed to Carrie. "You have cemented my genius. How does it feel?"

"Jesus is in my heart. I know it," Carrie insisted.

"Jesus is my creation, and we take care of our own, so long as we don't break our contracts. Hmph, kids? Who needs 'em? Currently, he's down below in the penthouse suite, where I'm having his flesh peeled off and eaten by the woman he thinks is his mother. That'll teach him to let God blindside me with the Pinheads from outer space. I've let my boy think he's really Jesus, and his daddy's abandoned him. But, I did promise him a mommy figure, and I'm a creature of my word – when it suits me. Some of us still have the gift of imagination, my dear." Mr. Grey proudly stuck out his chest.

"But you've given us a near-perfect world," Carrie scoffed. "You've fallen into your own trap. Food and water – abundance for all – a common purpose."

"My dear Carrie, I have transcended the transcendent."

"You've screwed yourself," she goaded.

"Never judge a book where I've written its cover." Mr. Grey suddenly looked bored and straightened the sleeves on his jacket. His expression filled with menace as he explained, "Wait until those villages in Tanzania get stampeded by herds of majestic elephants. See how quickly the villagers bring out the machetes and shotguns. Prides of lions in South Africa eating people three times a day, like ordering from a restaurant menu. The crocodile population is booming in India, and the people swimming in those pollution-free waters keep going missing. Changing weather climates with all that lush vegetation, more monsoons, more pollution, more power needed, more melting ice caps, seas rising, tornadoes twisting, hurricanes (a personal favorite) raging across mother earth. You, of all people, should know that you reap what you sow. I've got all the time in the universe to watch my crops grow – what about you?"

"You underestimate mankind," Carrie raged. Her phone buzzed in her hand.

"You should read that text. It'll be about James," Mr. Grey pitifully grinned. "So sad, especially as he just landed his dream job." Mr. Grey back stepped his way into the armchair and pulled his feet from the wet floor. The rats scurried from their hiding places and once more feasted on Senator Crowley.

Carrie looked at the text from Theo confirming James Gordon suddenly died of a heart attack within the White House. "This was you."

"I kept my side of our bargain, and James got what he was promised. I never said how long it would last," Mr. Grey looked around as if checking they were alone and whispered, "James doesn't know it yet, but he's joining my fraternity. It's all horns, tails, and tridents for him – people still hate that shit."

"Screw you!" Carrie turned and quickly walked away, her heart feeling like it could explode.

"Come back, Carrie; I've got some other projects you might be interested in?"

"Fuck you!" she shouted.

His cackling reverberated from every surface, filling the space and her head. "We make a good team. Think about it. We can repel the alien invasion, and I'm a great dancer!" Mr. Grey continued taunting her. "I can have the General's wife killed. You can have him ..."

Carrie kept moving without reply. His vile laughter followed her as she splashed through the puddles.

"Thanks for everything, Carrie Carter, fire starter. You were awesome! Give my regards to Mo and tell him to get his hair cut."

She flipped him a finger he couldn't see and shouted back into the darkness, "You'll never win!"

"I already did," came the sneering reply.

"Sometimes you have to lose the battle to win the war," Carrie muttered.

Carrie hurriedly inserted the badge into the reader and closed the elevator door with the vile laughter still ringing in her ears. Then, finally, she breathed a sigh of relief as the elevator moved upward.

When it reached the top, she rushed from the elevator into Mo's office and clutched herself into his arms.

"I just heard about James," Mo said but then pulled his head back to look at her. "Are you okay? You look like you've seen a ghost."

"God is great, isn't he?" Carrie whispered.

My ask to you dear Reader.

I am sure that you enjoyed this thought provoking and intriguing story. I would ask that you take sixty seconds of your time to leave a five star review that makes a huge difference for me.

Anything less than that and I ask that you keep your opinions to yourself.

In any event, I love you; Deal with it.

Thank you.

ABOUT THE AUTHOR

Vincent Redgrave is the author of The Angel Seedlings, The Third Coming, The Sideliners and A Texas Sunrise.

Vincent has fourteen other works of varying genres, time periods, and settings soon to be released. Each story is complete and under numerous iterations.

In the meantime, Vincent is likely hard at work on a novel or dancing to the beat of a rattlesnake's tail in Arizona.

For all the latest news on Vincent Redgrave's book releases and other shenanigans, click on the URL (if you're using an eBook), or type the following into your browser:

https://www.amazon.com/author/vincentredgrave

Reading a novel by Vincent Redgrave is like white water rafting in your favorite armchair. You know you're going to get wet and sustain a few bruises, but you can be reasonably confident about staying in the boat.

Coming soon:

Eternally Anonymous:

The prolific serial pedophile killer, known as the Demon Dentist, returns after a twelve month absence. The killer's pace rises to new heights, but the killer is collapsing under the burden of his mission. Nunez and rookie partner, detective Cam Sterling, have everyone breathing down their necks, including the dubious support of FBI profiler, Agent Harper. The killer, Nunez and Sterling are all battling personal issues. Unexpected events pull the central characters into an entangled finale, where everyone is faced with dire moral decisions, and nothing is as it seems.

Long Road to Vienna:

Twins, Livia and Luka are sold by their desperate father into the hands of Mr. and Mrs. Luknar. Everyone in the Austro-Hungarian valley dislikes the Luknars, and for good reason. Livia and Luka must use all their wits, guile, and determination in order to survive. Servant girl, Jirina, takes them under her wing, but soon the Luknars, along with invading Cossacks, and other dreadful people spin their insufferable world into a nightmare. Luka and Livia establish unbreakable bonds with a local wolf-pack - useful allies in the fight for life. The sanctuary of Vienna seems like an impossible dream, and dreams as we know are misleading.

Printed in Great Britain
by Amazon

17003800R00149